Praise for
The Sea Captain's Wife

"Epic in its emotional intensity. . . . Succeeds at painting a
vivid and vibrant portrait of the Atlantic Canadian landscape
during the last days of the Age of Sail."
The Chronicle Herald

"The best novel of 2010. . . . Powning's prose never misses a beat."
The Sun Times (Owen Sound)

"Powning is an extraordinary writer. . . . Her people are as
real as personal friends, neighbours or compelling strangers.
The watchful, visually engaged girl-child, Carrie, is,
through both descriptive power and economy of prose, one
of the most deeply affecting characters I've encountered. . . .
The book is clearly thoroughly researched, yet never reads
as written research but as lives fully and panoramically
lived. It reads as real. I am a witness to its truth and sweep.
I read, and was there."
Gale Zoë Garnett, *The Globe and Mail*

"An elegant piece of writing. . . . It is swashbuckling, it is
heart-rending and readers will shed tears. . . . Powning has
opened up a fascinating bit of history. . . . The details of
sailing are impeccably drawn."
National Post

"*The Sea Captain's Wife* is reminiscent of Ami MacKay's 2006
CanLit bestseller, *The Birth House*. . . . Powning skillfully
weaves both a harrowing and touching story about marriage,
obligation and devotion."
Winnipeg Free Press

"Beth Powning . . . is scoring another hit in the literary world. . . . Words roll effortlessly off the page into the reader's mind, combining into the rich sensory landscape Azuba inhabits. Powning's use of simple sentences, loaded with carefully placed sense imagery, creates a world beyond the matter-of-fact sense of the narrative."
Telegraph-Journal

"Beth Powning has the gift of drawing her readers into a work. The characters in *The Sea Captain's Wife* are enduringly memorable. . . . Powning paints scenes of sea life and its pains, fears, wonders, joys and tragedies."
The Coast (Halifax)

"As in her two wonderfully wrought memoirs, *Edge Seasons* and *Shadow Child*, and in her widely lauded first novel, *The Hatbox Letters*, the New Brunswick writer proves a master of descriptive dexterity. . . . [A] lively, well-researched chronicle."
Ottawa Citizen

"In history and in literature, the sea has always been the realm of men, but Beth Powning reminds us that women were there, too. *The Sea Captain's Wife* is both a brilliant and absorbing story of a singular woman's courageous entry into this alien world and of her growing sense of self-knowledge and strength as she encounters its demands. It is a tale of adventure and adversity, and of the terrors and deep satisfactions of life on the ever-dangerous and unpredictable sea."
Derek Lundy, author of *Godforsaken Sea* and *The Way of a Ship*

BETH POWNING

The Sea Captain's Wife

A Novel

VINTAGE CANADA

VINTAGE CANADA EDITION, 2010

Copyright © 2010 Powning Designs Ltd.
Map copyright © 2010 Paul Dotey

Published in Canada by Vintage Canada, a division of Random House of Canada Limited, Toronto, in 2010. Originally published in hardcover in Canada by Alfred A. Knopf Canada, a division of Random House of Canada Limited, in 2010. Distributed by Random House of Canada Limited.

Vintage Canada with colophon is a registered trademark.

www.randomhouse.ca

Lines from Seamus Heaney's "Lovers on Aran" used with permission of Faber and Faber Ltd., UK.

Library and Archives Canada Cataloguing in Publication

Powning, Beth
     The sea captain's wife / Beth Powning.

ISBN 978-0-307-39711-9

     I. Title.

PS8631.O86S42 2010a   C813'.6   C2010-900859-6

Book design by Terri Nimmo

Printed and bound in the United States of America

10 9 8 7 6 5 4 3 2 1

To Peter

traveller and companion
wind and stars

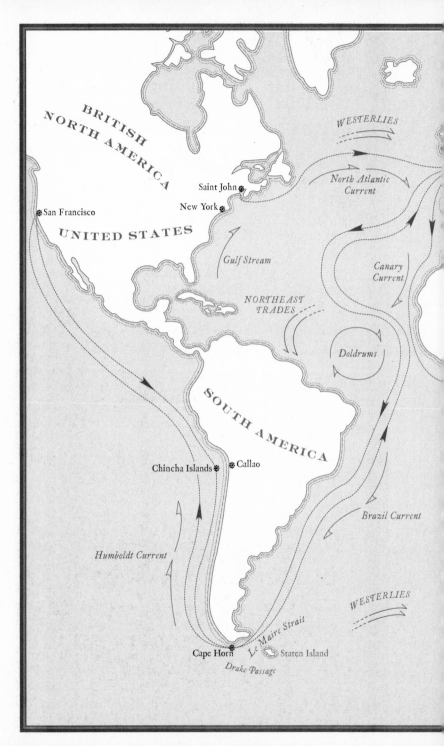

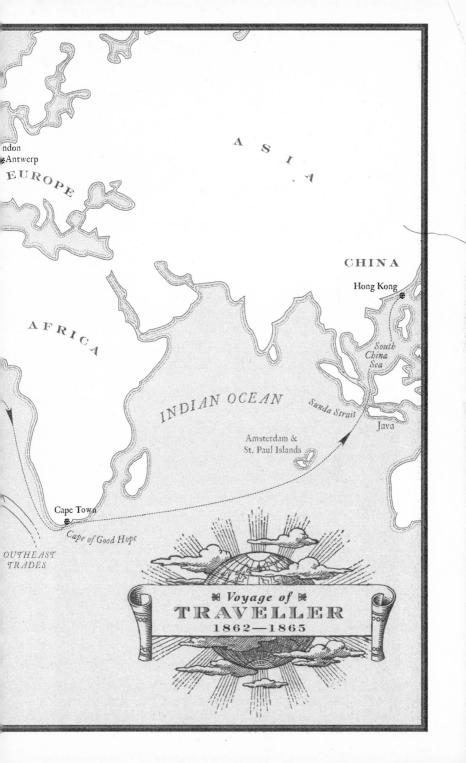

ndon
Antwerp

EUROPE

ASIA

CHINA

Hong Kong

AFRICA

South
China
Sea

INDIAN OCEAN   Sunda Strait

Java

Amsterdam &
St. Paul Islands

Cape Town
Cape of Good Hope

OUTHEAST
TRADES

Voyage of
TRAVELLER
1862—1865

The nearest dream recedes, unrealized,
      The heaven we chase
      Like the June bee . . .

      Emily Dickinson, *Poem 30*

Did sea define the land or land the sea?
Each drew new meaning from the waves' collision.
Sea broke on land to full identity.

      Seamus Heaney, *Lovers on Aran*

Contents

Prologue

Whelan's Cove is a place of departures.

On a windy June afternoon, Azuba goes with Father to his shipyard. She grips his hand as they wend their way between salt sheds. The air smells of oakum and is lively with sound: the ringing of mallets, the swish of saws. She stands at his side as he supervises his workers; then they walk to the wharf.

A ship is outward bound, and there is a crowd. People are hurrying, rolling barrels, lugging chests.

Captain Shaw is sailing on *Zephyr*, one of Father's ships. He and Father shake hands and then stand shoulder to shoulder, looking out at the black-hulled ship. When the captain bends to speak to eight-year-old Azuba, his bearded face comes close, and she sees how the skin is brown and shiny, varnished by weather.

His wife and two children are clustered by a pile of sea chests and trunks. Mrs. Shaw's face is as weathered as her husband's. She accompanies him on every voyage; both children were born at sea. The children, like their mother, are sun-browned, and Azuba longs to stare at them, but only dares furtive peeks. They seem foreign, more at ease with the wiry sailors than they would be with her. She sees the boy put his hand on his mother's sleeve and speak seriously, as one adult to another. And then Mrs. Shaw nods, casts a level look out at *Zephyr,* riding at anchor in deep water. She picks up a bamboo cage containing a red-headed parrot. Her shawl rises from her shoulders in a swirling billow; she has abandoned her hoops for the voyage and she presses her skirts with her free hand.

Captain Shaw climbs down into a rowboat. Mrs. Shaw ushers the children to the wharf's edge, watches as they go hand-over-hand down the ladder. Then she lowers the parrot cage and steps backwards onto the first rung, skirts over one arm. On the wharf, men lean to assist her; in the boat, Captain Shaw holds her at the waist. She laughs, her teeth flash white.

Father and Azuba walk to the end of the wharf amidst the on-lookers. Women wipe tears from their cheeks with hand-kerchiefs, wave them back and forth over their heads. The rowboat weaves between the anchored ships. Mrs. Shaw and the children bend forward, settling their bags, making room for their feet. Sailors lean to the oars. The bow of the rowboat rises, splashes down. Rises, splashes down. The little boat dwindles as it nears the square-rigged ship. It becomes barely visible, no longer part of Whelan's Cove once it passes into *Zephyr's* shadow.

Father does not wait to see the anchor raised, but walks briskly back down the wharf. Azuba follows, stumbling as she looks back. Perhaps one day she, too, will be rowed out to a ship—if not with her parents, then as a wife. This is not a fantasy that she conjures up. It is part of her, like the splintery boards beneath her feet, or the smell of tarred marlin.

When Azuba and Father return home, Mother is where they had left her, sitting at her spinning wheel.

After she has been sent to bed, Azuba kneels at her window. She presses her forehead to the cold glass, makes blinders with her hands. There's nothing to be seen, only blackness. Somewhere out there is the captain's family.

She climbs into bed, pulls up the quilt.

She lies listening to the sea's rhythmic roar, unchanged by darkness. It makes her feel loose, peaceful. As if she's become as large as the wind. She drifts to sleep, picturing Mrs. Shaw, skirt and scarf snapping like sails.

Part One

WHELAN'S COVE

1. Noah's Ark

IT WAS THE FIFTH YEAR OF HER MARRIAGE, WHEN HER child, Carrie, was four years old. The bleeding began in the privy. Azuba wiped herself with a square of newspaper and found a red gout. She ripped newsprint from the nail. More blood came, thick, flecked with black strands. She mopped, mopped. She stood, bent with pain, settled her hoops, petticoat and skirt.

Wind snatched the door from her hand. She left it unhooked, gathered her cloak across her breast. The house loomed against a grey sky, the path a pale string in the headland grass.

Blood surged, trickled down her legs.

She began to run, one arm clasping her belly.

"Hush, now, could've been worse," the midwife said. "You were only four months."

She set a tin basin on the floor by Azuba's bed, stooped and gathered the rags. "Baby's gone, but there'll be more bleeding. Stay still."

Azuba lay flat on her back listening to the midwife's steps going down the stairs. Mother was in the kitchen, feeding Carrie her supper. Soon the whole town would know.

Azuba Bradstock lost a child, people would murmur. *Years before she'll have another chance.* The next time she went into the village, women would lower their voices, clasp her wrist, touch her shoulder. *Such a pity.*

She rolled her head sideways to gaze at the candle flame. *Nathaniel. Oh, Nathaniel, my beloved.*

She pictured her husband reading the letter she had recently sent. Perhaps he'd been in Cape Town, where he'd planned to stop for provisions. *There he sits,* she thought, *at the rolltop desk in* Traveller's *saloon, holding the letter over a mess of business papers.* She pictured his fingers smoothing his moustache, wide mouth bent downward, studying her words. *His eyes lighten, he smiles. He reads the letter again. Then he folds it, tucks it into its envelope. Presses it to his heart.*

February 6, 1861
Whelan's Cove, New Brunswick

Dear Nathaniel,
I am with child. Carrie is excited to think she will have a brother or a sister. Oh my darling, if only you could be home for this child's birth.

Nathaniel had left six months after their wedding, and had been at sea when Carrie was born. Once he received news that he had become a father, he'd written to say that he'd be home as soon as possible. One thing, though, had led to another: a cargo of coal to Bombay; a long delay in port; a consignment across the Pacific. His letters became increasingly frustrated. Carrie had been a sturdy little girl of almost three when he'd finally arrived home.

Azuba thought of the tiny nightgown in her workbox. It

was a smocked nainsook, embroidered with a red rose, its stem unfinished. Her needle, piercing the fabric. Carrie's finger, tracing it.

"May I name the baby, Mama?"

The candle flame licked the air, blue at its base.

Azuba watched it through tears. She felt the heartbreak of motherhood—sorrow, now, not only for herself and Nathaniel, but for Carrie.

Ah, the day he left. He had been home for a one-year furlough and had left again just after Christmas. He'd carved Carrie a Noah's ark with all the animals and, before leaving, had clasped her to his chest, gruff voice in her hair and a rare tear glistening in his eye.

"I'll be home soon," he'd said to her. "Don't worry."

There Carrie had stood, waving to her father going out to his ship in a rowboat. Returning home in the carriage, she'd knelt to look back down the bay, too stunned to cry. And then, when they returned to the house, she had climbed onto his chair and made herself into a ball, pressing her face to the brocade, refusing to speak, eat or be comforted. For days afterward she had stood at the bow window, staring out over the headland pasture, asking for Papa. Expecting to see his sails, coming home.

And that night of his leave-taking. How I took his coat from the closet. She'd sat on the bed with her face buried in its black wool, breathing its smell of tobacco and cold air. And realized that her love for him had no expression now other than in words—scrawled or read.

Now she cried herself to exhaustion and lay staring at the ceiling. She longed to tell Nathaniel. Her shock, stumbling over the field. Her hired man, Slason, hurrying to the barn. How she'd waited, moaning, while the carriage went for her mother and the midwife. She longed to be held in his arms, to feel his hand on her forehead, smoothing, consoling. To feel the bitter comfort of shared loss.

Despair, she thought, was the inability to imagine. She pictured the nightgown she had been embroidering. The names she had thought to bestow on the new child.

I have no reason to despair.

The bedroom had two bow windows overlooking the Bay of Fundy with its spruce-cragged cliffs. At the age of nineteen, she had married Nathaniel Bradstock, who at twenty-eight was a seasoned captain. Her father had given them the house as a wedding gift, hiding it beneath a scaffolding strung with sails as it was being built. A big house meant to be filled with dogs, toys, music, guests, family. He had set the house high on a headland, fit for a sea captain's wife, where Azuba could look down at Whelan's Cove with its shipyards, hulls looming higher than the rooftops, gulls circling in clouds of sawdust; its harbour, crowded with fishing boats, coastal schooners, sloops—and farther out, in the deeper water, square-rigged merchant ships with their forest of masts and rigging. One of which might, on occasion, be Nathaniel's *Traveller.*

She could look down at the farmstead of her childhood, set within fields of oats and buckwheat, and the ribbon of shore road. She could see the salt marsh where, as a child, she had run with her older brothers, Benjamin and William, and the dunes where compass grass scratched half-moons in the sand. She could see the beach where they'd chased stilt-legged sandpipers, jumped the ropes of froth, watched ships beating up the bay with billowed, patched sails.

She pictured herself as a child—dark-haired, impetuous, with black eyes, different from her fair-skinned cousins—and felt pity for her hope. Her innocence.

I thought I would sail away on one of those ships. Married to a sea captain. I'd be Mrs. Shaw, with her red-headed parrot.

Her days, now: as they would unfold tomorrow, and next week, and next month. She saw herself working with her hired girl, Hannah—planting, weeding, scrubbing—her own hair pinned back, sleeves rolled, scissors and knives jingling in the deep pockets of her wash dress. How she made her choice to work from the wearisomeness of its alternative: tea parties, visits, carriage rides. She pictured Slason, with his crooked leg and loose-lipped mouth. He tended the pigs, the horse, the cow. His voice, submissive. *What do you need, Mrs. Bradstock?* And the violent headland winds, different from the winds of her childhood. Clothes on the line, twisted into knots. Doors, pulled from her hand. Often, she paused on the porch and looked out at the blue line of Nova Scotia and the silver gleam in the southwest where the bay widened to the Gulf of Maine: the sea spread before her, thundered in her ears; and sometimes she loathed it, since Nathaniel was at its mercy. At other times, she closed her eyes, tossed back her bonnet and breathed deep of the world's size.

Azuba drew up her knees, rocking from the ache in her womb, thinking of Carrie.

No brother. No sister.

The May wind blew onshore and there was a spring tide. Carrie was at her granny's for the day.

Azuba sat in an armless chair, a Paisley shawl concealing the opening at the back of her dress; she had left her corset loosely knotted. She wore a brown dress with purple piping. Her black hair was unwashed, parted in the middle, caught up in a net at her neck. Beneath her eyes were blue shadows. After four days, she still felt a low cramp in her womb.

The new Anglican minister, Reverend Walton, had come to visit. He had heard she was unwell, but would not speak of the reason. He sat upright, his ankles crossed and his arms laid precisely along the chair's carved arms. He was a slight, mild man, easily moulded by the parish women.

She and Nathaniel had paid a call at the parsonage when he had first arrived. He'd shown them his studio, a large room at the back of the house with an easel, drawing books and a table beneath a window littered with treasures he'd collected along the shore—feathers, shells, skulls.

Even when he's old, she thought, *he'll still look eager, innocent.*

Sunlight streamed through the windows, lit the carpet-draped table with its oil lamp and leather books; a japanned china cabinet; a pump organ.

"It's a beautiful house, Mrs. Bradstock," he said.

His composure was disarming and she felt an impulse to tell him her real feelings about the house. How, when her father had told her he would build it, she'd exclaimed, "No, no, we won't need . . ." And then had paused. Mother had looked up from her sewing, shocked, her face revealing all she hoped for in a married daughter: help, companionship, grandchildren. Father's smile paled. "What did you say, Azuba?" His voice was awry, like Mother's face, its tone incredulous. He'd laid down his pen slowly, his eyes had narrowed, and she had been caught by his prescient gaze. She saw that her intention to go to sea with her captain husband was so far from her parents' expectations that her words were like a foreign language. And she had not dared refuse the house, or announce her plan. *A house,* she'd thought. *Only a house.* "I meant that you needn't do so much for me," she'd amended. "Thank you, Father. We would be grateful for such a gift."

Or how, on the day of their wedding, in the midst of an October gale, she and Nathaniel and most of the villagers had gone up the headland road in horse-drawn carriages. Father had lifted his arm, men had slashed the ropes, and the sails had fallen from the scaffolding, revealing a large white house that would forever be known as "the sail house." It had gingerbread shingles, a porch and steep gables. In their enthusiasm, the men had cut the ropes tethering the sails and the canvas had risen like monstrous, demented gulls, flapping towards the horses. Drivers had stood, shouting, hauling on reins. Nathaniel had jumped from the carriage, seized their horse by the bridle, growling "Whoa! Whoa!" even as he stared up at the newly minted house with a complex expression— surprise, affront and then a dawning comprehension.

At that moment, she realized later, Nathaniel had glimpsed the implications of taking her to sea: the danger to her, the anguish of those left behind. Perhaps when the sails fell from the house, Nathaniel's mind had shifted like ballast throwing a ship off true. *A place he could safely leave me.* She wondered if her father might have hoped for such an outcome.

"My father built it as a wedding gift, as you know."

Reverend Walton leaned forward, picked a dead leaf from his pants. "It must be a comfort to you to have such a house."

He was studying the leaf, and she saw that he was unsure of his boundaries, as a minister and as a man.

She pressed her folded hands to the ache in her belly. She felt an upwelling of longing to be sharing the loss of the baby with Nathaniel, and it was borne upon her that she must learn to fold waiting into living, like a kind of stillness within motion.

It is the nearness, she thought, *of his last visit.* Only four months since he'd left. And then this loss. It made his absence more unbearable. And she wondered if the pain of parting, over the years, would increase rather than diminish.

She must begin again her work of maintaining love. Keeping Nathaniel alive in her memory, and now in Carrie's. Reminding the child how he carved the tiny animals, one eye squinted, critical; or knelt on the rug with his muscled thighs, being a horse for Carrie. His lovely baritone voice singing Irish ballads. And her own, private memories: silky flesh, his hands cradling her face, the way he lifted her shawl from the floor and tucked it around her. And to compose in her mind an imagined life that dexterously shrunk the years he was away and expanded the time he was home.

She began speaking nervously, as if confessing. "You know, Reverend Walton, I married for love. I wanted to be with my husband. I thought that I would go to sea with him. I've always wanted to sail; I still do. I've always wanted to travel, to see the world." She gestured at the window.

It came in a rush.

"I thought we would be a seafaring family, like so many others. Did you know that Captain Shaw delivered all three of their children at sea? They had a pet billy goat on board. Captain Shaw made a little cart for it. The children had a full-rigged model ship that they towed in the wake of their ship. Mrs. Shaw hung her wash in the rigging. She saw Buckingham Palace. The children rode on elephants."

Reverend Walton tightened his arms to his sides as she spoke. His eyes slid to the clawed feet of the organ stool. He brushed hair from his forehead, as one would a fly.

"Well," he said, after a silence. "Could you not? Go with him?"

"He changed his mind."

When Nathaniel had first bent his eyes on her, she had

felt a heat in her chest, fear mixed with elation. She had felt light as the wind, and as formless. *Oh, and I asked him, Will I come with you, on* Traveller? *Yes, he said. He took me by the elbows and studied my resolve. Yes, he said, I could not bear to leave you.*

Reverend Walton appeared agitated by her tone. His eyes flew to the window and remained there. "It would be a life filled with peril," he ventured. "For you and the children."

"I'm sorry," Azuba said. "I shouldn't . . . I'm not myself."

The minister rose. "Mrs. Bradstock, please." He stepped forward, took her hand, held it for an instant before shaking it. "I've tired you. Please come visit the parsonage. Bring your daughter. I'll show her my collection."

After he had seen himself out, Azuba rose and sought her sewing box. She sat on the horsehair sofa, lifted out a bundle of Nathaniel's letters tied with blue satin ribbon.

My dearest Azuba,
I am at lat. 35 11,' long. W. 126, in the vicinity of Pitcairn Island. We are in the S.E. trades and the weather has been beautiful.

She skimmed through the letters, seeking words.

Love. Sweet. My dear wife. Home, soon. Our wedding. Wish that I. Forever.

Azuba dropped the letter into the sewing box and replaced the lid. It was her secret, what she had told Reverend Walton. Everyone assumed her contentment. There was not a girl in the village who would not have married Nathaniel Bradstock. Sea captains' wives were envied, whether they sailed with their husbands or not. Nathaniel was the youngest of three boys, all sea captains. When he was twelve years old, he had served as cabin boy on his oldest brother's ship; at fourteen, he was sent away to the academy in Sackville. And was a second mate at nineteen. The Bradstock brothers, Nathaniel included, were renowned for their hard-driven voyages, extravagant items brought or shipped home, adventures spiced with rumours of ruthlessness. Their parents gave balls and dinners to celebrate their infrequent visits.

Azuba thought of her plaid silk wedding dress, hanging in her bedroom closet. Green and purple, with a shimmer of gold thread.

The following week, Azuba and Carrie drove to visit Azuba's grandmother, Grammy Cooper. Slason offered to drive, but Azuba refused. She loved to collect the mare's energy, tightening the reins, snapping the whip. And it was only five miles, through the village, up along the needle-softened road.

Far below, Whelan's Cove was like a toy village, and off to the west, Grand Manan spliced the silver sea.

"I loved to come here when I was little," Azuba said. Carrie sat straight-backed with excitement. She held her doll, Jojo, face-forward to see the view.

They turned down the lane. Budding hardwoods held the light tenderly. Half-wild cats slithered away beneath the barn. Grammy was stumping lopsided towards the house. She clutched a bunch of parsnips by their tops.

"Come along in," she called. She waved her cane.

Azuba unhitched the mare, led her to the barn. Carrie squatted by the sill making chirping noises for the cats.

They crossed the hen-scratched earth. The poplar leaves funnelled the wind with a soft roar. They went up the wooden steps, holding their skirts.

The house was placid, vital: knitting needles spiked a sweater; carded wool was piled by the spinning wheel.

Geraniums lined the windowsills. By the stove was a pail, a bucket of potatoes and a narrow, high-sided cradle.

Carrie took her doll to the cradle. It had been Grammy's as an infant and had kept her warm during that first terrible winter in Saint John. Carrie had heard her great-grandmother's story, the words incantatory as prayer. *Log house caulked with seaweed. The autumn fleet. Loyalists. Grammy, child of refugees.*

Grammy made tea while Azuba poured cold water from a pitcher into a bowl, washed the parsnips. They sat at the table to chop them. Grammy's fingers were twisted, the knuckles swollen. She held her knife by tucking it in her palm. It flashed in the sunlight, cut as fast as Azuba's.

"Lost a baby. Probably something wrong with it, Azuba. Nature knows. Think it's something you did?"

Azuba looked into the beloved face with its splotchy brown marks. Skin fanned beneath Grammy's chin in parchment folds; her eyes were tucked deep beneath loops of flesh.

"Every woman thinks the same, Azuba. I began bleeding once after I'd lugged a bushel of potatoes."

"Why—" began Carrie.

Grammy raised a finger at her. "Take these to the hens." She swept the peelings into a bowl.

Carrie went out to the sunshine and the cats. They saw her wandering towards the barn, strewing parsnip skin. The wind lifted her dress, revealed her tiny boots.

"No. I don't think it's something I did," Azuba said. "I think it's the way I was feeling."

Grammy darted a look, but said nothing, only pursed her lips with their white waxy patches.

"Maybe wanting the baby so that Nathaniel would hurry back home." She laid the white, rubbery parsnips in a row and aligned the ends. "When he was home, it was as if it was *my* house, or Father's house. Not his. I could feel it. He was only a visitor. And I will never tell Father, but I have not yet reconciled myself to my life. I don't live to fill my rooms with silver tea sets and satin cushions, delivered to me by my husband from Paris or Bombay." She lowered her voice, spoke as if to herself. "I want to go to those places. *With* him."

Grammy put down her knife. "He's a good man, Nathaniel." She spoke firmly, as if she had once doubted. "Some say he's too hard, or too blunt, or too used to command. But I've watched him look at you, Azuba. No one else except Carrie gets that look from Captain Bradstock. Do you think you made a bad choice?"

"No. Never."

"Still. You're not like those peacocks in their pretty pens."

They both watched Carrie. She was skirting the rooster, whose yellow and black tail feathers fluttered.

"I could see you on that ship of his. Do him good."

Azuba remembered her small, bright-faced grandfather and how Grammy had broken into a keening at his burial, her cries unfurling into the sky. She'd been urged to come down off the mountain when he died, but had refused. She said she would live her life the way she wanted.

After they had eaten dinner and washed the dishes, Carrie and Azuba said their goodbyes. There were deep, oval holes in the soil where hens had scratched out dust baths. Carrie held up Jojo. Nathaniel had carved the doll's face, arms and legs. He had painted its cheeks red, given it a wispy smile. Azuba had stuffed the body with dried peas.

Grammy took the doll in her hand. "Father made that for you?"

"Papa makes my toys," Carrie said. She spoke solemnly and as if her Papa were not far away, nor would be long in returning.

Grammy kissed the doll's head. Carrie hugged her great-grandmother and Grammy put one arm around the child. She set her cane, looked deep-eyed at Azuba.

"Never let men frighten you, Azuba. They're boys at heart. Just boys."

May 16, 1861
The Sail House
Whelan's Cove, New Brunswick

Dear Nathaniel,
I have sad news for you, my dear. I am no longer with child. There was no fall or apparent cause. The baby slipped away, and I am left well but sorrowing. Carrie is heart-broken, for she had been hoping for a little brother, and had begun choosing names.

I am well. I am back at work with Hannah and Slason. I know you will think I should not be, but it is my wish to be outside and vigorous, and so we have begun break-ing up the soil with the mare for a new garden.

Nathaniel, I missed you so during this misfortune. My heart ached for you. If I could have made a miracle, I would have lifted you from the seas and set you here in your chair. I hope you can find a way to make a shorter voyage, although I know it is not always in your control. This past year that you were home, although we had not agreed upon our future, was so blessed, not least the joy of seeing you and Carrie together. She misses you terribly and plays with her ark every night as she promised you she would.

I know that after you changed your mind about my coming with you, we had many discussions. I know that you tire of hearing my views on this, and hesitate to write them down, but I must say that I continue to believe Carrie and I would not be such a burden as you think. If you cannot find time to come home, please know that I am still ready to pack up and join you so that we may be a family. I am not afraid, as you know. No storm seems as bad as having to live day after day with no husband, and no knowledge of when he might return.

I am sorry; perhaps I should not write this letter, but these are my feelings at the moment, and were you here I would be telling them to you.

I love you, always. I miss you. I pray for your safety.

Your
Azuba

"Oh, Mr. Marr has ridden an elephant, too." Crumbs blew from Mrs. Marr's lips. She was tiny. She patted her mouth with a linen napkin. "He assured me he was not a bit frightened."

Azuba and Carrie had been invited to tea at the home of Mrs. Black. Mrs. Holder and Mrs. Marr were present. All were sea captains' wives.

Their skirts rustled, releasing the scent of lavender. They sat forward on their chairs to accommodate their bustles. Carrie's feet did not touch the floor. She sat with a biscuit forgotten in her hand, staring at the cut glass chandelier, the fringed lamps, the stuffed pheasant, the clocks, mirrors and waxed fruit.

This house, Azuba thought, holding a teacup and saucer, was as large as hers, similarly ornamented with gables and turrets, set back from the main street on a slope overlooking the harbour. But it was so stuffed with possessions that its rooms seemed smaller, darker. Nor could she think of herself as similar to the other women. They were as overly decorated as the room. They wore rings on every finger, gold chains around their necks, dangling jet earrings, lace collars, ribbons, beads. They swept their hands in negligent arcs and talked loudly, without reflection.

Mrs. Black resumed her husband's latest letter, lifting her chin to read from the very top of the paper. Fine silver chains looped from her pince-nez.

The cook baked tarts and gingerbread. I have a very atten-
tive steward who brought me these with my tea. I passed
the morning pleasantly, scarcely a ruffle on the ocean or a
cloud to be seen. Today some handsome birds have been
flying under our lee. I spied a brigantine standing to the
westward but could not make her out . . .

Mrs. Black swept the pages with an ostentatious rustle.

Later in the day came a heavy gale from the northwest,
attended with squalls of rain. I called the watch, but before
we could get all sail in, the fore and maintop split . . .

Azuba leaned forward. She pictured the black clouds, the rain-stippled waves.

"Oh, bother that part. Let me find something interesting."

"Oh!" Azuba said.

Mrs. Black lowered the paper. "What, Mrs. Bradstock?"

"No, I'm sorry. I just wondered what happened."

"Well . . ." She raised the pages, scanned them. "He doesn't say much more. They limped along, I suppose."

Mrs. Marr set down her cup and saucer. She frowned when she spoke, causing a wedge-shaped furrow on her brow. "I skip those parts too. They will go on about the storms."

"I like to read about the storms," said Azuba. She glanced at Carrie. "Although I always wonder what he's feeling, and he never says."

"Feeling!" Mrs. Marr's narrowed eyes slid sideways to Mrs. Holder, a stern-faced woman from Saint John. Mrs. Holder's expression held a permanent state of affront, her mouth pinched down at the corners. The two women exchanged a glance. "Don't expect to hear about *feelings,* my dear."

"Not a shred of fear in their bodies," said Mrs. Black, setting down the letter. "Annie?"

An Irish girl dressed in a starched cap and apron circled the room with the teapot and a plate of biscuits.

"It's not only his feelings," Azuba said, taking a biscuit from the maid. She wanted, suddenly, to needle these women. "It's the storms. He dismisses them in a word or two. 'Storm last night.' But I find them exciting. I always want to know what happened. Whether the sails shredded, or if they had to heave to."

There was a silence. The room was overheated, the windows closed against the spring air.

"What really happens, we don't care to know," said Mrs. Marr. She glanced at Carrie. "It's best not."

Azuba turned to stare at the bright little woman. "I wouldn't be afraid to know."

"Wouldn't you? I suppose you would like to sail with your husband?"

Azuba saw that Mrs. Black's mouth was opening, a change of subject in her eyes.

"Yes," she answered, quickly. "I wouldn't mind. I'd love to see London, Paris. Antwerp."

The women laughed. They made clucking sounds, glanced at Carrie, who had not yet finished the biscuit she held in her hand and whose dress, Azuba noticed, was covered in crumbs.

"Have you met any of those women who sail with their husbands?" Mrs. Marr hissed. "Have you seen their skin?

Observed their manners? And think, Mrs. Bradstock, of what we read in the papers." The wedge on her brow raised, hardened.

The voyages that went dreadfully wrong, Azuba thought. Fire at sea, women put off in lifeboats, captains shot dead by mutineers, dramatic rescues in icy waters. These land-bound wives could not conceive of the excitement of such drama, or imagine the lives of the families who sailed without mishap. They saw no challenge, no thrill; only the evils of weathered skin, the pity of coarse manners.

"Will you grow your heliotrope this year, Mrs. Marr?" Mrs. Black turned the conversation to Flower Sunday, in July, when the church would be decorated with blooms from their gardens.

" . . . lovely new rose. Mr. Marr brought some rootstock from England . . ."

" . . . Love-Lies-Bleeding. So foggy in Saint John, can't grow . . ."

Azuba looked at Carrie and raised her eyebrows. *The biscuit. Eat it.*

She pictured Nathaniel sitting in a hotel parlour in San Francisco. Perhaps he was speaking to a woman with sun-browned cheeks who was sailing with her captain husband, telling her about his own *beautiful* wife, Azuba, back home in New Brunswick, and of their fine house on the headland over-looking the Bay of Fundy, and of Carrie, his little daughter. Perhaps the sun-browned woman bowed her head demurely and then slid him an admiring glance. And Nathaniel was free to think of Azuba as privileged, safe, fortified by wealth, glo-rified by her absent husband.

Carrie nibbled nervously at her crumbly butter biscuit. Azuba felt sudden rage at the sight of her little girl, already burdened by the weight of expectation. *Expectations.* These tiresome women who clucked so disapprovingly expected her to come to their sewing circle. They expected her to grow formal flowers suitable for ornate vases or placement in the church. Like her parents, they expected her to spend Nathaniel's money on carriages and dresses, and to stand proud at village events—ship launches, cotillions. Like Nathaniel, they expected her to produce children on whom a father might lavish attention when he returned on his infrequent visits.

Sun broke through a bank of clouds, quivered in the rain-bowed daffodils. In the room, the light illuminated the stuffed partridge and the powder on Mrs. Black's cheek.

Azuba leaned forward and set her cup and saucer on a table whose heavy cloth silenced the motion. She sat staring at the wrinkled pages of Captain Black's letter, lying beneath Mrs. Black's pince-nez.

Never again. Never again will Nathaniel set sail without me.
She glanced at Carrie.
Without us.

2. A Family of Sorts

THERE WERE TWO SHIPYARDS IN WHELAN'S COVE: Azuba's father's, the Galloway yard; and Nathaniel's father's, the Bradstock yard.

Azuba's parents lived in a large farmhouse with well-maintained barns, sheds and outbuildings. It was a mile from the village, set on the shore road overlooking the salt marsh, the harbour snugged into the fields, and the town that clung to the coast beneath Grammy's forested hill. Azuba's mother, Grace, had a hired man who helped with her hens and cow; her gardens were protected from the sea wind by wooden palings. She made her own butter, spun her own yarn.

Nathaniel's parents had built a mansion at the east end of the town's main street. It was gabled, turreted, filigreed. Townspeople called it "the castle." Shipbuilders and sea captains were set apart from the rest of the village: they were people of wealth and status.

Every Friday morning, Azuba and Carrie went to visit Ida Bradstock, Nathaniel's mother. In the front hall, they gave their coats to a maid. Through a door, they could see the gleam of a varnished floor in the room where Azuba had danced, one night, with Nathaniel. Ida met them in a conservatory filled with wicker furniture and orange trees. Boston ferns sprayed from hanging planters. The maid brought toys for Carrie: a chess set with ivory pieces, a toy dog with a red leather harness and a cart.

Ida Bradstock was tall, with a long, white-skinned face and sardonic eyes. She was impatient, spoke rapidly, was always, it seemed, on the cusp of some more important duty. She did not laugh; her forehead bore a vertical crease. Carrie was frightened of her. Azuba was affronted. In her own family, sentiment flashed easily, whether anger, love or laughter.

Mrs. Ida Bradstock, it was said, had great influence in the family business.

Ida removed her pince-nez, motioned with it at a pile of papers. "I received a letter from Nathaniel," she said. "You know, of course, that our shipping company asked him to go to Peru. For guano. So lucrative, just now. He's arrived in Callao. Have you heard from him?"

"I received a letter sent from London," Azuba said. Her voice was sharp.

"Ah. Well, then, if he wrote you from Peru, it must have gone astray."

"Or perhaps he wrote earlier and gave it to another captain, whose mailbag has not yet landed."

Azuba spoke clearly, sitting straight and looking hard-eyed at Ida.

What kind of a mother would she have been? she wondered. Had she ever brushed lips to Nathaniel's brow, rocked him in her arms, sung lullabies to him as he drifted to sleep? No, she answered herself. He had never known tenderness. She thought of the village gossip—that Nathaniel had not married because his mother sought out wives for him and presented them to him on his every furlough. How Mrs. Ida Bradstock was mortified by her childhood on a ramshackle hill farm, and sought—with her mansion, her belongings and her unloving mien—to forbid any trespass into either her past or her heart.

There was a pause.

"Are you well, Azuba? You have a straitened look. I believe you have not quite recovered from the . . ."

Azuba's eyes fell. She could not maintain her sense of herself under her mother-in-law's eyes. She felt undeserving, disappointing. No girl that Nathaniel had picked himself, she guessed, would have satisfied Ida.

"I am well, thank you."

When the visit was finished, Carrie pecked her grand-mother's cheek. *Grandmother,* she had been told to call her.

Slason waited with the carriage. Azuba did not dare drive herself to the Bradstock mansion. She knew Ida would think it ill-befitting a captain's wife.

Always, after being with Mrs. Bradstock, Azuba felt scoured. It was a warm June day, and she and Carrie changed into simple dresses. They put on their bonnets and went to the headland field, where they knelt in the wind, picking wild strawberries.

Azuba caught sight of a man coming up over the lip of the cliff. It was Reverend Walton, carrying a wicker creel, wearing a straw hat.

"Reverend Walton," Azuba called. She waved. "Reverend Walton."

He waved back and brushed forward through the daisies, buttercups and redtop grasses. Azuba and Reverend Walton shook hands. He knelt and spoke to Carrie. He accepted Azuba's invitation for tea.

In the kitchen, he hung his hat on a hook, sat in a rocking chair, the creel at his feet. Carrie knelt as he folded back its hinged lid.

"This is called a sea urchin."

"And this?"

He handed her the egg case of a skate.

"See, the lovely lines?" His narrow finger followed the crisp black tendril. "They call it a mermaid's purse."

Azuba set down his tea, the cup slippery on its saucer. "Here," she said. "Do come sit at the table."

He sat with legs crossed, one finger exploring the cup's scalloped rim. His eyes brightened as Carrie brought him a periwinkle shell she'd found.

"The biggest one," Carrie said. "The biggest one I ever found."

The young minister studied the periwinkle lying in his palm. He turned it, held it to the light. "It is the biggest one I have ever seen," he said. "You must keep this very carefully, Carrie."

Bread was rising. Puffs of steam came from the kettle on the wood stove, and sun lay on the spool-legged table.

Azuba sat across from him with her own cup of tea. "We were picking wild strawberries," she said. "See?" Her hands were stained red.

His hair, fine as a child's, fell forward across his brow. In the light, she could see that his eyes were hazel, brown flecked with green. Azuba contrasted her recent sense of diminishment in the presence of Ida Bradstock with how she felt with this young man: capable, lively—wanting to push the hair back from his eyes and ask him, as she would ask Nathaniel, if there was anything she could do for him. Was he hungry? Was he happy?

"I love wild strawberries," he said. "My sister and I would visit our aunt on the Kingston Peninsula. We would pick them."

"Come pick them here," she said. "Anytime. And please

visit us, Reverend Walton. Anytime you're down on our beach. Carrie and I are always here."

"Your beach, Mrs. Bradstock, is a wonderful collecting ground."

"I know," she said. "I collect things, too. I have a collection of feathers. And pebbles. And dried flowers. See?"

She rose and lifted a vase filled with dried sea lavender. She placed it on the table next to him. She was made peaceful by the motion of his hand. Rising, so gently, to touch the fragile spray.

Reverend Walton raised his eyes, caught hers and saw their expression. He smiled in response. "I'm unused to being called Reverend Walton," he said. It was a confession of his own. "You might call me Simon. At least when we're having tea."

"Only if you will call me Azuba. When we're having tea."

"Where's Papa?" Carrie said that night, when Azuba put her to bed.

It was their custom, after kissing Nathaniel's picture, to slowly spin the globe, guessing.

"Oh. We forgot to spin the globe, didn't we?"

They would run their fingers over the continents and the wing-shaped seas. Azuba's finger would come to a stop, say, in the Indian Ocean, and Carrie would pat the place, her hand making a dry tapping. Azuba would see both seriousness and serenity in Carrie's face and realize that the child truly believed she had comforted her father.

"Mama," Carrie said, sleepily, "was that where the dance was?"

Azuba puzzled through Carrie's train of thought. *Ah. Today, in Ida's conservatory.*

"No, the dance was across the hall, Carrie. In the big parlour."

Carrie loved to hear the story of when her parents had first met. The story was a strand of bedtime, woven through drowsiness, and crickets, and the cries of evening gulls.

"Papa saw me, Carrie, and he came straight towards me across the room."

"Straight to you, Mama."

"I wasn't expecting it, because he was nine years older than me. And all the other girls were hoping for his hand in the dance."

"His blue eyes were looking at you."

"Yes. And then we danced. All night long."

And Azuba told the story—a man and woman, gliding, whirling, until they became one. Carrie's thumb slipped into her mouth. Her eyes glazed, wavered. The lids fell. Azuba folded her hands and sat in the gathering dusk. Carrie's room faced west, overlooking the shore road and the harbour. Dappled clouds drifted in a sky that was silver-blue at the top of the window and peach-pink at the bottom.

Before Nathaniel, she had never been in love. He had come towards her across the ballroom, restless, quick-footed. He was muscled, decisive. One eyelid drooped, marred by a fellow sailor's fist; his face was wind-burnished brown, his beard newly trimmed. As he crossed the floor, she wondered if another girl stood behind her, but it was to her that he bowed. It was her waist that his hand cupped, her hand that he gathered in his.

And after the dance, she had lain awake all night long listening to the teeming chime of the marsh frogs. The sound came in waves, loud, then diminished, then gaining strength—like her own wonder and disbelief. Could it be? Would he come calling? Had she truly seen him looking at her, in his stern face a softening, a wild, hazarded speculation?

And he had come, the next day. Then she was swept into a state of ecstasy, where love and freedom had seemed the same thing. He was a sea captain. The world began at the harbour's mouth.

She went to the window, bent her forehead to the glass. She could no longer see the wildflowers. The headland was in darkness, yet still she could see waves on the bay, lifting up red, running down silver.

August 4, 1861
The Sail House

Dear Nathaniel,
I send this letter to Bombay, but hope that some kindly captain will intercept it and find you somewhere at sea. Carrie turned five this month, as you know. Hannah made her a wind cake, since we are getting a dozen eggs every day. We had dinner with my family, and went up to your parents' house in the evening. Your brother Charles has returned for a furlough. He brought your mother a new parrot. I wonder how your canaries are. You told me once that you talk to them and tell them of your day. Have you carved them any new perches? I am glad you have Mr. Dennis on this trip. I'm happy to think you have a first mate you both trust and like.

Nothing much happens here to write about. Visits to one house or another. The garden is growing. We haven't had any really bad storms to rip down the corn or the sunflowers. The ships are almost done; they will be fine ones. Reverend Walton, the new minister, will bless them. Do you remember we went to his house? He is working on his sermons for the ceremonies, and is a bit nervous about such important events.

Mother is piecing a new dress for me from some old ones. I don't need it, but she intends that I go to the tavern this winter with my brothers to hear some of those lectures. I go up to Grammy's. She's teaching Carrie to hook.

Nothing much else has happened. I can't think of anything much to tell you. Even though she is only five years old, our little Carrie is truly my best friend.

The house proved hard to heat last winter. Next month Slason and I will get up the baize over the doors and put on the storm doors and windows. Mr. Titus brought up the wood last fall and it is well cured.

I miss you. I think of you always. I think about how you would read aloud to Carrie and how you taught me to play cribbage. We were only halfway through that last Dickens novel. Carrie and I guess at your place on the globe every night.

I hope this finds you well, and that you will find a way to get home as soon as possible.

With love,
Your,
Azuba

"There I've got it." Reverend Walton stood before his easel. He touched a part of the sky. "There I have the oncoming storm. But here, you see. It's . . ." He batted his hands around his head, wrists loose.

Azuba came up closer. He was displeased with the grass, the blowing flowers. It was a piece of the western headland, as if one were sitting there on a summer afternoon, squinting into the wind. As, she thought, she and Nathaniel had once sat in that very field. Nathaniel had lifted his hat from his head, held it on his lap. He had stared at it, brushing it with the side of his hand until he could say the words he'd held back from any other woman. *Marry me.*

She turned to the cluttered table. On it were bottles of sable brushes, sketch books, tin trays of drawing implements, pickled creatures. There were bleached bones, lobster claws, fish skeletons, teeth, sand dollars, sea urchins.

"But you can fix it," she insisted. She was pleased to be asked, to be giving advice and reassurance to a man. "You can paint it again. The rest is so beautiful."

She had left Carrie at Mother's house, spooning butter into wooden moulds patterned with acorns. Mrs. McKiel, the parsonage housekeeper, had answered Azuba's knock and had led the way down a dark hall hung with paintings of cathedrals and English landscapes. Azuba had followed, apprehensive, even though she had been invited. Simon was in his work room. He had risen from his desk, with its cubbyholes and gilt-embossed theological books.

After shaking his hand, she had stood absorbing this room that was unlike any she had ever seen.

"I'm no good, really," he said, still regarding his painting. "I wanted to go to Europe to study art, but my father wouldn't hear of it."

"Why not?"

"I was always intended for the ministry. I was a small, meditative child—"

He broke off, suddenly silent. He took a bone and held it to the light. "This is a sparrow bone," he said. "You see? It's translucent. Hollow."

His fingers, she thought, were finer than her own. Their skin was white, and she could see blue veins mapping the backs of his hands.

"Well," she said, "it seems you've found a way to do both things. You're doing what you have to do. And you're doing what you love to do."

"But I do love what I have to do," he said.

"Of course." She glanced at him. He was still studying the bone. She wondered if he had told her the truth.

"And also," he laughed, abruptly, "I have to do what I love. I have no choice in the matter."

She stroked the head of a stuffed bird. She remembered her admission when he had visited her after the miscarriage, four months ago. *I thought we would be a seafaring family.* She had been careful never again to speak in such a way.

He was pointing at the easel with the sparrow bone. "Do you really think I can fix it? I was prepared to start again."

She studied the painting. "Make the flowers sharper, perhaps?"

He placed the bone on a small white saucer and opened a drawing book. It was filled with pencil drawings of flowers. "*Cypripedium acaule,*" he said, turning the pages. "Pink lady's slipper."

She touched the page with her finger, keeping him from turning it. "Oh. This one. So lovely. You have caught the . . . quiver. The frailty."

He glanced at her. Then he reached for a penknife and a ruler. He cut the page from the book and handed it to her.

She stood close to him with the drawing in her hands, so touched that she could not speak, even to thank him.

Summer passed. One day the swallows left; that night, the air was edged by the breath of winter. Goldenrod held tufts of seed fluff and the hawthorns bore shrivelled berries. In the morning, there were frost ferns on the window panes. Later, it was warm, and the air smelled of woodsmoke.

They were at Sunday dinner, after church, at the Galloway house. All the family was present: Azuba's parents,

Grace and Joseph; her brother William, who had no wife; and her brother Benjamin, his wife, Sara, and their two red-headed children.

Azuba sat at the table, facing the picture of the woman she'd been named after. She was a worn-looking person with five children who looked as if they had never once smiled. Grace had said, laughing, that the name "Azuba" meant "the deserted." "A poor meaning," she'd said, "For a beautiful name." Azuba stared at the picture as she took a plate of squash pie from William. She was remembering how, as a child, she had climbed on a chair to examine her namesake and had been disappointed—Azuba Galloway Price did, indeed, seem deserted. Azuba set her fork to her pie, struck by the thought that as a child she had renounced the person she was meant to be. She'd pretended instead that she'd been named for a queen, since her black hair was rumoured to come down the family line from shipwrecked Spanish pirates. She remembered herself clutching one of mother's red silk scarves to her shoulders, twirling until it flamed. *Queen Azuba. Queen of the seas.* And she would pretend to be this queen when she ran on the sands with her brothers, combing the wrack line, collecting shards of soft-edged china from the wrecks of ships.

She was exhausted, had not slept the previous night, could not attend to the family chatter. The night before, Slason had not gone home, worried about Dolly, the dapple grey mare. He'd pounded on the door at midnight, and Azuba shook Carrie awake, not daring to leave the child alone in the house for fear she might wake and call out. They slung round their wool capes, went down to the barn. Slason held the lantern. The mare was stumbling around and around in a circle, head low, gobbets of yellow foam on her lips. Clouds of steam rose from her slick, glistening sides. Her legs tangled, she tripped and fell.

A glaze had crept over Azuba, making her decisive, capable. She had told Slason to go for the gun. She put her hands on Carrie's shoulders, pressing the child's face into her skirts, watching as the mare went down, falling so heavily that the ground shook. She knelt by the dead mare and tugged at her rubbery eyelids, but they would not close.

In the morning, Slason had borrowed a team of oxen to haul the mare into the woods. Azuba and Carrie had stood on the porch to watch. Dolly's legs trailed and bounced on the soil, like the hinged legs of a doll.

"Poor Dolly," Carrie said. She was sad, Azuba saw, but resigned. "The wolves will eat her."

Azuba realized that her brothers had begun discussing Dolly's demise and where to find a new horse. She looked up, but they were speaking to one another and ignored her.

"Mr. Cotter has a yearling," William said.

"Untrained."

"Well, then," William snapped. He leaned forward. He had crabapple red cheeks and black eyes, like Azuba's. "I saw a good mare down at McBride's."

They spoke, she thought, as if she were not sitting at the table. As if she had no mind of her own. She felt anger, a sudden vibrant bloom. She was expected to live alone, waiting for her man to return, while remaining in a state of dependency. She laid her hands beside her plate.

"I can find my own horse," she said. "I don't need you men to do my thinking for me."

There was the indulgent laughter of older brothers who have not accepted that their sister is grown.

"Where do you think Nathaniel is, Azuba?" Her father had white mutton chop whiskers growing spade-shaped on his red cheeks.

"Heading eastward," Azuba said. She spoke coldly. She felt

invisible, as if the person she really was could not be seen and the person they thought she was, or would like her to be, was as non-existent as the vanished Azuba Galloway Price, mute on the wall. "Towards Hong Kong."

There was a clattering of forks, scraping. The ticking clock marked the slow Sunday.

Benjamin and William had acquiesced to Father's demand that they stay in Whelan's Cove, learn the business, become ship builders. Not sea captains, as they would have wished. They were intimidated by Nathaniel. They resented his reticence when he sat at the dinner table, beard jutting as he chewed. In his presence, they talked heatedly, arguing over things that had little import.

I'm a married woman, Azuba thought, *but I might as well not be.* Carrie was swinging her feet, scraping her plate with minute movements of her fork, although there was nothing left. She knew, Azuba could see, that something was being said about her father.

That afternoon, the surface of the sea was a fretwork of fine wrinkles, like the drawings Azuba had seen of elephant hide. Then the wind wiped it clean, dug furrows, changing it into an old person's face. Carrie and Azuba walked on the beach at the foot of the cliffs. Carrie ran ahead. Azuba stood turning pebbles in her pocket.

Rising from the glittering water was her childhood sense of being poised on the cusp of a boundless, beckoning future—wondrous, without shape, particulars or flaws. Like Mrs. Shaw, who had scudded through her child's mind. A woman who turned to face the sea and then stepped down off the wharf—backwards, laughing.

She thought of the coming winter. The days shuttled across

her mind: sewing in the grey light; cold-fingered carriage rides. *Visits, church, family. Visits, church, family.*

She lifted her skirts, took two steps back. The tide was rising.

"Carrie," she called. The wind snatched her voice.

Her leather soles were slippery on the beach stones, her ankles twisted. Overhead, cliffs rose against the sky. In their crevices were pale tufts of grass.

She angled up to the tide wrack where there was firmer sand, bent to pluck a feather from crunchy seaweed. She turned to face the sea, gathering the collar of her cape close around her throat, tracing her lips with the feather's tip.

Captain Nathaniel Bradstock had come to call after the dance. He'd sat in their parlour drinking tea. He was a man who was by necessity a judge of character, and saw her more clearly, perhaps, than her own family did. Later, when they drove to the headland, he told her about herself. "I saw you watching, sharp as my lookouts," he said. "You were not preening and waiting to be admired." He acknowledged her intelligence, her energy. They sat side by side in the grass. "I think you are both headstrong and sensible," he said. "So many girls are only one and not the other." She was in awe of him, half-frightened. He was larger than her brothers, heavy through the chest and shoulders. He fell into brooding silences, one eye half-shut, thumb and finger drawing down the ends of his sun-bleached moustache. His lips were habitually grim, yet curved into a lovely sweetness when he turned, tugged at the ribbons of her hat and lifted it from her head. Wind loosened her hair from its combs. His hand had gone to hers, where it lay in her lap. She turned her wrist. Their fingers gripped, made a fierce fist.

After he'd asked her to marry him, his eyes were softened by tenderness, and she'd imagined the boy he had been. He delivered letters to her in person, in which he scribbled words he could not say. *You are soft and wild, my Azuba. You are like a morning sky. I would have you at my side, always.* There was never any doubt that they would stay together, that she would sail with him. Once he had rowed her out to visit the barque *Eudora* to show her a saloon that had been refitted for a captain's wife. She had followed him about the deck, talking eagerly about sailing families—women who brought children on board, along with their pets: goats, kittens, dogs. He'd smiled, tucked a hand under her elbow, held her by the waist as he followed her down the companionway to the elegant saloon.

She stood watching the red triangle of Carrie's cape. She brushed her cheeks with the feather, enumerating to herself the events that had made him change.

The first was the day of their wedding, when the sails were cut from the scaffolding surrounding the house and Nathaniel had realized the extent to which her father had provided for her comfort.

The second was when, the following month, one of Father's ships went down off South America after only two months at sea, with all hands lost.

And the third. Three months after the wedding, she told him she was pregnant. He took her in his arms. "My dear," he murmured into her hair. And then was silent, as if he could not trust himself to speak.

One evening, a few days later, he rose, took down a book from the shelf and thrust it onto her lap. He opened it to a picture and stabbed at it with his finger. It was an etching of Cape Horn in a blizzard. A ship was foundering, her sails shredded, her masts parallel to the water. A woman sat alone in a lifeboat, clinging to the sides.

"This is Cape Horn," he said.

"I know," she said, putting her hand over the picture, looking at him, puzzled. "I don't want to look. I've seen these pictures. They are horrible."

He lifted her hand. He turned the pages until he reached a picture of a ship wrecked on rocks. Women and children were lashed to the masts. People knelt on shore, hands clasped or raised to their mouths, weeping.

"Ships run into icebergs, go down in flames. I heard of a woman who drifted in a lifeboat for months." His voice was harsh.

"You're thinking only of the bad things. What about—"

He had interrupted her. "Azuba. I have changed my mind. It is madness for me to take you with me."

He was like a different man, she thought, stunned. He paced to his desk, stood with his back to her.

"Nathaniel. I am not afraid. Not in the least."

He turned and raised his hand, palm out. "Don't argue with me."

"How dare you? How dare you speak to me like—"

"Azuba. I regret . . . you can't know how I regret letting you think that I would take you."

"You make me sound like a piece of baggage. I think of myself as your companion. In life."

"Yes, you are my wife. But not my first mate."

"I never for an instant thought of myself as anything other than your wife. Since I am your wife, you should not be commanding me as if I were—"

"It is *my ship* we are speaking of."

She saw him become a different man. A man of absolute authority, who could wield punishment and fear, and was accustomed to doing so.

"Why?" she said. She felt wild, like the women in the picture, kneeling, hands clasped at their breasts, disbelieving what was before their eyes. "Why have you changed your mind?"

He had come, then, and knelt on one knee. He put one hand on her waist and the other to her cheek. His face softened; he was distraught. "Because you are my treasure. Because I want you and my children to be safe on shore."

And she. Equally distraught. "But this is not a marriage. I would be alone. Perhaps for years."

He had pressed fingers to her lips, stopping her speech. "You don't know," he said. "You can't possibly imagine what it is like at sea. I was mad to think of it. It is my fault."

She had wrenched away from his hands, struggled from the chair. "You can't be bothered. It is simpler to leave me here."

Her sense of who she would be and how she would live was like a picture gone up in flames. She had protested, argued. He said that he had made his decision for her own good. She raged that she could decide what was good for her and held up examples of other sailing families. And then she had seen a side of Nathaniel she had not known. He became closed and hard. As he would be had he assessed a situation at sea and given his orders. He expected them to be carried out.

An element of fear crept over her. And a layer of self-protection, a shield to salve her wound and protect her pride.

After he sees the baby, she had thought, *he will not be able to leave me behind.* But he had left before Carrie was born. And when he returned, he had not changed his mind. He had left again, even after having fallen in love with his little daughter.

Azuba threw the feather, watched it cartwheel on the air. She pulled up her hood, tied it firmly under her chin. She walked into the cold wind, watching Carrie, who had turned and was coming back. Running, veering, light as a bird.

"Mama," she shouted.

She held her hand out, fist clenched.

They knelt, backs to the sea. Carrie opened her hand. In it was a minute periwinkle.

"It's a baby!"

"It's smaller than your littlest fingernail, Carrie."

"I'm going to give it to Mr. Walton," Carrie said.

By the end of November, winter gripped the coast. Ice slicked the cliffs, cauled beach stones.

Every Sunday, Azuba and Carrie went to church and afterwards to dinner with her parents. During the week, she took Carrie to visit Nathaniel's parents, or visited her married friends or the other captains' wives. She went to sewing circles and quilting bees. She went with her brother William to a few lectures at the tavern, one on phrenology, another on history. She had a new horse that she had discovered and chosen herself. She kept busy—spinning, sewing, helping Hannah— and yet was preoccupied, serious, her brows drawn.

In the ship news, there were tales of brigs and barquentines due in to Saint John that had not arrived; of the same ships discovered in flames, or reported lost, or found broken on rocks. Passenger lists were published. One family lost a son on one ship and, two months later, a daughter who was a passenger on another.

On winter mornings Azuba woke from dreams of Nathaniel's death. He clung to a spar in shark-infested water. *Traveller* sank, and he hung lifeless in the flooded saloon, face-down, arms drifting. Or the ship sank off the Horn: icebergs loomed from whirling snow and at their feet a lifeboat drifted, containing Nathaniel's frozen body.

She scratched a hole in the frosted parlour window, watched the grey waters of the bay. She went to the desk, took up the daguerreotype of Nathaniel. The downward turn of his lips accentuated by his moustache. Short square beard; guarded eyes. A hard face, made grim by the burden of decision.

She thought of the life she might be sharing with him. And how it would change them: how she would be able to understand his world; how she herself would flower. He had described cities with sun-warmed stucco walls, cathedrals, oleander-perfumed air, markets. She felt a twist of jealousy, thinking of the captains' wives he might be walking beside at this very moment, and their children, whose hands he shook. And then pictured Nathaniel and his first mate, Mr. Dennis, companionably sitting in the saloon, drinking wine and playing chess.

She glimpsed a whore—rouge-cheeked, full-fleshed, reaching for his face with lacquered nails.

Does he miss me? Did he truly love me, or was it just a passing fancy?

She put back the photo, smothering the sense that the longer he was gone, the more she was beginning to think of him as the man in this picture.

The beaches and coves along Azuba's stretch of coastline became Reverend Walton's favourite collecting grounds.

Often they heard the stamp of his boots on the porch. His cheeks would be red over an icy muffler, the wet leather of his boots frozen, his mittens hard as boards.

"Come in, come in," Azuba laughed. She opened the door and slid an arm into the frigid air, pulling at his sleeve. Carrie, too, laughed at the sight of Simon's frosted eyelashes. Steam wheezed from the kettle. They sat him in the rocking chair. He smelled of frozen soil. Carrie knelt to inspect his day's collection without having to ask permission. Azuba resumed her knitting or sewing, her face bright.

Sometimes Simon came to supper, and occasionally stayed on after Carrie had been put to bed. He had asked which was Nathaniel's favourite chair and made sure not to sit in it. He made Azuba feel comfortable. He discussed ideas for his sermons, as he would commune with a sister. She curled on the couch, watching the firelight. She confided in him—spoke of her loneliness, her worries for Carrie and fears for Nathaniel, the difficulty of keeping up her spirits, her guilt about what she had been given and did not fully appreciate.

They kept the fact that he was her minister scrupulously in place, like a folding screen; yet it occurred to Azuba that in the years stretching ahead before Nathaniel's return, this configuration might come to feel like a family of sorts.

April 10, 1862
c/o Mrs. Drummond
The American Captain's Boarding House
Tavistock Square
London, England

My dear Azuba,
Here I am at the American Captain's Boarding House. Mrs. Drummond has now reached 382 pounds, as she is pleased to announce. We all lay bets, as I told you, as to her weight. I lost my wager.

I have very good news. I heard of a load of mixed cargo for Saint John, and I jumped at the chance. I won't be able to stay home long, but at least might spend the summer with you.

Also I have been worrying for some time about your news of last May, and wondered how you are getting on. I got a letter from Mother saying you were looking thin and tired.

I should arrive sometime around the end of June. I will

take the summer to have Traveller *seen to. She is a bit worn out. As am I. I am ready to put up my feet for a while and get to know my beautiful wife again.*

Please believe me when I say that I look forward with the greatest pleasure to being home.

I last wrote to you from Peru. We had a remarkably good passage round the Horn, but a long haul across . . .

Azuba had ripped open the letter. It was a windy morning, and clouds raced over the headland, making the dandelions flash like a beacon.

She held the letter close. Coming home, so soon.

Was this a sign? Did he realize, perhaps, that he could not live without his wife and child? And it rushed up on her. Excitement, anticipation of conflict. She stared down the bay at the place where she would first glimpse *Traveller*'s sails. She felt the weight of all that comprised her life: house, chores, garden, family. Friends. Ties, knots. That she must have the determination to unbind.

3. Davidson's Beach

AT THE BEGINNING OF JUNE, CARRIE BEGAN DRAWING A picture in an old store ledger. She coloured it with chalks Reverend Walton had given her.

At the top of the page was their house. A path wriggled down the page, lined with flowers. On the path were three stick figures: Carrie, Nathaniel and Azuba. Nathaniel wore a top hat. A pipe jutted from his mouth, black smoke coiling from it.

The drawing covered the spiky brown handwriting, reducing once-vital statistics into a ghostly underlay.

She opened the book on Azuba's lap.

"This is a cat, this is Papa's canary bird. This is me and Papa on the beach. This is Papa's horse. He's taking me to Grammy Cooper's. That's the garden. This is Papa's ship with a flag on the mast."

Every day, Carrie pointed at the ships coming up the bay. "Is that Papa?"

One day soon, Azuba thought, *it will be.*

She knelt in the garden, grubbing weeds from a row of peas. Yesterday, Simon had asked if she would care to go on an expedition to Davidson's Beach. At the end of the beach was a "flowerpot," a high-cliffed promontory that jutted out into the sea, accessible by a steep path. At the top were wild-flowers and nests that Reverend Walton wanted to explore.

An expedition, he'd called it. Too arduous for Carrie, but they would be back in time for supper. Mrs. McKiel was making up a lunch.

"Yes, of course, I'd love to come," she'd said, wondering with a twinge of guilt if he, too, realized that going without Carrie would make this the only and now perhaps the last time they would be alone together.

It is easy, Azuba thought, half-smiling, *to be with Simon.* His attention was focused on flowers and birds. On the beauty of the world. Sky, sea and forest became abstractions. "See the white line?" he would say, drawing a line in the air and peering.

And she followed his finger. She nodded—"Yes, I see!"—pleased by his assumption of her understanding. And concealed as the beach pebbles she carried in her pockets was her pleasure at being his friend. Friendship—with all its demands and obligations. The sharing of confidences. The avowal of need.

"Look, Mama!"

Carrie was pointing. A ship hung between water and sky at the end of the bay. It was ethereal, its sails like light-filled thistledown.

"Could it be?"

"Not yet, Carrie."

She wiped her nose on the cuff of her gardening dress. She felt her heart jolt and speed. It turned before her: the first night. How Nathaniel would untie her corset cover and draw it off. Then, slowly, he would unfasten the ties of her corset. Would unpeel the whalebone husk from her body, leaving only the worn chemise. Her arms lifting as he slid it up. A red mark between her breasts where the busk had pressed. Her body, so soft. Fumbling at the waist button of her ankle-length drawers. They would drop to the floor. The next part was like a storm with winds coming from all directions. Hands, mouth, wrists. She and Nathaniel, each opened by the other, cracked, as if broken. Cries. And then, in the morning, she would feel rich, tilthy. He would gaze at her, his eyes sated and sly.

She returned to pulling weeds. And the other part. Their life, and how it was to be lived. Arguments remembered and foreseen shunted their eyes sideways. She remembered how it was, always, when she brought up the subject of her coming on the ship—how his face darkened and the corners of his nostrils turned white, silencing her. *But this time,* she thought, stirring the soil between the green pea tails with her fingertips, *I will not be deterred.* She would tell him about Carrie's torrent of heartbreak. How she had curled on the chair, standing at windows—asking, asking, for Papa.

Perhaps. Perhaps he is ready.

After a year. Who would he be? A stranger, it seemed, came to share her bed.

They scrambled up a slippery slope of scree and boulders. At the top of the flowerpot was an open space of grass and flowers shaded by a few spruce trees. It was like being on an island that floated in the sky. They could look down at the expanse of beach they had just crossed. Seaward, red mud stretched to the glinting ocean, a half mile out, so far away that they could not hear the breaking waves.

It was hot, windless. Simon removed his wool jacket, loosened his black tie and rolled up his sleeves. Azuba sat in the grass, arms around her knees. She watched him as he pulled aside the branches of shrubs with his narrow hands, exclaiming, putting feathers, flowers and eggshells into his bags.

"My brothers would never let me come up here with them," she remarked. "They said it was too dangerous for a girl."

"You had no trouble. You're a fine walker, a good climber."

He's like an aspect of myself, she thought. *We always agree.*

Hungry from their long walk, they devoured the enormous lunch Mrs. McKiel had packed. There were slices of chicken pie, pickled fiddleheads, molasses bread spread with butter, hard-boiled eggs, ginger cookies. They drank tea from tin cups.

"Nathaniel will be home any day now," she said.

Simon sat cross-legged. He held his cup in both hands, blew on the surface. She saw him look at her with curiosity, quickly veiled.

"How wonderful for you. And for Carrie."

"Yes. But I can't bear the thought that he will return, and then we will have to endure the sorrow of parting once again."

And then they talked of other things. Of his parish, of the women who frightened him with their rigid expectations, of the summer teas he must host, of how the women had begun to ask when there would be a Mrs. Walton.

The light was rich on the cliffs. "Burnt sienna," Simon remarked.

Azuba was overcome with drowsiness. She yawned, curled on the grass, put her face in the crook of her arm.

"I'm just going to have a little nap. Watch the tide," she murmured, already so sleepy that her voice was like someone else's.

She was awakened by chill. She sat up abruptly. Simon was asleep, with his head propped on his bag, ankles crossed.

The pools were glinting gold, and the feathers of the browsing gulls were edged with late afternoon light.

"Simon!"

She ran to the edge and looked down. The flowerpot was surrounded by water.

Simon woke with a start, scrambled to his feet. Wordlessly, horrified, they packed up the lunch, and Simon's bags, and began the descent. Simon went first. Azuba came up behind him. She steadied herself with a hand on his shoulder, looked down. At the foot of the scree, there was no sign of the sand on which they had left the prints of their soles. The rocks were submerged beneath silver-grey water. Implacable waves curled.

"There is no other way," Azuba said. "The other side is sheer cliff."

Shock spread from her fingertips, constricted her lungs.

"Surely . . ." he said.

"No. My brothers were trapped here once. This is the only place down."

She made her way back to the top, stood looking up the coast. She saw the headland beyond which, hidden, was Whelan's Cove and her own house, where Carrie sat on the porch in the afternoon sunshine, waiting. Simon came up behind her. He set down his bags, went past the spruce trees. She glimpsed him leaning precariously, looking down.

They would have to stay here overnight. Until dawn.

What will happen?

Carrie would wait for her to come home for supper. She would wait and wait. Hannah would try to make her eat, but she would not. She would think that her mother had died. She would be put to bed and her heart would break. She would sob. She would kneel at the window and weep into the darkness, in a desolation of terror.

Hannah would send Slason down the road to Father. They would mount a search party. By daybreak, every person in the village would know that the minister and Mrs. Bradstock had gone missing.

Nathaniel would hear of it.

She could hear the incoming tide, a dark lap and chuckle. A gull flew past, so close that she could see the red spot on its beak. Shadows deepened, became sharper.

No shawl, she thought. *I brought no shawl, we have no blanket. We have no more food.*

He came up and stood next to her. Then he took off his coat and pulled it over her shoulders.

"It's the least I can do," he said, when she protested, seeing him in his shirtsleeves. "It is my fault."

"I could have said no," she said.

I should have said no.

She couldn't remember if she had told Hannah where they were going. He had not told Mrs. McKiel. They watched as water crept over the places where they had jumped from rock to rock.

"It is strange to think that where we walked now lies beneath seven feet of water," she said.

"And the seaweed is no longer flat, but has become a swaying forest," he said.

After a while, they sat, facing southwest with their backs to Whelan's Cove. Azuba put up a wall in her mind. She would break down if she thought of Carrie. Darkness came, and with it, the deep chill of summer night on the Bay of Fundy. She felt him shiver.

"Reverend Walton," she said. "Please. Take back your coat."

"No."

"Then I will have to sit closer to you."

She slid close. He paused, and then gently raised his arm

and put it around her. She could feel his leg through the fabric of her skirt. A sweet, flowery fragrance came from his clothes. *Mrs. McKiel must place sachets in his dresser drawers.* She felt how slight he was compared to Nathaniel. Almost, it seemed, she supported him, rather than the other way around.

She whispered. "We'll freeze, otherwise."

"Yes," he said. "You can put your head on my shoulder," he added. "You can fall asleep. "

She woke.

They were lying together. Her head was snugged to his shoulder. His arm was beneath her. Her skirts were drenched with dew.

She pushed herself up. The sun broke from the sea and trembled in dew drops. There was a smell of wet bark.

She sat cross-legged, watching him. She saw a fine bristle of hairs on his upper lip, on his cheeks. His skin was like the flesh of pears.

And a longing for Nathaniel came over her. What would he have done during this night? The strength she felt with Simon was too easily won. It would wear, and become a burden. Nathaniel would never have let such a thing occur in the first place. And if, for some reason, they were stranded together, he would have wrested the situation to his advantage. He would have broken branches from the trees, made a shelter. He would have made a fire and squatted beside it, grinning at her, holding his hands to the warmth. Made her bristle, perhaps, resenting his command and so insisting on helping. She would have gathered sticks, dry spruce cones.

She gazed at Simon's hands. Nathaniel's were muscled, with white scars. She had watched them bend around a small knife, carving Carrie's toys, a latency in their deliberation, like the smoulder of decision.

He would hear of this.

But nothing happened, she thought. *I went on a walk with the minister and was trapped by the tide. I will tell him so.*

And then she realized that she felt shame. The condemnation she and Simon would return to was something they had begun to expect. This was more than a simple friendship, and she had sensed, for some time, that it was bound to end.

Azuba began to run as soon as she turned the corner and saw the house glaring white in the mid-morning sun. A figure moved behind the kitchen window.

She ran until the stitch in her side was insupportable. She stood, panting.

Three figures spilled onto the porch. Carrie, Grace and Hannah. Grace and Carrie ran down through the blowing grass. Azuba resumed running, and at the bottom of the lane fell to her knees in time to gather Carrie, clutching the small, solid body with a consolation akin to grief.

"Where were you, Mama?"

Azuba panted. "We were trapped by the tide."

"I tried to stay awake, Mama. I tried to watch for you, but Hannah wouldn't let me. She put me to bed."

There were blue bags under Carrie's eyes, and her eyelids were swollen.

She blames herself, Azuba thought. *As if she might have brought me home with her patient vigil.*

"I'm sorry, Carrie," she said, hugging the child. "I'm so sorry." She heard Simon come up behind her.

"Foolish!" Mother raged. "It was ill-considered, Reverend Walton."

Azuba buried her face in Carrie's neck. Her mother was speaking to Simon as she would speak to one of her own sons, with no trace of a parishioner's respect, no sense of Simon as a man above her, superior in station.

"I'm sorry—" Simon began.

"My husband, and my sons, and half the men of the village . . ." She could barely speak for the press of her agitation. " . . . up all night. Thinking to find your drowned bodies. They're still out there."

Azuba looked up to see her mother's thin face. Her cheeks were like an apple after frost, skin made useless by shrunken flesh. In her mother's eyes she saw for the first time the enormous implications of this night, irrevocable as the taking back of spoken words.

"Mother." She stood. Carrie bunched up beneath her arm, stared silently back and forth between Reverend Walton, her granny and her mother.

"Mother, please let me explain. We . . ." Mortified, she could not meet her mother's eyes. "The truth is that I fell asleep after lunch. I'm afraid Reverend Walton did too. When we woke, the tide had already reached the foot of the flowerpot. We were trapped."

"Where was your mind, Azuba? What child who grew up by the Bay of Fundy wouldn't know not to nap in such a place?"

Grace turned, her hand rising as if it held some object she would hurl. She began to storm up the lane to the house. Her fury sifted back, dusted them.

"I'm sorry," Simon said, again. He looked at Azuba. He seemed drained, helpless.

"It's all right," Azuba said.

Halfway up the lane, she glanced back. Simon remained standing, watching her. She winged her hand, half-hidden in her skirt.

He was so slight, buttressed with his easel and bags. She turned once more. The road was empty.

A week later, Reverend Walton disappeared from the village. Azuba learned of it from Nathaniel's mother. She and Carrie were sitting in the conservatory. Dark clouds brewed up over the bay. Rain spattered the windowpanes randomly, like warnings.

The maid brought a tea tray. Carrie was offered a vanilla biscuit.

"We're to have a new minister," said Ida. She slid her eyes at Azuba, spoke sparely, expecting pain, as one might press a bruise. She wore a dress of gold silk with flecks like beaded water drops. "Reverend Walton has returned to Saint John. I saw him leaving on this morning's ferry. With a considerable parcel of boxes and chests."

Azuba looked at the saffron-coloured tea. *Will she accuse me? Or will she toy with me? With Carrie present?*

"Too young," Ida said. Lightly. "He was too young to bear the responsibilities of such a large parish."

Not a soul in Whelan's Cove would not know. *The minister and Captain Bradstock's wife. Had a nap. Got trapped overnight on the flowerpot.* Azuba had gone to her father that same day and explained what had happened. She had told him there was no disgrace. She and Reverend Walton, she'd said, had sat side by side until morning.

Joseph had closed his eyes as she spoke. When she finished, he would not look at her. He had stared at the upper panes of the dusty window. "Yes, yes," he had said, finally. His voice was edged. He licked the corner of his mouth and touched the wet spot with a finger. "I will be sure to broadcast the story as you reported it to me." Both felt that the other, for the first time in their lives, had concealed the truth.

"When do you expect Nathaniel?" Ida stirred her tea.

"I have as little idea about that as anyone," Azuba replied, nastily. She glanced at Carrie. She had taken a small nibble of the frail biscuit and was brushing the crumbs from her lower lip with her forefinger. She tried, Azuba saw, to keep her feet lined up neatly, but since they dangled could not help the way one toe splayed.

"Reverend Walton was a good friend to me and Carrie," Azuba said. Her anger with Mrs. Bradstock was so long-held that it was liable to explosive collapse, taking with it judgment, inhibition, sense. Colour rose in her face. "I will tell Nathaniel about the night on Davidson's Beach," she added. "There's nothing to hide."

"Oh, I never for a minute . . ." said Ida. A sweep of her hand. Its passage was like a hand scattering the crumbs of Azuba's meagre days.

How we lie to one another, Azuba thought. *The captains' wives, who say they do not miss their men. Nathaniel's mother, who thinks she has made a good life. With her servants and exotic birds. Eight cages, in this room.*

The birds, Azuba noticed, were subdued on this rainy afternoon.

4. Sea Chests

ON THE MORNING OF JUNE 24, 1862, THE SAIL HOUSE
was filled with masculine clutter: chests, boots, coats, twine-
tied parcels, a portable writing desk. Nathaniel set his belongings down randomly—tobacco pouch on the hall table,
calfskin trunk on a footstool—as if he were a visitor in Azuba
and Carrie's home.

His presence made ceilings seem lower, furniture smaller.
Azuba felt a wild excitement, as if she had lost every normal
habit. She stared at her husband, so close, sitting in the
morning sun, pipe in his teeth as he bent forward to
rummage in a satchel. A cedary tinge rose from his clothing. His cheeks were scorched, and there was a whiteness
around his eyes, like salt, and flakes of dead skin on his lips.
The hair on his arms was silver, glistening against dark
brown skin. She had forgotten the redness of his beard, the
way the long muscles in his forearms bunched and slid.

He took out a small, square package wrapped in brown
paper, shifted his pipe to his back teeth.

"Ah, this now. For you." He handed it to Carrie.

Azuba's excitement folded, calmed. She felt that she might
weep, watching his gentleness with the little girl, seeing
Carrie's joy. He put his hand to the child's cheek, a wonder

in his eyes akin to anguish.

"My little girl," he said.

Carrie stood at the arm of his chair, gazing at him. *He must seem enormous to her,* Azuba thought—thick-chested, arms like branches, his eyes fanned with white squint lines that narrowed and vanished when he grinned.

Carrie opened the parcel. It was a doll-sized leather purse—brown, with a zigzag of black stitches. He pointed at it with the stem of his pipe.

"My sailmaker made it by skinning pigeon's feet. He dried the skins and patched the shreds together."

Carrie bent her head, stroking the black stitches. "It will be Jojo's purse," she said. "She's going to keep her button collection in it."

Nathaniel looked up at Azuba. His eyes crinkled in a smile. *He is not cold and hard,* Azuba thought. Relief swept over her, and she realized that in her mind he had become the man in the daguerreotype. She had forgotten both his charm and his power. He was vital, alert: an explosive mix of competence, intelligence, impatience.

"Carrie has started her own button collection," said Azuba. "Show Papa."

Carrie turned to run upstairs. She paused, looking at Nathaniel. "I'll be right back," she said.

Nathaniel took her by the shoulders, spoke gently. "Don't worry. I will be here when you return."

The child's feet trampled on the stairs.

Nathaniel looked at Azuba. She took a quick breath that lifted her chest. He rummaged in the bag, came and sat next to her on the sofa. He lifted her hand and slid a bracelet over it.

"Shark's teeth."

In his eyes, just as Grammy had said, was the look that no

one else received. Burning, direct, nothing else within it but the woman he saw before him and the wonder that she was his wife.

"You are so beautiful, Azuba," he said. His face was softened by sleep and the cessation of exacting concerns.

Her cheeks flamed. *His hand on my belly, in the curve of my back, tipping me.*

"It was your letter that brought me home early," he said. "When you wrote that you wanted to make a miracle and lift me from the seas."

She felt a stab of terror. *I have to tell him. The sooner the better. Get it over with.*

He trailed his fingers up her arm, along the bone beneath her eye. His eyes followed his own finger as it traced her eyebrows and lips, looped her ear, followed the part in her hair. She watched him, fingers exploring the shark's teeth encircling her wrist. She thought of her first sight of him. He was coming towards the wharf in a rowboat. He'd stepped up onto the wharf and their eyes had met. Their hands had flown forward. They'd gone on a whirl of visits— up to his parents' house for wine and biscuits, then back through the village and up along the shore road, stopping at the Galloway house for tea. And then, finally, up the headland road, the right-hand turn into the lane. The house bulked against a sky pearled with summer dusk.

And this morning. They'd lain beneath the quilt. The room was cool, over the sea was a shoal of pink clouds, and the air smelled of daisies.

He had reached over and pulled her onto his shoulder. They had not spoken, but had lain listening to the cold rattle of pebbles in a bright, small surf. She felt his contentment. Hers was broken by fear. Words formed in her mind, telling him of the night on the headland, still so alive in the village, people's eyes slying away from hers, the story like a delicious treat. How angry would he be? Surely he would understand?

"I have been worried about you," he said now. "You're still too thin."

I will have to tell him. Before he goes to the village and sees it in someone's face.

"After the baby . . ." she murmured.

They sat looking at one another. She drew in his smell of tobacco, musty wool, a sear of perspiration.

"I didn't want to eat for some time," she said. "And I've been working in the garden. And all the rest."

Her hand, erasing with a flick—firewood, hauling laundry, kneading, scrubbing. Taking care of this place, and her life, and Carrie.

Carrie ran into the room, carrying a lacquered box. She went to Nathaniel and placed it on his knees. She busied herself opening it. "I like this button," she said. "See, Papa. This is a pretty one."

"That *is* a pretty one," he said. He held it to his eye.

After opening their gifts, they hitched up the horse and went for a drive. Nathaniel wanted to go to the headland where he had proposed to Azuba.

Nathaniel turned frequently to Carrie. He grinned, told her his boyhood memories. Sliding on that hill. The bull he had been chased by. The pig shed he had hidden in, there in the hollow, half-buried in wild roses.

The words pressed in Azuba's mouth. Where should she start?

You remember the minister, Reverend Walton.

He asked me to go . . .

One day we were up on the . . .

You know how the tide out by Davidson's . . .

From the headland, they could see their own house on the

opposite promontory. Nathaniel pointed out *Traveller,* like a miniature ship in the harbour. They sat in the grass and looked out over the dark blue waters of the bay, rimmed by the far-off, alluring swell of Nova Scotia; up and down the coast, red cliffs faced the sea, white scarves at their feet where waves met rock.

Nathaniel put an arm around Azuba's waist. Carrie curled with her head on his knee.

That afternoon, Nathaniel went to the Bradstock shipyard, and still she had not told him.

At suppertime, when Nathaniel had not returned, Azuba felt fear darkening her mind, interfering with her good sense. She was busy, rushing. She snapped at Hannah, and Hannah tripped over the broom and dropped a pitcher of milk.

Azuba apologized, at the point of tears.

Carrie stood by the window waiting for Nathaniel. She cried out, "Mama, here he comes!"

Azuba went to the window. She saw Nathaniel hand the horse to Slason. She saw how he walked through the wind-whitened grass. He was resolute, yet resisted each step. Carrie ran to the door.

"Carrie," Azuba said. "Papa is . . . Papa will be tired tonight."

Nathaniel's boots on the porch. The latch, lifting. He came into the kitchen. He looked down at Carrie, his glance careful to exclude Azuba. He did not smile, but put his hand on the child's head.

"Papa?"

He walked through the kitchen, went into the parlour. Carrie began to follow.

"Papa's tired," Azuba said. "As I said he would be. Leave him alone."

Azuba saw such disappointment in Carrie's face that she felt the welling of an apology, not to Nathaniel, but to Carrie.

And Azuba thought of how there might have been Carrie's happy shriek, and Nathaniel's laughter, and now there was only the child's hurt face. And the wind. A log shifting in the stove.

In the bedroom, Azuba sat with one foot tipped sideways on her lap, untying her shoe's ankle laces.

"Nathaniel," she said. "I was going to tell you."

He had undressed in complete silence, his back to her. He spoke in a hard voice, without turning. "I could not have imagined you would have such bad judgment. I feel as if I did not know you."

"Yes," she spoke quickly. "I should not have gone. I'm sorry, Nathaniel. But that is all it was, too much lunch, falling asleep. We never—"

"Never mind," he said. "I heard more than I wanted to."

Now she heard the anger. Her heart thickened, her saliva tasted of blood.

"There was nothing," she said. "Only a long, cold night sitting on the—"

He turned, took a step towards her. She saw that if Simon were present, Nathaniel would smash his fist to the young man's head. He fixed her with his captain's eyes. "There's no need to explain, Azuba. I don't want to hear. Ever."

"There is, though," she said. Her heart hammered. She stood, the shoe in her hand. "There is much to explain. Much to say. Reverend Walton is my minister. And my friend. Only my friend."

"A married woman doesn't make friends with other men."

"I am a married woman, Nathaniel, but I am alone. I am lonely."

He went to the open window. The sleeves of his nightshirt were rolled to his forearms, the collar open. The hollow wing-whistle of snipes stitched the darkness.

"You should make friends with other women."

"Ah. Yes. And do I tell you what you should do?"

He said nothing.

Her voice rose. "How do I know how you live your life? How do I know if you befriend women in Paris, or Hong Kong? I have nothing to say about where you go, what you see, how you spend your days. You are not trapped in the same place day after day. Your life is one of continuous interest. Challenge. Change."

"You are spoiled." His lips made an ugly twist, exposed his turmoil.

"If I'm spoiled, then so are you. I'm like a pet. You come home to visit me in my pretty pen. Peacocks, Grammy calls the other captains' wives."

"The other captains' wives don't traipse out to headlands and spend nights with young men."

"The other captains' wives are not me, Nathaniel. Perhaps you're right. Perhaps I'm someone other than the woman you think me." Like the daguerreotype, she thought, suddenly. "You don't know me."

They held one another's eyes, a bald stare, each making their eyes crystalline, impenetrable.

He went to the bed, picked up a pillow and then struck it with the flat of his hand and hurled it against the head-board. He went to the chest of drawers and took off his nightshirt. He began to dress, speaking rapidly.

"It seems we will get to know one another very well, Azuba.

Very well, indeed." He thrust an arm into a sleeve. Stepped into his trousers, savaged their buttons shut. "You'll get your wish. You and Carrie will come with me."

He went to the bedroom door.

"Nathaniel."

"I've spoken to your father."

She stood listening to his steps on the stairs. The slam of the kitchen door. The crunch of his boots, going down the lane.

No, she thought, stunned, staring at the door. *I didn't mean, I wasn't trying . . .*

She felt as if he had taken her desire like a beloved toy and torn it and thrown it in her lap. *Have it, then,* he'd said.

He came to bed, but left before she awoke.

The next morning, she was kneeling on the parlour rug, agitatedly pairing the animals and putting them into the ark. He came to the door, paused, then went to his desk. He picked up a paper knife.

"There was nothing," she said, sitting on her heels. "Nathaniel, we went in the morning, meaning only to be gone for a few hours. I was helping collect—"

"There was something." His voice was tight. "Something to set a whole village talking. I told you not to speak of it."

She turned a giraffe in her hands. There was a silence in which they could hear Carrie talking to Hannah and the sizzle of bacon.

"Since we cannot discuss what happened, I will tell you that I am glad for your decision," she said, finally. "I'm glad to be going with you."

His eyes were remote, his lips pinched down at the corners. "I have no choice. Therefore, it is your choice. Remember that."

He told Carrie at the breakfast table.

"How would you like to come to sea with your Papa?"

Carrie's mouth fell open. She looked at Azuba.

"Mama too," Nathaniel said. He spoke evenly. His eyes burned straight into Carrie's. "You will have to do just as I say on the ship. I'll be your captain as well as your father."

That is for me, Azuba thought.

"You'll have to live in a tiny cabin with no fields to run in. No cousins. You'll have only Mama."

Carrie sat so still that she trembled.

"We'll leave in September. We'll sail to London. Likely we'll spend Christmas there."

He set knife and fork to a slice of ham. Azuba watched his hands on the knife, sawing. His chewing. The muscles in his cheek. His beard, bobbing up and down.

Yesterday seemed so far away. When he had traced her lips with his finger. When she was like treasure, and he was holding her, turning her—like a jewel to light.

"Mama?" Carrie was watching Azuba. Her eyes were anxious. "Are you afraid?"

Nathaniel glanced at Azuba.

"No, darling," Azuba said. "No, of course not."

"What will happen to Hannah? And Slason?"

"They'll . . ."

She realized what she had set in motion, and how much would need to be decided. Set in a new configuration.

"They'll be . . ." She lowered her voice, even though, in the dining room, they were out of Hannah's hearing. "They'll go somewhere else to work."

"Will we come back? Will they be here when we get back?"

Nathaniel put down his fork. He looked out at the bay,

his mouth grim. He was motionless, as if stilled by possibilities.

"Yes, of course they will, Carrie."

Carrie looked at her father. "Will we take my cat on the ship?"

He returned her gaze, half-smiled. "Best leave her with your Granny, Carrie. She'll need a nice haymow for her kittens."

"But . . ."

Carrie, Azuba saw, was bewildered by the extent of the changes.

"Carrie, my darling. We're going to be with Papa. We'll be with Papa every single day. We won't have to wave goodbye to him."

Carrie looked between her mother and father. *She knows,* Azuba thought. *That something is missing. Or wrong.* She reached for Carrie's hand and patted it. "It will be wonderful," she said. "We will have a wonderful time on *Traveller.*"

She looked out the bow window. The sea was different, more present. Its menace and its beauty filled her mind, even as the house, the garden, the horse and the village began to fade, separate, diminish.

All summer, Azuba remembered the first day of Nathaniel's return. It grew blurred with the remembering, like a much-handled letter. She remembered the moment he had slid the bracelet onto her wrist, had traced her face with his finger— reading her, it seemed, by touch. They'd had one night in which they had slid hands on flesh, lost within one another, crying out, laughing. And one day to feel wonder.

Then she had wounded him. He would not forgive her. He was humiliated, his equanimity shattered. In his eyes, and in the set of his shoulders, she read brutal questions he would never ask. *Who am I to you? On what is our marriage based?*

I did not betray you, she wanted to shout. *You have no reason not to trust me.* But every face in the village, even those of her own parents, could not help but tell him otherwise.

Most of every day, Nathaniel was down at the wharf or at the shipyard. He became the man of the daguerreotype—brusque, impatient—leaving barely enough time to visit with Carrie before it was her bedtime. His civility to Azuba was elaborate.

Decisions had to be made. The horse, the cow and Carrie's cat would go down the road to the Galloway house. The hens and the barn cats would be taken to Grammy Cooper's. The pigs would be killed at the end of August. Slason was to work in the Bradstock shipyard. Hannah would move back to the village, where she had secured a job with another captain's wife.

The rest of the summer was not for Nathaniel to rest, as he had planned, or to spend time with his wife and child. Everything tended towards departure. The garden, now, was for *Traveller.* Nathaniel spoke to Azuba peremptorily, motioning towards the feathery carrot tops. "We'll need potatoes, carrots, turnips—anything that will keep in the hold. We'll need jam, butter, relish, pickles. Put down the eggs in water-glass. I'll purchase salt beef, lard, salt, sugar, flour."

The house would need to be shut down for an unknown length of time. Slason hauled the beds outside, took them apart, scrubbed them with cold water and brown soap. He caulked, painted, made repairs. Azuba put her hair in a cap, wore her oldest dress, worked from morning until night. She and Hannah washed windows, dusted wallpaper, organized cupboards and closets, took up carpets and beat them and stored them away. They washed curtains, bedding and clothing, sun-dried them, folded them with twists of tobacco, sewed them into clean sheets, laid them in chests.

As she worked, she wondered about Simon. She did not dare ask anyone if he had been transferred to another parish or had given up the ministry. Every day, she intercepted the mail, even though she was certain he would not dare to write to her. She assured herself that she had never been in love with him and so was clear in her sense of righteous indignation. Truly, he had been a gentle friend. She knelt in the garden soil, hands filled with weeds, and felt an almost pleasurable sorrow that would be easy to dispel if she could write to him. She wanted to end the story; to tell him, simply, that she had enjoyed his company. And longed to know if he felt the same way about her. She hid the drawing of the lady's slipper in a drawer beneath her corset covers.

Azuba and Nathaniel were neither companionable nor tender. Occasionally, and by mistake, they caught each other's eye. In the dark, steady looks he cast at her from under his sunwhitened eyebrows, she guessed that in his mind she was still gathering flowers for another man. Lay, perhaps, in another man's arms, an image so outrageous that he could not bear even to hear it disavowed. The only subject on which they could speak easily was Carrie, and her doings and accomplishments. Often, Azuba was frightened by Nathaniel's tone and tried to hide the fact from Carrie by speaking in an offhand, pleasant voice. She heard her own falseness and hated it in herself.

There were nights of intimacy. And then, afterwards, a day when they could half-smile at one another or sit in the parlour of an evening and speak with equanimity about the day's events.

All summer long, Azuba's heart was heavy. Once, she apologized. She admitted that she had made a terrible misjudgment. He heard her out, and agreed with her.

"Yes," he'd said. "You did. You and your Reverend Walton."

She had risen from her chair, stormed from the room. Of the voyage to come, they were silent.

In September, Grace, Azuba's mother, came up to the house to help. They stooped in the garden, skirts and shawls billowing, filling baskets: onions, potatoes, beets, carrots, squash. In the kitchen, they made jams, chutney, pickles, and packed the jars into crates. They spent hours on their knees in the autumn sunshine, laying away last-minute linens and woolens, packing china in newspaper. Slason carried chests and trunks to the attic.

In Azuba's bedroom, they selected clothing for the voyage. There was a large sea chest for Azuba and a smaller one for Carrie.

"Best put this away," Grace said, running her hand over the Star of Bethlehem quilt. "Pack it down with pepper. Keep it for when you come home."

Azuba went to the window. Her mother came up to stand beside her. They watched Carrie pulling a wagon down the lane. Goldenrod and blue asters tossed beneath white cumulous clouds.

"Getting long-leggity," Grace said. Her voice was barren. "I won't know her when you come back."

For the first time, Azuba realized how she had taken for granted the presence of family. Her familiarity with the hills, the harbour, the smell of the air. The spacious rooms of the house, and its sturdy timbers, and the view framed by its windows.

The reason for their departure lay exposed, everywhere.

Only recently had her father been able to look Azuba in the eyes. Only in the last week had her mother asked for a forwarding address, and then ventured her opinion that Azuba and Carrie would go only as far as London, then come straight back home on another ship. William and Benjamin had become distant, not wanting to be drawn in to family dissonance. Nathaniel was barely present, his focus cast forward.

Grammy Cooper gave Azuba her medicine book. Every October, as a child, Azuba had spent a few days at Grammy's to help make winter medicines. Pinch of alum, tincture of rhubarb. Salve of gingered butter for erysipelas. Azuba had lined up the little glass bottles, loving how words came solid and plain from Grammy's mouth: *burned flesh, milk fever.* Now, Azuba turned the pages of the small, leather-bound volume, its stained, tattered pages covered with Grammy's handwriting. Notes, reminders, advice, recipes. She felt Grammy's eyes studying her. *Ear ache. Putrid sore throat. Toothache. Seasickness.*

"Nathaniel will have a medicine chest," Grammy said. "With the ingredients."

And she gave Azuba a hooked rug. It was a picture of Whelan's Cove, houses tippy on the hillsides, white-capped waves, gulls and a church.

"Don't let Nathaniel say you can't take that," she said. "He does, you have him come speak to me."

"He won't say no, Grammy."

"Remember us by," Grammy added.

They said goodbye in Grammy's kitchen. Grammy kissed Azuba's cheek, and then Carrie's. She turned her back and would not watch them go. She was standing at the stove, stirring apples in an iron pot.

I'm sorry, Azuba thought, to all of these people. *I'm so sorry.* But she would not say it, fearing that in the sound of the words would be a ring of vindication. For whatever reasons, she had fulfilled her desire. She and Carrie were leaving on

Traveller, with Nathaniel. And beneath everything—
Nathaniel's anger, Simon's disappearance, the sadness of
leaving her family, her worry about Carrie's safety and apprehension about the perils of life at sea—beneath it all was an
exultant sense of release. Of freedom.

Part Two

OUTWARD BOUND

5. Chalk Line

ON THE AFTERNOON OF OCTOBER 20, 1862, NATHANIEL, Azuba and Carrie left the house. Azuba looked back through the carriage window. Mist hung in the spruce trees, fog loomed across the fields. The cedar shingles of the roof were dark, drenched.

They spent that night with Azuba's parents. Supper was a quiet meal. Her mother's face was drawn; she ate slowly, watching Carrie. Her father put down his fork and stared at the chicken carcass. They listened to the drumming rain. Nathaniel spoke, once, to Carrie. He told her of the sights she would see in London. Carrie listened, but asked no questions. Over the last few days, Nathaniel had been fierce—issuing commands, stating what could and could not be taken.

Carrie looked back and forth between her parents.

"Eat, Carrie," Azuba murmured. Her own stomach was a knot of tension.

The next morning, Nathaniel left the house in darkness. Azuba woke, later, to the bleak light of a cloudy day. Her mother made buckwheat pancakes, but only Carrie could eat them. After breakfast, William and Benjamin came to help carry their small luggage: carpet bags, portmanteaus. Their footsteps left black holes in the grass. The horse hung his head, half-asleep.

When they stepped from the carriage, it began to spit rain. Azuba, Carrie and Grace walked towards the end of the wharf, hearing the suck of chopping waves, rain pattering their hats and making cobwebs on their wool capes. They could see *Traveller* out in the deep water, heavy-laden with a cargo of deal lumber.

The wharf was crowded with family and friends. There was a babble of tearful laughter, joking comments, heedless and unheeded words. Azuba put her arms around her mother, struck with a sense of doom. The pictures Nathaniel had shown her came into her mind: women and children lashed to masts; the people on shore who wailed and tore their hair and held out empty arms.

I might be taking us to our deaths.

"Write to me, Azuba," Grace whispered. "Write to me, my darling." They hugged for a long time without speaking. Then Grace turned, knelt and gathered Carrie.

Joseph stood with chin raised.

"Father," Azuba said.

He bent, hugged her. She laid her cheek on his lapel, felt his quelled emotion.

I could turn back. Her thoughts, like the words being spoken—"Write. Safe journey!"—were like sparrows: lightly perched, then a scattering.

Nathaniel climbed into the rowboat. He reached up for Carrie, lifted her down, settled her on a thwart. Azuba turned backwards, set a foot on the ladder's rung. Nathaniel took her by the waist, helped her to a place beside Carrie. She felt the breathing of the sea, the boat like a living thing—quivering, precarious, riding up, slipping down. Two sailors bent to the oars. A gulf of water grew between the wharf and the rowboat. Still they were close enough that Azuba could see the lines in her parents' cheeks, the folds of Grace's skirt and the glass beads on her bag, her father's beaver hat, his watch chain. Grace raised her arm, waved a handkerchief. Gulls hunched in the rain, crouched on the shipyard roofs. On the hills, yellow-leaved trees emerged from the mist, and from the village came the day's muted sounds: ring of hammer on steel; rumble of wheels over cobblestones; the barking of dogs.

"Goodbye, Azuba! Goodbye, Carrie . . . home soon . . . write . . . safe voyage . . ."

Azuba and Carrie waved until the faces became like specks of paint in a landscape.

Rain-stippled waves slapped *Traveller*'s hull. Azuba and Carrie were hauled, one by one, up onto the weather deck in a gamming chair—broad-seated, with wooden arms. They stood by the rail, holding hands, gazing up at the masts that towered 120 feet overhead. The decks were piled with coils of rope, casks, barrels of coal, crates of chickens. A small man stood in the deck house doorway, sharpening a knife, grinning at them. *The cook,* Azuba thought, *Mr. Lee.* In pens beside the deck house, sheep huddled and piglets dashed, colliding with each other, squealing.

Nathaniel strode to meet them. He pointed at a line scrawled across the deck with chalk. "For now," he said, "you may stand at the bow rail if you wish to watch our departure. But you'll never again cross that line. Your lives will be lived in the aft section of the ship."

He pointed beyond the chalk line to a small door in a raised deck in the ship's bow. "That is the fo'c'sle. The sailors eat and sleep there. You and Carrie *will not* fraternize with them."

Azuba was shocked by his tone. She could not believe he had chalked the line. She put a hand on his sleeve, felt a wave of rage. "We are not your prisoners." Her voice trembled. She kept it low for Carrie's sake. "May I remind you that I am your wife. This is your daughter."

"What I tell you is for your own safety," he muttered, his own voice lowered. "You ignore me at your peril. And Carrie's. Learn this now. On board, I do not have time to explain. Nor to argue. Do you understand?"

He did warn me, she thought, staring at him as he turned away, barking orders. *I will be your captain.*

Sailors clustered on the deck, passing a thigh-thick rope, the hawser, down to a steam tug that lay at *Traveller's* bow, waiting to tow the ship into the bay. A shudder went through *Traveller* as the hawser came taut.

The rain came hard now, wind-lashed. Whelan's Cove was a vague sketch behind the grey veils. Azuba thought she could see their house, out on the promontory, but could not be certain.

The aft cabin was like a small house that rose up from the deck in the ship's stern. In it was a door, and they went through and stepped down the companionway, a short stairway at the bottom of which was another door that opened into the dining cabin. Azuba and Carrie crowded into the room, stopped to absorb their new world. Azuba took a deep breath, recovering from her shock at Nathaniel's tone and her realization of her changed status. *As if I were a common sailor.* She thought of the sailor's superstition: *a woman aboard ship is bad luck.*

The ceiling was low. There was no colour, only the wood of a long, narrow table that filled the room's centre, bolted to the floor, as were its chairs. An oil lamp swung from a white-painted ceiling. There were no windows, no play of light, and so the lamp was the only thing responding to the sea: swinging, creaking. There were two doors on the port side and two on the starboard. Azuba had been taken aboard in the summer so that she could decide what to bring. She pointed to the doors. "Those are the mates' cabins, on that side. First mate, Mr. Dennis. Second mate, Mr. Perkins. And these are for the steward's cabin and his pantry."

A door at the far end of the cabin opened into the saloon, the captain's private quarters. In the saloon, bleak light fell from rectangular ceiling-level windows and a central skylight. The room was darkened by the purple-reds of a carpet laid over a round table. Swinging from the ceiling, like the room's heart, was the canary cage. There was a dry thunder of wings, a yellow blur, as the birds hopped, made sweet trills.

Azuba pointed to a door on the starboard side of the saloon. "Your cabin, Carrie. Why don't you go explore?"

Carrie took off her coat and hat, stood on tiptoe to hang them on a hook. She made her way across the room, eager, staggering from the motion.

Azuba untied the strings of her own hat and passed her fingers through her damp hair. Just before leaving, she had asked her mother to cut it so it would be easier to care for.

She stared at the dark, airless room. *Nathaniel's world.* It was like a miniature, tipping parlour, pictures shuffling back and forth on hooks, a book shifting on the table, the bamboo cage and a shaded lamp swinging from the ceiling. There was a smell of leather and lamp oil, and the percolating rustle of water just beyond the walls. Furniture, clamped to the floor.

She went to Nathaniel's rolltop desk. She pushed it open, stood with her feet set wide apart as the ship began to lift and fall, entering the swells of the bay. Her husband—his privacy exposed to her gaze, to her fingers. She picked up his protractor and compass. She opened the log, read his entries for each day at sea. She picked up a leather-wrapped stick with weighted ends. Then set it down, realizing it was Nathaniel's billy jack.

She sensed the part of him she didn't know, the man who lived alone in this cabin for years at a stretch. She plucked at the worn memory of his finger tracing her face, his wonder at the sight of her. *How frail the tie of trust was,* she thought. *How easily it broke.* She picked up his pen. He had written those loving letters from this very desk. He had sat at this chair dreaming of her and the sail house, and of the precious time he would spend there with his family.

And in her mind, she sent a different reply to Reverend Walton. "No," she wrote, "I am sorry. I cannot come with you." And in her mind, she changed herself into a woman who was strong, self-reliant, even while waiting for her husband. And who respected him. For his fortitude, his discipline.

Beside the desk was a set of shelves containing the ship's library. She studied the spines. Books on navigation. Novels, poetry. And what he called his "doctor books." She pulled out a few, leafed through them. Saw notes he had scrawled in margins. "Monday admin. laudanum."

On the bottom shelf was a mahogany box with a hinged lid and inset brass handles. *The medicine chest.* She knelt, slid the drawer partway open, glimpsed a bone-handled knife, a pestle.

Carrie was calling. "Mama! Come see."

Azuba slid the drawer shut. She scrambled to her feet, made her way across the room, putting a hand out. Carrie had opened a door in the centre of the aft wall.

"How elegant!" Azuba said, peering in. "Nicer than our outhouse."

The toilet had a high wooden back and wide arms. It sat atop a cupboard whose latched door opened onto a porcelain pot.

"Now look, Mama." Carrie was important, opening doors.

On the starboard side, one door opened onto a storage room—there were baskets of nuts and apples, and shelves with fiddled edges to keep jams, pickles and preserves from sliding to the floor—and the other opened onto Carrie's stateroom. The bed had two berths, the lower one made up with a pillow and a patchwork quilt. Jojo lay with outstretched arms. Carrie's trunk was buckled to the floor with leather belts. The walls were white, and there was a small, rain-streaked porthole. They pressed together to look through it, Carrie standing on her sea chest in order to see. The porthole was at the level of the deck. Sailor's feet passed by; the ship heeled and they found themselves looking directly down at the grey water.

They crossed the saloon to the port side, where one door opened onto a bathroom, with a tub and wash basin; and the other to the captain's stateroom. Narrow shelves ran along beneath the low ceiling, and there were built-in drawers on whose surface was a rosewood box with brass carrying handles. Azuba lifted the lid. Inside was a round clock with roman numerals and solid gold hands and a ratcheted winding key. "The chronometer, Carrie."

Carrie stood on tiptoe to see it.

Mr. McVale, the steward, had made up the bed with two pillows and a quilt made by Grammy Cooper. Squares of yellow sprigged with white, squares of white sprigged with yellow. Red triangles sprinkled here and there, like hawkweed in a field of daisies. Grey light lay on the quilt, whose colours would make the room snug in lamplight but now were hard and without warmth.

She went to the window. *Water,* she thought. *Tipping up, falling away. This will be our landscape.*

"Carrie, let's unpack. Let's make up our house. It's our home, now. Not just Papa's anymore."

Azuba folded back the lid of her trunk. Four dresses, she

THE SEA CAPTAIN'S WIFE

had packed, for a voyage whose duration she could not fore-
tell. Two wool, two cotton. Wool socks, capes, petticoats, split
drawers. She took out her combs, her hairbrush, a box of
hairpins and a Bible. She handed them to Carrie, who set
herself to arranging them.

Then they went back into the saloon.

"What should we do now, Mama?"

The floor tipped, buckling their knees. Azuba staggered,
found herself sitting in an armchair. Carrie made a few
running steps. Azuba closed her eyes, a thickening in her
chest and throat. She clenched her jaw against nausea. The
canaries made questioning trills. Azuba squinted, saw how
the birds cocked their heads, examining her. Nathaniel must
have cupped them in his hands, releasing them into the cage.
He was precise and careful with small, delicate things. Birds,
children, carvings. Once, his hands, cradling her face.

Carrie climbed onto the armchair, burrowed up against
her mother. They sat together, subdued. They sat listening to
their new world. It was a place of motion, whose sounds—
the ship's long-drawn, moaning protests—made Azuba think
of childbirth.

The cabin darkened as the afternoon passed. Nathaniel did
not come below to visit. Azuba felt their superfluousness. The
lack of welcome.

Her breath shallowed. With queasiness. With anger.

At supper on the first night, Nathaniel sat them at the table
as they would be for the rest of the voyage: captain on the
starboard side and whichever mate was not on duty across
from him; Azuba at one end of the table and Carrie, far
away, at the other.

Mr. Dennis, the first mate, was off watch, so it was his

turn to join them. He made a slight bow to Azuba before taking his place. He was a small man, with quick, irritable motions. He gave a double-handed flick of coattails as he sat, staring around the room with an air of belligerence. He held his blue eyes so wide that the whites showed. Azuba nodded back, disheartened by the male brusqueness, the curt nods exchanged by Nathaniel and his mate.

Mr. McVale came down the companionway wearing a glistening oilskin, carrying a tray with a cloth over it. He was a fresh-faced young man from Halifax—competent, with a quiet demeanour. He had round, healthy cheeks, a tidy beard shining with raindrops. His eyes skimmed over the table.

He was followed by the cabin boy, Andrew Moss, who carried a large pitcher of tea. The Moss family lived down the road from Azuba's parents and had asked if Nathaniel might take their son on this voyage. At twelve, it was the boy's first time on a merchant ship. His face was sprinkled with freckles. He went around the table pouring tea into mugs, keeping his eyes on the pitcher, trying not to spill. He gave Carrie a quick glance. She bit her lips, repressing her longing to speak to him.

Nathaniel was this age when he left home to go on his brother's ship, Azuba thought.

She picked up her fork, trying to imagine her husband's childhood spent in the company of men. Or at home, with an unloving mother.

The wind had risen and the oil lamp swung. Shadows stretched and quivered over the walls. *Traveller's* wooden pegs and mortised timbers made creaks and groans, the sounds rising, falling, mixing with the moan of wind and snap of canvas. Azuba could hear the faint shouts of the second mate, Mr. Perkins, an enormous young man with friendly, pig-like eyes that slanted up in the corners with an expression of bland surprise.

She put out a hand to stop the slide of her water glass. Nathaniel and Mr. Dennis drank their tea, listening, glancing at one another at each of Mr. Perkins's shouts. A silent conversation, Azuba felt, flowed between them. Were she not present, they would be discussing the ship—how she was trimmed, how she went, the shifting wind, the treacherous bay currents.

She leaned forward, caught Mr. Dennis's eye. "Where are you from, Mr. Dennis?"

"Saint John."

"And your wife? Is she from Saint John as well?"

He glanced at her and she saw his impatience with idle conversation. His mind was on the ship and she had interrupted his train of thought.

"She is, and has family there. Mr. McVale?"

Mr. Dennis's finger tapped the edge of his mug. Mr. McVale motioned to Andrew, who came to the mate with the pitcher of tea.

Steam curled from beef stew. There were mashed turnips and biscuits.

"Papa?" Carrie asked. "Do the canaries have names?"

Nathaniel wiped his moustache with his fingers. There were no napkins, Azuba noticed, and she surmised that clean laundry was a luxury.

"The mother canary is Ernestina. The father is Horatio. Their last name is . . ."

Mr. Dennis glanced up, surprised by the sudden gentleness, and Azuba realized that he had never heard Nathaniel conversing with Carrie.

Nathaniel pondered, and Azuba saw that Carrie and her father were like friends who had reached complete understanding of one another.

"It's the Featherby family," Nathaniel said.

"If they have children, may I name them, Papa?"

Azuba pressed the tines of her fork into the mashed turnips. Her heart ached, tears pricked the backs of her eyes. If it were not for Carrie, she would never see his eyes soften. She would never hear his voice become teasing. She was pinched with loneliness. A woman wanted more than a child's dependent love. A woman needed to see in a man's eyes what Azuba had seen in Nathaniel's when he had crossed the ballroom floor, drawn by her, as if she possessed a power he could not resist.

Azuba closed her eyes against a wave of queasiness. She rose abruptly as the smell of onions overcame her.

"Excuse . . ." She rushed from the cabin.

She put Carrie to bed without a proper wash. She went to her own cabin.

The captain's bed had a footboard and headboard, like any ordinary bed, but was stone-weighted and gimballed, suspended from a frame attached to ball bearings in sockets. The bed swung, the gimbals clanked.

She thrust back the quilt, pitched forward. She lay sprawled, sluggish.

Stay perfectly still.

Right now, her parents would be sitting in their parlour, Father reading out loud from the Bible, Mother tatting. Hearing the stillness where last night had been Carrie, Azuba, Nathaniel.

She bolted from bed, kneeled, vomited into the basin she had requested from Mr. McVale.

She fell back onto the bed, belly down, face in the pillow. Sweating, shivering. No one. No doctor. No Hannah to brew herbs, to lay warm cloths. No mother to soothe, and help with Carrie.

Only Nathaniel.

On her knees once again, her stomach wrung, twisting, the back of her throat raw. Retching, retching. Her hands shaking, folding back the quilt. Furious that he did not come. That he had not followed her when she'd rushed from the table, white-faced, hand over mouth.

The door opened. Mr. McVale? She froze, about to climb into the bed. A sailor? The person took away the basin as she fell onto the bed. She rolled onto her side. The door opened again. Click of the basin being set down. Hands on her head. Strong, warm, hard.

"Nathaniel."

He sat beside her, stroked her forehead. She held his wrists. A wave of nausea. On her knees again. Retching. He rubbed her back.

"I'm sorry," she said. "I'm sorry."

He helped her back into the bed. "South wind," he said. "Fog." His hand began at her shoulder, ran down her side, smoothed her hip. "You'll be better once we clear Nova Scotia," he said.

They lay listening to the rustle of water beyond the planks. Then he tensed, lifted his head. "Foghorn. We're passing another ship."

His hand resumed its slide—shoulder, waist, hip—and she felt sleep coming towards her, rising, stretching, like the waves that held them.

Azuba was awakened by Carrie. She opened her eyes, felt the relief of wellness.

"Mama. Are you awake? Papa is already upstairs."

"*On deck.* We say 'go on deck' or 'come below.'"

They dressed and went up. The air was so fog-filled that their hair was instantly veiled with droplets. Azuba licked her lips, tasted salt. She staggered, reached for the nearest line, felt as strung tight with excitement as the wet rope.

The deck stretched ahead two hundred feet. A long spar—the bowsprit—extended from the bow like a narwhal's tusk. The ship was on the starboard tack, and the deck slanted—wet, gleaming. Sails towered overhead, wind-pressed bunt-lines outlined against the canvas, a web of tight-stretched ratlines and shrouds rising from deadeyes on either side. The sea surrounded them, so close they could hear the hiss of expiring froth, the surface bulking higher than the railings, the waves solid, ridged, like heaving stone. Smoke rose from a stovepipe in the galley roof. The galley was in the forward deck house, a small white building before the foremast, flanked by its coops and stalls. The cook had his own cabin in the deck house, Nathaniel had told her. Born in China, he was fifty years old. His shuffling stoop was the result of years of managing pots and pans at sea; he took his pleasure in a pipe of opium after supper.

A sheep baaed, setting off the others. On the fo'c'sle deck, higher and so far ahead that Azuba could barely make out his features, a sailor baaed back, rudely. "Ah, shut it, you lousy . . ."

Smell of pipe smoke, coffee, boiling beans. Men she did not know, and to whom she would never be introduced, were at ease on the ship, moving about, busy with tasks she could not identify. Someone stood at the galley door, wiping a pan with a white cloth. Nathaniel's voice rang out. " . . . topsail haul . . ."

Azuba and Carrie went up a short flight of steps, emerged on the roof of the aft cabin—the quarterdeck, extending almost the width of the ship and from the stern of the ship to just before the mizzen, or sternmost mast. This, Nathaniel had told them, would be their place to sit, walk, jump rope, hang laundry; in warmer latitudes, they would erect awnings against the heat, sling hammocks, take meals, even sleep. Carrie knelt by the skylight, peering down into the saloon.

Nathaniel was staring intently into the fog. Years of squinting and the drooping lid had made his left eye narrower than the right. It was his compassionate eye, whereas the other, wider, was bold and hard. Since Azuba had first met him, he had lost flesh in his face; its bone structure was more marked, fatigue or anger more visible. His body, however, had become stronger—shoulders more muscular, chest thicker. Now his eyes seemed a paler blue, as if faded by an excess of light, and their expression here at command was complex: remote, edged with brutality, a steadiness balanced at the midpoint of two realities—the sea's force, the ship's frailty.

He looked away from the topsail, crossed the deck. He put a hand to Carrie's head, stroked her hair. "Better, Azuba? You missed breakfast." His distant politeness had returned, as if he'd forgotten how he'd comforted her.

"I'm well, thank you." *For the moment, anyway,* she thought, feeling the return of her queasiness at the sight of the heaving water, the tilting deck.

"Watch over there." He pointed, set his pipe between his teeth. The white fog on the port side darkened as a disturbance stirred within it. A ship resolved, less real at first than phantom, white sails indistinguishable from the surrounding opacity, its rigging like a dew-drenched spiderweb.

"And there," he said.

Off to starboard, another darkness.

"The cliffs of Grand Manan. These are treacherous waters. I was once trapped in the bay for thirteen days. You'd best keep warm. I'll send Mr. McVale with food."

"I'd like to watch for a while."

He watched the cliffs as if he had not heard. His pipe shifted.

"Nathaniel?"

"These are dangerous waters, Azuba," he repeated, his voice sharpening. "I need my mind on my work. I wish you and Carrie below decks."

She put a hand to her cheek, felt the slick of spray on her skin. *What can I say?*

Men, everywhere. She sensed them glancing up at the captain and his family on the quarterdeck. "They will resent you," Nathaniel had told her. He'd explained, when she'd asked. He had spoken with a tight voice, as if seeing it from the sailor's point of view. "They will have to curb their language. They are accustomed to bathing in the nude—on deck, after rainstorms. Their outhouse consists of a urine barrel on deck and a sling in the bowsprit."

"Look, Mama!"

Nathaniel had gone to stand beside Mr. Dennis. Both watched the ship through spyglasses.

Azuba leaned on the rail. *Where is she from?* she wanted to ask, feeling hungry fascination. *Is there a woman aboard? Are they outward bound, or coming home?*

Carrie was pointing excitedly at the bright signal flags.

Azuba glanced at Nathaniel. Spyglass to his face. His lips turned down at the corners as he studied the ship.

So. Another chalk line.

It was not as she had imagined it. The stuffy cabin where her seasickness would worsen and she must keep Carrie occupied. Handwork. Knitting. Books. She had never thought of the confinement. Or the vomiting. Or the fact that every man on board was intimidated by Captain Bradstock. She was startled by her own fear of him.

Everything will improve, she told herself. She could not bear to admit disappointment. *With time, sunshine, health.*

"Come, Carrie. We'll go below."

It was a stormy passage across the North Atlantic. Azuba was seasick again. Carrie sat at her side, stroking her mother's forehead with a cool hand, crooning.

Later, weakened and frustrated by her illness, Azuba began to drink tea and thin soup brought by Mr. McVale or Andrew Moss. Carrie became adept at entertaining herself. She cut out paper dolls, worked at her embroidery hoop, lay on the floor, singing to herself or telling stories. She curled in the armchair, drifting to sleep.

After twelve days, when she had fully recovered, Azuba occupied herself with exploration of Nathaniel's books, sitting on the floor by his desk, bent over the pamphlet that came with the medicine chest, *A Companion to the Medical Chest, with Plain Rules for the Taking of Medicines,* or opening the chest itself and removing the instruments and the little phials, each one marked with a number rather than a name to simplify things for the captain. She compared the book's recipes with those in Grammy's book.

From his books on navigation, she filled her mind with things hitherto unknown to her. Dead reckoning. Celestial navigation. Uses of the sextant. She opened the rosewood box in her cabin and studied the chronometer, realizing that without it they would not know their longitude. She studied the points of the compass. Nathaniel and Mr. Dennis held debates at the table about what they called "Maury's book," so she sought it on the shelves. He was an American, Lieutenant Matthew Maury, whose writings explained the workings of the sea. She sat with elbows on the carpeted table, learning how winds were borne; or that air flowed from high-pressure cells to low; or about the rotation of the earth and how the seasons of the year influenced the wind's direction. Ocean currents, she learned, were as regular as roads; deserts and ice sheets affected wind and rain. Nathaniel and Mr. Dennis, she noticed, both admired and were irritated by Lieutenant Maury. The man's writings could not be ignored, since his findings allowed captains to make decisions based on science. The sea, in Maury's view, was not a place of random wildness. There were new certainties.

She slid the book back into place, making certain no black hair remained in its pages, no drop of tea, no feather to mark her place. At the table, she said nothing during discussions of Maury's conclusions, although many times she might have supplied answers.

The weather continued rainy, windy. Azuba and Carrie spent much of their time alone. They could hear the sailors roaring out shanties when they did any job requiring coordinated effort. Carrie's favourite was "Rolling Home."

Call all hands to man the capstan,
See the cable run down clear,
Heave away, and with a will, boys,
For old England we will steer.

"Rollin' home!" she would shout with the chorus. "Rollin' home across the sea."

During the day, Nathaniel seldom came below decks. He saw them only at meals and sometimes missed those.

It was cold in the saloon. She dressed Carrie in a woolen undershirt and a heavy sweater. During days in which the ship rolled and plunged, she felt an edge of regret that would become despair if she examined it, and so instead turned her mind to London and read aloud from her *Harper's Guidebook for Travellers*. As Carrie listened, her paper dolls became the Queen, or the Prince of Wales, or the Princess Alexandra.

"We are going there, Carrie," Azuba said, putting down the book, returning to her knitting. "Going to London!"

It was more exciting, now, to think of the city itself rather than the fact that she was going there with Nathaniel. His eyes were still bitter, as if he could not look at her without seeing Reverend Walton. Occasionally, though, she would wake at night and find herself curled around him, head on his chest. "Nathaniel?" she would whisper. He would murmur, half-conscious, and pull her closer. She would touch him with her fingertips, a graze along his cheek.

She thought of the love that softened his face as he knelt and spoke to Carrie and wondered if it were the same, this love, no matter on whom it shone.

One month after leaving Whelan's Cove, on November 20, 1862, *Traveller* arrived in London.

They settled in a fine hotel, Thomas's, on Charles Street, near St. James's Park. Azuba was stunned by the enormity of the city, its vast, endless clamour. On the first night, she woke clutching at the bed, which seemed to rock beneath her, as did, for the first days, floors and pavement. Thomas's was opulent, with hot and cold baths, a reading room, a lady's drawing room and an elegant dining room. There were chandeliers, hothouse flowers, letter boxes. Nathaniel engaged a dressmaker to make city dresses for Carrie and Azuba. They would ship them home, he said, once they returned to *Traveller*.

In the evening, after putting Carrie to bed, Azuba stood at the window watching the tangle of carriages passing below, their lanterns like burred stars. She had never imagined such crowds, such chaotic energy. Home now seemed like a tiny oil painting ridged with brush strokes: a house with staring windows, wind-twisted trees, brown fields. Her parents were as Nathaniel had become when he was at sea: miniature as the painting, their voices fading as time passed.

Nathaniel told Azuba that he would be occupied with business, but that he had found a retired gentleman, Mr. Cookson, who would take her and Carrie to see the sights. Every morning, she woke half-wild with excitement, chivvied Carrie to dress and hurried through breakfast. Mr. Cookson was red-faced, with a round belly and mild eyes. He peered through his spectacles at Azuba's finger on her guidebook and obligingly fulfilled her requests. Carrie and Azuba pressed their noses to the window of their hansom cab as they were jostled through the streets of a city inhabited by three million people, calling each other's attention to the passing scene. Mr. Cookson took them to the Thames Tunnel, where they entered the shaft and went down many flights of marble steps, ending up eighty feet below in a gas-lit rotunda. The tunnel stretched away into a shadowy distance, and they crossed the Thames in a flood of sightseers, passing alcoves in which pale-faced women called in soft voices for them to purchase trinkets or view dancing monkeys or have their fortunes told. Carrie grasped Azuba's hand tightly, wide-eyed, and did not say a word. On another day, they visited Tippoo's Tiger, a life-sized wooden beast devouring a European man. Carrie was fascinated, and was allowed to turn a crank on his shoulder, making creaky shrieks and a horrid wheezy growl. They went to London's central post office in St Martin's le Grand; passing beneath its massive Ionic columns, they felt dwarfed, awestruck. They were dwarfed again in Westminster Abbey, and at the Crystal Palace in its new home on Sydenham Hill, where they strolled past fountains beneath the soaring glass and cast-iron roof. At Mr. Cookson's insistence, Azuba and Carrie ventured into the "Retiring Rooms," where for one penny they sat on the new "water closets" and were given a towel, a comb and a shoe shine.

Over dinner, they told Nathaniel of their adventures. He smiled at Carrie's chatter and kept his eyes on the little girl when it was Azuba's turn to speak. "Is that true?" he said. "Is Mama telling the truth? You didn't really walk beneath the Thames!" Azuba imagined him thinking, *Wouldn't it be nice if your Reverend Walton were here to go about with you?* and felt the urge to take him by the shoulders and shake away his pride.

December 26, 1862
Thomas's Hotel
St. James's Park
London, England

Dear Father and Mother,
Nathaniel now has his orders. We will be sailing to San Francisco via Cape Horn, carrying a load of coal. Nathaniel informs me that we will be embarking in the middle of February. I will be sorry to leave the comforts of this hotel, which have spoiled me! Christmas was peculiar without snow, but we hung a stocking on Carrie's bed and told her that Santa could find her anywhere. He brought many gifts.

I dreamt of home last night. Nathaniel gave me the idea of returning on a steamer . . .

Azuba struck out the last sentence with x's and circles.

I dreamt of home last night. I am happy to think that once on board Traveller, *Nathaniel, Carrie and I will be close once again, for he is much occupied and worried about provisions, crew and cargo. We are all well, and hope you are too, and that no one in the family has succumbed to any illness.*

With all my love,
Azuba

p.s. Carrie sends love. She has kissed the paper, just here.

They left London on the evening of February 17, 1863. Azuba went above the next morning in time to see the Isle of Wight. She glimpsed its green fields beneath a cloud of grey oak branches. The island slipped into the sea as *Traveller* sailed westwards down the English Channel.

In Gibraltar, Nathaniel hove to near a floating mail cask. He sent two sailors off in the rowboat to deliver the last letters they would be able to send until they reached San Francisco.

Then he turned *Traveller's* bow towards Spain.

It grew warmer, once they headed south, and Azuba shed her wool cloak. Carrie spent as much time as possible standing at Nathaniel's side. She had grown taller and had lost a front tooth. He taught her to coil a rope over the belaying pins, to name the sails, to call the thrumming ropes supporting the masts "shrouds." He told her the names of the lines used to work the sails: "halyards," "braces" and "sheets"; that to "reef" was to take in the sails and "hove to" meant the ship had ceased its forward movement. Nathaniel's mood lifted. He stood on the quarterdeck, legs braced, pipe in teeth, hair wind-blown, watching the bowsprit's twisting rise against the blue sky, and Azuba glimpsed, as she had not on the stormy crossing of the North Atlantic, how at the best of times he and his ship were like companions.

And she experienced, at last, what she had dreamed of all her growing-up years. Life at sea. The great sails like the wings of swans, cupping the light. The sounds of snapping and swash. Simplicity. The bells—*ting ting, ting ting*—monastic and serene.

Nathaniel's course, as advised by Lieutenant Maury, speared towards the coast of Brazil, thence catching the South Equatorial and Brazil currents that would sweep them towards the Drake Passage and the Horn.

Azuba wrote to her parents:

Be at peace in your hearts. I read my Bible, Carrie and I send our prayers heavenwards and our thoughts to you, and be assured we will be together before . . .

She lifted her pen. She was writing on the round table in the light of the ceiling lamp. Carrie was asleep in her berth; Nathaniel lay back in the armchair, eyes closed, the newspaper he had been reading spread out on his chest. She remembered another peaceful moment, when Simon had sat on a kitchen chair, lifting sand dollars from his creel. She felt her face soften at the memory and then repressed a prick of regret. She bent back to her letter. Usually, Simon came to her only in her sleep, unbidden, a kindly presence emanating admiration and concern.

Nathaniel, she wrote, *is teaching me . . .*

She and Nathaniel had made tentative approaches to one another. Once, she had asked him to show her how to take a sun sight. Surprised, he had handed her the sextant, shown her how to use it. Later, as he sat at his desk, making his calculations, she leaned over his shoulder, watching. Not without pride, he had explained what he was doing. He'd set her a problem and corrected her as she worked it out. Yet the next time she asked to take a sight, he was impatient and had no time.

On another warm day, she'd stood beside him at the binnacle, a wooden stand housing the compass and its light, and he'd shown her how to box the compass—recite the points in the right order. Every day, as he taught Carrie the names of the sails, masts and yards, Azuba stood by, listening, studying the web of lines, following each one from its block to its culminating point, seeking patterns in the maze. She began to understand the actions of the men who stood strung out along the yards with their feet on bouncing ropes. Sometimes she could not help making a remark indicating her comprehension, and she noticed a startled expression in Nathaniel's eyes, yet he made only slight response.

"Mr. McVale will see to that," he said curtly when she asked if she might stir up a molasses pudding on the coal stove.

He was annoyed to come below decks and find sewing projects strewn over the backs of chairs; sometimes, stiff with the glaze of command or exhausted from a night watch, it was difficult for him to unbend even to Carrie, to see or appreciate her drawings, to understand her stories or speak with a gentled voice.

One night Nathaniel showed Azuba the map. He ran his finger westward across the Atlantic Ocean; down the coast of South America, around the Horn; up past Chile, Peru, Ecuador, Central America and the thin tail of Baja California; on across the Tropic of Cancer and so to San Francisco. Their ship, on such a map, would be so tiny as to be invisible, and she appreciated, with sudden humility, how its canvas, rope, planks, masts and yards constituted a creature as frail as a butterfly. And that without Nathaniel's indomitable, ferocious will as its heart, there would be no hope for such an enterprise.

Still.

Reverend Walton stood between them, a ghostly presence that would not fade.

6. Cape Horn Snorter

THEY BEAT DOWN TOWARDS THE SOUTH ATLANTIC AND
for six weeks saw nothing but water and sky.

What had once seemed monotonous changed in Azuba's
eyes to a landscape of transcendent beauty. She stood at the
railing or sat in a chair with shortened legs, watching spilling
shawls of iridescent froth. Shadows raced, lifting or darkening the sea's mood. Occasionally, whales or porpoises rolled
from the depths.

"Carrie! Look! Look!"

The waters parted and they glimpsed grey flesh, or a small
eye. It was like being granted a glimpse of divinity. And they
waved and called out, as if at the sight of friends.

April fifteenth.

Azuba and Carrie, in the saloon, heard excitement in the
sailors' voices, and shouts—"Land! Land!"

They scrabbled in Carrie's chest for mittens, a wool cap
and a creamy white sweater Grace had knitted. Bundled, only
Carrie's round eyes and straight, serious mouth could be seen.
Azuba, too, dressed warmly, and they climbed to the quarterdeck, squinted into an icy wind. *Patagonia.* It broke from

the sea, a band of brown, barren hills looming off the star-board bow. Farther, rising above the hills, they could see the glitter of snowy mountains.

Nathaniel stood at the rail, brass speaking trumpet tucked under his arm, spyglass to his eye, so intent that Azuba kept Carrie from running to him. He glanced up at the sails. They were headed for the Strait of Le Maire, a shortcut passing between Tierra del Fuego and Staten Island. Nathaniel had determined upon this course. Azuba had heard him discussing it with Mr. Dennis. The strait was dangerous if the wind blew against the current, but it might save them seventy miles.

All that day, except for meals, they stood on deck and watched as the land grew near and passed along their star-board side. Once, Azuba saw Nathaniel staring intently west-ward. He called the mates and they stood in a cluster, faces strained, hands cupping ears. Then she, too, heard it: the faint, heart-stopping roar of surf. Nathaniel reached for his trumpet. The mates hurried down off the quarterdeck.

Traveller changed course, headed farther offshore.

The next morning, Carrie and Azuba went up the compan-ionway and saw that they had entered the strait. It was a windy, grey morning. They could see featureless brown land some miles away on both sides. There was a quiet on board, and Azuba felt the presence of fear.

Eight bells were struck, for the watch was about to change. Nathaniel, jacket buttoned to his chin, was staring to the northwest through his glass. "Hold," he roared suddenly to the men going off watch. "Hold!"

Azuba reached for Carrie's hand. She looked in the direc-tion of Nathaniel's glass.

"Mr. Dennis," he called, pointing. "Mr. Perkins. Look there!"

Under the hills of Tierra del Fuego, the sea was blackened by a squall. It raced towards them, edged with a line of foam-whipped water.

"All hands on deck!"

"Let go the topgallant halyard!"

"Stand by your clew lines!"

"Haul down your outer jib!"

"Let go the stay sail halyard!"

Azuba kept her voice calm. "Quickly, Carrie." Carrie's face was stricken. She looked towards her father. "Quickly, quickly."

They hurried below. Everything was just as they had left it: scissors on the table, newly cut paper dolls, chalks in a wooden box.

The squall hit. Azuba was thrown to the floor. She slid up against the wall, Carrie pressed beneath her. She heard dim, confused shouts mixed with a seething roar as wind and water flattened the ship.

The roar died away. Slowly, *Traveller* righted.

The floor was strewn with scissors, paper dolls and the contents of drawers: ribbons, hair clips, beads, buckles. Sofa cushions were flung, and music books from the organ, and a porcelain vase of dried roses. Azuba and Carrie huddled on the floor, waiting for the next onslaught.

After several minutes, when the wind seemed to have died away and they could hear nothing but the slap of waves against the ship's sides, Azuba kneeled. She held Carrie by the shoulders. "Are you hurt, Carrie?"

Carrie was too shocked to speak, her eyes wide. She shook her head.

"All right," Azuba said, pulling Carrie to her breast. "All right, we're all right."

A continuous stream of orders came from above: Nathaniel's voice, then the mates.' Carrie relaxed.

"You begin picking up your paper dolls," Azuba said. "I'll go see what's happening."

She made her way up the companionway, opened the door. Dark sky, black clouds. A silver light, metallic on the wet deck. Ropes thrumming in a cold wind.

One of the topsails was blown to ribbons.

Mr. Dennis passed the doorway where Azuba stood clutching her cape. His hat was gone, his hair blown into two horns.

"All's well, ma'am," he shouted. "We'll soon be on our way again."

The ship lurched, making no headway, her sails in disarray. Mr. Dennis staggered, reached for a shroud. Men were swarming towards the shredded topsail, racing hand over fist up the swaying rope ladders. The measured calm—Nathaniel in his place on the quarterdeck, the watch about to change—had been thrown into chaos. The seas were building; ahead in the open water of the Drake Passage, Azuba could see white-capped waves beneath the lowering sky.

Fear made the taste of blood in her mouth. Moments were discontinuous—one instant she was speaking to Mr. Dennis and the next she was looking up, shocked by the ragged canvas strips, like entrails against the clouds.

She was steadied by the thought of her own task. *Reassure Carrie.* She went below, found Carrie on her hands and knees busily picking up the mess in the tipping cabin.

"Good girl," Azuba said. "The topsail is shredded, but the men are fixing it."

She braced herself, hands on table. There was no way to know from which direction the next swell would come.

Carrie was holding a paper doll's dress. She looked up at Azuba. Questioning, trusting.

"Didn't I do a good job, Mama? I found every single chalk."

The sailors bent on a new topsail. By late afternoon, *Traveller's* sails were again filled with wind and she surged up and over the great swells of the Drake Passage.

Mr. McVale made a fire in the coal stove. At this latitude the days were short, and already the saloon was dark, lit only by pools of light cast by the lamps and the stove's glow. Carrie bowed her head, and Azuba unpinned her bun. The child's black hair tumbled down. The silver-backed brush pawed, making a crackle of static. Azuba felt, suddenly, that the ship was fragile, a thing of tenous parts. She pictured the shipyards. Hulls like whale skeletons with steam-curved ribs, planks pegged with hemlock treenails. She imagined the cabin flooding with icy water, the unstoppable inflow making a mockery of their parlour. Trapped. Water filling their lungs. Their arms and legs scrabbling towards life. Floating, in death. As they plummeted down.

Think of home. Spring air smelling of soil.

"It's April sixteenth," she said. She spoke in a pleasant voice, imbuing her tone with warmth. "Today Grammy Cooper planted her peas. Do you know why?"

"No. Why?"

"Because when she walked to the barn to collect the eggs—"

"All the cats came out to see if she had meat scraps!"

"Yes, and she noticed that the snow had melted in her garden. *Time to plant the peas,* she thought."

The saloon door opened and Nathaniel stepped in, bringing the smell of cold air. His eyes adjusted to the light, and Azuba saw in them a strange, sweet sorrow. For an instant, he said nothing, silenced by the loveliness of Carrie, who was sleepy after the soothing brush.

Azuba waited for his eyes to travel from Carrie to her. An instant of shared compassion would be equivalent to a long span of time in the heart's equation.

But when he looked at her, his eyes had darkened, and once again he was in a hurry.

"What?" she said. The moment fled. "What is it?" she demanded. She tossed down the hairbrush, her mouth set in a hard line.

"Nothing to worry about," he said. He grinned. "Bundle up. Quick. There's a sight for you to see. We're about to pass the Horn, and if we have thirty-six more hours of this wind, we'll be safely around and bound for California."

Azuba swept her cape and bonnet from a hook by the door, wrapped a blanket around Carrie and followed Nathaniel on deck.

The sun had set, although it was not yet pitch dark. Fire still burned in a ragged hem of cloud; directly overhead, the sky was clear, star-pricked. Away to the north the forbidding face of Cape Horn gleamed in the remnant of light, a black cliff sweeping straight up.

Nathaniel pointed southward, where the sky was dusty. "The Magellan Clouds. Another galaxy that you can only see down here."

Carrie settled on the skylight, as composed as if she were in her own bedroom. She held Jojo in her lap, busied herself making a hood around the doll's head with an end of the blanket. Azuba stood with one hand on a shroud. She wore a quilted black bonnet with satin laces. The dying light picked out red glints in her hair.

"The tip of South America," Nathaniel said. His voice was sober. "Many lives have ended here."

They stood side by side. Away on the foredeck, sailors had come up from the fo'c'sle to see the wreck-haunted cape.

Azuba remembered how Nathaniel had told her, back home in their parlour, that any person who had seen the Horn was forever marked.

Surf broke at the feet of the cliff, shot hundreds of feet upward against the ice-streaked basalt. Gulls, wild ducks and albatrosses flew low over the water, like sparks in the sunset. Snow on the mountain peaks—a cold burning.

"The light," Azuba said. "Oh, Nathaniel. The light. So savage, so beautiful."

She lifted her collar and pulled it forward.

A crushing silence, here on the earth's wild margin. Essentials. Rock, water and light.

"It seems that human beings were not meant to inhabit such a world," she said.

Nathaniel glanced down at her. She had stepped closer, but did not touch him since the mates were nearby and the sailors were on deck.

"See, Azuba." His voice was spare, shed of human concerns. He put a hand on her shoulder, pointed.

Heading westward were three other ships. Red and green running lights swayed from their bows. Their sails laddered up, tier after tier of canvas. They crept across the cold sea, frail as spiders.

Azuba felt a chill at the sight. *So brave. So lonely.*

Every eye on *Traveller* went to them, and no one spoke, as if not wishing to acknowledge how they mirrored themselves.

"Dear Lord," Azuba murmured, "thank you for our safe passage around the Horn. Bless, oh Lord, my husband, Nathaniel, for although he may not have time to speak to you, I know that love for you is in his heart. Bless Carrie."

The pound of water against the hull lulled her to sleep. She woke when Nathaniel slipped in beside her, fully clothed save for his boots.

"What time is it?"

"Nine o'clock," he said. "The barometer is low and dropping fast. I'm afraid . . ."

She was instantly wakeful. "Afraid of what?"

He mumbled, sighed.

"Nathaniel?"

She pressed her back to him, pulled his arm tighter around her waist, thinking of the forbidding cliff. Cape Horn. She rolled towards him, put a hand to his cheek.

"Nathaniel," she whispered. "I love you."

She heard the words, like an echo in the darkness, breathed on a sigh. "Love . . . my dear . . ." Then his slow, deep breath.

She woke, later, pressed to the edge of the bed, held from rolling out by the preventer board. Nathaniel was gone, and she could hear that everything below decks was disturbed: unlatched doors clapping, the clatter of objects sliding back and forth, and over all, the hollow, insistent moan of wind.

She rose, lit the lamp, looked at a pocket watch hanging from the wall.

Midnight.

She dressed, holding herself in place with one hand on the built-in chest of drawers, the other pulling dress and cloak from their hooks. In the saloon, it was as dark and cold as Whelan's Cove on a January night. Ice pellets flicked the skylight. Embers smouldered in the stove, but she did not dare stoke the fire. She clung to the table, releasing her hold long enough to reach up with both hands, a lighted match in one, the other steadying the lamp. In the dim glow she saw the ship's cat on the sofa, black-pupilled, claws digging into horsehair. The ship began a long downward plunge. Azuba turned to Carrie's cabin but was precipitated into a run. She threw herself forward into an armchair. The cat leapt from the sofa, slapped onto its side, then sprang into Azuba's lap.

She struggled to rise but was trapped in the chair, clinging to its arms as it tipped backwards with the ship, her body pressed against its cushions. She heard a dull, heavy thud as *Traveller's* bow crashed down, then a shudder as tons of water poured across her decks.

Men's shouts came dimly, intermittently. Sheet music slithered from the pump organ. Albatross feathers propped behind the family photographs slid out of place. The canary cage swung violently, and the birds were thrown from their perches and beat their wings, colliding with each other and the bars of the cage.

"Mama! Mama!"

Azuba crawled to Carrie's cabin. Carrie lay across her bunk, head touching the floor, arms flung out.

"Mama!"

Azuba pulled the child into her lap and sat on the floor, with her back pressed to the sea chest. "Papa will take care of us. Papa will take—"

The ship tipped forward and the tilt continued.

A mirror jumped from its nail, crashed against the wall before them, now a floor. Azuba threw out her arms, flew forward, landed on the bunk, Carrie beneath her.

"Mrs. Bradstock?"

It was Mr. McVale.

"Captain sent me."

He was breathless, had removed his soaked mittens and was standing braced in the door. His oilskins ran with water; his moustache was stiff with frozen mucous.

"He says to get in your bed and stay there."

He helped them stumble across the saloon, handed them into the jolting gimballed bed.

"How bad is it?" Azuba asked.

"The captain says it's a regular Cape Horn snorter, coming up out of the southwest, just what you'd expect down here." She heard fear in his voice, although he spoke as if such words were matter-of-fact. "We're hove to, all the sails are furled, save the storm spanker and fore topmast stay sail. He said he's seen worse. He said to tell you not to worry, he'll see us through."

The ship's bow went down again. This time, *Traveller* shuddered and paused for so long that Azuba clutched at the young man's soaked wool sleeve. The ship slewed as if no longer buoyant but carrying a sudden, intolerable weight.

They spent the day sleeping, making their way to the toilet and sipping water. Azuba hardened herself against fear by closing her mind to all but the moment at hand—keeping Carrie warm, fed and occupied. In tiny, lingering nibbles they ate the last pieces of crystallized ginger they had bought in London, while reminiscing about sweets shops, pigeons and marble horses. They took an imaginary walk through St. James's Park, reminding one another of its placid, round ponds, its ducks, swans and golden-leaved willows.

At five o'clock, Andrew Moss came. Strands of hair clung to his wet forehead; his wool cap was furrowed with melting snow. He carried a canvas bag.

"Cook sent what he could," he said. "He can't keep a fire going in the galley."

He was not frightened, Azuba saw, but excited. His exuberance made her think of her brothers. She remembered the tomboy she had been, running on the sands, climbing fences, herding cows with sticks. She imagined herself recounting this adventure to her family.

"You'll have a tale to tell your ma," she said, grinning at him.

"Yes, ma'am, I will." He grinned back. There was a gap between his front teeth.

"I remember . . ." Azuba paused. *Something to restore normalcy for Carrie.* "Your ma's garden. She has such pretty zinnias. And your barred rock rooster. He might be scratching around in her garden right now."

The boy sent Azuba a wary glance, ducked his head. "He were a mean one, that rooster."

Carrie knelt, clung to the headboard. "What did the cook send?"

"Well, now, wait till I see." Andrew dug into the bag, lurched up against the built-in drawers. He grinned at Carrie, handing over the thick, crackery slabs. "Hardtack," he said. "Cold beef."

"Can you stay?" Carrie asked. "Stay and eat some with us?"

"Captain needs me," said the boy. He straightened a bit. "I'll come back again."

Carrie fell asleep, later, with a piece of hardtack in her hand and crumbs on her cheeks. Azuba tucked blankets tight around the little girl, took her own shawl from a hook. Her heart raced with fear and compulsion. Nathaniel would be furious, but she would only look out through the aft cabin door. She had to see a Cape Horn snorter with her own eyes. She had to be able to describe it to William and Benjamin.

At the top of the companionway she leaned against the door but could not push it open. She forced a crack, slipped through and crouched in the lee of the deck house. Icy snow flew, and she raised her hand to protect her face from the stabbing pellets, recoiling from the howl from which she and

Carrie were insulated. She could not imagine how Nathaniel and the mates could make themselves heard over the scream of wind in the rigging. Water struck the bulwarks, spouted fifteen feet in the air. The ship was lying on her lee side, the deck steeply tipped. There was still enough light in the sky to see, a grey luminescence making everything both sharp and unfamiliar: water streaming over the tilted deck, the ice-coated stays and shrouds, men labouring at the pumps.

A wall of grey-black water towered ahead, crested with a white fringe. *Traveller,* even lying on her lee as she was, rose to meet it. Azuba was pressed back against the deck house wall as the bow lifted. The ship breasted the wave. From the swirls of mists and spray came another ship. It was heading directly towards them, flying before the wind, so close that Azuba could see the men on her decks waving their arms, mouths open in horrified, soundless roars.

She had no memory of tumbling back down the companionway, only found herself on her knees in the cabin, her heart so swollen with fear that it pained her—wet, pulling clothes from drawers, trying to think what they would need in the lifeboat, while Carrie sat bolt upright in bed.

"Mama, what is it? What's happening?"

Any minute. Any minute I'll hear his voice commanding us.

Leggings, extra socks, woolen undervest.

"Mother, *my* mother, Carrie, when she dressed me for sledding, she would put two pairs of mittens on my hands, like this, she would be sure that my nose was covered . . ."

"Why are you dressing me, Mama?"

"We may have to . . ."

Then she realized that Nathaniel had not called and that the ships would have collided long ago and that she could still hear the clanking of the bilge pumps.

She slumped back against the wall. She looked out the

porthole, saw the grey mist, the black waves. Her fingertips tingled and the world returned—hunger, crackers, hope— and she felt a flood of relief and the certainty that this terror would end. That one day she would look back at it and see only a picture, small and insignificant as a rain-wrinkled postage stamp, of herself and Carrie, a messy cabin, a storm somewhere in the Drake Passage.

Carrie stood staring at her, mittens on her hands. "I'm hungry," she said. "Why are you putting mittens on me, Mama?"

"Oh, Carrie. I think I went a little crazy. I thought we were going to . . ." Azuba stripped the mittens from Carrie's hands. "Never mind. Let's go forage in the storeroom."

They scrambled up the sloping floor, stumbled across the saloon, went into the storeroom, gathered nuts, cranberry chutney and crackers. They took them back to Azuba's bed.

"A picnic, Mama. We're having a picnic in your bed!"

Carrie hummed and patted the cat, so sure, Azuba thought, that her father would save her. And if any man could, it would be Nathaniel, she realized, suddenly under-standing what it meant to put one's life in someone else's hands and why Nathaniel had not wanted her and Carrie aboard his ship.

Azuba woke.

Cracker crumbs were pressed into her cheek. Her nose was icy, the quilt and blankets had slipped from her shoul-ders. No fire had been made up in the saloon. She struggled to her elbow. She lurched, tossed. Her body was flung side-ways as she scrabbled for covers, making a nest over herself and Carrie.

She huddled under the covers, thinking of Nathaniel.

He must be sleeping on his feet or slumped on the floor of the deck house. He had no time for them.

Just then she heard steps in the saloon. The door opened, Nathaniel looked in.

"All right?" he said.

"All right."

They both looked at Carrie. She lay sprawled on her belly, her cheek pressed into the food-smeared pillow.

"She's been so good," Azuba said. "Not crying, keeping busy."

They exchanged one swift look of shame and shock that their child was at the mercy of the southern ocean rather than safe in her stout, four-poster bed in the house her grandfather had built.

It was in Nathaniel's eyes and in her own—the terror that their child might be lost to the sea.

On the third day the storm intensified. Everything that was movable on the fore deck, Andrew Moss reported, had been smashed to kindling or had gone over the side. The ship became sluggish; at every rise, she made a drunken, sodden lurch. By now, *Traveller* was like a wounded animal, and Azuba feared that she was slowly drowning, that water was in the hold, soaking the coal. Nathaniel had been so long without sleep that she imagined him collapsing from fatigue and being washed overboard. Carrie sought refuge in sleep, or in telling stories to Jojo, or in lying on the floor of the saloon, studying the underside of the sofa and munching on crackers. Andrew had been unable to empty the chamber pot, and chaos was compounded by stench.

At midnight, a wave swept over the quarterdeck. Carrie and Azuba were crumpled together in the armchair. The boards over the skylight gave way. Water poured into the saloon, drenching the horsehair couch. Instantly, the roar of the gale and the shriek of rigging filled their ears.

"The cat, oh, Mama! Save the cat. The canaries!"

Azuba snatched the cage from the ceiling. The cat tangled with their feet as they stumbled into Azuba's cabin.

The gimballed bed clanked, its cracker-strewn sheets damp from spilled water, sticky and stained with chutney. The ginger tin rattled across the floor. The pitcher jiggled in its rack beside the sink, and the doors of the washbasin slammed.

Sleep. Wake. Carrie's little voice, no longer humming. Whimpering.

"Mama, where is Papa? I want to see Papa."

"He can't come to us, lovey. He's too busy."

"Mama, I'm so hungry."

"Me too, Carrie. It will be over soon. Cook will start up his big stove."

"What will he make?"

"What would you like?"

"Apple pie."

Azuba rolled onto her side, snuggling Carrie up against her. "And I would like to be lying in a bed that does not move, hearing robins, smelling lilacs."

She imagined Grammy Cooper's garden when she was ten years old. Grammy had sent her to pick raspberries. Early August clouds were piling over the hayfield, and Grampa and other men were scything. She could see the flash of their blades, and their white shirts and black caps. Barefoot, she tucked up her skirt into her sash. The earth burned. The rain-fattened raspberries were easy to pick, and she plucked them from the canes. Worked them onto the tips of her fingers.

The next morning Nathaniel came below and sat on the bed, working at the laces of his boots.

"The storm has weakened. The worst is past. We've been blown backwards; we've drifted maybe a hundred miles sideways." He heeled off his boots, sat in soaking socks with his arms folded across his chest. "Good job, ladies," he said. "Good job."

"Lie down," Azuba said. She brushed crumbs from the bed, tidied the sheets, plumped the pillow. "Sleep."

He hauled off one sock. "Wake me, will you? Give me two hours."

He pitched forward on the pillow, arms straight at his sides, one leg draped over the side of the bed. Carrie stroked his wet hair, leaned to press a kiss on his cheek. Azuba lifted his leg, put it on the bed, took off the sock. She worked the quilt out from under him and pulled it up over his shoulders.

Mr. Dennis came below. He surveyed the saloon, its floor strewn with glass and splintered wood. Azuba sat on the couch, wrapped in blankets. Carrie huddled at her side, sleeping.

Mr. Dennis's staring eyes gentled. He stepped forward, touched Azuba on the shoulder. "We're through it, Mrs. Bradstock."

"Are you certain?"

"There's a break in the clouds. I've seen blue sky."

Icy wind whistled through the broken skylight.

"Let him sleep," he said. "I'll send someone to fix the skylight."

"Won't he be angry if we don't wake him?"

"I will bear the responsibility."

Exhaustion reduced the small man, stripped him of his irritability. Azuba saw how he was Nathaniel's partner more than she herself. She glimpsed the man he might be—in his drawing room, with his wife. In the warm light of a winter's dusk.

He lowered himself onto a chair, put his head in his hands. "I should go on deck," he muttered.

"Did you . . ." she whispered. "Mr. Dennis, did you see that ship?"

His body stilled, as if her words had frozen him. His mouth warped. "It was a close shave, Mrs. Bradstock."

They sat in silence.

"I'll send someone," he said, rising.

There were fair winds, the sun broke through. Gradually the ship was returned to normal. The skylight was repaired, Mr. Lee cooked an enormous hot meal, and in the saloon Carrie and Azuba propped wet cushions, blankets and clothing to dry in the pulsing heat of the coal stove. The watches resumed, the bells tinged, the decks were swept. *Traveller* surged westward.

One afternoon, Azuba and Carrie dressed warmly and went on deck. Dolphins played in the waters about the ship. Off to the west, the sky was clear even as a hail squall pelted them and then passed.

Nathaniel stood by the man at the wheel. He pointed at the fore topsail. He was subdued with exhaustion. Once again, they were attempting to round the Horn.

Azuba stood with one hand on the rail, the other cupping Carrie's shoulder. She glanced at Nathaniel. She heard his clipped words, the sailor's response.

Last night at supper Carrie had said, "I'm a good sailor, Papa."

He had smiled at her. "So you are."

"So is Mama," she'd added.

Nathaniel had glanced at Azuba and half-smiled but said nothing.

And Azuba had realized that whether or not she was a good sailor meant nothing to Nathaniel. Her presence added only a burden.

Azuba watched the dolphins. She felt bitter. Torn.

Where is home? Where do I belong?

She thought of how she and her hired man had worked together to winterize the sail house—like an outline of the partnership she'd expected to have with a husband. She had helped Slason, or rather, Slason had helped her. Together, they had hung the storm doors and windows. She had stood on chairs to hang baize over spare bedroom doors. She had made the decision to put down Dolly. She had determined what Hannah was to do of a day. She had paid their wages, kept her accounts. She could harness a horse, hoe potatoes, haul heavy boxes into the root cellar. She had killed chickens, scooped out steaming guts. She could stitch a wound.

Nathaniel must know this, even though he had not been there to see it.

She had been pondering other captains and wives in a new light, wondering how it was they could sail together in equanimity.

So far, she was allowed to do nothing but sit in the saloon. She could read, teach Carrie. She could iron on the saloon table. She could satisfy his needs. And only then was he tender: beneath the covers, where their eyes did not meet.

Now she realized how he perceived his world and women's place in it. Year after year, he had visited home, reacquainting himself with his domineering mother, and had been relieved to leave her and her ilk behind, to re-enter the vigorous world of men that he had known since boyhood. Settle back into his solitude. Love had no part in his life as a captain. Azuba saw that he knew this about himself, that it was why he had resisted marriage.

He had left the man at the wheel and was coming towards them along the deck.

It crossed her mind that, once they reached San Francisco, she could take Carrie and make the arduous overland journey home.

Just then, he reached them at the rail. He swept up Carrie in his arms, pointed at the shoals of leaping fish.

No.

It was patience she needed. Not flight. She must wait for his wound to heal. She felt a lightening of her heart. It touched her face just as he looked up from setting Carrie back down, and he was surprised into a smile.

Three weeks after the evening they had first sighted the Horn, *Traveller* passed the black cliff once again, rising dim through sleet. This time they rounded it and headed north, battered, towards California.

7. Yellow Dust

August 15, 1863
The Palace Hotel
San Francisco, United States of America

Dear Mother and Father,
I enclose this photograph of Carrie. The photographer
insisted that she place one hand on the table and hang the
other down. She said, "But I want to wave!" That is why
she has such a disconsolate face. Her dress is brown with
red flowers. As soon as we arrived, Nathaniel had dresses
made for us, since we had no room on board for our
London ones, which we shipped home. Have you received
the parcel? . . .

The hotel was on a hill overlooking the new park being laid
out on the west side of the city. It was to be called "Golden
Gate Park" after the entry to the harbour, which *Traveller* had
sailed through one windy afternoon, passing between high
cliffs and the Farallon Islands. Every night they dined at the
hotel, where, to Azuba's delight, there were people from
home: captains from Halifax and Yarmouth, Captain and
Mrs. Holder from Saint John, Captain and Mrs. McBride

from Tynemouth Creek. Over tea, Azuba and the other captains' wives talked avidly, comparing shipboard accommodations, stewards and cooks, and their respective passages round the Horn.

Azuba woke every morning with a sense of childlike anticipation. Nathaniel was less occupied than he had been in London. Perhaps, she thought, he was less determined to avoid her than he had been then. One day they hired horses, an extravagance at five dollars—a mare with sidesaddle for Azuba, a grey pony for Carrie and a roan for Nathaniel—and they rode through dunes to the beach, where enormous green rollers finished their journey from the Orient with such violence that the ground shook. Nathaniel lifted Carrie from her pony, offered Azuba his hand. They tethered the horses and walked on the beach, watching Carrie skirting the foam, her bonnet coming loose and lashing against its strings, wind snatching their voices so they had to shout to be heard, exclaiming over the sand dollars the child proffered on a sandy palm.

"Would you and Carrie like to return home by train?" Nathaniel asked Azuba. It was the evening of the same day. He was sitting at a table in their hotel bedroom, writing. *Traveller* was to go in ballast as far as Callao, Peru. From there, Nathaniel would sail to the nearby Chincha Islands to take on a load of guano. "The Chinchas are no place for a child."

Azuba was wearing her new city dress, its hoops so large she sat in a chair with no arms. She felt a pleasant ache in the small of her back from the sidesaddle.

"Why . . ." she began. In Nathaniel's mind, the ship itself was no place for a child, so she would not give him the chance to augment his reasons. "No. I think the dangers of Carrie and me crossing North America on a train without you are greater than . . ."

She turned down the wick of her lamp, which had begun to flare.

His pen resumed its scratch. Guano. Highly profitable fertilizer, much needed in the depleted soils of Europe. The cargo was consigned to Antwerp. Nathaniel would not be stopping on the east coast of North America, but would cross the Atlantic where, as Lieutenant Maury advised, he could best take advantage of the currents somewhere in the vicinity of Bermuda.

"All right," he said. His pen paused, he gave her a quick glance, and she caught a glint of acquiescence in his hooded eye. "It's the easier way to go 'round the Horn. Heading east. Wind will be behind us."

Us. She knew, then, that he, too, could not bear the thought of bidding farewell to them on the platform of a train station.

In Callao, Nathaniel found a hotel whose proprietor was an English-speaking native of Colorado with a Peruvian wife and four children. The hotel was two storeys high, its rooms opening onto a patio with a fountain, stone seats, a cage of parrots, cascades of bougainvillea. One entire wall of their room opened onto a balcony, and Azuba pulled back the drapes, happy to see Carrie playing with the other children, making Jojo squeak Spanish words.

They stayed in Callao for two weeks. One day, they went to visit a ship that had long ago been swept inland by a tidal wave. Houses surrounded the decaying ship, clotheslines were strung from her rotting ribs, chickens scratched at her keel. Azuba stared, thinking of her own father's ships, their wood still moist with sap and smelling of the forest.

November 4, 1863
The American Hotel
Callao, Peru

. . . and we will be leaving soon. This is the last letter I shall send until we reach Antwerp, unless we speak a ship at sea. I shall keep a record of this next stage of our voyage and will send you my own "log" of what will, I am confident, be a quick and easy passage. How strange it is to think that while I am sitting on a stone seat, enveloped in the sweet scent of flowers, the air warm to my skin and my ears hearing the croon of parrots who pick at their plumage, so brilliant beneath the blue sky, you are reading this by the grey light falling from the south window, if it is not yet obscured by frost. I can hear the fire ticking in the stove and imagine the smell of baking pumpkins. Please read this letter to Grammy, Benjamin and William. I miss all of you, and send you all my love, always.

Your devoted daughter,
Azuba

Traveller dropped anchor, swung around to her resting place. Birds wheeled over the barren Chincha Islands. A ship being loaded was anchored close to the cliff face, canvas chutes angling down into her hold. Clouds of yellow dust belched upward with each rushing load, enveloping the ship until she became only a vague shape, masts spiking the dust. The air was humid and Azuba covered her face with a handkerchief, gagging on the stench. Unseen, deep in the trenches, men shovelled the greasy guano into wheelbarrows. On the rocky surface, Azuba could see black straggling lines, persistent as ants—men staggering at the handles of wheelbarrows, heading for the loading chutes.

Nathaniel had tried to forestall Azuba's shock by describing the conditions before their arrival. His voice had been harsh.

"Some of the workers are convicts or army deserters. Most are coolies. Some are slaves, stolen from the Pacific Islands by blackbirders."

"What are blackbirders?"

"Unscrupulous captains who lure islanders aboard their ships. Azuba, I make no apologies for the place. The conditions are foul. If a man can't shovel, he's yoked to a wheelbarrow like a mule. If he's too weak, he works on hands and knees, picking stones from the guano. The overseers use whips. You'll hear the guard dogs."

There were twelve ships before them, more than Nathaniel had expected. They would have to wait their turn. It might be as long as two months.

Most evenings, a strange fog crept in, reducing the pestiferous islands to black swellings in a molten, red haze.

After supper, despite the humidity, they sat in the saloon for privacy. Yellow dust blew through the windows. Azuba ran a wet cloth over picture frames, the arms of chairs, her tea set. She had unpacked the coronation teacups and her best teapot and laid out Grammy Cooper's rug. She took shallow breaths, imagining clean air, astounded at how she had never before appreciated it. The stench was constant, like the heat.

Nathaniel sat in the armchair reading a newspaper they had brought from Callao. Carrie knelt on the hooked rug, where clouds and seagulls floated in a blue sky, brightly coloured houses tipped on a hillside, and boats lay in a harbour, wavy lines making the water dance. She and Azuba wore head scarves. They had been warned by the other captains' wives that the dust would cause their hair to fall out.

"Whelan's Cove," Carrie said. Her finger described patterns on the rug's flattened loops. "Here's our house."

The wind shifted and they could hear the thudding of picks and the harsh shouts of overseers. Azuba tensed. Horror lodged in the back of her throat. She had been on board adjacent ships and noticed how at such times the other women lifted their teacups and spoke of home, ignoring the sounds.

The previous night, fifty slaves and coolies had held hands and jumped to their deaths from one of the cliffs. An American woman had come to their ship. She had whispered the news to Azuba, advising her to keep Carrie below decks in case any of the bodies should float by.

The barking of guard dogs came on the sultry air, a slim chain of sound. Their own dog made a growling deep in his throat. Nathaniel lowered his paper.

"Best guard dog I've ever had on a ship," he said. He put down his hand, wiggled his fingers. The dog lurched to his feet, went panting to Nathaniel.

They had bought the dog in Callao. A man selling fruit from a gig had called up that he had a puppy for sale. Nathaniel bargained, and the man returned with a thin, eager dog, not a puppy, sitting in the bow. The dog was half-starved, flea-ridden. Carrie had leaned down, arms spread.

"Poor thing, poor thing!"

"She needs a creature to love," Nathaniel had muttered and motioned to a sailor to heave the dog aboard.

Azuba had given Carrie an old hairbrush and the dog had grinned with pleasure as the child brushed his short black hair. Carrie named him Gig. They soon realized his worth. The dog slept on the quarterdeck and would bark at a mouse.

"Papa?" Carrie walked on her knees from the rug to her

father, folded her hands on his lap. "Why couldn't I come above decks today for my arithmetic lessons? Or even to play?"

Azuba looked up sharply. She was dipping her cloth into the pie crust edges of a kerosene lamp.

"Something bad happened last night." His voice hardened, repressing questions. Carrie observed him steadily, as if guessing at the horror he tried to conceal. "Nothing for little girls to know about. You were best off playing with your doll down here."

Azuba went to the horsehair couch and sat with the cleaning flannel wound around her hands like a bandage. Through the windows she could see the red sky, made lurid by spinning dust.

"Show Papa what you did today," she said. She wanted him to realize that even here they could live a normal life.

Carrie went to her cabin, rummaged, returned with her chalkboard. *Chinchas* was written there. *Careful, confuse, console.* She took lessons in the cabin with Azuba until eleven o'clock and then went above decks to study mathematics with Nathaniel. She sat on the roof of the deck house. It was the closest she ever came to the sailors, and as she did her sums, she peeked at the rough men who were not allowed to speak to her. They, too, were intrigued by the child at their captain's side.

Nathaniel took the slate. "What's this one?"

"*Careful,*" she read. She coughed from the dust until she bent double. "*Confuse. Console.*"

He patted her back. "Good girl."

Azuba spoke quietly. "Will you sing for us, Nathaniel?" He had a tender baritone, well tuned. At home, he sang bedtime songs to Carrie. And, early in their marriage, to her.

He took a sip on his pipe. The smoke wreathed on the yellow-hazed air. He did not answer, but she saw that he had heard her and was considering her request, watching Carrie—thinking, perhaps, the same thing she was.

Fifty men, leaping to their deaths. Their little girl, in a place where such things could happen.

He cleared his throat, set down his pipe. The fingers of one hand pinched his moustache, smoothed it outwards, snugged down to grip his beard. He patted his knee and Carrie climbed into his lap.

He began to sing an Irish song, "Shule Agra."

But now my love has gone to France,
to try his fortune to advance,
If he ever comes back,
'Tis but a chance . . .

The music was the sound of longing. She wondered if Nathaniel had chosen the song for the women whose men had jumped from the cliff. He sat with his eyes closed and lips pressed tight as the last note died away. His hand rested on Carrie's head.

"Bedtime now," Azuba whispered. Tears pricked her eyes. "I'll go too, Carrie."

It was eighty-five degrees Fahrenheit, day and night, too hot to sleep below decks. The air was heavy with humidity, although no rain ever fell. Nathaniel had had the sailors rig a roofless cabin on the quarterdeck, just behind the mizzen mast.

Azuba and Carrie went into their makeshift bedroom and climbed into their hammocks. Carrie pointed at the stars. "See, Mama? There they are, the fairy families. The littlest ones are the children fairies. They're swinging from the rigging, the way I will when I'm old enough to climb up the ratlines."

Azuba thought of the workers on the island. Sleeping on grass mats, in reed huts. Hungry, wretched, ill. She wondered if they lay as she did, picturing their homes and families. "*Shhh*. Sleep, sleep," she murmured.

Like a luxury, she riffled through memory, choosing. Christmas, she decided. The men preparing the church. They were stoking the wood stove that filled the aisle. She and some other young women were decorating the tree. It was snowing, each flake coming separately, rocking, easy on the air, making its own tremulous journey. Carrie was at Mother's, cutting out gingerbread men. Unexpectedly, Reverend Walton came into her imagined scene. He opened the church door. He wore a black wool coat, snowflakes dusting its shoulders. He stood holding his mittens in one hand, arrested by the picture he saw—the fir tree, the women's dresses. Azuba knelt, arm raised to hang a tin star. She smiled at Simon and he smiled back. Later, he showed her the picture he had painted from memory. The grey light, the tree, the women.

She laid her arm over her face.

What happened to him? Does he think of me?

As she drifted towards sleep, the image of Simon was replaced with another, something so close and enormous she could see only a piece of it: Nathaniel's careworn face and how he had closed his eyes, singing, snuggling his little girl. And how she had wanted to lean up against him and put her arm around his waist.

She was jolted wide awake by a sudden realization. She had missed her courses in November. Often they came late, so she had not been overly concerned. But by now it was time again.

"Don't ever be sure," the midwife had told her after the miscarriage. "Don't ever be sure until you've passed the third month."

Her fingers raised, one by one.

On Christmas Eve, Azuba and Carrie sat on deck, stringing popcorn that Mr. McVale had brought from the galley. Carrie wore only a shift. Beads of perspiration trickled down Azuba's neck.

"Good thing you sent Santa that letter. So he'll know where you are," Azuba said.

The smell of boiled ham and roasting chicken rose from the nearby ships.

Carrie tugged a piece of popcorn down her thread. They were going to wind popcorn chains around the handle of a basket and set the basket on the saloon table, hoping Santa Claus would see it.

"Shall I hang my stocking, too?"

Water lapped *Traveller,* a calm chuckling, while from the islands came the thuddings and bawled commands, the breeze-borne horror rising and fading.

"Yes, Santa will be looking for it."

"Will he go onto the island?"

"I don't think reindeer can land on guano. Besides, Carrie, there aren't any children there."

On Christmas morning, Azuba woke to the sound of Carrie's happy shriek. She reached for Nathaniel's hammock, found his dangling arm, squeezed his hand.

Carrie was kneeling in the shade of the flimsy walls, pulling treasures from her stocking—candy, nuts, a silver bell, a bead bracelet.

"He came!"

She urged them from their hammocks to see if Santa had thought to go down into the saloon. Mr. McVale was crossing the deck with a tray of coffee.

"Happy Christmas, Mr. McVale."

Smoke came from the galley stove. Mr. Lee had begun preparing Christmas dinner.

In the saloon, the popcorn-trimmed basket was bulging with gifts wrapped in brown paper with red ribbons. Nathaniel sat on the couch. He wore a knee-length cotton nightshirt. He ran his hands through his red-gold hair, pushed out his chin and worked at his beard with his fingers. After a minute, he reached for Azuba, pulled her close. She leaned against his shoulder. They relaxed, watching Carrie. He took Azuba's hand. "You made a nice Christmas for her," he murmured. Azuba looked up to see that he was looking not at Carrie but at her. Pain in his eyes, and confusion.

Carrie opened her presents, clapping her hands. Dominoes. A cup and ball. A cast-iron horse and a toy carriage to match.

Azuba's mind went to the men on the island. She had heard they were fed two meals daily: a cup of maize and four unripe bananas.

"Surely," she murmured to Nathaniel. "Surely those workers will receive something extra today."

Impatience touched his sunburned face, and she wished she'd kept her thoughts to herself. She ran over in her mind the rest of the day: she'd conferred with Mr. Lee about a traditional menu and given him a few recipes. Turkey and ham, boiled onions, wine jelly, vanilla pudding, ginger beer. At dinner, Carrie would slip Andrew Moss a tiny box wrapped in red silk, containing an elaborate key she'd found in a Callao gutter. The sailors, too, would have a special meal and would come to the cabin, Nathaniel had told her, for a drink of rum.

Azuba thought, but did not say, that it would never matter where they were, land or sea, as long as she could be with her husband at Christmas, watching their child's happiness.

On sunrise of the day *Traveller* was to be loaded, two weeks after Christmas, a sailor rowed over from the ship *Suzanna.* Azuba and Carrie were to stay with Captain Marshall and his wife during the three days it would take to load eight hundred tons of guano.

Crossing to the *Suzanna,* they sat in the rowboat, facing one another, bags and sewing baskets at their feet. As the sun rose from the sea, Azuba could hear the half-starved, vicious dogs on the island begin their barking. The first rays of sun were tender, a shimmer. Then, as the sun rose higher, heat came like a furnace, an orange glow on Carrie's cheeks. *Suzanna*'s crew lowered a gamming chair, hoisted them up one at a time.

They were led to the cabin to take breakfast with Mrs. Marshall.

"Sit, sit, just in time." Mrs. Marshall made a flurry of her hands towards the bolted bench running alongside the table. She was a strong, heavyset woman. She wore a brown dress tight across the bosom, its lace limp, missing buttons revealing a coffee-stained chemise. She loved the seafaring life, was her husband's navigator.

"Porridge," she said, ladling gummy brown wheat grains into bowls. "Coffee. Going to be hot as a pocket today. On your way soon, I'll wager. We'll be following; our turn is next."

"Where are you going?"

"New York," Mrs. Marshall said. "Then back to Yarmouth for a bit. Must see my little ones, see if they're behaving themselves."

"What do you mean, little ones?"

"My children. Emma and Tom. They stay in Yarmouth when Mr. Marshall and I go seafaring."

"Oh," Azuba said, shocked. The woman spoke so easily, as if it were commonplace for a mother to leave her children in safety and place herself in danger.

"We're going to Antwerp," Azuba said.

Mrs. Marshall leaned forward, elbows amidst the crockery. The sharp smell of perspiration rose from her soaked armpits. "Do you wish you were going home?"

"Oh, no." Azuba glanced at Carrie. "Well. Eventually, it will be nice. We do have a lovely house. But Carrie and I prefer to be with Captain Bradstock."

Mrs. Marshall studied her with open curiosity. "What kind of a crew do you have? How are your mates?"

Azuba turned her face away from Carrie, lowered her voice. "At first, I thought the first mate hated me. But he's not as bad as he seems. He was kind to me after a storm. Sometimes I notice that he's a bit put out with . . . well . . . Nathaniel is sometimes a little too much in charge."

"I've seen that in captains. He's still young, your man."

"And, Mrs. Marshall, I did not enjoy rounding the Horn."

"Don't like having your face smashed up against the wall? Don't like seeing your crockery flying off the table? Well, Mrs. Bradstock, what kind of a woman are you?"

The women burst into laughter. Carrie looked up, spoon in her porridge. Azuba had put on her gold hoop earrings. She felt reckless, confessional.

"Are you ever frightened?" Azuba asked.

Mrs. Marshall crossed her arms. She considered Azuba. "I once spent two weeks in an open lifeboat. Ship went down in a storm off Bermuda. We were picked up by some Spaniards. I kept the men going with my jokes. No, I don't worry. We're the stronger sex, Mrs. Bradstock. Men won't admit it."

Stained teeth in a sunburned face. Azuba had heard that Mrs. Marshall went out on deck and hauled lines with the men. She thought of Father. He would not approve of this woman. And she did not think Nathaniel would want her to become like Mrs. Marshall.

Yet I think I could be like her. In my own way, she thought. And felt a small change inside herself.

After breakfast, they went back on deck. *Traveller* by now lay at the cliffside. Mrs. Marshall peered intently through her glass. She was a font of information on every port she had ever visited. She had amassed a large collection of curios, including a human skull and several enormous whale's teeth, one carved with a full-rigged ship, another bearing the Lord's Prayer.

She passed the glass to Carrie. "Look there, now. Could be you can see your Papa."

Carrie screwed the glass to her eye, pointed it at the ship.

"Carrie," Azuba said, suddenly, after squinting naked-eyed at the ship. "Give it . . . give me . . ." She snatched the glass from Carrie, peered through it affixed with shock. The crew had retreated high into the rigging, their faces covered with cloth. Each time guano was dumped from the chute, a belch of dust obscured *Traveller's* masts, her delicate fretwork of rigging, the deck houses. As it thinned, men appeared through the clouds, trimmers staggering up from the hold, ripping away masks made of hemp plastered together with tar, tied with rags to their noses and mouths. One man had blood pouring from his nose. Another, gasping, fell on all fours. They seemed to be naked, although she could not tell for sure, since they were plastered with guano.

Carrie tugged at Azuba's arm. "Where's Papa?"

Azuba pointed to a man on the main royal yard. She did not know if it was Nathaniel, but she leaned to direct Carrie's eyes. "There he is," she said. "Quite safe."

"Where's Andrew?"

"Oh . . ." Azuba paused, pointed at random. "There."

"Who's Andrew?" said Mrs. Marshall. She had retrieved the glass and was watching the ship.

"A boy," said Carrie.

"Cabin boy? Sweet on him?"

Carrie frowned up at the large woman.

"He's a boy from home," Azuba said.

"Some of 'em go blind," Mrs. Marshall said, paying no attention, scanning with the glass. "Trenches cave in, bury them alive. Trimmers have been asphyxiated from the vapours, I've heard tell. I've seen them come up vomiting. They get dreadful infections from the cracks in their hands. Sores, ulcers, wounds. Won't heal. Terrible."

She protects her own children. But not mine. Good Lord. The insensitivity of some people.

"We're going below," Azuba said. "We brought our sewing baskets. Come, Carrie."

Carrie opened her mouth, startled by Azuba's sharp tone. Mrs. Marshall did not seem to notice, nor did she lower the glass, but only waved vaguely over her shoulder as Azuba and Carrie turned and went back along the deck.

The cluttered saloon smelled of unwashed clothing. It was dark, only a slice of light falling from one window. Its surfaces were dull, dusty. Azuba had brought shirts she was making for Nathaniel. She had made six so far this trip, and the last two needed buttons.

"Now, Carrie. Papa is all right. Take out your button box."

Carrie's mouth was warped, her eyes dark. She had seen the men coming up from the hold. "Mama. Those men were like the pigs when Slason came to kill them."

Azuba was silent. She had not known that Carrie had been watching when the pigs had staggered around the pen, screaming, their eyes bright and aware, so frantic that they fell onto their knees.

"The men will be all right," she said. "They had face masks on to help them breathe. Don't worry."

Carrie sighed, took out her lacquered button box. There

were all sorts of buttons—bone, brass, horsehair—but her favourites were vegetable ivory, corozo or taugua palm nut, impressed with designs of stars, moons and animals. She would take these out and arrange them in patterns, making star-hung, moon-silvered worlds for the deer, rabbits, horses and dogs.

Carrie was staring at her precious buttons, biting her lips. Azuba laid her hand on Carrie's head, ran it down to cup her cheek. She gave a gentle pat. She handed her a set of steel buttons packed in strips of cotton. "Never mind your buttons, lovey. We'll use mine for Papa's shirt."

She set Carrie to unwrapping them.

"When we get home—" Azuba began.

"When *will* we get home, Mama?"

"After Antwerp." Azuba took thread from its packet of brown paper. She selected a needle from the wool pages of her needle case, passed it through her hair to oil it.

"Let's talk about home," Carrie murmured. Her head was covered in a pink-flowered scarf; her fingers, unrolling cotton, were brown, their tips unworn.

Azuba threaded her needle in the dim light, pondering Mrs. Marshall, who travelled the world at her husband's side, both of them at ease with her role. But she let another woman raise her children. It would be the children who would be like strangers to her, rather than her husband.

"I was thinking of roses. Do you remember the wild roses between the house and the road? And the ones Papa planted on the trellis by the kitchen door?"

"I would collect the petals before they blew away," Carrie said. "For our sachets."

"Yes. You were very good at it, too."

Azuba's needle pulled through the fabric with a small tearing sound. They could hear the distant, rushing thunder as another load of guano slid into *Traveller*'s hold. She and Carrie had dusted the saloon last night. Now, close beneath their home, the hold was being filled. Load after wet, stinking load.

"Perhaps the roses will be blooming when we get home. They have such a sweet scent," Azuba said. Her voice trembled and Carrie looked up. Her eyes were as round as pennies, fringed with black lashes.

Our empty house, she thought. *Nothing more, at this moment, than a square density around which the December wind moans. No flicker of candle flame.*

She put her needle down, watched as Carrie pressed a button to the fabric, pricked her needle up from beneath. Azuba put down her own work, reached to help. Their kerchiefed heads touched—red flowers, pink flowers. Black curls licked flat by sweat. Her fingers touched Carrie's. She saw how earnestly the child worked to set her father's button straight, to snug her stitches tight.

Oh, my sweet little girl.

Nathaniel was right, and she had not listened. She felt small before a sense of her own selfishness. She had brought Carrie to this monstrous place, thinking to make a family. But it had been for herself, not Carrie. Not Nathaniel. It had been for her own vision of freedom. She had seen how she might fly from her cage, and what it might make of her.

There was no way to erase horror from a child's memory.

8. Moonstones

Fair wind.

It was the second morning out from the Chinchas. Azuba lay in her bed, listening. There was a settled regularity to the creaking of timbers. The light was lively, no longer hazy, and sea wind had blown away the island's stench and the smell of guano in their hold. A sailor was sluicing the quarterdeck. She heard the swishing of a broom and then water showered past her porthole, carrying chicken feathers, broom bristles, bits of twine.

She rolled onto her side, closed her eyes and drew up her knees, nauseated.

For the third time, her courses had not come.

She used a finger-shaped sea sponge encased in a tasselled silken net. On days of heavy bleeding, she wore a waistband with an attached napkin strap to hold her grandy rags. She washed her rags and dried them, hidden inside pillow slips, on a line strung on deck. The cloths were stacked in her dresser drawer. Two weeks had passed. She had needed neither the sponge nor the rags. She had felt prickly pains deep in her womb.

This is not seasickness.

She lay waiting for the nausea to pass. She absorbed the

enormity of her changed circumstances. She felt the wonder of a new being, a brother or sister for Carrie. And for an instant she was washed with peace, sending her thoughts to the new child. *Who are you? Boy or girl?*

Then her eyes flew open. She imagined herself, Carrie and Nathaniel shipwrecked and cast up on an island. Or, God forbid, cast adrift like Mrs. Marshall in a lifeboat. She would have only Nathaniel as midwife and doctor. No chloroform. No strong, wise women's hands. No recourse but to books. Or luck.

She thought of her miscarriage, her own initiation into nature's random cruelty. And the stories she had heard recounted—women leaning close, voices grim. Breech births. Stillbirths. Bleeding that could not be stopped. Milk fever. Labours that ended in exhaustion and death for both mother and child.

She rolled back to stare at the white-painted ceiling.

She could stay in Callao. She could have a house with a cook, maids, a gardener. She would meet other English-speaking people. Carrie would go to school, have other children to play with. She would find a midwife.

Yet.

Nathaniel would miss the birth of his child. And how would they get home again?

Carrie came to the door, hair like a gone-to-seed dandelion. "Good morning, Mama. May I go barefoot?"

Carrie loved the feel of the decks on her bare feet, soft as cloth from being scoured with holystones, Bible-sized blocks of sandstone. All the sailors went barefoot in the hottest climates. It was still summer off the coast of South America, although they were heading for the perpetual cold of the high latitudes.

"Yes, Carrie. You may go barefoot. Get dressed and don't forget your bonnet. Wait for me, I want to come too."

Azuba took a steadying breath through her nose. She stood, staggered slightly, put a hand to the wall. She dressed and followed Carrie through the dining cabin and up the companionway.

Azuba squinted up at the tiers of white canvas. "Look at the clouds, Carrie! Like castles." She smelled a tinge of woodsmoke coming from the galley as she and Carrie climbed the steps to the quarterdeck.

Nathaniel stood in his usual place on the deck's wind-struck weather side; Mr. Dennis stood on the lee side. A helmsman, aft, held the wheel. Nathaniel came towards them, smiling as he watched Carrie struggle to disentangle skirts from her legs, unwind hair from her mouth, settle Jojo properly in her arms so the doll could see the view and ward off Gig, who came bounding, saliva stranding from his tongue.

"Down, Gig! How are my ladies? Got your sea legs back?"

He glanced at Azuba, did a double take. "You're white, Azuba."

"No, I'm well. Really. I just had a touch of seasickness."

She crossed the deck towards her chair. If she did not tell him soon, he might make the discovery on his own, sliding his hands over her in bed and feeling her swollen breasts. She imagined his face at the moment he learned the news—first pleasure, then worry.

And she felt certain, suddenly, that were he to know, he would put her off in Callao.

Nathaniel squatted at Carrie's side, directing her eyes to a raft of birds skimming low over the surface of the water. Mr. Dennis glanced at father and daughter. Last night he had taken his flute from its velvet-lined case and let Carrie make a breathy blow.

Mr. Dennis would smile if we were below decks, away from the eyes of sailors, Azuba thought. She lowered herself into the rush-seated chair, with its sawed-off legs. She watched Mr. Dennis. Increasingly, she lost her fear of him. He had a quick, focused mind, and it teemed with concern for the ship. His voice lashed the men—raw, brutal.

Once, Carrie had clutched Azuba. "Listen to Mr. Dennis, Mama!"

"It's all right," Azuba had reassured her. "Papa wants him to roar at the men like that. The officers have to command the sailors."

Mr. Perkins, on the other hand, was shy, awkward. His fingers were the size of sausages. At the table, he kept them curled into fists and hidden in his lap. He was twenty-three, and without being asked had told Azuba that he lived on White Head Island, off Grand Manan, where his wife was expecting their first child. He had wistfully told Azuba his wife's name—Jane—and had described their small house, so close to the shore that spray coated its back windows with salt. Now he stood in the ship's waist, gesturing, shouting, directing men to winding spun yarn around lines to prevent chafing, or to painting, tarring, oiling, cleaning.

Azuba shook out her skirts, laid her hands on the arm-rests. The backs of her hands, she noticed, were sunburned. She spread her fingers, pleased, observing the white skin between them. She had bent to peer into the cabin mirror and seen that her face, too, was darkening, despite her bonnet and despite the shadow of the sails that fell over her like the roof of a shed. There was no escape from the water's glare.

How odd, she thought, watching the sailors, *that I am only just beginning to learn what those men are doing, although they work at their tasks as easily as breathing.*

There were twenty people aboard: aside from the family, there were the two mates, the cabin boy, the steward and the cook. And there were twelve sailors, a rough lot of men who had replaced their New Brunswick crew, reeling aboard in London, "full," as Nathaniel muttered. Two were Swedish, several Irish, one African, the others English.

There was a pause as the bells imposed discipline— ordering the day and minimizing the reality of their precarious situation, how the ship and all aboard her were at the mercy of forces close at hand—long swells, gentle air; insouciant and sinister.

Azuba's workbox lay beneath her chair, but she left it untouched and sat watching the water. Wind swept the surface, made a hundred wavelets. Cloud shadow was a darkness quickly relieved. She thought of how, later, she would wash her clothes and hang them in this lovely wind. She pictured her mother, who at this very moment might be standing on a path trodden into the snow beneath the clothesline, pinning laundry with mittened hands on this January day. A cat might slither past her mother's skirts as she went back into the warm, quiet house—clock ticking, soup on the stove. Azuba imagined herself coming into the kitchen and removing her own winter-smelling cloak. *Mother, I'm going to have a baby . . .*

"Mama? Will we get more animals in Callao?"

The pens by the deck house were empty. They had grown used to the domestic clucking and baaing of a farmyard but had killed the last pig, the sheep and all the chickens during the two months at the Chincha Islands.

"Yes, Papa will get more animals."

"We won't name them."

"Oh, Carrie," Azuba shook her head, rueful. "Wasn't that terrible? No, no more naming." She felt a pang, remembering Carrie's tears when Mr. McVale had reported that Mrs. Smith, the barred rock hen, was on their plates.

Carrie sat cross-legged, one arm around Gig, her cheek on his head. She was gazing up, squinting into the sun, watching Andrew Moss. He inched along a yard, wearing a red neckerchief, a blue ribbon on his straw hat.

Azuba watched Carrie's wistful face as she gazed up at the only other child on *Traveller*. Nathaniel had spoken to every man on the ship and told them to look out for Carrie. Children had been known to wash overboard. Mrs. Lattimer, a grim American woman at the Chinchas, had told Azuba of her son. "I was standing on the deck with my little boy beside me," Mrs. Lattimer had said. "He was three years old. A great wave came, and the next thing I knew he was overboard. I screamed and rushed to the side. He was on his back, and I could see his little face and hands just below the water's surface."

Azuba closed her eyes at this thought. Perversely, she replaced the image with one of herself in labour, in the midst of a storm such as the one they'd had rounding the Horn. Nathaniel stood in the door, roared at her to wait, wait, he had no time to help her; she screamed back, *I can't help it!*; Carrie said, *I'll help, Mama.* Azuba shook her head, dispelling the thought. She reached into her workbox and took out her knitting. *Or,* her mind nagged, only last year, the ship *Anne,* loaded with guano, had taken water into the hold, and a flash of combustion had blown off the entire stern. Passengers and crew had escaped, like Mrs. Marshall, in open lifeboats.

She put down her knitting and stared out over the glittering waters. Imagining herself in a lifeboat, with Carrie and an infant.

Three days later, Carrie and Azuba sat under an awning on the deck, watching the coast of South America grow from a motionless blue line on the horizon into hills and islands with discernible features. All the sailors were on deck; men of the off watch sat on capstans or lifeboats, hands shading eyes. They passed a promontory capped with the fortress of Castillo de Real Felipe. They entered a large bay, sheltered by La Punta, a tongue of land on the south, and the islands of San Lorenzo and Fronton. Nathaniel stood beside Azuba, pointing, reciting these names, lifting his glass to study the passing landscape.

"Listen," he said, cupping his ear.

City sounds came over the water: the hiss and clank of a rail yard as trains arrived or departed for the Andes; braying mules, barking dogs.

A tug brought *Traveller* into the harbour, eased her along-side the new three-hundred-foot floating dock imported from Glasgow. Carrie and Azuba rushed to the railing, mes-merized by the sight of so many other human beings. Men driving mules, shouting, laughing. Women walking, their skirts licking the dust. Boys running after wagons. After two months anchored at the forsaken, desolate islands, it came as a shock to realize that such activity had never ceased, even as desperate men laboured in trenches, or leapt from cliffs.

Azuba reached down for Carrie's hand. "Mail!" Azuba said. She gave Carrie's hand a little shake. "News from home!"

"And we'll take Gig for a run," Carrie said.

"And eat fruit and cheese."

"Wine," Nathaniel added, overhearing. He spoke briefly to Mr. Dennis, resuming command as the pilot boat dis-engaged. Carrie turned up her face to look at him. He folded back one side of her bonnet, brushed a wisp of hair from her cheek. "Chocolate?" he said. "And a new doll? For my brave sailor girl."

"And solid ground beneath our feet," Azuba said. "Remember, Carrie, you might trip and fall, at first."

They stood on either side of their child, smiling down at her. Azuba felt the gentleness in Nathaniel that fatherhood drew forth. And wondered if he felt the same change in her.

The ship's routine was thrown into disarray. Nathaniel's energy was bent towards the next leg of the trip. For him, there would be no time for sightseeing or for making any purchases other than what would be needed for the long passage. He set up an outdoor office under the deck awning. The mates were transformed into clerks, taking inventory as vendors arrived with blocks of ice, meat, vegetables, eggs and fruit. Barrels of provisions were stacked on the dock. The sailors became farmhands—repairing stalls, wrestling animals over the gangplank.

Azuba and Carrie took tea with other captains' wives on board their ships or went with them on walks and excursions. Azuba became friendly with Mrs. Davis, of the ship *Magnolia,* from Bath, Maine; Mrs. Lattimer; and Mrs. Troop, of *Electa,* from Liverpool, England. There were even three little girls for Carrie to play with.

Azuba saw, but did not meet, a few of the older women who had sailed with their husbands for twenty years and more. Like Mrs. Marshall, they had become somewhat like men themselves, in their brash confidence and the way in which they were too busy with duties to attend tea parties, even hiring crew or bargaining for provisions. She observed them, fascinated, thinking that they seemed more content than any other women she'd known. She wished she had the chance to tell them that she studied Nathaniel's books on navigation, set herself mathematical problems, listened to Nathaniel's orders and was attentive to the way in which the men carried them out. And that, in the back of Grammy's leather book, she had drawn a picture of *Traveller* and, turning her nib upside down, had labelled sails, lines and yards.

Is this, she longed to ask them, *how you became who you are?* And she wondered how they had revealed their skills to their husbands.

Some evenings in Callao, Nathaniel relaxed in the saloon with Carrie and Azuba. He taught Carrie to play checkers, exchanged proud glances with Azuba when Carrie made a clever move. Azuba wondered if, surrounded by other captains' wives and their children, Nathaniel was becoming resigned to and even pleased by the presence of his own.

She pictured the older, competent women. *He won't be able to help it. I will become like them.*

After a few days in Callao, Azuba realized that the brief fantasy she'd had of staying on and having her baby in this strange city was unthinkable. The idea had been conceived in the Chinchas' miasma of death and despair. Now she could not imagine living here alone with Carrie and a newborn baby. She thought of the stories she'd heard of women giving birth at sea; so many captains had made safe deliveries of sons and daughters, and given them proud, out-landish names to commemorate their place of issue: *Woodhull, Samoa, Valparaiso.*

She decided to keep her condition hidden until they were well under way.

She would be months away from other women. *I'll need nour-ishments for the mind and soul—books, plants, projects.*

Small boats swarmed *Traveller,* filled with grinning men who held up handfuls of apricots or trinkets. *"¡Flores!"* they called. *"Leche, naranjas."*

Carrie pressed against the railing on tiptoe. "Look, Mama, look! A monkey! A parrot!"

"Goodness, Carrie, imagine the trouble a monkey could get into."

But Azuba beckoned, and men came aboard and spread serapes on the deck.

Once, to Carrie's delight, a man picked at the knot of a rag bundle and released a wash of milky moonstones. "*Mira*," he said, smiling at Carrie, gesturing. "Take! You, gift."

Azuba bought a potted rose, an English ivy and rose geraniums, remembering how at sea she had yearned for colour. She bought a canary and Carrie named it Bonita. She bartered with the other captains' wives: exchanged a skein of blue yarn for red sewing silk, preserves for books, thread for newspapers, fruitcake for fabric. Women gave Carrie pieces of cloth with which to make a quilt. "You teach your papa how to turn a needle," they said, laughing, comparing anecdotes of husbands who had taken to needlepoint, knitting or quilting.

Wearing light shawls and carrying lace-trimmed parasols, the women took their exercise on the dock. They were light on their feet, their hands like drifting feathers, actual feathers fluttering from their hats. Azuba and Carrie walked with them, enjoying the companionship of soft-bodied, soft-skinned females. Azuba did not tell even these women of her pregnancy, fearing that, in the inevitable way of secrets, word would reach Nathaniel.

They were invited to dine on board an American ship, *Day Break*.

"Come, Carrie," Azuba said. It was time to dress.

Carrie was watching an altercation. Down by the provision barrels, a man was fraternizing with the crew. Nathaniel, at his desk beneath the awning, growled to Mr. Dennis, who rose to his feet with one flex of his legs, and strode down the deck.

"*¿Qué quiere usted?*"

The man narrowed himself, arms to sides. He stepped sideways into a group of bystanders.

"Keep an eye out," Mr. Dennis snapped to the sailors. It was nearing sundown and there were still barrels to load.

"Come, Carrie," Azuba said, even though she, too, watched uneasily. They hurried below, and Nathaniel came behind, followed by Mr. Dennis, who had also been invited to the American ship.

Azuba and Carrie had nothing fancy to wear, since they had sent home the dresses made in San Francisco. Azuba selected a flower-print dress for Carrie. She wore her black bombazine, without hoops. At his request, she straightened Nathaniel's silk ribbon necktie.

They set off down the dock, leaving Mr. Perkins in charge of the ship. It was a warm evening, with a cool, onshore breeze. Schooners were returning from a day's fishing. Still, they did not have their land legs, and the boards of the dock seemed to rise up and meet their feet.

Day Break's dining saloon was enormous, far more luxurious than *Traveller's*. At the table were the American captain and his wife, their four-year-old daughter, the ship's doctor and the first and second mates.

"Please call me Louisa," the captain's wife murmured, laying her hand on Azuba's wrist. She was a young, open-faced woman with a sprinkling of freckles over her nose and an innocent, pleading expression in her eyes.

The little girls sat side by side, the younger child gazing up at Carrie. Their faces were flushed by the evening light falling from the cabin windows. They ate roast turkey and boiled ham, stewed pumpkin with cranberries, buttermilk biscuits and Indian pudding. The steward brought cruets and bottles of wine, port and ale. The American captain chewed with his mouth open, roaring a tale of his rotten tooth: how the dentist had sliced the gum around the tooth before screwing his instrument onto it, causing a shower of blood, then hauled the tooth to the right, left, back, front, and when the tooth had neither broken nor come out, the captain had snatched the instrument and yanked out the tooth himself.

Azuba glanced at Carrie, who was not eating. She stared at the captain. *Not knowing,* Azuba thought, *whether or not to be frightened.*

"Little girls don't have rotten teeth," she whispered. "Yours just fall out by themselves."

Talk, as was natural with Americans, turned to their civil war, now in its third year. Dangers off the American coast. Ships sunk by Confederate raiders.

Louisa and Azuba rose, held out their hands to the little girls and swept from the table.

In the saloon, Louisa had spread red brocade on a table and laid out curios. There was a long, slender leaf from a South African Table Mountain silver leaf tree, painted with a miniature of *Day Break*. There were sailor's valentines made of shells, and the dried wings of a flying fish.

Louisa and Azuba sat side by side on a sofa.

"I could have stayed home, you know," Louisa said. "We have a new house in Stonington, Maine. My husband didn't care one way or another. 'Come if you wish,' he said."

"Mine . . ." Azuba began. "My husband was at first opposed to me and Carrie coming, but I think—I *hope*—he's beginning to see that it's not so bad having his family on board."

"I'm terrified to go 'round the Horn again," Louisa said, after a silence in which she stared at her hands.

"I've heard that it's much easier going the other way 'round. The wind will be behind us." Azuba heard authority in her voice. A hint of experience, a bemused toughness.

"Truly?"

"And then we'll be on our way back to Europe. I enjoyed crossing the Atlantic when we came from London. We had fair winds and peaceful days. Nathaniel had time to teach Carrie the names of the sails and how to box the compass. He gave her brass to polish—all manner of things." She lowered her voice. "I'm teaching myself about navigation. I'm studying my husband's books. His doctor books, as well."

She looked at Louisa's anxious eyes, so close to hers. "I'm pregnant," she whispered, glancing at Carrie. The words blossomed.

"Do you have a midwife on board?"

"No."

"Oh! You mustn't go." Louisa was shocked. She reached for Azuba's hands.

"I hope we'll arrive in Antwerp in time," Azuba breathed. "And if not, many captains have delivered babies at sea."

She remembered Nathaniel turning the pages of the book. Pointing, distraught, at the dreadful pictures. The woman clutching the sides of the lifeboat. The women and children lashed to the mast. She remembered his voice, so long ago. *You are like the morning sky, my Azuba. You are my treasure.*

"Anyway, I have no choice," she whispered.

"You could stay! You could stay in Callao."

She could not speak for the sudden prickle in her nose and tears in her eyes. She shook her head.

They talked, then, of the families and houses they had left behind. In the light of the hanging oil lamp, the cabin was warm, homelike, glowing with its Persian carpet, inlaid wood walls, silver samovar and velvet pillows.

When it was time to leave, the women hesitated and then threw their arms around one another.

The men were noticeably louder in their speech as they returned down the dock.

9. One Man Short

IT WAS THEIR FIRST DAY OUT FROM CALLAO.

Carrie sat doing her lessons. They heard Mr. Dennis bark an order, and the helmsman's echo: "All hands on deck! Wear ship!"

Azuba knit, listening to the men singing a shanty as they hauled the yards.

*My bonny bunch of roses, **oh!***
*Hang down, ye blood-red roses, hang **down!***
*Time for us to turn and **go**.*
*Hang down, ye bunch of roses, hang **down**.*
Oh! Down! Go! Down!

The canary cage began a slow cant. Carrie and Azuba grasped the table as *Traveller* made a wide, lumbering turn. The sails luffed, a disorganized snapping and cracking as eighteen sails were hauled across, took the wind and headed the ship onto her new course.

An hour later, Nathaniel came below. "Come see what I made for you, Carrie." His eyes were half-hidden by the brim of a linen hat. He was relaxed, pleased to be back at sea. He wore a white shirt open at the neck, the knot of his tie tugged loose. He caught Azuba's eye, cocked an eyebrow in invitation.

They went on deck to find a swing, hung from the mizzen yard. Nathaniel led Carrie to it, set her on its wooden seat. "Now, you have to hold on tight," he said.

He pulled her back, let her fly.

The sky was blue, cloudless. They were in the variables, sailing south against the Humboldt Current, which had borne them northward. Carrie shrieked, Nathaniel and Azuba laughed. The sailors and mates looked up.

"Hang on, little girl," Mr. Lee yelled from the galley door, where he stood stripping feathers from a hen.

Andrew Moss stood beside the cook, holding a dishcloth. Nathaniel gave Carrie one final push and then called down to Andrew. "Job for you, my lad," Nathaniel grinned. "Keep her flying."

Carrie looked back under her arm as Andrew came running, caught the swing's seat and pushed.

Azuba saw how differently Carrie reacted from when her father had pushed her. Now she was throwing herself into the motion, wanting to show Andrew that she was not afraid, no matter how high she flew. And Andrew, she noticed, threw a glance at his captain.

Nathaniel stood grinning, in a fine mood.

As perfectly at home as the birds and fish, Azuba thought.

Carrie was singing now, leaning forward against the ropes, pulling back, bonnet hanging by its ribbons. Nathaniel's and Azuba's eyes met, sharing the instant of happiness. Azuba tugged down the brim of her straw hat. She turned to squint out over a landscape whose only features were formed by light, a coruscation of silver and obsidian.

All four jibs were set, and the bowsprit plunged, rose, plunged down. *Traveller's* voice was contented: straining blocks, rufflings, clanks. Carrie's voice stitched the quiet, *close,* farther, *close,* farther: *My* bon*ny lies over the ocean. My* bon*ny lies over the sea. My* bon*ny lies over the ocean. Oh* bring *back my* bon*ny to* me.

A shout.

Mr. Perkins, on the main deck, threw his arm upward as if thrusting aside a branch. He strode aft, mounted the steps to the quarterdeck.

Nathaniel frowned, stiffened. "What is it?" he demanded.

"Samuel Davis, sir," Mr. Perkins said. "He was sick last night in port, and I told him he could bunk in this morning if it was a fair wind. He is not aboard, sir."

Nathaniel's teeth set, a muscle moved in his cheek.

"I am sorry, sir. I bear the responsibility."

Nathaniel stared at the big man. "As you should, Mr. Perkins. As you damned well should."

He let Mr. Perkins stand before him for some time, holding his eyes. Everyone present—Azuba, Carrie, Andrew, Mr. Dennis by the jigger shrouds, himself, the helmsman—absorbed the fact that they were heading towards the Horn one man short.

"I am very sorry, sir. I should have—"

"You will be sorry indeed if we encounter another snorter," said Nathaniel. "We may all pay the price for your oversight."

He repeated the same gesture with his arm that Mr. Perkins had made to the sailors, made more expressive by curtailment in order that the crew not see disunity among the officers. "Go back to your station," he muttered.

Mr. Perkins went back down. Nathaniel and Mr. Dennis stood half-turned away from one another. The helmsman kept his eyes on the sails.

Carrie brought the swing to a stop, stubbing her boot toes on the deck. Andrew glanced at Nathaniel, slipped back down to the main deck. Azuba lowered herself into her chair, and Carrie came and sat next to her in her own small chair.

"What shall I do now, Mama?" she whispered.

The sudden hysterical cackle of a hen announced the advent of an egg.

"Take up your sampler," Azuba whispered back. Carrie had reached the letter *O* in blue thread.

The wind shifted and Nathaniel ordered the helmsman to change course and set the crew to bracing the yards around to keep sails to the wind.

Azuba looked up from her work, pondering her husband. *He is never easy for long,* she thought.

He would turn thirty-six this year and looked far older. His skin was burnished, seamed and cracked. She had noticed how his restless impatience increased with the years, engrained by the necessity of making split-second decisions bearing life or death import.

She looked down at her needle. Her spirits plummeted. First day out and one man short. Nathaniel's fury. He would not know what to do with it once he came below with her and Carrie. And she reached for familiar thoughts, like checking a recipe for reassurance: *no understanding of women, so many years in the company of men, cabin boy, boarding school, straight to sea, hardened brothers, no sisters, that mother . . .*

His tenderness, when it broke through, was as surprising to him, perhaps, as it was to Azuba.

That night, it was Mr. Dennis's watch. Azuba, Nathaniel and Carrie sat at the dinner table with Mr. Perkins. Azuba brooded on the contrast between this meal and the meal of the crew. The officers' table was glossy walnut, with a fiddled edge. It was set with china plates and silverware; the crew hunkered on coils of rope and ate from the kid, a wooden tub sent out from the galley. They had brought aboard their own tin plates, their own mugs, their own clasp knives, with removed tips. They reached into the kid with their knives and sawed off slabs of salt pork, or fresh meat. Every man was above decks for supper, since watches were rotated every evening. The two dogwatches were from four to six, six to eight.

Mr. McVale crabbed down the companionway, carrying a tray. His face was earnest, and he was noiseless and swift. He slid a basket of hot biscuits onto the table, set down plates of chicken and potatoes. The cook had killed several of the pullets.

Too small to be killed. Azuba lifted her fork, stared at her plate. Anger rose. So often, she noticed food on her plate that she could have better prepared herself. Underbaked bread. Chickens killed too young.

The sound of clinking silverware filled the narrow, tipping room. Drops of tea trembled from Mr. Perkins's beard. After setting down his mug he did not pick up his fork but sat with his hands fisted in his lap.

Nathaniel's mouth was sour. His hand sprawled forward, two fingers tapping. Veins bulged on the backs of his hands. "Mr. Perkins," he said, "I want you to remember that *no detail,* let alone one so onerous as the loss of a seaman, can be overlooked."

Carrie looked up at her father.

"One frayed rope can sink a ship."

Azuba could not reach for Carrie's hand since the child sat at the far end of the table. Nathaniel had resumed eating and would not, she could see, speak again.

That evening, Azuba stood on deck watching Carrie and Nathaniel. They were at the railing, etched black against a red sky. Nathaniel squatted to speak to the child. They exchanged earnest words. Every night after supper Nathaniel invited Carrie on deck. They watched the sunset or he showed her phosphorescence or the misty plumes of spouting whales. He taught her the constellations, the names of currents, prevailing winds, planets, birds.

On previous journeys, Azuba thought, *when angry he would have gone to the saloon and worked himself back to steadiness with his carving knife and a stick of bamboo.* She felt a yearning love, watching him pat his daughter's shoulder and seeing how Carrie stood so sturdily, as if understanding how she was helping her papa.

Azuba went below. She stood in her cabin, listening to the faint, sweet pulse of hidden crickets. She opened her workbox and took out a letter from her mother that she had received in Callao. The paper was still crisp, not yet soft as cloth, as it would be by the time they reached Antwerp.

My dearest Azuba,

She read phrases twice, lingering over every word like a person eating when they know there is no more food to be had.

My dearest Azuba,
How I miss you. I have just now finished hanging three plum puddings to drain, and am having a rest before cleaning up.

Grace had written this letter in early December, facing her second Christmas without Azuba and Carrie. In the parcel had been a pair of red and white striped mittens. Azuba pressed the paper to her face, fancying she could smell pine boards and molasses. She pictured the town wreathed in woodsmoke, masts standing up above the roofs. She saw the harnessed horses, noses frost-bristled, hooves cocked, waiting before the general store.

She folded the letter, slipped it back into her sewing box. She set the box inside her sea chest. The belts securing the chest to the floor tightened and loosened as the ship dipped, rose and rolled. The air was tinged with the scent of guano. She laid her hand on the chest. She did not move, but stared down, thinking of the passing of time.

And she realized that today's incident had both quickened her need to tell Nathaniel of her pregnancy and intensified her fear of his reaction.

Carrie was calling: "Mama! Mama! We saw my friends. The whales."

She came to the cabin door. Behind her was the young steward. He wore canvas trousers and a pale linen jacket. He contrived, Azuba noted, to keep himself clean, his face always washed.

"Mr. McVale saw them too. They were off the port side."

"It's a good thing we aren't on a whaling ship," Azuba said, smiling at the young man.

He was between the sailors and the crew in status, and while this made life difficult for him, for Azuba and Carrie it was a blessing, as he ran errands for Azuba when she did not dare trouble Nathaniel, and he kept an eye on Carrie.

"Bedtime," Azuba said to Carrie. "Thank you, Mr. McVale."

He tipped his hand and lifted it partway towards his forehead. "Good night, ma'am," he said.

"I *must* change her," Carrie said. Her tone was aggrieved. Azuba said nothing, but waited while Carrie put Jojo into night-clothes, taking a long while, fussing with a ribbon, arranging the doll's hands and knees into prayer position, whispering a prayer, laying the doll on the pillow, singing it to sleep.

Then she rolled onto her back, pulled the quilt to her chin.
"Mama?"

"What, lovey?"

"Are there any frayed ropes on *Traveller?*"

"Of course not! Do you think your papa would allow a
frayed rope on his ship? You are safe. Now go to sleep."

Azuba leaned, kissed Carrie's cheek. When there was a fair
wind, the child slipped into sleep as peacefully as if rocked
in a cradle.

"Good night, Mama."

Azuba went to the saloon and sat in an armchair. She
picked up an old Toronto newspaper. October 1862. News
of the war in the American states; discussion of confederation in British North America. She wondered whether the
dreadful civil war still continued; wondered if her father, who
was in favour of confederation, would have his way. She put
down the paper and listened to the creak of stretching rope
and a groan, as Nathaniel had told her, at the "jaws of the
boom." She loved the term. It made the ship seem like a
fellow creature.

The ship's bells rang and Azuba rose, checked on Carrie
and went on deck.

Traveller was moving in a quiet sea, running at about eight
knots with a long, easy pitch and roll. Red and green bow
lights were lit and swinging, the sails hidden in the darkness.
She climbed to the quarterdeck and sat in her chair. Gig
shambled to his feet and came to her, toenails clicking. She
sat stroking the dog's head. She smelled the tang of pipe
smoke and heard the murmur of voices and the regular boom
and wash as the bow lifted and fell.

Nathaniel came and stood beside her. She could see his face
in the light of a swinging lamp. She wished that his fingers
would tease at the edge of her cap. She untied its strings,

shook her head and felt the air cool her scalp. *Put your fingers in my hair. Cup my head with the palm of your hand.*

She reached out. His fingers closed around hers.

She saw that his mind was roving over potential problems: broken bilge pumps, shipworm, shifting cargo, rotting canvas. A missing sailor. He was sifting through his collection of impressions and instincts: the smell of the wind, the underbelly of evening clouds, the surface of the sea.

"It's like reading the mind of God," he'd muttered once, when she asked how he predicted the weather.

Stars glittered in the new moon blackness.

They had not seen another sail for two weeks.

Sometimes it was hard to believe that any other place existed, and Azuba fancied that they had died and gone to the afterlife, and found it to be a place of stormy petrels and albatrosses, of clouds, rain and porpoises. Or else she imagined that back in the old life their families spoke of them with diminishing frequency and decreasing interest, as if they had become like scissor portraits: always facing the same way, without features.

Since leaving Callao, they had had winds from east-southeast, so fresh that Nathaniel set every sail. Good weather had held, with light trade-wind clouds and mild temperatures. In seven days, they made twelve hundred miles. Nathaniel showed Carrie how they had sunk the North Star and the Great Bear and had gained the Southern Cross, which had appeared just above the horizon.

One day, the sailors changed the sails. Nathaniel was fierce, hurrying the men. Beginning at daybreak and continuing until dusk, the soft, fair-weather sails came down and the crew bent on heavier canvas. It was like preparing a house for winter—tightening doors against blizzards, putting up storm windows. Azuba watched, memorizing the ropes, sails and yards. Starting at the top and working down, she murmured the names she had learned and written in her little book: *royal, topgallant, topsail, mainsail.* The rigging, too, was overhauled, every old or frayed rope replaced or mended. High above, men stood spread-legged on the footropes. Others kneeled on deck, folding the old canvas, laying out the new. Nathaniel and Mr. Dennis had debated the decision to change sails at the dinner table: it was a subtle matter, not using the heavy canvas too soon, yet allowing time for the hemp and canvas to become supple before encountering freezing temperatures.

Carrie, too, watched the sailors. She sat cross-legged beside Azuba's chair.

Freezing temperatures, Azuba thought, reaching to rub Carrie's back reassuringly. *Or the Horn's ferocious gales.*

On the day of the sail change, it was so cool that Mr. McVale made a fire in the coal stove. That evening Nathaniel read to himself from *The Mariner's Chronicle,* and Azuba curled on the horsehair sofa wearing slippers, wrapped in a black wool shawl. The little room was more homelike since she'd added the sweet-smelling rose geraniums and the potted rose.

She was bent over the pamphlet that accompanied the medicine chest, *Plain Rules for the Taking of Medicines.* Then she opened Grammy's compendium.

For Ear Ache—Tobacco and roasted onion, drop one drop into the ear

She turned the pages of the leather book.

To Paint Bee Hives
To Make Treacle Beer
To Prevent the Fly on Turnips and Cabbage
To Fix a Cracked Stove
To Make a Gaspereau Net

And her grandmother rose before her. Stubborn, feisty. Challenging Azuba to be the same.

"Listen, Azuba," Nathaniel said.

Azuba slid a paper into her book to hold the place. Took up her knitting.

"*The captain,*" Nathaniel read, "*Shouted: 'There is the land! My God, we are lost!' His wife ran for the baby and wrapped it and herself in warm shawls. The captain came to the door and took the infant from her arms, saying, 'We are lost. In two or three minutes, it will be over.' He bade her good-bye and was in the midst of prayer, when the sea came in, the deck gave way under their feet, and they went down in the wreck. The captain's wife was in the water long enough to swim thirty or forty feet towards the bow. When she came up, her clothing caught in the wreckage, but she tore it loose and searched for her husband and child.*"

Azuba lowered her needles and stared at him. He was truly fascinated with the stories, so caught up in them he seemed to be reading to himself. He was not reading them as the cautionary tales he might have used to dissuade her from joining him.

"*She saw her husband on top of the deck house, alone, and without the child. She could see that he was hurt. He motioned frantically for her to get onto the rock upon which the ship had foundered. The mate and some of the men had got on shore, and called to her, and so she ran for the rock on floating pieces of*" *wreckage. On shore, they found shelter in a hovel and her husband was laid by her side. With his last breath, he asked if the little one was saved."*

They sat in silence. Nathaniel picked up his pipe, pulled at it as he turned a few pages.

"Now this one. Took place in the North Atlantic. They were carrying coal, heading out of Boston."

"Nathaniel?"

He looked up, sipped on his pipe. He stared into the flame of the oil lamp. Calm, calculating.

"Why are you reading these accounts, Nathaniel? Why are you reading them out loud?"

"I'll read them to myself if you don't like them."

"No, I didn't mean . . . I love to have you read to me. They *are* distressing, though. They make me think of our families. How they must be worrying."

"Ah." He glanced at her, raised an eyebrow. "I suppose I simply find them interesting. It's my trade, my life. I ponder such eventualities. I find them instructive. I'm pleased to see how many people survive. I like to think that I would have the same presence of mind and courage."

"And some, of course, don't."

"What? Don't what?"

"Survive."

She picked up her needles.

She'd been looking at her breasts in the privacy of her cabin, either in the lamplight before going to bed or in the dim light of dawn. A blood vein snaked over the plump white skin, and the nipples were darkening.

"Nathaniel." She dropped her knitting, waited until he put down the paper.

"What? Something about Carrie?" Sharp. "Tell me."

"I am with child."

"You . . ."

She put both hands on her belly. "Pregnant. Going to have a baby."

He said nothing. He laid his pipe down on a saucer. He put his elbows on the table and ran fingers through his hair.

"Good Lord, Azuba," he said, finally, not looking at her. "When?"

"After we arrive in Antwerp, I believe. Not before. Not at sea."

He slid his hands over his eyes.

She rose from the couch, stood by his chair. She pried one hand from his eyes, opened his fingers and laced them in hers.

"A little baby, Nathaniel," she said. "A little boy or another little girl like Carrie. Blond hair, this time, like yours. Blue eyes."

"Did you know in Callao?"

"Yes."

"Why didn't you tell me? You could have stayed there."

"That is just why I didn't tell you."

"There are no assurances that we'll make Antwerp in time."

"Then I'll have the baby on board. Women do. You know that, Nathaniel."

She remembered saying this before. *Women do.*

"It's your fault as much as mine," she said.

He sat with his fingers laced in hers, staring at her, and seemed younger, no longer a captain. She slid onto his lap and laid her head on his chest. Just under her ear was his heart and she felt it beating rapidly but did not remark on her discovery. She felt his breath hot in her hair.

"They say the second birth is easier?"

"Yes, yes," she said, knowing that her reassurance was not necessarily true. "Always."

The motion of the ship pressed Azuba, at times, closer to Nathaniel. His heart rate slowed, but she felt his body tense, slowly claimed by this new burden.

He sighed, lifted her from his lap and stood. They looked at one another. He was thrown off-kilter, uncertain how to feel.

"I'll come back down in a minute," he said. His voice was agitated, one hand half-raised. "Must speak to Mr. Dennis."

He shut the door behind him with care.

Azuba stared at the place he had been, and then went to Carrie's cabin. She sat on the sea chest and leaned against the wall. She folded her arms over her belly.

He had been shocked. Even, perhaps, frightened. She thought of the savagery they approached as they sailed towards the realm of endless winter.

Have I made a terrible mistake?

Later that night.

Four bells of mid-watch. Two lookouts stood motionless in the bows, half-lit by the running lights. On the main deck, on a quiet night such as this with a fair wind, the other sailors of the watch paced quietly fore and aft. The first mate stood on the quarterdeck, speaking trumpet handy, legs braced, arms folded.

The second mate and the captain had bunked down.

The ship began plunging, her bow digging deep.

10. Ice Barque

A WEEK LATER, NATHANIEL STRUCK OUT IN HIS SLEEP with both arms. Azuba woke with a cry. The grey light of dawn was coming through the porthole. He lay staring at the ceiling with a stricken expression.

"I dreamed the ship went down," he said. He put an arm over his face. "I put you and Carrie in a lifeboat. I was in the water trying to swim, but I could not catch up to you."

He threw back the quilt, dressed, frowning. She watched his face as his fingers dug at the buttonholes. Since she had told him she was pregnant, he had become grimmer, doubly preoccupied. He would have had such a change in any event, she realized, since they were entering the southern seas; yet he looked at her with only worry in his face, and no delight at the thought of a new child. As he opened the cabin door, she saw that he had already forgotten his dream, and the words he had spoken, and the way he had said them.

The saloon windows and the skylight were boarded over with deadlights. Everything on the ship was battened down tight, boats double-lashed, lifelines stretched along the main deck. Nathaniel spent almost no time below; Azuba and Carrie were isolated for hours on end, save for brief visits from Andrew Moss or Mr. McVale. Yesterday, they had rummaged in their sea chests seeking wool socks and mitts. The crew, too, had been digging out their cold weather gear: wool pea-coats, oilskins, socks, sou'westers. Last time they rounded the Horn, Azuba had watched the men climbing into the rigging, furiously pounding the canvas to get the sails under control, and had seen that they were bare-handed. "Why?" she'd demanded, horrified. "Frozen mittens are slippery," Nathaniel replied. One slip could be fatal, either a crash to the deck or a long fall into the icy waters. She'd watched as they beat their bare hands against the canvas to restore cir-culation, as if tenderizing lumps of meat.

After breakfast, Azuba went on deck to see the dreary sight of a February sky hatching weather; despite the fact that this was austral summer, the rain now striking the ship was mixed with sleet. *Traveller* bucketed southward, riding up one side of a wave, sliding down the other. Azuba held herself against the aft cabin, squinting out at the brutal waste. Close by, the waves rose, black-sided, a filigree of froth breaking, the bubbles sliding, expiring.

She went back down the companionway to find Carrie "coasting," as she called it, tobogganing on slippery sock feet down the slant of the floor, having begged Azuba to pull back the carpet. The cat perched on the sofa, claws flexed, eyes flick-ing back and forth between Carrie and the canaries in their wildly swinging cage. Gig lay beneath a chair, muzzle on paws.

Azuba sat by the stove, took out needle and thread.

"They will be sledding at home," she said. She tried to keep her tone matter-of-fact. Her hand swung in the air, not of her own volition, but like the gimballed compass. She made several attempts to pierce the cotton of a nightdress she was making for Carrie. She pricked her thumb, exclaimed, stuck it in her mouth. Carrie fell to the floor in a heap. Gig lifted his head, watching her with white-rimmed eyes.

"Carrie. You're worrying poor Gig. Stop, now."

Carrie crawled to the dog, took his head in her lap.

"Where did you go to slide, Mama?" she asked. She fussed with Gig's ears, lifting them straight upward, pig-like.

Azuba put aside her sewing. She took her cap off when they were alone in the cabin, and her hair was free to curl, as it did in the perpetual dampness. *Time to snip it again,* she thought. She arched her fingers and stirred her itchy scalp, trying to remember the last time they had bathed. Already, she was uncomfortable in her clothing, the waistband and bodice too tight.

"Up the road," Azuba said. *Other children. Carrie needs to remember their existence.* "The road was rolled for the sleighs, and we pulled our sleds to the Jacksons' pasture. Our eyelashes would be thick with frost. From up there we had a view of the town, and we could see the white snow-covered roofs, and the headlands, and the glare of the icy cliffs. We could see the ships in the harbour, their rigging glittering like the branches of the apple trees. And the sea, smoking. It was so nice, coming home. Our mittens were hard as boards, just like Papa's are when he comes below. We hung them on a line strung over the cookstove, and Mother gave us hot cider."

Carrie crawled across the floor and sat at Azuba's feet, thumb in her mouth, head resting on her mother's skirt. She gazed at the stove's isinglass.

So nice, Azuba heard her own words, *coming home.*

Steps came down the companionway and through the forward cabin. A knock.

"Come in," Azuba said.

It was Andrew, carrying a pot of tea in one hand and a

lumpy, steaming package wrapped in threadbare red cloth. He was covered in slush, his grey mittens so sodden they had turned black.

"What is it?" Carrie asked, scrambling to her feet, eyes on the steaming cloth.

"Aren't you the lucky one, Miss Carrie?" Andrew said. "Cook thinks you're pretty special. Smells like ginger."

Carrie crowded against him as if he were a brother as he leaned to set pot and bundle on the table. She folded back the cloth. Gingerbread, cut into squares.

"Won't you have a piece? Mama? Couldn't he?"

"Please," Azuba said. "Sit, just for a minute. Captain Bradstock won't mind." She held the teapot's spout against the edge of a cup as she poured, thinking that she should ask Nathaniel if she might include the boy in their lessons.

He sat on the very edge of a chair at the round table. Carrie sat as close beside him as she could. She lifted a square of gingerbread, held it out to him.

Carrie watched as Andrew put the entire square in his mouth. She took a small, prim bite of her own.

"You could come to my house when we get home," she said. She sat very still with her hands in her lap, watching the boy wipe his mouth with the back of his hand.

"Thank you, miss. Thank you, ma'am. I'll just . . ." He nodded aft.

"Of course," Azuba said.

He opened the door of the head. Carrie and Azuba busied themselves with the tea and called their thanks as he departed, carrying the chamber pot. The bell sounded the half-hour.

"Lessons, now," Azuba said. The farther they sailed into dangerous waters, the more she was steadied by the ship's routine. She adhered to her lesson plans, scheduling them in the tidy slices of time made by the bell.

Noon dinner was their main meal. Mr. McVale came down the companionway, carrying a tray with plates of bread, roast chicken, boiled onions and potatoes. On his coat's wool was the cold breath of snow.

They bowed their heads and Nathaniel mumbled a blessing. He was not a churchgoing man and Azuba knew that, were she and Carrie not aboard, he would not bother with grace.

". . . in the Lord's name, amen."

"Amen."

Nathaniel stared at the food on his plate. His hands were in fists, his elbows snugged tight to the table's fiddled edge.

Mr. Dennis raised his fork, held it suspended. He and Azuba exchanged a look.

"Nathaniel," she said. "What's . . . ?"

He sent her a swift, open glance. "I've found out what that man was doing, back in Callao."

"What man?"

"The man," he turned to Mr. Dennis, "you spoke to. Hanging around the ship. Slipped away like a stray dog."

Mr. Dennis set his fork back down. The skin of his forehead lifted. "I made short shrift of him, Captain."

Azuba heard the edge in Mr. Dennis's voice, saw in his face that if they were not captain and officer he would say more. He would snap or rise to his feet. His own voice would become as aggressive as Nathaniel's. Her appetite vanished.

Nathaniel stared unblinking at Mr. Dennis, excluding Azuba. "I was speaking with Mr. Lee. He tells me that he opened a barrel of beef and found it filled with dirt. It may be that that man colluded with Samuel Davis on the night we were aboard the American ship. After dinner, Mr. Dennis, you will be so good as to go below and take inventory. I fear that won't be the only barrel weighted with something other than food."

Mr. Dennis lifted his fork but did not eat, only stared at his plate. His lips pursed and his eyebrows lifted as he relived his actions—rising from his desk, striding towards the man, surveying the wharf.

Azuba was swept with guilt. It was on Mr. Perkins's watch that this had taken place. Mr. Perkins's father was a Grand Manan shipwright, and it was at her own father's urging that the young man had been hired as their second mate. Nathaniel had every right, now, to demote him and put a man from the crew in his place. He would not do it, though, as the crew, she had learned from a few terse hints from Nathaniel, were increasingly at odds with the officers and such a move would weaken a captain's authority.

Nathaniel raised his fork and they began to eat.

Azuba thought of how few chickens were left in the coop. When they had set sail from Whelan's Cove, *Traveller*'s pantry had been filled with Grammy Cooper's blueberry jam, with jars of applesauce and pickled beans. Azuba thought of her mother's garden, the cow, the chickens, and realized how she had been blessed with good food. There had always been rich, fresh milk—as a child, she had run a bent finger around the bucket's rim of cream. Eggs, warm from the hens. Sap boiling, in March, for maple syrup, and then the bowls of snow and the lacy candy.

Mr. Dennis was eating rapidly, his eyebrows arched as he conducted an interior conversation. On deck, the first mate's voice was violent and contemptuous, peppered with foul words. Sometimes she wanted to put her hands over Carrie's ears; yet the sound of the officers' voices was part of the ship's truth. "If frayed ropes sink ships, Carrie," she explained, "then so does an order not followed." Yet she had begun to think of Mr. Dennis as a man who was not merely alone but lonely. She thought of his fleeting kindness, as when he sat with her after the storm and let Nathaniel sleep. His hardness with the men revealed not an evil temper, but his desire to be safely finished—to do his job and return home.

Nathaniel laid down his fork. The silence had extended throughout the meal. He looked at Carrie, and Azuba's heart lightened as she saw his struggle to regain a easier tone for the child's sake.

"I was reading of the tribes that frequent Tierra del Fuego. They do not wear clothing, even in the harshest weather. No one knows the reason."

Carrie's face lit with interest. "Do the children go without clothing?"

Just then, Mr. McVale returned with a steaming pot of tea. Azuba had told him she would like to be responsible for providing dessert. Without informing Nathaniel, she'd begun mixing up pies and puddings, getting Mr. McVale to run them forward to the galley to be baked. She rose, opened the door to the steward's pantry. Light furred the edges of the deadlights. She could see that the shelves were emptying. Still, there were enough jars of blackberry preserves, bought in California, and enough flour and lard for her to manufacture a few pies. There were pickles and dried fruit. She took figs and dates, set them on the table.

Nathaniel watched her, a hint of curiosity in his eyes. He ducked his head to the steaming tea, took a sip. He wiped each side of his moustache with a forefinger.

"Mothers lower their babies into the icy water to toughen them. Yes, apparently the children go naked. You watch carefully when we go back 'round the Horn. Maybe you'll see a Yahgan."

After dinner, Nathaniel went on deck with Mr. Dennis and then came below, brushing snow from his sleeves. He hung his sou'wester on a hook behind the stove, went to his bed for a nap. He often slept during the day, since he spent much of the night on deck. Carrie, too, went to her bed. Azuba sat cross-legged in her favourite chair by the stove.

Smiling.

Last night, she had risen from bed when she heard Nathaniel coming down from the quarterdeck. She had lit the lamp and he'd entered the cabin and stood behind her, facing the mirror. Slowly, he'd gathered up her gown. In the mirror's tarnished glass, they were reflected from neck to waist. He'd slid his icy hands over her breasts and lifted them with care, as if the skin might burst. She'd wound her fingers between his. She had turned, then, and he had bent and kissed her on the lips.

Mr. Dennis wants this voyage over so he can leave the ship and return to his wife. Nathaniel, she thought, *thinks of* Traveller *as his home. Thus, the journey has no end. Only visits, furloughs.*

And what will be home for me and our children?

She watched the pulsing coals, thinking of how only yesterday she'd caught herself watching the birds, envying them their freedom to fly away home, and then remembered how she had stood on the beach in Whelan's Cove, outlining her lips with a feather, still envying the birds, thinking of freedom as flying away to sea.

That night, the wind rose. Carrie and Azuba ate a solitary supper in the saloon, for neither mate nor captain would leave the deck. After Carrie was in bed, Azuba wrapped herself in her warmest shawl and settled in her chair.

She had just opened her workbox when she heard a scream, a cracking thud on the roof, frantic shouts. Running feet.

She stood, hands pressing her cheeks.

A barked command. Footsteps in the companionway. She rushed to the saloon door. They were coming through the dining room, men shuffling, some walking backwards, stooped, carrying a body.

"Who is it? Who is it?"

"The boy."

She was pushed against the wall. The men laid Andrew Moss on the saloon floor. Someone held a mirror to his mouth.

"He's breathing."

"What happened?"

"He fell from the mizzen topmast."

Carrie came to the door of her cabin. She stood wide-eyed, Jojo clutched to her chest. Sailors were present who had never before set foot in these quarters. One removed Andrew's boots while Mr. Perkins covered the boy with a blanket. Nathaniel knelt, holding a flask of brandy.

"Hold his head higher."

Brandy filled the boy's mouth, oozed from the corners of his lips. Mr. Dennis knelt beside Nathaniel, holding smelling salts. Nathaniel slapped the boy's face. He tipped the flask again. Andrew was not swallowing.

"Bloody hell," Nathaniel muttered.

He slapped the boy again. Everyone, kneeling or standing, stared, frozen in the agony of helplessness, in the midst of which the boy remained present but beyond summoning, and then Nathaniel said, "The mirror. Where's the mirror?" One of the sailors passed it to him, and Nathaniel held it to

Andrew's mouth, then took the boy by the shoulders and shook him violently, and then again positioned the mirror at his mouth. He lifted the boy's wrist, pressed his thumb against the vein. He laid the arm down, so respectfully that Azuba turned to Carrie.

"Come," she said.

"Is he dead?" Carrie whispered.

"Yes."

Carrie's eyes darted past Azuba. Nathaniel pulled the blanket over Andrew's face. Freckles, hair and mouth disappeared. Heavy hands pinched at the edge of the blanket, tucked it, snugged it around his feet. Nathaniel bowed his head, face in hands. The men lifted the parcelled body, set it into Mr. Perkins's arms.

Carrie crawled into bed and lay knees to chest as if she had a pain in her stomach. She said not a word. Azuba pulled the quilt over her shoulders. The room tipped up and then down, with a twisting motion just before the descent.

Azuba stroked Carrie's hair. Her hand shook. She stroked, stroked.

"Shall I sing?" she whispered.

Carrie shrugged.

"What shall it be?"

Nothing.

"I'll sing 'Brightest and Best,'" Azuba murmured.

"*Brightest and best, Of the stars of the morning,*" Azuba began, but her voice swelled and caught. Carrie's shoulders began to shake. A moan ripped from the child, and then sobs.

"Mama, Mama."

Azuba pulled Carrie into her arms.

Together, they wept, moaned, rocked, breathed deep.

He was buried the next morning. Azuba found the funeral service in her Bible and marked the pages by sliding pins through the paper, thinking they would need them again before reaching Antwerp.

It was a cold, grey day with heavy seas. The ship was hove to. They clustered around the main mast, the men with uncovered heads. Azuba had asked Nathaniel to make sure the boy was in his best clothes. She wanted to be able to tell his mother he had gone to his Maker neither disfigured nor unkempt. A sailor had sewn a canvas bag, weighted it with leads. Nathaniel read the funeral service, and the body, resting on a board, was tipped into the sea. Azuba watched, gripping Carrie's hand. Carrie was white-faced, but did not cry. The small canvas pod slid beneath the cold waters, and Azuba thought of Mrs. Lattimer's description of her child—how she saw his little face just beneath the surface of the water, mouth and eyes wide open.

The day progressed as every other day that preceded Andrew's death: Nathaniel and the mates following their patterns— two men on the quarterdeck, one on the fo'c'sle; men's feet trampling, distant shouts—"Stand by for stays! Mainsail haul! Get down on the main deck! Get down there, son of a . . ."; the clanking of the bilge pumps, ringing of the ship's bell, the ship heaving and rolling. Carrie and Azuba could not pursue Carrie's lessons but worked instead with needles, as if small, tight stitches, set in place, one after the other, might secure their minds to simple things.

For a week, Carrie would not talk. She clutched Jojo— staring, haunted. When Azuba put her to bed, the child reached out her arms and held tight, face burrowed into her mother's neck.

As they sat sewing, Azuba spoke quietly, telling stories from her childhood, making word-pictures: cows shambling down dusty roads bordered with goldenrod, the smoke of a supper fire rising over fir trees.

Carrie said nothing, only bent closer to her work. She was sewing together bits of material for a patchwork quilt. Women at the Chincha Islands had given her remnants. In Callao, Azuba had bought a basket from one of the vendors in which to keep the pieces. Before Andrew's death, Carrie had spent hours playing with the squares, kneeling on the floor and arranging them in various patterns, making imaginary landscapes. Now she picked her pieces from the basket only after Azuba told her that it was time to sew. She took the first one her fingers encountered and then, randomly, a second. She joined the pieces, sewing without care, tugging too hard or making large, loose stitches.

Mornings, now, were so cold that Azuba woke with her breath smoking. She reached for blanket and quilt, thinking they had fallen off, but found them already covering her shoulders. She rolled onto her side, lay curled with hands cupping her belly. It was round and smooth, like a small watermelon she had bought in the Callao market. As she wakened, anxieties arrived one by one. Provisions: Mr. Dennis had brought Nathaniel the results of his inventory—other beef barrels were filled with dirt, and there were missing quantities of coffee, tea, dried beans, flour and molasses. And their position: it had been raining, snowing or sleeting for days. Nathaniel was on deck fifteen minutes before sunrise and fifteen minutes after sunset, seeking star, planet or moon in the mirror of his sextant, but day after day, the horizon blended with the sea and he could not get a fix. Nor had he been able to shoot a good sun sight at noon. He was continuing on a southerly course, not turning eastward until he was certain they were clear of False Cape Horn. Two men stood in the bows all day, straining their eyes and ears. Visibility in the low, scudding clouds was only one mile. Nathaniel kept sail laid on.

Azuba listened to discussions between Nathaniel and the first mate. Once, Mr. Dennis enumerated the dangers of laying on sail and was treated to a belligerent stare. Now she noticed that Mr. Dennis had become wary: he narrowed his eyes and made a curt acquiescent grunt in the base of his throat. His shoulders were tense as he went to do Nathaniel's bidding. Azuba herself said nothing to Nathaniel, but from her covert studies of Nathaniel's books, from her attention to the accounts he read aloud, from the questions she asked as she watched him plot their course and from the evidence of her own senses, she knew they were flying in forty-knot winds like a blind man running.

She dared not accuse him of recklessness, even though she knew that if Nathaniel were wrong in his calculations he risked driving them straight into the coast of Chile. She feared floating ice; with the speed they were making, the bows would be ripped open before the men could haul the sails around. She remembered the ship they had missed so narrowly on the outward voyage and feared that they might breast a wave and find themselves on a collision course with a westbound vessel. She envisioned the ice walls of Antarctica, looming like an apparition from fog or spreading the miasma of their cold breath in the dead of night.

And she was astounded by the monstrous greybeards. They built behind the ship, walls of water that seemed to tower as high as the mastheads, dwarfing the thousand-ton ship, flinging *Traveller* forward, so steeply at times that her rudder upended. One mistake by the helmsman and they would broach, and in such seas, would roll.

The greatest danger was to carry too much sail, and this, she was certain, from the feel of the ship, they were doing.

She felt her anger growing day by day as she thought of the words she would use to query his decisions and yet said nothing, knowing how he would respond.

Who are you to question my judgment? How many years have you been sailing merchant ships? And, worse: *If you were not here, I would not have such need of speed.*

And she imagined the contempt and frustration in his voice, and how perhaps Carrie might overhear. And then, later, how they would be burdened with the memory of the exchange, the peculiar, dragging grief of words that pricked at a festering irresolution.

She lay in bed, shuddering with cold. Such simple thoughts had drifted into her mind when she had surfaced from sleep back on land—small pleasures comforting her like patting hands. Taking Carrie to visit Grammy Cooper. A quilting bee. Or the chance that Simon might come up over the edge of the cliff, wicker creel in his hand. How he might paint a watercolour for Carrie. Of ducks, or donkeys wearing hats.

Azuba wore her warmest dress, made of alpaca and sheep's wool, whose waist she had altered. She and Carrie spent every day bundled in sweaters and shawls, even though they kept the stove stoked. After they finished their lessons, Azuba took out her sewing and Carrie bent over her scissors, cutting out paper dolls. Just over their heads, sailors climbed a hundred feet in the air, balancing on bouncing footropes as they fisted canvas with bare hands. Or they clustered on deck, roaring shanties, hauling lines, stepping on one another's feet, waist-deep in freezing water as waves rushed over the bulwarks.

While I sit here letting out waistbands. Just as I would be if I were at home on land.

She felt that she was two people, the one who listened and smiled and bent to Carrie, and the other who was attentive to her womb's odd, dark fissures of pain. She was always hungry, craving food she would not have until they reached land. The sweet, bready flesh of a pear. Rabbit stew, made with new potatoes. A fresh-baked cinnamon bun—yeasty, steaming, butter sliding into its oblong holes. Water, cold from a well, tasting of earth.

She was tired, and a torpor crept over her. She wanted to sleep all day. There was a heaviness about her body, her breasts ached, and her belly began to swell.

Nathaniel kept his private possessions, business papers and navigational instruments in the rolltop desk that took up most of the forward wall of the saloon: compass, sextant, ink, pen, ruler; pipes and tobacco; papers pertaining to the cargo and the crew; pistols, ammunition, brass knuckles and billy jack in case of mutiny or piracy; and the ship's cabin log, more personal than the one in the deck house. The precious chronometer was kept in the captain's stateroom so that it would not be drenched if the skylight were smashed. Azuba had asked Nathaniel if she might be entrusted with its winding. After a third request, he'd agreed, saying only that Carrie was never to open the box.

After supper, whenever possible, Nathaniel sat at his desk, poring over nautical charts of the winds and currents of the region, and studying Maury's *Explanations and Sailing*

Directions to Accompany the Wind and Current Charts, pondering new routes and the science on which they were based. He was considering coming as close as possible to Cape Horn, as on their previous trip, and cutting up northeast for the Strait of Le Maire.

During one clear night and then a clear day, he managed to take a fix on sun and stars. That night, he sat at his desk, covering sheets of paper with plain and solid geometry and spherical trigonometry. He made small stars connected by lines, charting their actual course against his planned course. Across the map, *Traveller's* passage scratched a chicken track.

He sat staring at the spiky pattern, pipe in teeth, the corners of his mouth roped. The ship—massive, momentous, manned by seasoned sailors, deep in the water, filled with tons of bird manure—did it now have, for him, another dimension, making him indecisive? Colour—the red, blue and yellow of quilts, necklaces, geraniums, frocks, toys? Delicacy—blue veins, slender arms, Carrie's coral fingers?

She saw that he could take chances and make speed, or be cautious and waste time. Both courses were perilous now that *Traveller* bore the dry rattle of potential starvation and the spectre of birth at sea.

"Are you done?" Azuba asked. She looked up from her needlepoint. She was making a cushion top: a house, with clouds and apple trees. The house was finished, and the outline of the trees. She was filling in the apples with the brightest of the red silk she'd bought in Callao. She longed to speak of the greybeards, of False Cape Hope, of currents, cliffs, fog.

He tapped the pencil against the chicken tracks. "We're not making . . ." he began, and then broke off. "Never mind, Azuba. Never mind."

"I only—"

"This is a discussion I need to have with Mr. Dennis. Not with you."

He pulled down the slatted rolltop. He rose from the desk, stood with knees flexed as the ship began a long, ponderous climb.

"Why not have a discussion with me? I have read Maury's book."

He frowned. "Have you."

"Yes, Nathaniel. I am capable of reading. And of understanding what I read. I would be less frightened if I could share your worries."

His eyes skimmed past her, ignoring her words. He made a cursory study of the saloon. "Are you and Carrie warm enough?"

His wide mouth was stretched with fatigue. The bold eye narrowed, the compassionate eye dimmed, making him seem perplexed, fraught. She guessed his desire. To be free, alone in this saloon, with no concern for the safety of wife and child.

She felt a blaze of hatred, even knowing his distress, and its cause. They might be in a warm parlour, safe on shore, and still she would feel this frustration. He was a man who made his decisions in private, even if they concerned her. And then saw to their execution with no discussion, no second thoughts. Assuming that she, like his sailors, depended on him.

She nodded, her own mouth splayed with anger.

Nathaniel pulled on his mittens. He swung an arm into his stiff black jacket. "We made it 'round the Horn once," he said. His voice lost its bite, was only weary. "I'll get us 'round again."

"I don't doubt it, Nathaniel," she said. Her anger cleared; she was appalled by her own burdensomeness. She said it to his back, but the door shut. Perhaps he hadn't heard.

She picked up her needlepoint, then threw it down. She drew up her knees, curled in the chair's embrace. One hand on her belly, the other cradling her cheek, wondering what they were doing back at home.

She pictured a winter storm when the cold was so severe that Mother had made up beds for them in the parlour. Hers had been a pad of sheepskin on the floor beside the Franklin stove. Cold air eddied, thin streams wavering like ice water from walls and windows. The door to the kitchen was open, and in the night she had wakened to see Father stooped over the range, a shower of sparks as he worked sticks of wood into the firebox. The wind pressed against the house, hurled snow.

Blessed with safety. Deep-rooted in our little village.

She bent her head, listening to the wind, a moaning that rose to a shriek and then fell to a hollow whistle.

The next afternoon, Nathaniel came into the saloon. He stood at the hooks, putting on more clothing. Mittens, a wool cap, a scarf. He spoke to Azuba without looking at her. "The barometer is falling. It's getting colder."

His voice was curt, and he left without speaking to Carrie, although she had looked up. The cabin, after his sudden appearance, seemed darker. They had not yet lit the oil lamp.

"Let's go tuck up in bed," Azuba said. "Let's go get some crackers."

They went to the pantry. It was the last tin. They gathered pillows from the saloon, and books. Azuba stood with a pillow hugged to her. "Go get a sweater, Carrie, and a shawl."

The light in Azuba's cabin was dull, the sheets were soft and greasy. Azuba sat cross-legged, scratching her scalp. "I don't remember the last time we had a bath," she said. She spread out her hands next to Carrie's. Twenty black fingernails.

They opened a book, *Mother Goose's Melodies.* A smell rose from the paper, reminding Azuba of the shop in London. It had been before the Horn. Before the Chincha Islands. Before Andrew.

There was a picture of a tree, with fish growing on it. Azuba read aloud:

The man in the wilderness,
Asked me,
How many strawberries grow in the sea?
I answered him as I thought good,
As many red herrings
As grew in the wood.

Carrie touched the fish on the tree. "Why did he let go, Mama? Why did he fall?"

Azuba lifted Carrie's finger and turned the page. "His mittens were slippery," she said. "He didn't mean to. He closed his hand on the rope and it slipped."

"Who is going to tell Andrew's mother?"

"Papa has written a letter. He said what a fine . . ." Her voice caught, she stopped talking for a minute. "He told her what happened. We'll give the letter to the next ship we speak, or else we will mail it from Antwerp."

Carrie traced the letters of the next rhyme. "His Mama. What will she do?"

Azuba leaned back against the pillows and closed her eyes. She put an arm around Carrie and pulled her close. "She'll weep, Carrie. She'll plant flowers in the graveyard. They'll have a stone carver make an angel."

Azuba thought of Mrs. Moss's little house on the bank over the marsh, its windowless back to the sea so she wouldn't have to see the dangers endured by her fisherman husband. She pictured the woman's good-natured round face, freckled like her son's. Azuba had passed the house many times, seen clothes on her line dancing over the mud bank, puffed out with salt wind. She couldn't tell Carrie. How Mrs. Moss would likely go to her son's room and sit on his bed. How she would lift his clothing from the drawers and hold each item to her face. How she would read the letter and change, in an instant. Become a new and different person, forever grieving. As, Azuba feared, had Carrie.

She picked up the book. Read aloud.

Carrie was sucking her thumb, staring at the page without seeing it.

That evening, the wind rose to a gale, and then the gale became a full-fledged Cape Horn snorter. Boarding waves thundered onto the cabin top, sent concussive shudders down the saloon walls. The wind built into a many-voiced shriek. Men's voices were desperate, thin, mingled with the cracking of snow-lashed canvas.

The following day came with a worsening of the storm. There was no fire in the stove and the saloon was so cold that breath bloomed on the air. Azuba staggered around the room securing anything still loose—workboxes, books, Carrie's drawing paper. Water leaked from the weather-boarded sky-light, dripped onto the table.

They sat on the floor, wedged against a wall with their feet against the bolted armchair. They lowered their faces to the mugs. The rims jarred against their teeth. Carrie howled, put a hand to her mouth.

Later, they lay together in Azuba's bed. Azuba put an arm around Carrie, pulled the child close.

She dug deep into her store of humour and beauty. She smoothed Carrie's hair. "Do you remember the last batch of kittens, the yellow tigers? Their mama hid them in the back of the cupboard? We could hear their peeping mews. Like this." She mewed. Carrie mewed, higher.

Together, they recounted their favourite stories.

"The time . . . Auntie's false teeth in the stove, sifting through the ash bucket to find them? The time . . . the china platter went out the window with the wash water? Found it unbroken in the sweet williams . . ."

She would not be frightened. She would not think about the fact that they had not once seen Nathaniel.

Traveller was knocked down. She lay on her beam ends, wallowing. They were flung against the wall in a welter of blankets and cracker crumbs. Azuba pulled Carrie to her breast. She could not speak. Her ears roared with prayer.

Save us, Lord, save us, save us.

The ship righted, slowly.

A bawling bellow. "Hello down there! Hello!"

The shout came dimly from the companionway door. Azuba made up her mind.

Out of here. Get ready to face it.

She and Carrie struggled into their outer clothing. They crawled over the saloon floor to the dining cabin. The ship tipped so precipitously that they set one knee on the wall and the other on the slanted floor, fending off jam jars and sodden onions spilled from the steward's pantry. They went up the companionway. The door was ajar.

"Captain wants to know if youse are all right."

Shouting into her face. Foul breath. Skin slimy with sweat and water. Frozen beard.

"Yes, yes."

"He says stay close to here."

The sailor backed out. Through the door's crack they caught a glimpse of lamplight; within its shaft, they could see snow whipped by the unholy howl.

Sit. We'll just sit here for the night. The dog had followed them. Azuba saw that Carrie was waiting—childlike, trusting.

"We'll sing, Carrie."

"*Out on an Ocean,*" she began, "*All Boundless We Ride.*"

They sang-shouted every hymn and song Azuba could remember, hysterical with exhaustion. Waves broke against the door as the southern ocean buried the deck. They heard the tuneless, harpy shriek of the wind, felt the ship's laboured heave. They were still there, slumped, sleeping, when Nathaniel opened the door the following morning. He shook them awake and they stumbled after him. He fell into bed. Azuba thawed the frozen laces of his boots with her hands, hauled them from his feet. Then Carrie and Azuba went to Carrie's bed and slept, clasped in one another's arms.

Traveller plunged onward into the icy seas of the planet's most desolate realm, and just before slipping back into sleep, Azuba felt that they were the last people left on the earth's surface, and that everything else—horses, church bells, white houses, mud-snouted pigs, dandelions—had ceased to exist.

Several days later, on the first morning of a steady, fair wind, Azuba woke in her own bed. She lay in the bliss of half-sleep, picturing a January day when she was eight years old and she and her mother had set out on foot to Grammy's house carrying apple pie and biscuits, goose grease and camphorated liniment. The snow-packed road was ridged with the marks of sleigh runners. Bits of ice came pelting from the sky, and then a fine snow began and came on so fast and thick that they could barely make out the silver-barked alders. Dark fell and they missed the turn. They tramped in a small circle, round and round, staying awake, eating the apple pie and then the biscuits until the snow died and they saw the moon through ragged clouds and finally heard the jingle of sleigh bells.

And she remembered how Simon could not believe this story.

"You must have dreamed it," he said, stroking between the ears of a purring cat with two fingers. "Why did she walk? Why didn't you take the horse?"

Azuba had shrugged, watching his hands. "Often we walked."

She lay now in a bliss of drowsiness, lulled by regular waves and the distant sound of shanties and shouts and creakings and slattings as one by one the great sails were spread. She let her mind drift like a spent blossom. *Home.* And then, from home, to Simon. How strange it had been, she thought, rolling onto her side, opening her eyes and smiling; how strange it had been listening to Reverend Simon Walton when she sat in the family pew. She'd kept her eyes fixed on her glove buttons or else flicked dust from Carrie's shoulders that had risen from the summer roads, churned by the hooves of horses.

She was awakened by Nathaniel shaking her.

"Come up, Azuba. Get Carrie and come up. There's a sight for you to see."

His cheeks were wind-chapped; his coat exuded a wintery sharpness.

Carrie and Azuba hurried into warm clothes. When they stepped onto the deck, Azuba put a hand over her eyes, dazzled. In the night, they had changed course and were finally heading eastward; and for the first time, their world had a limit. All along the southern horizon was a field of broken ice. Azuba and Carrie climbed the slippery steps to the quarterdeck where Nathaniel and Mr. Dennis stood with spyglasses to their eyes. Gobbets of ice hung from the ends of Nathaniel's moustache.

He handed Azuba the glass. "Look over at that berg."

She paused before putting the glass to her eye. Several miles off was an immense iceberg, like a drifting island.

More men than usual stood on lookout duty in the bows and on the fo'c'sle.

"Put the glass to your eye," Nathaniel said. "Look to the right of the berg."

She raised the glass, squinted through it. The berg was a hundred feet high or more at one end, higher than the main-mast, and slanted downward; its jagged crest bulked against the sky; waves broke at its base. Her glass moved, and stopped. There, filling her sights, was a ship that had run up onto a shelf of ice. It was black, tipped at a grotesque angle. A few frozen sails hung from the fore and main topmast yards. Every line, spar, halyard, stay and shroud was thick with ice. The ship glittered.

Nathaniel stood close to her. "A barque," he said.

Azuba returned the glass to Nathaniel. He looked at her, but she said nothing. She drew Carrie close.

Mr. Dennis spoke, glass to eye. "The lifeboats are missing."

Nathaniel studied the stricken barque. "No lifeboat could have lasted in such a sea," he said, keeping the glass to his eye. "They would not have survived long."

"It could have been us," she said.

"It could have," he agreed. "But it wasn't. And will not be."

He handed the glass to Carrie. "I have never seen such a sight," he said. "A ship stuck in ice. You'll tell your grand-children of this, Carrie."

Why? Azuba felt a stab of protective outrage. *Why show Carrie?* That ship had carried men, cabin boys, dogs, birds, livestock, perhaps women. Perhaps a little girl. Everyone on that ship was dead.

Mr. Dennis looked down at Carrie, who was now eagerly

scanning with the glass. Azuba saw disapproval mar his face. Then he glanced up, roared out a warning to the men on the main deck as heavy seas threatened to break aboard.

Nathaniel took the glass from Carrie, found the ship. He knelt beside her, balancing the glass while arranging her head behind it. He put an arm around her, energy in his shoulders, a grim light in his eyes.

"What happened to them, Papa?"

"Captain made a miscalculation, I suppose," Nathaniel said.

Carrie looked up at him. She braced herself, mittened hand on his shoulder. He motioned, turning Carrie's eyes to *Traveller*'s deck—ice-coated lines, smoke coming from Mr. Lee's stack, and the bowsprit rearing up against the wintery sky.

"I have to keep my ship from such a fate," he said.

"Carrie, we're going below," Azuba said. "It's too cold."

Nathaniel did not hear her tone. He had seen some crimp or slatting of the sails and reached for his speaking trumpet.

Azuba crabbed down the steps, half-turned to hold Carrie's hand. Carrie came reluctantly, chattering of the frozen ship.

Who is this man I married? Azuba thought. *He shows us a ship of death, wanting to make me proud.* She remembered Mrs. Marshall and her heartless fascination with the guano trimmers. She felt a sickening, thinking how she'd dreamed of *Traveller*'s saloon, imagined it to be as comfortable as the sail house parlour. She and Nathaniel would sit on the sofa, her head on his shoulder, and the ship, in her mind, had been rocked by easy waters, sometimes anchored within sight of palm trees, tropical flowers and the plumage of parrots.

She felt pity for the person she had been. And a wistful, bitter sorrow, since no vision replaced the one that had vanished.

For days, they travelled past the icefields. Carrie and Azuba stood by the mizzen mast, mittened hands tucked round their waists, faces bound in scarves, watching the shining landscape. It was a glittering wasteland of ice chunks—some flat, others tipped and wedged like ship's hulls. Vast bergs separated from the icefields and drifted northward, spray booming upward through crevices.

One morning, they came on deck to see that the ice was only a gleam at the horizon. The wind was strong and steady, and when the bow spanked down, spume rose and flew back as far as the gangway. It had rained in the night, and the sky was dappled with shoals of white clouds. In between, the sky was blue, but a shower chased up, a steel-grey band of cloud luminous in the sunlight.

Nathaniel stood by the weather rail, pipe in his teeth. "Look," he called to Carrie, pointing. A double rainbow had appeared.

"Pot of gold!" Carrie cried, running across the deck, her hood blowing back. Nathaniel put out his arm for her. He grinned at Azuba, his tension lifted. She smiled back, laid a hand on her belly.

Nathaniel had promised that on the next day they would see Staten Island, off the east coast of Tierra del Fuego. Then, at long last, they would pass into the Atlantic.

"You'll be born in Belgium," Azuba murmured to her baby, squinting into the sun-shot spume.

"Bennett, if you're a boy. Dorothea, if you're a girl."

Part Three

THE ATLANTIC

11. A Dead Ship

IN THE EVENINGS, NATHANIEL POINTED AT OLD constellations sinking into the sea behind them as new ones rose in the north. Ice melted from spars and rigging. The days lengthened, and Azuba felt the air grow soft.

The wind was hauled almost dead astern and remained constant, so Nathaniel ordered the yards squared in and gave the crew time off to clean. The men tied their dirty laundry to ropes, tossed it overboard. Later, the rigging was alive with pants, shirts, blankets, neckerchiefs. At last, Carrie could sit on deck in a wooden tub, splashing in sea water heated on the galley stove.

By mid-March, they were nearing the equator.

Lately, Azuba had begun to worry about her father. In the few letters she read, over and over, there were only a few lines from him at the end, as if he did not know how to strike the right tone. Azuba pictured him sitting at his desk, lifting his pen, holding his beard, eyes dark with anxiety. She saw her own behaviour in a new light. She had abandoned the house he'd built for her—closed the door on beds, china, wardrobes and linens; shocked him with her friendship with Reverend

Walton. She imagined him opening the paper to the shipping news with a daily torment of fear, reading aloud to
Mother, who would listen in silence and then sigh, setting
pudding before him, touching his shoulder.

She felt the baby kicking.

"Carrie! Quick, the baby's kicking."

Carrie was sitting on the skylight, brushing Gig. She
hurried across the deck, put her hand on Azuba's belly.

Nathaniel left his place on the quarterdeck and crossed to
where Azuba sat in her chair, hands on her belly, a rapt expression on her face. He laid a hand on her shoulder. She slid a
hand up to cover his.

"Feel your little brother, Carrie?" he said. He tipped back
his hat, scratched the white, shaded skin of his forehead. He
smiled at her and then turned his attention back to the sails
towering overhead.

Carrie went back to Gig.

Azuba closed her eyes, enjoying the peace that washed over
her like sun from lifting clouds. The touch of Nathaniel's
hand on her shoulder had brought a memory of a moment
when she was in her mother's garden, laying stalks of bee
balm and snapdragons in a basket, and he'd appeared on
horseback, coming along between the lupines. He had drawn
his horse to a standstill and sat watching her.

My husband, she had thought. *He will be my husband.*

She wondered if there would ever be a time when they
would sit together on the sail house porch in a similar
configuration—parents and children—neither she nor
Nathaniel yearning to be elsewhere. She pictured the house:
its steep gables, its gingerbread shingles and bow windows.
How long would it take before it was inhabited by mice and
bats? Before the roses went wild and the shingles tugged loose
in winter storms and lay like silver shells in the grass?

Sunshine slanted through her porthole. A motionless spear of light angled from the mirror.

The bed was not rocking.

She felt only a wallowing sway. She heard Nathaniel's voice and Mr. Dennis's reply; they were speaking in normal tones, and yet sounded close. The stench of guano rose from the hold.

Azuba passed a hand over her beaded forehead. There was a slick of sweat beneath her breasts. She could hear the scratchings of the rats who climbed the saloon walls and slithered into coat pockets to nibble at handkerchiefs.

She rose, dressed. She peered in at Carrie, who still slept as if drugged by heat. She left her sleeping and went on deck.

Traveller lay becalmed. The old, patched sails that had been bent on after they left Cape Horn hung like aged flesh. The water bore no waves but gleamed like oil on metal, rising in a long, slow swell.

"Lay aloft to sluice the sails," Nathaniel was shouting. "Lay aloft!"

The men of the watch dipped pails over the side, climbed the ratlines with slopping buckets, heaved water over the sails to close the fibres of the canvas. Water rolled down, dripped from the spars onto the deck, or plinked into the water, making a wavering necklace.

Each bucketload left a dark patch the size of a postage stamp.

Azuba climbed to the quarterdeck. Nathaniel stood hands on hips, staring at the limp sails. Mr. Dennis stood beside him.

"Good morning, Mr. Dennis," she murmured.

"Good morning, ma'am."

Tension between the two men was as palpable as the unseen, odoriferous bird feces. She opened her mouth to speak, but

Nathaniel answered her question before she could ask it.

"We've been speaking of what is to be done." His voice was like a hand raised, palm out. "It seems my calculations went awry. We're just north of the Equator. I had thought to catch a current."

The doldrums. Maury's book, Azuba remembered, had written of them as a formidable obstacle, like a mountain range with gaps and passes that could be found only through experience or by dint of painstaking navigation.

Captains, Nathaniel had told her, prided themselves on their ability to find a way through.

Traveller floated in a sunlit circle, light glancing from her brass fittings. There was a mutter of thunder. Azuba looked westward, where the sky was dark. Smoke rose from the galley stovepipe, and she felt a twitch in her womb, as if the baby had been roused by the unaccustomed stillness.

After seven days of drifting and whistling, Nathaniel wedged a coin under the foremast. It was a superstition to appease the men; a tithe to the god of winds.

Small puffs of breeze teased. Nathaniel kept the sails spread and sluiced, even though the water quickly faded into crusts of salt. The mates kept the men occupied with busywork—sail-mending, caulking, scraping barnacles from *Traveller's* sides, mending spars. Chips, sawdust and coffee grounds swayed on the water around the ship. Nathaniel had the mates erect awnings, including one over the aft skylight to keep sun from the saloon. Meanwhile, it grew hotter, and the stench from the hold grew stronger, and a torpor struck, making every task require an effort of will that began with Nathaniel and was transferred to the mates, and ameliorated in conviction as it went.

They drifted from March twenty-fifth to April twenty-fifth.

Never, in all his days at sea, had Nathaniel been becalmed for so long, nor had he heard of any other ship suffering such a fate.

"Perhaps there's a Jonah aboard," Azuba said. "Maybe it's me."

"Cracker hash," he said. "Sailor's talk."

He was relieved, she thought, that she had said it. Like lancing a blister.

For two dreadful days, he put sailors in the lifeboats and ordered them to tow *Traveller*. He left them at it all morning, and then, in the late afternoon, went aboard himself with the second watch. Singing voices rang out over the greasy swells:

Oh, the times are hard and the wages low,
Leave her, bullies, leave her;
I guess it's time for us to go;
It's time for us to leave her.

On the third day, he gave it up.

The sailors kept to their end of the ship, but the dead air made an uneasy intimacy. Azuba could hear flatulence, belches, snores, grunts and the sour notes of displeasure in their voices. She pointedly turned her chair to face aft if she noticed a man making his way to the slings in the bow or to the urine barrel. The door to the fo'c'sle stood open to admit any breath of air; the men off duty did not go below but dispersed themselves about the deck, sleeping in shady spots, handkerchiefs covering their faces, or sitting cross-legged, bent over their mending.

The mates kept the men of the watch at their tasks.

Mr. Lee came from the galley, apron tied under his armpits. "Catch fish," he urged, waving a wooden spoon at the men off watch. "Lazies."

But the fish swam deep. Occasionally a shark would pass, and all hands would stand by the railing to watch its languid swirl. Twice, the men caught one, and Mr. Lee prepared steaks.

Nathaniel paced, lips drawn back in frustration, exposing his teeth on the stem of his pipe. He supervised the scraping, painting and carpentry, or stood cross-armed, staring north towards Antwerp.

Azuba and Carrie sat beneath the awning on the quarterdeck. They sneaked glances down at the lower deck. They knew nothing about the sailors, save their nationalities, and learned their names only by chance. Azuba had heard other captains' wives speak of them as "scum of the earth" or "peasants" or "pigs." Azuba felt pity for them, thinking of how they spent most of their lives without wives or children, had no one to mend their clothes, and bathed only when it rained.

She pictured Simon's hands, smooth as white butter. Saw the tidy young man peering into a mirror, drawing a shaving knife over his cheeks. *Was it for me?* she wondered. *Oh, to speak of him, as I speak of the others at home. Just to reminisce with Carrie.*

One day, in the saloon, when Carrie had fallen asleep, Azuba removed even her shift and sat naked. Her naval was beginning to flower into a tiny rose.

She sat cross-legged, a large book on her lap for a writing tablet. She began to write.

Dear Simon,

She ran her finger over the name, as, in Nathaniel's absence, she had once traced his presence—fingers stroking his desk, a pipe, the cuffs of his coat.

We are becalmed. It is stifling in the saloon. I can barely breathe. I am frightened because the steward says we are running out of food, even salt beef. The water in the butts is thick and brown and tastes dreadful. The chickens were laying, but then the crew decided to clean the coop. They stuck it on a pole and hung it over the side and poured water on it. I think it terrorized the hens, and now they are sickening. The sailors are so sunburned that peels of skin hang from their faces. Nathaniel sent them out in the lifeboats and made them row, trying to tow the ship. He kept them at it all one day, and then all night, and then another day. Finally he gave it up, but not until the men were enraged. He was happy for a while, but now it begins to seem that he is going crazy with frustration. Sometimes I'm afraid of him. He hardly speaks to me and Carrie.

Oh, what are you doing, my friend? Trying to draw the petals of a rose? Painting a storm sky? I see clouds, and I think of you. I wish I had not . . .

She put her face in her hands.

She went to the stove, tore the letter into tiny pieces and buried the pieces beneath the ash.

Nathaniel came into the saloon. He stopped and stared. Azuba whirled, pulled on her shift.

"I was so hot."

He grinned, slightly, but seemed in a hurry. He went to his desk, took out his billy jack and slipped it into his sleeve.

"Azuba," he said. "Button my cuff, will you, please?"

"What is going on?"

"Nothing. Just a precaution."

He went out, quiet in his bare feet.

Azuba sat on the couch, ran her fingers through her short hair, lifted it from her scalp. Her belly hilled the fabric of her cotton shift, a proud growth in a place of shrinking flesh.

Carrie was peering from her cabin. "Mama, is Papa going to hit one of the men?"

"He might."

"Why?"

"They have to obey him."

"Why?"

"He is the master."

Azuba felt tears starting. She had not cried since the death of Andrew Moss. She would not cry now, but her throat ached.

"He is the master," she repeated.

Thunder brewed, muttered and sometimes blew up a light, cool wind accompanied by a brief shower. The men kept the roof of the deck house freshly painted and clean; it was fitted with spouts and gutters so that rain could be collected and tipped into the water butts.

In mid-April, not knowing how long they were likely to drift, Nathaniel ordered half-rations for all hands. He said Azuba was to have any eggs the hens might lay. For a while, Mr. McVale brought her one every morning. She broke it into her single cup of coffee and gagged it down, thinking of the child stirring in her womb.

The ship rocked, encased in turgidity like an egg in

waterglass. Day after day passed with no wind. Once, a sailor called out, "Barque to the west!" and everyone paused, arrested in mid-motion, but the sails shrank until they were white needles, fading to nothing. At night, Azuba lay alone in her bed and thought of the schools of fish that swam in the sunless waters far below *Traveller*'s hull.

One night, Nathaniel's fingers began roving and he pressed his hard member against her thigh. She rolled away, huddled on her side, closed her hands in fists and crossed her arms over her belly.

"It's too hot."

He made a sound of rage in his throat. He threw himself onto his back, lay staring at the ceiling with one arm under his head.

She huddled away from him, picturing his hard, chapped lips. The lines beside his slitted eyes—white against scorched skin, deep as knife slits.

Nathaniel was a commander, but without wind, he had nothing. A dead ship. Men without purpose. Provisions running out.

She saw cruelty coming upon him like fever.

He began to spend his nights on deck. The off watch, too, slept on deck, since it was too hot in the fo'c'sle. Carrie and Azuba took to spending the day in the fetid saloon so they could wear as little clothing as possible. No one wore shoes. The men wound handkerchiefs around their foreheads to keep sweat from their eyes.

Azuba saw Carrie lay Jojo in the precise spot on the saloon floor where the cabin boy had lain. She cradled the doll's head in one hand, tipped a teacup to its mouth. She slapped Jojo's cheeks. "There, now," she muttered, lifting the doll to her feet, making her black cloth shoes tap-tap across the carpet. "Walk, walk."

One morning, even Carrie felt the sting of Nathaniel's wrath. At breakfast, she banged her hardtack on edge and weevils came swarming out. She shrieked, and said, "Bugger off, you scum!"

"You don't use words like that," Nathaniel said. He thrust himself to his feet and touched the child on her breastbone. "Do you hear me?"

Terrified, she looked at Azuba.

"Yes, Papa."

Men's voices. Raised in anger, up in the forward part of the ship, coming back aft. Azuba struggled sticky limbs into clothing, went on deck. Mr. Dennis and Nathaniel stood on the quarterdeck. She looked forward to see the sailors frozen, Mr. Perkins trying to put them back to work.

"I know my place, Captain Bradstock, and by God you should know yours." Mr. Dennis's voice shook. "You give me my orders, and I carry them out, and if you can't trust me to do so, put me down with the men. I'm ready to step down. Find someone else to be your mate. You'll find no one else as qualified on this ship, but by God I'd rather serve under a man who trusts me than one who does not."

"Lower your voice," said Nathaniel. "I command this ship. If it is my desire to inspect your work, then so be it."

Mr. Dennis spoke in a voice so low Azuba could barely hear. "I respect your command, Captain Bradstock, but do you think I can retain the respect of the men if you question my competency?"

Both men glanced down at Azuba. Nathaniel made a violent dismissive motion, brushing his fingers backwards as if flicking away a fly. His face was contemptuous. "Go below, Azuba," he snapped. His eyes were wide and blind, crushing.

She paused.

"Go," he said.

She went slowly down the companionway. She sat on the sofa in the saloon, gripped with trembling like a dog. She could see Carrie in her cabin, lying face down, sleeping, her limbs sprawled. The ship lolled and drifted, and the sound of Gig's panting was loud in her ears.

Nathaniel entered the saloon. He went to his desk, thrust open its top. He picked up his compass. Azuba looked at the back of his head. His blond hair, matted with grease and salt, lay in hanks.

"How dare you," she said. "How dare you flick your fingers at me and send me below like a common sailor."

"On my ship, you have no place being privy to a discussion between me and my officers."

"I have been privy to many a discussion. Should you lay on sail; should you change the canvas. I understand far more than you think. Both about you, and about this ship. It's only that, this time, you didn't want me to see the truth."

"What truth?"

"That you don't respect your officers. That you won't let them do their jobs. That you second-guess their decisions."

He turned towards her, eyes narrowed. "You are not an officer on my ship. You are not a sailor on my ship. You are my *wife*, Azuba. I won't have you making judgments on me. Remember that you are aboard this ship only because you disgraced yourself and disgraced me."

"Ah," she said. "There, you have just proved my point. You have never allowed me to tell you the truth. Just as you will not allow Mr. Dennis the freedom to exercise his judgment."

He took a step towards her. She folded her arms over her breast, too furious for fear. "I saw it coming," she said. "Between you and Mr. Dennis."

"Did you," he said.

A canary hopped onto a new perch with a thud. The empty perch swung to a standstill.

He turned back to his desk. He pricked the blotting paper with the compass. She heard the small implosion of pierced paper. His voice was low, gravelly from thirst. "Azuba, in this situation that we find ourselves, you have to trust me. You have to keep silent in these matters."

Azuba lowered her voice. She felt a flood of fury, nullifying censorship. "I'm neither foolish, Nathaniel, nor stupid. You know this about me. It's why you married me. Or so you told me. You harm Carrie, you harm yourself, and you harm me by your attempt to keep me in what you see as *my place.* I think it is your way of punishing me. If you ever again dismiss me with the flick of a finger, I promise that I will rage at you in full view of all the men on this ship. And I will truly begin to hate you."

Carrie stood at the doorway of her cabin. "Mama?"

"Go to your cabin and shut the door, Carrie. Papa and I need to talk."

She heard the silence above and wondered if the sailors and crew had heard their raised voices. Her shaking was like the quiver of taut rope. "I'm sick of it," she whispered, turning to the sofa and sitting. "I'm sick of the way you have been treating me."

"You see me as I am on my ship," he said, finally. He had been thinking, gathering himself, drawing back from cruelty. "It is one of the reasons I decided even before the . . . incident . . . that I didn't want you to come with me."

"You are kind enough," Azuba whispered, "to Carrie."

Her eyes filled with tears.

Carrie came from her cabin. She clutched Jojo and walked towards her father, steadily, as if she had thought through what to do. She did not look at Azuba. Nathaniel heard her footsteps. He turned. Then he knelt and pulled her to him.

Azuba crouched forward, staring into the darkness of her cupped hands. She saw no way forward. She felt loathing. For herself, for her husband. For her life.

12. Creature of Barnyards

CARRIE CLIMBED ONTO A CHAIR TO TALK TO THE
canaries and found that two of them had died in the night.
They lay on the floor of the cage, their claws curled.

"Mama!"

Azuba came at Carrie's cry. She reached in and lifted out
the birds, laid them on the couch. Carrie knelt, stroking
them. The yellow feathers were vivid against the black
horsehair.

"Poor little . . . poor little . . ."

She pressed her face into Azuba's lap.

Azuba sat with one hand on the mound of her belly and
an arm around Carrie. The booms made a monotonous
creaking. Swinging, aimless. Nathaniel told her it was called
the singing of the doldrum birds.

The next morning, Azuba did not get out of bed. She lay on
her back, one hand trailing to the floor, the other thrown up
on the pillow. Her legs sprawled, the touch of flesh on flesh
intolerable.

Nathaniel came to the door. She covered herself with the
sheet, pushed herself up against the pillow.

"Are you ill?" he said.

Over the past week his face had become masked, his eyes cold, even when he played checkers or sat reading the tattered newspapers. Carrie had ceased going to him with requests to be pushed on the swing, or to be sung a naptime song.

"No," she said. He would have no sympathy for her, since what she felt—hot, hungry, fractious—was felt by everyone on the ship.

"I'm putting everyone on quarter-rations," he said. "I've been inspecting the stores with the mates and the steward. We'll be lucky to—"

"Papa." Carrie wore a grey cotton shift that had once been white. It hung from one shoulder. The tops of her feet were dry, dusty, cracked with sunburn. Her eyes grew larger in a thinning face, purple smudges beneath them. "Gig is hungry," she said, speaking to her father. Each word was distinct. "I can see all his bones." She stood up straight, spoke to him as an equal. She was the only person on board who was not afraid of Nathaniel in his present mood.

Some captains would throw a dog overboard, Azuba thought. *Some captains would throw horses overboard.* Yet what she saw in his face was the expression that came whenever he looked at Carrie—a restfulness that lightened his eyes, made them hopeful. And Azuba remembered the day he had taken Gig, and had explained, as if ashamed of his feelings, *She needs something to love.*

"I'll give Gig some of my portion," Nathaniel said. "I'll—"

There was shouting on deck, a confused sound that might have been either desperation or exultation. Nathaniel froze. He turned, was gone.

"Quick, Carrie," Azuba said. She pulled a dress over her head, snatched up her bonnet. They hurried through the forward cabin, stumbled up the companionway holding their skirts.

Men lined the starboard railing. They pointed, shouting. Everywhere on the sea, dark patches formed where the wind blew. The patches grew larger until the entire surface of the ocean darkened to a deep blue. Nathaniel fired words at Mr. Dennis. Mr. Dennis and Mr. Perkins began shouting orders. The sailors swung the yards to present canvas to the wind, and the sagging sails fluttered, flapped and suddenly boomed out with great snaps. *Traveller* began to move through the water with a murmuring wash. She leaned to the wind, gaining speed.

Carrie screamed. She ran back and forth, jumping invisible puddles, waving her arms. Azuba stood with her arms out, fingers stretched, taking breaths of the sweet wind that blew away the stench of guano and all of the ship's stale odours: perspiration, latrines, chicken manure, filthy clothes.

The men piled together on the deck, hauling lines.

The northeast trade winds stayed steady. *Traveller* heeled, once more on her way, bound for Antwerp. That night, Nathaniel came to bed, and they lay listening to the rush of water past the hull and the rhythmic creak of working wood.

On the first day of heavy rain, Azuba and Carrie stayed below so the men could wash. They heard laughter, the sound of rattling buckets, sluicing water and outraged roars in various languages. There was an open-air barbershop, resulting in cuts and jabs, Nathaniel told them later, as the African sailor acted as barber and the men came to the capstan to be shaved and shorn.

Mr. McVale brought hot rainwater. Azuba and Carrie bathed in the tiny bathroom, and later Nathaniel came down and sat in the tub. Azuba scrubbed his back, poured warm water over his head and washed his hair. She slid her fingers down his soapy back, let them stray into the groove of his buttocks. She pressed a kiss on the back of his neck, stifled laughter as he bent forward, arms shielding his lap.

For days, Azuba was filled with energy as she restored her home. Mr. McVale washed sheets and towels and Nathaniel's trousers, while Azuba scrubbed all the smaller articles of clothing and hung them in the rigging to dry. She covered the saloon table with flannel, and Mr. McVale brought hot irons. Carrie folded the ironed clothes and helped Azuba stow them away, tucking lavender sachets into pockets, between handkerchiefs.

They resumed Carrie's schooling, which they'd abandoned during the days of grimy lethargy. They ate meals at regular hours with whichever mate was off watch. They observed every formality, bowing their heads for grace and talking of the merits or perils of confederation, expeditions to the north and south poles, or the customs of royalty. Mr. McVale continued to wear his apron and arrived as usual with his tray.

But on it, now, was nothing more than salt beef and biscuits, and he placed miniscule portions onto their plates. And as the water in the butts sank and there was little rain, he poured brown, mouldy-smelling liquid into their mugs. Azuba cut her meat into cubes the size of her smallest fingernail and held each forkful on her tongue, swallowing beef-flavoured saliva, waiting for the piece to soften. No one mentioned what was on their plates, or spoke of the thing foremost on their minds.

Starvation. Like a hidden vice.

"Remember . . ." said Azuba. She was stitching a green vine around her needlepoint house. For the first time on this voyage, Carrie had taken out the ark and its animals, and set them on the saloon floor.

Azuba's mind was snagged by food: blueberry grunt, she saw, served hot, with fresh cream. "Pound cake," she said to her needle, and glanced up to see if Carrie would join the game.

"Gingerbread," said Carrie, after a moment's thought.

Lemon pudding, baked shad, fiddleheads sprinkled with vinegar, apple pudding made with sour milk and cinnamon . . .

Carrie sprawled on her stomach, chin in hands, waggling her bare feet. The cabin was neat; fresh air stirred the papers on Nathaniel's desk. Yet in Azuba's gut, knife stabs of hunger kept her from sleep and plagued her with worry for Carrie and for the growing child in her womb.

Now that people and clothing were clean, Azuba lost her energy. The men's voices became like clouds on the horizon, too distant to decipher; her feelings swayed as if on a fulcrum, descending on one side towards fear, tipping on the other into hope. She did not dare ask Nathaniel if he understood what to do if the baby was born on board. Pregnancy pre-occupied her as much as hunger, and each augmented the other in the entirety of their compulsion. Her belly grew, blossomed. Her breasts became too large for her dresses, their material stretched across her bosom until she had to make darts or add panels. Yet her stomach sent forth hollow vines of hunger. Her mouth ached with the desire for texture; her hand went to her dry, swollen throat.

In the saloon, light fell from the skylight.

"Mama," Carrie said. She laid her head on her arms. She was weak, and tears were close to the surface. "I'm so hungry."

Azuba felt a flash of terror. *What can I do?* The sea's bounty was unavailable, capricious. They could not rely on sharks, or albatross, or flying fish. The fish swam too deep, the ship went too fast.

At home, there was always food. Always. Her root cellar. Her pantry. And, everywhere, fresh water: a spring, a well, snow to melt, or a stream.

"I need to get my . . ." she said, vaguely, setting down her scissors. She rose and went from the saloon into the dining room. Quietly, she slipped into the steward's pantry. She opened the jars. They contained nothing but the whispery odour of jam, pickles and raisins. She ran her fingers along the angle of shelf and wall, remembering how at home, molasses had spilled there, making a paste where nuts or raisins lodged. Mr. McVale was a competent young man, though, and the shelves were clean. She knelt and felt in the back of a cupboard. *Paper!* In the paper were a few dried figs.

She went back to the saloon. Carrie still sat at the table with her head cradled in her arms. The ship rolled; the stern lifted and spanked down. Azuba staggered, slapped the hand holding the figs on the table. Carrie sat up. She snatched a fig and crammed it into her mouth, biting and gnawing at the rock-hard fruit.

Azuba watched her, anguished. Like Carrie, she, too, was weakening.

It's my fault that Carrie is starving.

It was stormy, too rough to sew or knit. *Traveller* plunged and rose; warm rain mixed with spray.

Carrie was asleep. Azuba sat in the saloon with her hands folded in her lap.

In New Brunswick, the pin cherries would be in bloom, their frail, pink-white blossoms rippling on a cool wind while dandelions made yellow blankets on the fields.

If I were home. Hannah was spooning oatmeal into a wil-lowware bowl. Carrie sat pouring maple syrup from a jug.

Azuba opened the kitchen door; the moist air was scented with seaweed and spruce. Four ships headed down the bay, their sails billowing.

For a while, Azuba held this spring morning in her mind, imagining it as if it did not contain longing, loneliness and fear. Then the woman of her vision put hand to mouth, went into the kitchen and picked up a letter from Nathaniel. It had been two months since he'd written it, and as she read, she wondered where he was, and if he were still alive, and if he would ever come home to be a father to Carrie.

The way it really was. The way it would be if I were home.

Nathaniel came below, streaming with water. He took off his oilskin. "We're making good progress."

"Nathaniel. How much food is left?"

He sat. He took his pipe from his shirt pocket. "Enough."

"What do you mean, 'enough'?"

"If we keep on like this—" Nathaniel began.

She spoke rapidly, keeping her voice low so as not to wake Carrie. Her words came as if from a conversation recently interrupted. "How much? How many bags of beans? How much rice? How many potatoes? How much hardtack? Nathaniel, I provided for myself when I lived alone. I'm not accustomed to being treated like a child. *Quarter-rations.* A quarter of what? When will we run out? What will we do then? How . . . what if Carrie . . ."

"Everyone on board this ship has to trust my decisions, even you. You are not the cook, Mr. Lee is the cook. You're—"

"I am . . ."

"My wife. You are the captain's wife. I'll give Carrie my food if it comes to that. But it won't. We will not starve."

"We are beginning to starve."

"Call it what you will."

"I am feeding the goat Carrie's grass petticoats, Nathaniel."

A muscle moved in Nathaniel's cheek, but still Azuba spoke, hands gripped in her lap beneath the curve of her belly. "Carrie is becoming weak, my hair is beginning to fall out, all day long I think, *How is the baby, how is the baby?* You pretend we aren't dying of hunger, Nathaniel. You've never once acknowledged that your little daughter is bravely suffering. You treat us like baggage."

"I understand what my daughter is suffering." He pointed the stem of his pipe at her. "I would advise you not to assume what I feel for my daughter."

Grey, rainy light fell from overhead. Her face was beginning to lose flesh. Her hair was salt-laden, without lustre.

The entire argument went through her mind in a dull, wordless rumble, like wagon wheels over cobblestones. *We must not start; it has no finish, I have no energy.* She closed her eyes and put her hand on Nathaniel's arm. She spoke in an even voice, without emotion. "Nathaniel, I ask it of you. For my sanity. Let me inspect the stores. Let me see with my own eyes. Let me confer with Mr. Lee. Please."

He filled his pipe, tamped the tobacco. "All right," he said. He glanced at the door of Carrie's cabin. He looked back at Azuba, and she saw his anger dampened by respect. There were pockets of blue exhaustion beneath his eyes. "I'll speak to the others. Mr. McVale will take you around."

"Thank you."

Azuba and Carrie were on the quarterdeck, sun warm on their faces, wind from the west. It was mid-May. Azuba had picked all the tucks from her calico dress and raised the waistline. The hunger pains in their bellies made all things hostile, even the caressing wind and easy clouds.

At the taffrail two sailors were trailing the log, gauging the ship's speed. Nathaniel stood with one foot raised on the wooden grid where the helmsman stood with arms spread to the wheel. Save for the slap and splash of rushing water and the occasional snaffle of canvas, the ship was quiet. No one had the energy to sing, laugh or even talk. Footsteps were slower. Shoulders slumped forward, bodies cramped by hunger.

Nathaniel bent over the binnacle, spoke to the helmsman. He squinted up into the sails. Azuba sat surrounded by net bags. She was picking through the remaining onions, setting aside the ones with sprouts or blackened skins.

Carrie was trying to put a piece of cloth into a nail box for Jojo's bed. She fussed, frustrated, not getting the folds the way she wanted them. She threw down the cloth and sat with her chin in her hands.

Azuba looked up, about to speak.

A chicken flew at Carrie with a flurry of bony wings. Carrie screamed, batted with her hands. The chicken attacked again, pecking at the child's chest.

"Get away! Get away! Papa! Mama!"

Nathaniel ran from the binnacle, snatched up the hen. "You bloody—"

"No, Nathaniel!" Azuba screamed. "Don't throw her over—she's still laying."

Carrie ran to Azuba. "Harriet is my friend, Mama. Why did she attack me?"

Nathaniel stood with the hen under his arm. Azuba looked from the hen to Carrie, then held the sobbing child at arm's length.

"She's not harmed is she?" said Nathaniel.

"No, I'm not looking for injury," Azuba frowned. "It's her buttons."

"Her buttons?"

"They're made of bone. That hen is looking for calcium. She has no shell on her eggs."

Carrie looked down. "My buttons?"

"Give me the hen, Nathaniel," Azuba said. She rose, brushing onion skins from her skirt. She took it in both hands, repressing the bird's wings, then bundled the hen like a box under her arm and put out a hand for Carrie. "Come, Carrie. We have to go feed this bird."

They went below. Azuba set the hen on the floor, went to her sea chest. "Carrie," she called. "I'm going to find every edible button I can. Get your button collection. Find the mortar and pestle—it's in the pantry."

At the saloon table, Carrie opened her button box. "They're my friends, Mama." She touched the antelope, with its slender, backward-curving antlers. The rabbit, the eagle. The moon, the stars.

"We'll save them for last," Azuba said. "Look, here are some plain white ones from my nightgown. Harriet can have them."

Azuba lifted the pestle and smashed the buttons. She put the dust in a bowl and set it on the floor. Harriet pecked at it with sharp raps of her head. Her crepe-like eyelids crawled down, folded up.

All morning, they cut buttons off shirts, dresses, capes. They collected the powder in a crock. The sharp gut scent of chicken manure quickened the air. Azuba mopped up the squit with a rag. Carrie ran on deck to throw the rag overboard.

The chicken pecked at the powder.

For days, Azuba fed Harriet white powder. Her eggs began to have shells. When there were no more white buttons, they smashed up ones with red and blue stripes, or black figures or green stars, and laughed to see that the eggshells bore odd flecks of colour.

Azuba insisted on sharing the daily egg with Carrie. When it was Azuba's day for the egg, she drank it in her coffee. When it was Carrie's day, Azuba broke the egg into a tablespoon of the goat's milk.

They took turns until the button mash ran out. Their clothing was stripped. Carrie had no more animals, only ten brass buttons.

It was late afternoon, five o'clock by the ship's bells. All day, the wind had been rising, making a heavy head sea. Wind keened in the rigging, and long-drawn cries ribboned from captain, mate and second mate as Nathaniel finally put the men to furling the sails. He had courted danger, pushed the ship to her limits all day long.

Weakened, Carrie had taken to her bed.

A slap and slash of rigging landed on the deck, or the saloon ceiling, just over Azuba's head, and Azuba heard Nathaniel shouting. *Traveller* was pitching, the seas striking the bows hard, the ship coming up and then rolling half onto her beam ends. Azuba snatched at Gig's hairbrush, which Carrie had left on the table, but it sped from her hand and knocked against the wall. The calendar and photographs tilted on their nails. She held the arms of her bolted chair; at one moment, she was looking down on the wall, and then it rose up over her.

She made her way to Carrie's cabin and tucked the blankets tightly around her, then went forward through the dining room and up the companionway. Spray dashed full into her face as she opened the door. She shrank back against the aft cabin. Nathaniel was shouting orders from the quarterdeck;

Mr. Dennis was away up in the fo'c'sle, roaring; Mr. Perkins was in the waist, at times knee-deep in green water. The bowsprit plunged and reared, and the ship rolled until the lee scuppers were under water and the fo'c'sle was buried in foam.

Harriet came fluttering from her coop. It was her feeding time, and she began to make her way over the deck.

"No! Go back, Harriet!" Azuba thrust her hands at the little hen. "No, no, Harriet. Please, please. Go back!"

Wind blew up the hen's tail feathers. She persisted, coming towards Azuba, half-hopping, half-blown. Nathaniel roared out an order. The men were dispersed across the fore top-gallant yard, fighting to furl the sail. The ship rolled. Wind lifted the chicken, and she spread her wings for balance and was sent flying over the railing. Azuba ran to starboard. She saw the hen, brown feathers incongruous against the black waters, wings flapping, trying to regain the ship. Azuba leaned over the rail, watching, until the hen became a tiny brown speck, suddenly obliterated by the spume of a breaking wave.

Before going to bed that night, Carrie knelt by Gig, stroking his head. "Poor Gig," she whispered. "Poor Gig."

The dog's skin sagged between each rib.

Azuba sat on Carrie's bed watching the porthole, which first framed the night sky and then tipped down to frame black water, while the pinpoint of the lamp's flame stayed steady, a pupil at its centre. She had not told Carrie about Harriet.

In the saloon, Azuba slid to the carpet. The dog came, put his head in her lap. She bent her face into her hands and wept soundlessly, wiping her nose on the back of her hand, drying her cheeks with her shawl.

By midnight, the storm had weakened and Nathaniel came into the saloon. Azuba was still sitting on the floor.

He stepped over and peered down, fingers working at his buttons. He was soaking wet, haggard, peremptory from command. "Why are you sitting there?" His fingers paused. "Are you ill? The baby?"

"No." She pulled up her knees, wrapped her arms around her skirt, buried her face in her lap. He went into their cabin, returned wearing his nightshirt. He sat on the sofa and stretched his legs. "The storm is passing. Should be quiet by morning. Wind's still in a good quarter."

"Nathaniel. What would you be doing if you were alone?" Azuba said.

"Just what I'm doing now. Stretching out my legs. Thinking about sleep."

"Would you talk to the canaries?"

"Yes, I'd say good night to them. Tell them they were good little birds, I suppose."

"You're at home, Nathaniel. You're at home on this ship. You go on just as you always have, living here on *Traveller.*" She had realized this on the night the cabin boy fell to his death, and had been on the point of saying it many times since, but had not.

His chest lifted in a sigh. He closed his eyes. She saw him thinking the tired words: *It was your choice, Azuba, not mine. You left me no choice but to agree to your coming. If you had not . . .*

"I always thought that you longed for me when you were alone on your ship. As I longed for you when I was alone on land. Weren't they true, those letters? *These* letters . . ." She lunged to her knees, crawled to her workbox beneath a chair. She opened it, took out the bundle of letters. " . . . tied with a ribbon I went expressly to the store to buy, thinking about whether it should be blue or red, and which I have carried close to my heart even when—"

"When giving your heart to—"

"*No.* Don't you dare say that." She held out an arm, forbidding his words. "I never gave away my heart to anyone but you, Nathaniel." Her voice bent but did not break. She held his eyes, kept her arm extended.

Nathaniel crouched on one knee beside her. He put his hands on her head, tipped her face. "Were you crying when I came in? You never cry."

"Harriet went overboard."

He drew back, incredulous. "The chicken?"

She tried to speak, but this time choked on the words. She pictured the little hen beating its wings, a creature of barnyards, swallowed by the sea.

He put his arms around her. "You never cry," he murmured, like a reminder to himself. He rocked her. "You never cry."

They held each other in the shadowed saloon, hearing the shouts of men, feeling the shock of the plunging bow. And Azuba felt that for the first time they understood one another, and drew comfort from each other's presence, their grievances dwarfed by the enormity of their peril.

13. Crazy-Quilt Sails

THE SUN HAD RISEN IN A RED HAZE, AND THE AIR WAS humid. *Traveller* canted to windward, all sails set. Azuba stood on a footstool to look out the ceiling-height window. The sight of another ship would be like looking in a mirror— as she had done in the years when she lived alone in the sail house, confirming that she was more than a collection of feelings and thoughts.

Azuba turned to see Carrie slumped back in a chair. She lowered herself into her own chair and pushed her hands against her belly, where hunger made an ever-present nausea. She opened her mouth to offer comfort to her child but was overcome by the desire to sleep.

Carrie drew up her knees, hugged them to her chest. "I'm so tired, Mama."

" . . . five children," Mr. Dennis said.

Dinner was watery pea soup. Maggots floated on the surface. Carrie held her spoon over her bowl and glanced at Azuba. *Maggots or rice?*

Maggots, Azuba mouthed.

Carrie skimmed the white bodies with the side of her

spoon, tapped the spoon on a saucer set in the middle of the table. Mr. Dennis tapped his spoon at the same time. After dinner, Carrie would put the saucer on the floor for Gig.

" . . . came up before the magistrate on the same day, for stealing. They were aged thirteen . . ." He balled his hand, held it up and began with his thumb, then extended a finger for each child. "Twelve, eleven, ten and ten. And do you know, they were all sent to jail. In our city of Saint John. There is a need for a reformatory. When I get home, I shall write to—"

There was a pounding at the cabin door. Mr. McVale and Mr. Perkins, roaring: "Out of there! Get back!" Sailors, shouting: "Captain Bradstock. Come out!"

Nathaniel and Mr. Dennis jumped to their feet. The companionway door slammed open and a sailor burst into the dining cabin, four others pressed up behind him. The room filled with the smell of tobacco and sweat. The first man had close-set dark eyes and a flat, broken nose. Black beard and moustache, a whiskery fold in each cheek. Last week, Azuba had seen him standing nose to nose with Mr. Perkins, Nathaniel heading towards them with his billy jack.

"Youse are filling your bellies," the man said to Nathaniel. "Letting us starve."

"We are eating the same rotten food you are," Nathaniel said. He reached forward and picked up the maggot-filled saucer. "This is for the dog," he said, violence beneath the pleasant sarcasm. "We'll give it to him once we've finished. As for us," he nodded at the table, "you see." He set down the saucer and picked up his own bowl. "Pea soup, with a sprinkle of rice. You're welcome to taste it." He lifted a mug. "Water. From the same barrel yours comes from." Nathaniel set down the bowl and mug. "Go look in the steward's pantry."

Mr. Dennis stood with his head thrown back, restraining himself with one hand on the table. The man stepped into the pantry. He rummaged along the shelves, overturning empty glass jars, rattling crock lids, shaking empty tins. He came out and shrugged his shoulders at the other sailors bunched in the doorway.

Nathaniel fixed each man with a stare. His words hung, a space between each. "We're all extremely hungry. That's why I'm driving the ship to make speed. We're on quarter-rations, just as you are."

A sailor in the doorway shoved forward, mouth open to speak, but the spokesman shot out his arm. "Lots of places on board this ship to hide things," he said. Now he raised his eyes and looked into Nathaniel's. "Could be you knew we were coming to pay a visit."

Mr. Dennis lifted his hand from the table, flexed his fingers. Nathaniel stepped forward, stabbed a finger into the man's chest. He narrowed his eyes. The man's hand flew up, checked. He stepped back.

"You're welcome to search," Nathaniel said. "If you find something more to eat on this ship than is already accounted for, take it. We won't ask to share. Now go. Commence your search."

The men wavered.

"Go!" Nathaniel roared. "And God be with you," he snapped, as they turned and began to file out.

"For it seems," he muttered, as he sat back at his place and lifted his spoon, "that He has abandoned us."

The next day, at suppertime, it was again Mr. Perkins's watch, and Mr. Dennis sat with the family. They were waiting for Mr. McVale to come from the galley with his tray. Azuba and Carrie glanced back and forth between the men. Mr. Dennis sat on the edge of his chair with his feet back as if to spring.

Nathaniel lifted his spoon, tapped the handle against the table. He made no effort to begin a topic of conversation.

"We've been making good time today," Azuba said. "Did you trail the log?"

Nathaniel's eyes turned to her. They were wide and did not register her question other than as an irritant. He made a slight, impatient grunt. She felt sickened by the sight of him, enraged by the blankness in his eyes. She felt the urge to hurl water into his face. *Look at me. See me.*

His spoon continued its irritating tattoo.

Mr. McVale entered, carrying the tray. On it was the same pea soup they had had for the last week, and smaller pieces of hardtack, and a pot of tea made with the last scrapings of molasses. Carrie sat up at his entrance and then, seeing what was on the tray, collapsed back in her chair, chin falling to her chest. No one spoke as he set a bowl before Azuba.

She lifted her spoon.

Shouts. Stamping, a trample of feet. Mr. Dennis and Nathaniel leapt up. Men kicked open the companionway door, surged down the steps brandishing blunt-tipped knives, Mr. Perkins in their midst.

Nathaniel and Mr. Dennis flew at the men. Shouted threats were cut short; there were thuds and roars as fists smashed into faces. Mr. McVale dropped his tray and joined in. The men were borne back up the companionway.

Azuba and Carrie ran after the men, stood in the doorway watching as the melee swept down onto the main deck. Nathaniel was swinging his billy jack. A bloody slice opened on the ringleader's cheek. Another man was felled by Mr. Perkins's huge fists. The cook stood in the door of the galley, screaming in his own language, and Gig barked and flew at a sailor, burying his teeth in the man's calf. There were twelve sailors to the two mates, the steward and Nathaniel. Azuba screamed, not knowing what she said. She saw a knife lifted and the wrist that held it caught and smashed to the deck by Mr. Dennis. The sailors were overcoming the officers. Mr. Perkins was battling two men. Mr. Dennis was on the deck with a sailor's knee on his throat and a knife rising, and then Azuba saw Nathaniel pull out his pistol and aim it at the sailor.

"No!" she screamed. She took Carrie by the shoulders, pushed her towards the companionway. "Go below. Stay there." Then she flew down the steps, ran to Nathaniel.

His arm wavered, distracted. He roared at her. "Get away!"

"No!"

She reached for his forearm, pulled it. He slid his finger from the trigger, raised his other arm to push her away. Every man stopped to watch. The man holding a knife to Mr. Dennis's throat lowered his arm. Mr. Dennis scrambled to his feet. Azuba stood on tiptoe, wrenched the pistol from Nathaniel's hand.

"Azuba," said Nathaniel.

"No!" She looked for Carrie. The child had returned, and clung to the frame of the companionway door. "Carrie, I told you to go below! *Go.*"

Carrie vanished. Every man stood silent, panting, staring at the pregnant woman who had taken a gun from the captain's hands. They held hands to bleeding mouths or cheeks.

"No killing," Azuba panted. "There will be no killing on this ship." Her voice was hoarse, came on gasped breaths. She handed Nathaniel the pistol. He did not look at her, but aimed it over the men's heads, moved it back and forth.

"Drop your knives!" He shouted over the cracking of the sails, backed and flapping since the wheel had been abandoned and the ship had come up into the wind.

Azuba put her arms around her belly. Trembling began in the stem of her neck, swept to her shoulders, her knees. She stood beside Nathaniel, watching as knives clattered onto the deck.

"Mr. Perkins," Nathaniel snapped, motioning.

Mr. Perkins stooped, half-rose, stooped—retrieving the weapons.

"Mr. Dennis. Irons."

Mr. Dennis passed Azuba, heading for the aft cabin. He did not glance at her, yet she felt that his awareness of her was more acute than it had been since she had stepped on board. He returned with the irons that Nathaniel kept in his desk. He went to the men who were not injured, and they offered no resistance.

A groan came from the man whose wrist Mr. Dennis had smashed. The ringleader's face was covered with blood.

Azuba stumbled as the deck heaved and put one hand to a shroud. The ship—her decks littered with kneeling and cuffed men, her sails slatting, her officers half-stunned—was like an overturned family dinner table. Tureens smashed, silverware scattered. Azuba put a hand to her breast. She did not dare look at Nathaniel, could not believe what she had done.

He lowered his pistol, looked at Azuba. She saw that he was not angry with her, but could not read his expression. He seemed muted, cast down.

"Azuba."

"I'll go," she said. "I'm sorry."

"No," he said. He made a nullifying slice with his free hand. "No. Don't . . . I'm going to need you. Would you get the medicine box? I may need you to . . . I'll send Mr. McVale to watch Carrie."

She went, veering with the random motion, dress looped over one arm. Carrie had reappeared in the companionway door.

"Go," Azuba said. Her trembling began to change to hysterical laughter, and she took a quelling breath. "Hurry."

Carrie ran ahead through the dining cabin, followed by

Mr. McVale. Pea soup pooled along the fiddled edges of the table. Underfoot, the floor was tipping with the choppy rise and fall of waves as the ship drifted, directionless.

Azuba carried the medicine box to the forward deck house. Nathaniel had swept charts and navigational instruments from the table, where the bloody-faced ringleader now lay mopping his face with a wet cloth. Mr. Dennis watched over the handcuffed wounded men, and Mr. Perkins, armed, was setting the others to trimming sails.

Azuba took out her smallest needle and thread. She threaded the needle and handed it to Nathaniel. Mr. Lee poked a hand through the doorway with a jar of grog and lingered to watch as Nathaniel—white-faced, a glistening of sweat on his forehead—tugged thread through the wounded man's skin. The man winced, yelled. Azuba said nothing, but stepped forward and took the needle from Nathaniel's hand. She bent low over the wound, stitching with quick, neat hands, as Grammy had taught her.

That night, Azuba knelt on a small hooked rug next to her bed. Her knees rested on the roses in the centre. They were "riz roses," *hoven up,* as Grammy Cooper said, higher than the background. The cabin was silvered by a moon almost to the full. She wondered if aloneness was something separate from loneliness. If it were a condition of life, a thing one must come to terms with, no matter where, or how, or with whom one lived. If she had chosen a life with some gentle man— more like Simon and less like Nathaniel—once passion had faded, would she have arrived at the place she was now? And then she realized that what she thought of as Nathaniel's selfish determination to live as he pleased was no different from her own desires; that lack of compassion on both their parts was the fertile ground in which loneliness thrived.

The door of the companionway clicked open. Footsteps came down the stairs, through the forward cabin and the saloon. Nathaniel came into the cabin. He knelt, put his arms around her, buried his face in her hair. She reached back to touch the face that at supper she had viewed with loathing.

He sighed, a long breath. He rose to his feet and began to undress. Azuba slid into bed. Her belly was a fist of hunger. Her joints felt loose, as if no effort of will could make wrist bend, fingers clench, toes curl. He climbed in beside her, lay on his back with his arms folded behind his head. There was the groan of timbers as *Traveller* rode a heavy swell.

"You're thinner than Carrie," he said, after a minute. "She can hold out longer than you. You will have all the goat's milk. We have to think of the baby."

"Carrie's such a brave girl," Azuba murmured.

"Have you visited the lazarette?" he said.

"Yes, I went down this morning."

The unlit lamp swayed with a rusty squeak. "You saw, then," he said.

"Yes, I saw."

All that was left was a bit of lard, the last of the hardtack, peas and onions.

"The onions are mouldy, but good enough for lobscouse. And there's still a bushel of peas."

"And the goat," he said. "We'll eat her if we have to. God willing, we'll speak another ship before we run out completely."

"I'm not really hungry anymore." This was not true, but would be, soon. "Neither is Carrie. We're only weak."

Traveller's bow rose. Azuba's feet pressed against the footboard.

"We've lost one man. For a while anyway, thanks to

Mr. Dennis," Nathaniel said. "That wrist is broken. It will take some time for it to heal."

He laid an arm over his face, covering his eyes. "I should thank you, Azuba. It took courage to do what you did."

She said nothing. She had assumed command. For an instant, she had taken the ship. Her strength, pulling his arm. Every man—paused. The knives—clattering. *There will be no killing on this ship.*

"I might have killed a man today," he said.

"I didn't think," she said. "I found myself standing with a pistol in my hand, and I had no idea how it came to be there."

"That is what commanding a ship is like, Azuba. You can't wait when the ship is on her beam ends. Your mind makes decisions almost before you have time to think. You have to use the men like tools."

He had never spoken to her of this.

Their voices were changed. Stripped and yet not harsh. Azuba felt the knot of loneliness unravel. She lifted his hand, laid it on her breast and held it with both of hers. "Why did you marry me?"

When he answered, his voice was younger, simpler, as if he were not listening to himself—the way he spoke to Carrie. "I fell in love with you. You were a black-haired beauty with an intelligent face and eyes that sought truth."

"I was in love with you, Nathaniel. You were everywhere, in everything. It must be like that when a person is insane. I scoured turnips and they were your cheek. I leaned against my bedpost and it was your shoulder."

He smiled.

She felt a light touch at her temple. His fingers, stroking her hair.

An uneasy peace pervaded the ship. Nathaniel had ordered the irons removed, but the mates were never without their pistols. Still some weeks from the westerlies, they were heading northeast through the dark blue seas of the North Atlantic. Nathaniel had considered making a detour to the Azores for provisions, but since clear skies and fair winds held, decided to press on towards Antwerp with all possible speed.

One day, the lookout shouted. Off the starboard bow was a ship, bound to the south.

"Carrie!" Azuba shook the child's shoulder. "Carrie! A ship! A ship!"

She stuffed away her work, hurried to the rail.

Nathaniel called out, "Raise the signal flags!"

The other ship changed course, came towards them. Azuba and Carrie ran to the rail, leaned forward, waving, shouting. Clothing fluttering in the rigging—dresses, aprons and petticoats with arms and skirts dancing.

"Oh, Carrie! There's a woman aboard."

She was the *Marianna,* from Liverpool. The sails made a hurricane roar, snaps like gunshots as both ships hove to, halyards flapping, yards jerking. The other captain was pointing up at their distress signal. There was the squawky sound of men bellowing through speaking trumpets.

A woman came from the aft cabin. Azuba waved her arm over her head so wide and hard that the armpit of her dress ripped. The woman ran to her own railing. Her blond hair was in a net, and she wore a lacy cap and a lilac dress over hoops. "Hello," she called. "Hello!"

"A woman's voice," Azuba said to Carrie. "Oh, can you hear it? A woman's voice! Hello, hello!"

A lifeboat was lowered. Two sailors and Mr. Dennis climbed down. Mr. Dennis pulled out his shirt to conceal his pistol. They boarded the *Marianna* and returned after a brief interval. The sailors handed up a bushel basket and a barrel, and then they and Mr. Dennis came back aboard *Traveller*.

Marianna's stern swung away.

Carrie and Azuba made their way aft. They stood leaning against the taffrail, waving. The other woman was leaning against her taffrail. They waved and waved until she was only a tiny purple and white spot.

Azuba took a deep breath as the ship dwindled and she could no longer see the woman. *To have talked about my condition.*

"I wish there had been a child," said Carrie.

"Soon, my love. Soon we'll see birds. They'll land on the spars, and on the railing. Then we'll smell land."

"What will it smell like?"

"Like the earth after warm rain. Like sunshine on shingles. Like . . ."

"Like plum pudding," Carrie suggested.

"Gingerbread."

"Frogs!" Carrie shouted, stamping her foot.

"Mud puddles!"

They were shrieking into the wind.

"Goodbye!" Carrie shouted. Already the ship was nothing but a shard of light. "Goodbye, goodbye."

Nathaniel was back on the quarterdeck. "Keep her up to her course again," he was saying to the helmsman.

"Keep her up, sir."

"Run up the flying jib. Lay aloft . . . loose the royal . . ."

As they went back to the saloon, Mr. McVale passed, and Azuba stopped him. "What came aboard?" she asked.

"A barrel of flour and a bushel of dried beans," he said, his voice tight. "We had the misfortune of encountering a skinflint captain.

Nathaniel, too, began to be weakened by hunger. Occasionally he came to the saloon in the evening and sat, barefoot. Skin peeled from his feet where they curved like the bridge of a violin. He whittled, pipe slung from the corner of his mouth. The sweet tobacco smoke touched Azuba's nostrils, rich as the smell of food.

Azuba tried to keep up Carrie's spirits with stories of home. She infused her voice with strength, talked of people and places they could all remember.

Nathaniel's whittling slowed. He did not look at Azuba, nor put a hand to her arm. Neither did she look at him, nor place a hand on his knee. As if, Azuba thought, something as frail as a seedling might be distorted, or diverted.

The sails were so rotted that they barely held the wind. "A poor decision was made in the purchase of that canvas," Nathaniel muttered. "Mother's parsimony, no doubt."

Almost every morning, another had split from head to foot and the sailors were sent aloft to unbend it. Old Harry Steeves, who had not taken part in the melee, had been appointed sailmaker; all day, he leaned over the canvas, his hand dipping, rising, pulling. Whenever possible, Nathaniel and the mates joined him. They sat on the lee side of the deck house, leather palms strapped to their hands, at their feet a box of prickers and marlinspikes and string and needles. They worked together on one sail, sent it to the sailors when it was finished. "Haul it up." They started on the next. There was no canvas left that was not rotted, so Nathaniel asked Azuba to ransack their wardrobe. She and Carrie sat by the men with their scissors. They cut trousers, skirts, blouses and capes to fit, and the men laid the fabric over the rents and tears and sewed it into place.

They were barely able to stomach the food that Mr. Lee continued to cobble together from the scrapings of various barrels. They drank rainwater: every awning was stretched and filled with shot to make hollows to catch the afternoon squalls. Buckets and bowls were wedged beneath waterspouts.

Birds appeared. They flew high over the masts or scudded close to the water. Bent on their own purposes, they were incurious, unaware of their own import. There were other ships in sight, once as many as six. They were too far away, though, to read *Traveller*'s signal flags—and unaware of her plight, did not change course. Gazing after them, Azuba felt like a beggar swept by the skirts of a passing woman.

Please, she thought. *Please, please. Bring us food.*

She could not bear to look at Carrie, whose skin was no longer velvety but rather like brown linen, stretched over cheekbones and the sockets of her eyes.

Fat Labrador herring, Azuba thought, *in wooden barrels.*

She was too weak to rise from bed.

Fat Labrador herring. She imagined herself pressing a knife against iridescent scales. The scales gave way, crumpling. What should she do with the heads? Save them for a chowder, using the last, rubbery potatoes and the sprouting onions and fresh chives. Nathaniel came into the cabin carrying a bowl of watery bean soup. He sat on the bed.

"Sit up. Were you sleeping? Here. I'll help you."

"Carrie?"

"She's at the dining table."

She sat up against the pillows. That morning, she had fallen to her knees as soon as she had risen from bed. She had lain on her side, while Carrie ran for her father. Nathaniel had helped her into bed, ordered her to stay there.

He passed the spoon between her lips.

"The sails are finished."

"I wish I could help sew . . . I am a good . . ."

"Eat."

She opened her mouth. The mirror slushed back and forth; the horizon sliced across the window, dropped away. Nathaniel's cheeks were sunken. Soon they would reveal the shape of his gums. His lips were white, patched with blisters. He held his eyes on the spoon, carrying it carefully to her lips. "I can smell land," he said. "We'll enter the English Channel within a day or two."

"I was dreaming that we were having . . ."

"Eat."

"Captain Bradstock?" Mr. McVale, respectful in the door. "Beg your pardon. Wanted on deck, sir."

Nathaniel nodded, and the young man withdrew. "We have one more day of food, Azuba. I plan to go ashore at the Isle of Wight." He watched the last spoonful of green soup going into her mouth. His eyes lifted to hers as he slid the spoon from her lips. "Do you need a doctor?"

"No. I'm only weak, Nathaniel."

He tested the fat left on her face, pressed her cheekbone. He squeezed her arm. "I don't know if it's been harder having to watch you and Carrie go hungry, or if it would have been worse thinking of you at home, reading the ship news. Thinking I had gone down." His voice was ragged. "Surely you see, Azuba, that on my ship, even when we're close, I have little time for you."

"Yes. I see that. I understand now. But I think of Carrie being with you. How you taught her the stars, the sails."

"I would have written letters to her."

"She was forgetting you. I would show her your picture every day, Nathaniel. But at the end, she looked at it only to humour me. Now she adores you. Think of how you stand together watching the sunset, looking for whales. Think of how you push her on her swing."

His mouth warped. He looked out the window, and she saw that he began to understand her needs, and love's demands.

"You've known the baby growing in my womb. You felt its first kick." She closed her eyes. *Not a time to argue, or persuade.* "You're a good captain, Nathaniel."

"It's my training. Being a captain is what I know."

The bleak brevity of the words, overwhelmed by an unspeakable truth. Now she knew. She had seen him engaging wind, clouds, sun, stars, the shape of waves, the colour of water—knowing, or pondering, how each affected the other and what his own place was within the intricate puzzle and how he might accommodate himself either to survive or to take advantage.

She thought of what land had to offer him. Desk, walls, dust. Bills of lading. Dim-witted cows. Horses in harness.

She drifted to sleep, pressed into the dark-walled corridor of dilemma.

I will never again persuade him to let me sail. He will never stay home.

Later, she woke infused with grief, as from a dream. Death had stooped over her, testing, the way Nathaniel had pinched her cheek. She felt profound surprise. The eventuality that lay beneath life rose to engulf her.

When will I die? Carrie will die.

She felt a blanket of sorrow, closer and more human than grief. And profound regret. Pictured her father, her mother. The house on the promontory, and the salt-sharp wind travelling through its rooms. How easy it would have been to stay there.

She struggled to sit and was overcome with dizziness. A rush of blackness, stars in her head. Head on the pillow. Seeking peace. Sleep.

She opened her eyes and found herself staring at a wool shawl. Blue plaid.

Two sailors, the African and the Swede, showed signs of scurvy. Their gums were swollen and their flesh drooped. Nathaniel pressed a fingertip into the African's leg; the indentation remained.

"Take them on deck," he said to Mr. Dennis. "Bunk 'em down in the lifeboats. Fresh air will do them good."

Later that day, Azuba was strong enough to leave her bed, and she and Carrie went up to the quarterdeck. They could see the two sailors lying in lifeboats lashed to the roofs of the deck house and the galley. Their heads were on pillows; grey sheets covered their bodies. They lay motionless, occasionally lifting a hand to the other sailors, who called down to them from aloft. "Lovely ladies ahead. Shoal of mermaids coming this way. I see one for you, boy. Look alive."

Azuba overheard Nathaniel mutter to the first mate. "The ones with scurvy . . . likely to die if . . . Isle of Wight . . ."

Two sailors were kept on the fore topmast yard with the sole task of watching for land and instructions to sing out at the slightest sign. Nathaniel stood with his glass pressed to his eye.

"I can smell it," Azuba said to Carrie. They sat side by side facing the bow, like people at a theatre.

"I can too," Carrie said.

The air was no longer brisk, pure, but had become as complex as wine, carrying hints of dust, horses, vegetation.

Every few hours her womb tightened like a vice. She slid her bony hands to the bottom of her belly and turned her face away from Carrie.

"Are you going to have the baby?"

"Don't worry, Carrie. Don't worry."

On the next day, birds began alighting on the yards.

Carrie ran below to rouse Azuba from her bed. "Birds, Mama! Birds!"

As soon as they opened the companionway door, Azuba could hear a vast squabbling. The ship was festooned with birds, dozens of gulls beading the yards beneath the spread sails, which were patterned like crazy quilts with squares and lines and zigzags of blue denim and black wool, odd bits of tartan, gingham and red flannel. The gulls ruffled their neck feathers and shrugged, taking small steps to one side or the other, claiming their space or consolidating their comfort, all the while glancing downward with heartless eyes, yellow beaks opening in mewing cries.

"Land," Azuba said. "I can *really* smell land."

They went to the rail and gazed eastward. Just then a sailor sang out. His voice cracked with excitement. "Land ho! Land ho!"

Every man went to the weather rail. There, rising from the water, was an unmoving, irregular blue line—the shape of hills.

Every vestige of order came to a delirious end. The mates flourished their pistols, but still the sailors shouted, whooped, slapped each other on the back. The sick men struggled from the lifeboats, fell onto the deck, were helped to places at the rail. Mr. Lee stood in the galley door, grinning. Mr. Dennis's voice became lighter, lost its demented, quelled fury. Nathaniel slid one arm around Azuba's waist and with the other pulled Carrie to his side. For a few sweet moments, every person on board faced the same direction and thought of home.

Then Nathaniel sent the sailors back to their stations, ordered the Swede and the African back to their lifeboats, sent the off watch to the fo'c'sle under the guard of Mr. McVale. He and the mates climbed to the quarterdeck and stood talking in low voices, with frequent glances at the sails, the wake, the looming land.

Azuba and Carrie remained at the rail, watching a distant fishing boat. Its masts rose from a cloud of milling birds.

Nathaniel came down from the quarterdeck. "I'm going to come up on that boat and see if her captain will take me and Mr. McVale ashore. It will be simpler and quicker for me to leave *Traveller* anchored offshore and go myself for provisions."

"Who will you leave in charge?"

"Mr. Dennis. I don't expect there will be any trouble this close to port, but just in case, I'm leaving a small pistol for you. It will be in my desk. I'll show you where it is."

"May I come with you to get provisions, Papa?"

He paused, looked down at Carrie. He put his hand on her head. "No, you must stay and take care of Mama."

They came up on the fishing boat. There were six men on board, English, not French, and they made arrangements to pick up Nathaniel early the next morning so that he would have all day to reach the island, make purchases and return before nightfall.

❀

That night, Nathaniel did not come to bed. He worked the ship as close to the island as he dared, making frequent soundings with the lead line. Sometime in the early hours of the morning he dropped anchor.

After six months at sea, *Traveller* came to rest.

Azuba was on deck before daybreak. The sea was quiet, with regular swells, and there was a light southeast breeze. The fishing boat was off the starboard bow. Even at this hour, the air was leavened with an earthy warmth. The African had been rousted from his lifeboat, and he stood by the rail, staring with bloodshot eyes as two sailors, Mr. McVale and then Nathaniel climbed down into it. In Nathaniel's breast pocket was the letter to Andrew Moss's mother. The men leaned and pulled, and the oars rose, glistening drops falling from their blades.

The morning clouds spread, and squalls passed across the face of the ocean. Carrie and Azuba wrapped themselves in wool capes. They gazed at the land. "Look, now I can see it!" one or the other of them said all day. The island was wreathed in mist, but when the clouds thinned and the sun touched its slopes, green fields showed behind the grey veils.

The officers were on edge. They kept their pistols visible, paced from one length of the ship to the other. The sails were furled, and all joined or swinging things on the ship made an idle, useless banging, a disorganized sound they had not heard since the doldrums. Mr. Lee passed out a tray filled with chopped pieces of hardtack. Carrie and Azuba sucked on the broken bits, pinching their noses before wetting their mouths with foul water. Occasionally, blackness fringed Azuba's vision and she closed her eyes and sat straight, trying to make room for her lungs. The ship's bell rang every half-hour. The sun reached its zenith and the day lightened, but then the rain became steady and all around the water was stippled. Land birds flew by—doves, crows.

By mid-afternoon, Azuba realized there was no danger of mutiny. It had been food the men wanted, not the ship and its odoriferous cargo. Mr. Perkins allowed the off watch onto the deck of the fo'c'sle. The men sat staring at the island through the drips falling from the brims of their hats. Mr. Dennis took into consideration the men's weakened state and mental exhaustion and set simple tasks: oiling, running the spun-yarn winch.

It was coming on to dusk when Carrie spotted the fishing boat. She had spent the day clutching her doll, sucking her thumb, never taking her eyes from the island. She cried out so loudly that for the first time it was a child's voice that roused every man to his feet. "Papa! Papa!"

In the dusk it was hard to make out that it was the fishing boat, or the direction in which it was moving—but as it came towards them, growing larger, they could make out Nathaniel's figure, his arm waving as broadly over his head as had Azuba's when she sighted the captain's wife. *Traveller's* gulls remained hunched on the yards, as they had all night and all day, even though the fishing boat was accompanied by the mews and harsh cries of its attendant flock.

"Barrels, Carrie," Azuba said. "Barrels and boxes and bags."

"Strawberries!" said Carrie. "I wonder if he brought straw-berries."

The lifeboat went over the side. Men jumped down into it and let fly with the oars. Lanterns in the bow of the fishing boat cast green and red paths over the water. There had been no sunset, only a gradual darkening of the grey sky. Voices came over the water. By the time the provisions were loaded, the returning lifeboat was barely visible. The splash of oars grew louder. The sailors on board *Traveller* surged to the rail, crowding Mr. McVale and Nathaniel as they came up over the rope ladder.

"I've got grub, boys, but you'll have to be sparing of it tonight or you'll be sicker than dogs. Lay back, now, and take your portions, and be happy knowing that there's more where it came from."

Barrels came up, and cloth bags, and one bag in particular that Nathaniel gathered to himself. "This one is for my child."

He left the rest of the task to the mates and came up the steps to the quarterdeck. By the light of the aft lanterns, Azuba could see that although his steps were weary, his eyes were lively with relief. He held out the precious bag for Azuba. He dropped to his knees and spread his arms for his little girl.

"Strawberries," he whispered into her hair. He held her to his chest.

Part Four

ANTWERP

14. Lace and Diamonds

THAT NIGHT, THEY ATE CHICKEN. AT FIRST THEY WERE unable to restrain themselves from tearing at their meat, from stuffing more into their mouths before they had finished swallowing.

"Carefully, slowly," Nathaniel cautioned.

The next day, they ate rabbit stew, and small portions of mashed potatoes, and one baking powder biscuit apiece, with butter. They ate Carrie's strawberries. They drank coffee, tea, fresh water.

They slept deeply, without hunger pains.

A few days later, *Traveller* was towed up the River Scheldt by a side-wheeler tug. The river wound between fields, where June grasses tossed in a warm wind and birds burst from reeds. The water curling at the bows smelled of mud and roots.

Carrie and Azuba wore their best bonnets. They were flattened by their long sojourn at the bottom of their sea chests and Carrie pulled at hers, spreading its sides back from her face. That morning, Azuba had sewn herself, Carrie and Nathaniel into their buttonless clothing.

Traveller rocked in the wake of a passing steamer bound for London. Merchant ships hailed them, outward bound. There were barges and small fishing boats. Blunt-prowed galiots passed, loaded with fresh-cut hay. Women wearing wooden shoes and white caps worked alongside the men, steering or hauling sails, sleeves rolled over sun-browned arms.

Carrie waved ecstatically at every person.

Azuba sat in her chair, thin hands cradling her belly, watching the cathedral tower rise from the meadows. It was at first a silver glint, featureless, part of the grasses like the sun-sleeked reeds, but it grew until it dominated the landscape, connecting land to sky in a monstrous stitch, signifying a world dominated by humans. She sensed the effort it would take to shed the life she had become accustomed to, where earth had dwindled to memory, where she had been tiny beneath the sky. And she realized what Nathaniel must feel each time he returned from the sea—relief for safe arrival tempered by regret for lost singularity. She saw herself as she would appear passing through the city streets: half-starved, her confinement coming, sun-scorched, oily-haired, wearing a salt-stiff dress with no buttons and accompanied by a starved, ragamuffin child. The only women she would be fit to visit would be the other captains' wives, who also knew the true size of the world.

Nathaniel stood with his arms behind his back, watching the approach of Antwerp. He seemed struck to silence. The mates, too, were motionless, tension drained from their faces, leaving only the expectation of what might await them in letters from home. The sailors leaned over the bulwarks, shoulder to shoulder.

The city rising from the fields was inanimate and peaceful, like a painting: stone buildings spreading out from the cathedral, over their roofs a lacework of the masts and rigging of ships moored in the basins; along the embankments, a wash of green lindens, flecked with red flags.

When they disembarked, Carrie lurched forward onto the wharf. She scrambled to her feet and stood with legs spread for balance. She took another step and fell again. "The ground is coming up at me!"

In the carriage going to the Hotel Antoine, Azuba clutched the seat, noticing the strange, jolting energy of horses, their hooves a clatter of steel on stone. She peered up out the window. The great sky was now barely visible, wedged in blue slices above the buildings. Tiny-waisted women passed wearing hoop skirts and leghorn hats, parasols delicate on their shoulders. Two little girls in lacy white dresses and button boots pulled a dog on a red leash. Carrie gripped the carriage windowsill with her brown hands, trying to keep the little girls in view. Not one of these people, Azuba thought, knew of what they had suffered or paid them the slightest attention.

She crossed her arms to cover the stitches on her dress. Nathaniel sat quietly, letting another man be in charge.

It was the city's most elegant hotel, three storeys high with ranks of tall windows separated by pilasters. The manager came from behind a mahogany desk. He bowed to Azuba. She nodded, arm tucked in Nathaniel's, realizing that their clothing exuded the smell of guano.

"We're happy you had a safe passage, Captain Bradstock. What was your route?"

"San Francisco to Callao, then round the Horn."

The manager handed Nathaniel a leather reticule containing their mail and the key to their suite.

They passed through the hotel lobby followed by two porters carrying their baggage. Nathaniel looked up at the ornate plastered ceiling. There were white columns, waxed floors, Persian carpets. Clusters of horsehair couches and rattan tables. Potted palms, ferns, peonies. Azuba saw people glancing up at them, balancing cups of tea or lowering newspapers.

Their suite had two bedrooms, a bath and a sitting room with tall windows. Azuba sat on the edge of a chair, dazed. She had never before realized the luxury of a room that remained still; of airy, clean space. She pulled a handful of letters from the leather bag. She laid her cheek against them, ran her lips over the red sealing wax and the raised ink of the address—*Captain and Mrs. Bradstock, Hotel St. Antoine.*

She ripped them open, regardless of date.

> . . . *fire. They got the horses out before the frame fell. To our dismay, it turns out it was the brother of Mrs. Caldwell, with whom her husband had some difficulty, who set the fire. He has left the country* . . .

> . . . *heavy rain, and then the full fray of the storm came in over the marshes. There was some damage to Father's* . . .

> . . . *shot a partridge. Father hired some boys to pull bushes on the hill back of the barn. I took molasses and tea up to Grammy. Her new rug is coming along very nicely. It is an antique posy* . . .

> . . . *The new minister has been keeping busy. There has been much sickness, and we fear the scarlet fever, for it has been* . . .

The porters carried their luggage into the room. Nathaniel threw open the windows, rolled back his sleeves and went into the bathroom. This hotel had indoor plumbing—a water closet, and a sink and tub with hot and cold running water. He turned on the water, emerged to pay the porters and sent one to make arrangements with a nearby restaurant to have meals sent to their rooms.

Carrie ran back and forth over the thick, soft rug. She tripped, fell, crawled on hands and knees, jumped up, twirled. She went into her bedroom, climbed on the bed and threw herself backwards onto enormous pillows.

"Carrie," Nathaniel called. "Come see!"

Carrie went into the marble-floored bathroom. Nathaniel took her hand and held it in the steaming, shuddering ropes of water.

Azuba shuffled the letters back into their envelopes. For the first time she realized the weight of fear that had pressed on her for so long that she had become accustomed to the dark cast of her spirits.

"They're all well, Nathaniel," she called. She heard the lightness of her voice. "No one has died."

She saw Carrie clamber onto the window seat, and rose with sudden excitement now that her worry was assuaged. She put her arm around Carrie's waist, and together they peered down at the cobbled square. Horses stood hitched to omnibuses, their necks bowed, their ears like tiny folded leaves. In the centre of the square was a bronze statue of Peter Paul Rubens, and just across, the cathedral of Notre Dame, whose tower they had seen like a needle shining from the grasses.

A carillon pealed the hour in a violent, cascading tangle.

"Papa! What is that?"

"Bells, Carrie. Bells in the cathedral," Nathaniel said. It was as if he were still on the quarterdeck, taking command.

"Azuba! You will be first. Hot water, soap, towels . . ."

His tenderness towards her had not left him. It had begun on the day that she had risen from bed and fallen, and he had spoon-fed her. *He has grown used to it in himself,* she thought, sliding through the door that he held open, feeling him pat her shoulder as she stared at the porcelain tub filled with quivering water.

She shed her clothing, left it in a sordid brown heap on the floor. She climbed in, swept with ecstatic gratitude as the hot water enveloped her. To be alive. And the baby within her. Nathaniel and Carrie, chatting on the other side of the door. To have survived.

Her hands and wrists were brown, her white belly ballooned from the water. She arched her back, sank her head underwater. She scrubbed at her legs with a thick cloth, frothy with rose-scented soap. She worked at the filth between her toes, daubed the crusty itch of her anus, gently washed the taut skin of her belly, wondering if the baby could feel the warmth and hear the splashing. She raised a lather in her armpits. She spread her knees, leaned forward, brought handfuls of water to her face.

Nathaniel cracked the door. Carrie's face appeared beneath his arm.

"Is it nice?"

"Are you happy, Mama?"

"Oh." The cool porcelain of the tub in the groove of her neck. She felt herself spreading, separating, like seaweed lifted on an incoming tide. "It's lovely, lovely."

In the evening, a doctor came. He was small, painstaking, with a broad beard splayed against his starched shirt. He frowned at their thinness, pinched Carrie's cheeks, murmured over Azuba's condition.

He proclaimed them to be anemic.

"Eat," he said. "Carefully, carefully. Red meat. The juice of limes, cow's milk, beef liver, oysters, spinach and dried fruit."

He bowed to Azuba. "Rest, Madame," he said. "Drink liquids for the breast milk. Don't worry about the baby. It is likely healthier than you."

Two weeks later, the baby was born. A boy.

Bennett Wight Bradstock.

Bennett for Nathaniel's grandfather. And Nathaniel thought of the middle name, to commemorate their salvation at the Isle of Wight.

It was not a difficult birth. There were no complications, and labour did not last long. Nathaniel had insisted that Azuba be cared for by a doctor and two nurses. He paced the corridor, sat in the lobby or strode around and around the square, and Carrie stayed with Mrs. Marshall, the captain's wife they'd met in the Chincha Islands, recently arrived in port.

When Nathaniel entered the room, Azuba was propped up against pillows holding a bundle wrapped in white flannel. She folded back the cloth. The baby's eyes were closed, their lids like grape skins. His scalp shone with red-gold down.

Nathaniel had not been present for Carrie's birth. He gazed at the baby, touched the wrinkled knuckles. The baby opened his eyes, spread his hand and then grasped Nathaniel's finger.

"Strong," Nathaniel said, moving his finger. His voice was humble. "Is he healthy?"

"Yes, only a little small."

Nathaniel cupped the baby's head with his hard, brown captain's hand.

Azuba saw all previous thoughts and feelings evaporate

from her husband's face. She glimpsed him as he might have been when he himself came into the world.

The bed was like a cloud—feather ticking, white woolen blankets and Belgian lace on the slips of large, down-filled pillows. Every morning, Azuba woke with her eyelids suffused with sunlight. Then her fears rushed up. Starvation. Storm. Waves to stave in the ceiling and fill the saloon with icy water. Mutiny. Carrie going overboard. Squalls, shredded sails. Death.

Then she was swept with relief.

And accompanied with the bliss of safety came a new conviction: never again would she and her children sail on *Traveller.*

She lay savouring her comfort, watching the young nursemaid, Lisette, bending in the sunlight to touch a finger to the baby's cheek.

Azuba had nothing to do but sleep, bathe and nurse. At noontime, while Lisette cared for Bennett, Azuba went to the parlour to eat. She took small, careful mouthfuls and then chewed slowly, gazing at the alien spectacle of a laden plate. Small white potatoes, sprinkled with parsley, shining with butter. Omelettes oozing warm cheese. Clear water in a crystal glass. Fruit tarts, made with raspberries so fresh they tasted of earth and sunlight.

Nathaniel had put the cargo in the hands of a broker and so did not have much to do. He and Carrie visited *Traveller.* She lay in the stone-lined basin, a 250-acre area accessible from the river by a sluiceway, packed with hundreds of ships, surrounded by tall buildings. Their ship was obscured by yellow dust as workers shovelled guano from her hold.

On other days he took her to the "Bourse," or exchange. It surrounded an open square, its lower storey open to the air, its balconies supported by carved stone pillars. Banners hung from balustrades, and doves fluttered into the square, where merchants and their clerks had stands. Carrie clutched Nathaniel's hand as men's voice rose around them.

Azuba did not know if he went there to seek the companionship of other captains or to arrange new cargo. She did not ask, did not want to know. She spent her days listening to the bells of the cathedral and the comfortable chatter of sparrows. *Antwerp.* Her mind offered pictures, blurred at the edges and soft as watercolours, borne by the bells and the birds: chocolates, lace, the smell of river water.

She felt free, drifting in and out of sleep, with neither desire nor regret.

Nathaniel and Azuba sat at the table in their suite. The waiter had cleared away their plates and had swept the tablecloth with a boar-bristle brush. He left only their wineglasses and a crystal vase of white roses. Through the tall windows, they could see balconied stone facades and evening birds wheeling in arcs, as if tethered.

Lisette came from the children's bedroom. "*Monsieur, Madame, les enfants sont profondément endormis.*"

Azuba had stopped the waiter's hand from lighting the tapers on their table, for within the room's twilit half-darkness and the fading fire of sunset were the gleams of silver and polished wood.

"*Merci, Lisette,*" Azuba said. She was learning French from a book Nathaniel had brought her from a bookseller's shop. "*Tu peux partir. A demain.*"

The door made a click as Lisette left the room. The night nurse would come at ten. She slept in the children's room, brought Bennett to Azuba for his nursing and attended to his needs.

Nathaniel had hired Lisette and the night nurse without asking Azuba and been surprised when she had protested that he was spoiling her. "You are a captain's wife," he had said. He'd raised his eyebrows. "When you're on land, you may live in luxury."

Nathaniel reached into his breast pocket. He slid his closed hand across the table, opened his fingers. Two white velvet boxes lay on the cloth. "Open them."

She opened the larger one. On white satin lay a Swiss-made watch hung on a gold chain, and a brooch and earrings, set with a matching pattern of pearls and turquoise.

She could not speak.

The smaller box contained a gold ring with a setting of delicate diamonds and tiny pearls.

"As a memento of our voyage," he said. "It is customary." He touched a diamond. "This is for Andrew Moss, our cabin boy." He touched the next. "And this is for the Horn, and the ship we saw there. This is for your little hen and her eggs. This is for . . ." He paused. " . . . saving a man's life. This is for weevils and pea soup. This . . ." He sighed. Touched another diamond. " . . . is for cold, heat, boredom and hunger, fear and loneliness."

Azuba lifted the watch by its gold chain and slipped it over her head. "And this is for watching you whittle, and for Carrie's swing, and for whales and albatrosses, and fair winds, and sails like marble in moonlight, and your bravery."

She reached forward for his hand, and he slid the ring onto her finger. He pushed back his dainty chair, came around the table and pulled her to her feet. He slid his hands down her sides, slow over her ribs, cupping her uncorseted waist. He brushed his lips to hers, like a bird's wing, fluttering; she felt the shell of his mouth, tasted wine.

She put her head on his chest. The tendril that had sprouted on the ship in the last days was still tender.

Oh, she thought. *I never want to endure another voyage like the last. Yet I love him, he loves me. I never want to be parted . . .*

She wondered if he felt the same way. And if so, whether he might be content to come home with her and the children. She did not dare to ask.

Eleven of the twelve ships that had been at the Chincha Islands had arrived in Antwerp.

Azuba and Carrie, with Lisette and the baby, spent a morning with the other captains' wives—"sister sailors," they called each other. Every woman had a small satin-lined box presented to her by her husband to commemorate their voyage, and the women passed them around, exchanging memories. They told of evenings in foreign ports, of pet monkeys in clothing, of backgammon games and Spanish wine. There were veiled allusions to rollicking nights. None bore the dark stories that glinted in Azuba's diamonds. She had thought she might speak of her voyage, share her feelings, but she could not, she saw, with any of these women. None had suffered hunger, mutiny or terror. With the exception of Mrs. Marshall, they seemed as willing to be glorified, commanded and eclipsed by their men as the captains' wives in Whelan's Cove.

Mrs. Marshall was glad to see Carrie and tickled the baby's cheek. She was no longer slovenly, as she had been on board *Suzanna,* but wore a green and red striped dress with enormous satin-bound sleeves. Her voice was as loud as if she still stood on deck, roaring advice to her husband.

" . . . at dinner," she said. "And Mr. Marshall said I was a damned fine navigator. 'She can haul sails as well as any jack tar,' he said. 'I'd never leave home without her,' he said."

Mrs. Marshall's husband was as large and loud as she.

Azuba opened the small box she held on her lap. Soon she would pass it around the circle of women. They would admire the ring—gasp, cluck.

A memento. To memorialize. And what it memorialized in her case, Azuba thought, was near-death, and rebirth. This was a story she could not tell.

"And Captain Bradstock," Mrs. Marshall was saying. "Does he enjoy your presence on board? Of course he does, what a question! A lovely young creature like you."

She stretched out her thick-fingered hand for Azuba's velvet box. Her eyes were shrewd, and Azuba kept hers lowered.

One morning, they went to visit Mrs. Lattimer, of the American ship *Wellfleet,* from Mystic.

"Remember?" Azuba said to Carrie as they rode through the streets in a carriage. "She's the one who taught us how to make moss pictures." They still had them, seaweed floated over paper and left to dry.

Azuba and Mrs. Lattimer sat with their handwork while Carrie occupied herself with a book and Lisette took the baby to a bedroom. Mrs. Lattimer was embroidering slipper tops for her husband.

"Did you see the engagement off Cherbourg?" She was sharp-faced, with quick, glancing eyes and a mouth soured by crooked teeth. After losing her child overboard, she had had no other children.

"No," said Azuba.

"Confederate ship, *Alabama,* put into the French port for refitting. Challenged to a ship-to-ship duel by the Union ship, *Kearsage.* The battle took place in the English Channel, and the Confederate ship sank after only an hour's engagement."

"We must have passed the spot a few days earlier," Azuba said.

"A notorious raider, the *Alabama*," Mrs. Lattimer remarked, after a silence in which her needle, pulling red thread through black silk, made a rough rasping. "Sank many an unarmed Union merchantman."

The woman seemed vengeful, with frightening energy. She had shown Azuba a diary she kept of the items she had sewn, knitted, embroidered or quilted on each voyage.

"Their captain, Captain Raphael Semmes, was wounded. He was saved by the British. More's the pity, I say."

Traveller flew the British flag. Azuba did not reply.

The woman seemed hardly to notice the room, with its graceful cornices, its marble fireplace and vases filled with bearded irises. As she watched Mrs. Lattimer's fierce stitches, Azuba's needle lay idle. She brushed one hand down her hoop skirt. Carrie wore a white dress with puffed sleeves, and white stockings, and black button boots.

"I've often wondered," Azuba said, "what became of a woman I met in Callao. Her name was Louisa. I wonder if she and her daughter have returned to their village in Maine."

"Don't know," said Mrs. Lattimer. "You heard about Mrs. Davis? She was one of us at the Chinchas."

"Yes, of course."

Mrs. Davis had been on board an American ship, the largest in the harbour. The ship had arrived towing a gigantic turtle upon which, one evening, they had all dined.

"Taken by pirates," Mrs. Lattimer said. Her voice darkened. "The captain and the mates were overcome." She did not look up from her work. "Pirates delivered them to the *Alabama*. Before their eyes, their own ship was burned. That beautiful ship, if you remember. Such a waste. Mrs. Davis was kept below decks in the Confederate ship for two weeks. She never knew what had become of her husband until they were reunited when the scum put them off on the coast of Spain."

Carrie was bent over her book. She turned no pages.

"Thank the Lord they did not have children," Mrs. Lattimer added.

Her skin was so sun-darkened as to make her seem to be suffering from some disease like gout. She had dressed the part best suited to the finery that surrounded her, but as if with mute exasperation. When she returned to Mystic, she would change into what was appropriate there, and then, once again, return to the pattens and loose dresses of her life below decks. Her permanent state of displeasure suggested that even within herself she was but temporarily lodged.

Azuba rose to leave. The woman's savage needle rendered her speechless.

She remembered her girlhood vision of captains' wives. She had thought they were independent, free. She saw now that shipboard life wrought changes of different kinds on different women. Even the few older women in Callao who had seemed content and confident might, like Mrs. Marshall, have made the choice to abandon their children. Their hearts might ache. They might be hardened by brutality, numbed by fear.

And even they, when on board, were within the domain of their captain husbands, and served under his command.

When Azuba had fully recovered from her lying in, they went on family excursions, embarking in one of the cabs parked in front of the hotel. The cabs had four horses, with hoods that could be removed for sightseeing. They passed the guild houses on the main square, their stone facades carved into the form of lace or in the shape of pillars and beams that sprouted stone statues, gargoyles and flower-boxed balconies. There were long flags and banners suspended from the halls for archers, coopers, tailors, carpenters. They visited the zoological gardens, where Azuba lingered in the palm house, and they happened on the sight of live rabbits being flung into the serpent cage. Nathaniel read from their guidebook that the collection of blue monkeys was the largest in Europe.

The square on which the hotel was located was called Place Verte. Every building on the square had window boxes filled with red geraniums, and the bronze statue of Rubens gleamed in the sunlight. The cathedral was so tall that from the tower, in clear weather and with a telescope, one could see Brussels. At the foot of the tower, chunks of brass were imbedded in the pavement, marking all the pieces of the body of a man who had fallen. Carrie was fascinated by this story and bent backwards with her hands at her waist, trying to see the top, discovering the illusion made by the passing clouds of the tower rushing forward to tip on her. She longed to climb it, but Nathaniel told her six hundred steps were too many.

In their hotel suite, Carrie swung a silver spoon over Bennett's face, exclaiming at how he began to follow it with his eyes. He was plump and healthy, and had begun to smile. Nathaniel loved to prop the baby on his lap and tell stories to both him and Carrie.

Azuba wrote to her parents of all these things. She added:

Yet in spite of this lovely interlude, I begin to miss home, and to think of you. Have the men begun cutting the marsh grass? Are your delphiniums blooming, Mother? I do not know what Nathaniel's plans are, but I am so happy, at this moment, that I have not troubled my state of mind by asking . . .

She put down her pen. They could go home on one of the new steamers, with doctors aboard, and hot and cold running water. She sensed that Nathaniel was ready to give up his life at sea—for love of his children. For love of her. He would come home, and this time he would stay.

Azuba looked down from her window to see Nathaniel and Carrie setting off, holding hands. They were going to the Castle Steen, now an archaeological museum. Sunlight limned them as they passed into the open square. She sensed that Nathaniel's gentleness with Carrie was in part informed by his regret for the things he had missed—her first steps, her first words; the day she had been put into a long dress, or had been given her own fork, or had celebrated her first birthday.

Azuba placed a chair so that the sun would fall on her and she could look out on the square as she nursed. She unbuttoned her dress. Lisette bent, lowering the baby into her arms. Everything was immaculate, cleaner even than Azuba or her mother could keep their own homes. Staff took their clothing to the hotel laundry and returned it washed, bleached, starched and ironed.

Her fingers relaxed against the lace-edged shawl that wrapped the child. Shed of her cumbersome belly, she felt weightless, easy in her body. A froth of bubbles outlined Bennett's lips. The baby's eyes flew open as the carillon began its morning concert. She hummed, ran a finger over his scalp. "My sweet Bennett Bradstock," she said. "Hush, now."

The notes were so lush and heavy that they spilled from the cathedral tower like shot birds, colliding with one another. She thought of the man who played the carillon. He was broad-shouldered, massive. They had been told that he wore heavy leather gloves to play, and that he was weary after fifteen minutes. She imagined him striving in his small, dark room, separate from the great sound he produced. And then her mind went to the women who spun flax for Brussels lace, rendering thread so fine, so gossamer, that it was drawn from the distaff over a piece of black paper, in a room pitch-dark save for a single ray of light focused on the emerging strand.

People who make beauty, Azuba thought, *alone, and in darkness. But at what cost?*

And it occurred to her that Nathaniel was like the man in the tower. Expending himself, alone on the desolate seas. Exhibiting, for no one to see, bravery, strength, endurance, skill. Talking to his canaries. His tenderness a dormant skill. Sending home money and precious gifts to his family.

And me, she thought. *If I were to return to the sail house and bring up my family alone, I would be like the lacemakers.* She pictured the way her hands would braid hair, spin wool, write accounts. How she would soothe arguments, mend wounded spirits. Efficiently, she would run her large house, pack Bennett's trunks when it was time for him to go to the Academy, prepare Carrie for her first ball. She saw patience turn to endurance, unleavened by joy.

Each would lose themselves, subsumed by the effort of sustaining aloneness.

She closed her eyes, drowsed into the half-sleep where sounds are exaggerated—Lisette setting a china coffee pot on the marble table, horse hooves on cobblestones.

Sunlight made a fiery world on the insides of her eyelids.

It was light that had kept her from despair, a particular quality of light, like hints of tenderness in a hard man. Sometimes this light had made a dusting around the cracks of the closed deadlights; sometimes it sleeked the canary's feathers or hung in a silver line between Carrie's half-closed eyelids. Sometimes it wavered, soft, pink, on dawn wavelets.

Sometimes it gathered in the moonlight that shadowed the folds of night sails, or pooled on the sanded decks. It signified something nameless that she had insisted on imagining, even when, as during the burning glare of the doldrums or in storms, it seemed to have been obliterated from the earth.

15. Chameleon

"I WOULD LOVE TO GO TO NOTRE DAME," AZUBA SAID. Nathaniel and Carrie had gone to the zoological gardens. "*Je voudrais . . .*"

Lisette put down her work, made shooing motions. "*Allez! Allez! L'enfant dort, Madame, vous pouvez partir.*"

It had rained in the night, and the air was cool. Azuba swept down the stairs, went through the lobby. She wore a cobalt blue dress with braided tabs and a red sweeper hem to protect the silk from the ground; a hat with rolled sides and velvet ribbons; and a shawl trimmed with Belgian lace. The manager raised his eyebrows and made a slight bow from the waist. "*Bonjour, Madame.*"

Home now seemed remote. She was enthralled by Antwerp, and once her health was completely restored, she spent her days sightseeing. Nights, as she drifted to sleep, her mind teemed with images: gilded clouds over the lowlands, inhabited by cherubs and angels like those of Rubens's paintings; martyred saints with bony sandalled feet; lambs, swords, demons and dragons. Names echoed like Gregorian chants—the churches of St. Andrew, St. George, St. Jacques, St. Augustine, Carolus Borromeus. She pictured priests and merchants, the city's cross-current of commerce and

Christianity, every square ringed with guild houses, yet every gate, pump and fountain inscribed with crosses or the figures of saints. She saw women wearing red boots, bolero jackets, straw hats trimmed with ostrich feathers; merchants in lemon yellow gloves; monks in robes and cowls.

She crossed the square. Behind the cathedral tower, white clouds loomed against an ominous sky. Light struck the stained glass windows and made the shadows deep and sharp. Azuba stood on the wet cobblestones gazing up at the Gothic profusion of spires. It was foreboding, ecstatic. She pictured her own white-painted church set in the midst of hayfields, a sky brewing storm, and the muttering of thunder as women descended from carriages carrying delphiniums and peonies.

In the cathedral, the air smelled of sweet, ancient wood, and she felt herself dwindle as she walked down the aisle, dwarfed by 125 pillars marching away into the gloom. She spread her hands over her skirts to quiet their rustling. Small knockings—a prayer stool, the snick of a latch—were magnified, reverberant. And she thought how their voyage on *Traveller* seemed a barely plausible memory: even as they had seen icebergs and abandoned ships, even as Nathaniel had raised his pistol, even as she had felt forsaken by God, sunlight had slanted through these stained glass windows and hung, dust-spun, between the pillars.

She made her way to Rubens's *Assumption of the Virgin,* hung on the high altarpiece. The Virgin Mary sat among clouds, surrounded by a choir of angels, her face blissful. Azuba stood absorbed in the painting's beauty, pondering how the mother of a murdered son could be at peace. She pictured Andrew's mother, Mrs. Moss, hanging out her laundry, and wondered who had delivered the letter telling her of her son's death, and whether she had derived any comfort from the simple service at their church.

Footsteps echoed on the stones. The crisp tapping of a man's heels. She closed her eyes, waited for them to pass, savouring the awe that had stolen into her as she contemplated the Virgin's face.

Peace. This is peace.

There was a touch on her arm.

She turned, startled. She opened her eyes.

A man stood close to her. He was neither smiling nor not smiling. Her heart swelled and shrank. She drew a deep breath and stepped back.

"Reverend Walton!"

It could not be, she was mistaken. She felt a deep blush sweep her cheeks.

In one arm, cradled like a palette, the man held a felt bowler. In the other, he carried a walking stick. He wore a cream-coloured linen sack coat, light woolen trousers, a black silk tie with hanging ends. His hair was neatly parted, slicked with oil. He seemed ghostly, pale, an apparition of Simon Walton.

His eyes were stricken, shocked. Veiled with apprehension.

He bowed.

"It can't be," she said. She did not take her hands from her breast, where they had flown. "But it is. It *is* you. It is too incredible. What are the chances of our paths crossing?"

His cheeks bore a burn of embarrassment. "Mrs. Bradstock. I saw you just as I was about to pass by. I wasn't sure it was you; you are so changed. I turned to see. If I hadn't, we would have been ships that pass in the night."

Azuba stood staring at him. In the dusty sunlight, he was blurred, as Carrie and Nathaniel had been crossing the square. His hair was hazed; she could see light in the down of his cheeks, a glistening along his half-parted lips.

He lifted his hand, the fingers open. She reached forward. Their hands clasped. She had last seen him as she stood in the lane, and he had been small in the blowing grasses, holding his easel and bags.

"I have thought of you." She heard herself speak and felt outside herself, overhead and looking down, like one of the cathedral sparrows.

"I thought of you, too," said Simon. He had dropped her hand, quickly. He stood straight-backed, his voice polite, guarded. She saw by the half-shy surprise in his eyes how she had changed. "I thought that you were lost. It was everywhere in New Brunswick. That Captain Bradstock took his wife and child, and the ship was lost."

"My parents," she said. "Oh, my poor parents. They know by now. They know we are safe."

She withdrew her hand, clasped her waist. She could not adjust to the fact of his presence: the folds of his jacket, the light in his eyelashes. He had drifted in her mind as a placatory vision summoned in times of despair. She had taken his image as her own and distorted it.

"Did you know we were in Antwerp?" she said.

"No, no." He stepped back. Agitated. "No, this is a complete surprise. I have been staying in Paris. I have recently relocated to Antwerp. I have taken rooms."

"What are you doing now?" she asked.

"I'm learning to become a photographer." He pointed at a stained glass window. "Light. I want to learn to use it. To preserve the world as it really is. Not as I render it in my clumsy paintings."

"Are you no longer . . ."

"No. I have left the ministry." He glanced back at the window, took out his pocket watch. "Would you mind if we walked as we talk? I have an appointment."

"No, of course."

The echo of heel-struck stone was portentous as they

exchanged news in brief sentences, as strangers do—her new baby, the well-being of parents and Carrie. Azuba could not bring herself to say Nathaniel's name, nor did Simon ask after him.

He stopped at the second chapel on the south side of the ambulatory, where there was a carved confessional and paintings of the descent of the Holy Ghost and the Adoration of the Shepherds.

"I confess that it's an appointment with time," he said. "This is where you must stand to see the *Assumption* when the sun strikes it at noon. See?"

They stood in silence, watching as Mary's face was touched by light.

"Just now, I was almost hearing the sound of the angels singing," Azuba said. She realized that she could speak to this man as easily as she spoke to Carrie. "It's my favourite painting in this cathedral."

"Mine, as well," Simon said. He pressed three fingers to his lips, gazing upward. He was clean-shaven, pale-skinned. He seemed more serene than when she had known him in Whelan's Cove.

He lowered his voice. "I have no wish, anymore, to explain or interpret God's will."

Azuba felt the familiar urge to confess to this man. To tell him things she could tell no one else, since his response was unjudging. She remembered how he made her feel stronger, more sure of herself. It was as if there were nothing she could say that he would disagree with.

"I am relieved," he said. "I felt an imposter. As I was."

He, too, tells me things I'm certain he tells no one else, she thought, hiding her pleasure.

He narrowed his eyes at a statue in Carrara marble of the Madonna and Child.

"What will you photograph?" she asked.

"Portraits. Still lifes. I've been studying Rembrandt's portraits, Brueghel's rabbits, Vermeer's interiors. I want to have a studio in Saint John."

They turned from the painting, walked down an aisle.

What am I going to do? Should I keep his presence a secret?

She stopped, turned to look into his eyes. "I have told my husband that nothing . . ." Her voice wavered. He looked away, and then back. " . . . happened . . ." She took a breath so quick it came as a tiny gasp.

He dropped his eyes.

Terrified of Nathaniel. He's terrified.

He stood with his walking stick planted on the worn stones, hat hanging from one hand. Azuba felt sorry for him, and wanted to bring him into her life, clearly defined as her friend. She could make Nathaniel see what an inoffensive man Simon was, she argued to herself; she could make him see how much Carrie enjoyed Simon's drawings of ducks in hats. She could make Nathaniel understand that he had nothing to fear from this friendship. The illusion rose before her of Nathaniel and Simon coming to like one another. She imagined the day when they would go to Mr. Walton's photography studio and he would photograph their family.

"How can we be in the same city and not meet?" She heard a new vibrancy in her voice—warm, bemused—and remembered grinding up buttons to feed her starving child.

"I don't think it is possible," he said. "I don't think I would enjoy meeting your husband, believing of me what he does."

"But he doesn't think badly of you . . ." Her voice failed, then strengthened. "I have told him, as I said. Carrie would adore to see you. Besides, you see, we will not be able to avoid one another. Unless you leave the city, it is only a matter of time until we meet. We live just there." She pointed across the square at the hotel.

"Well," he said. "You must pave the way for me."

And what will Nathaniel say. How dare I do this?

She felt hot prickling in her breasts and turned away, pressing the insides of her wrists to her dress. "The baby!"

"I beg your pardon?"

"It's time to feed the baby." She smiled. "I can tell he's awake."

She began to hurry back down the aisle, thinking of Lisette walking with Bennett in her arms, the dissonance of wailing and appeasement.

They parted outside the cathedral. The clouds were breaking, and sun warmed the Hotel St. Antoine. The bells were just finishing their noon chorus.

"Come to the hotel, then? At eight o'clock."

He wrote his address in a small notebook, handed her the page, bowed.

"I know that it will be awkward, Nathaniel. But it was a coincidence, and cannot be undone. He will be staying here for some time. We won't be able to avoid him."

"He should leave the city, knowing we are here."

"Who are we to ask that of him? He is a student of art. He needs to be here as much as we do."

He went to the window and looked down at the square.

"Nathaniel, do you think that if anything had happened between us I would have told you that I had met him? If I were guilty, I would not have dared to invite him into your presence. I will tell you straight out, I invited him so you might see what a harmless, pleasant person he is, so inferior to you as to make it a matter of ridiculousness for you to be jealous."

He was silent.

"To show you how . . . kind he is to Carrie. He draws such funny—"

He turned, stared at her. The weeks of growing tenderness seemed undone. "Let the wretched man visit. I will be civil."

She looked away. These were eyes she could not meet. She wished that she had not met Simon in the cathedral.

The night nurse shooed Carrie into the parlour just as Nathaniel and Simon finished shaking hands. Azuba was about to speak. Simon was in an agony of embarrassment, not knowing where to look. Nathaniel had begun to turn away, patting his pocket, seeking his pipe.

Carrie stopped, her mouth open. "Papa! It's Mama's friend!"

She ran to Simon, whose face opened in a smile. He swept forward, made an exaggerated bow. "*Mademoiselle Bradstock, je suis ravie de te revoir.*"

Azuba repressed a flurry of speech to cover Nathaniel's curtness, since at Carrie's words he paused and a half-smile shadowed his lips, an unconscious reflection of the child's delight.

"Will you draw me pictures?"

"Certainly, if your parents will allow . . ."

Nathaniel began to stuff his pipe, glancing from beneath his eyebrows. And Azuba saw it dawn on Nathaniel that Carrie, too, wanted to share Simon with him. That Simon was a part of their life—hers and Carrie's—as it had been, once.

Several days later, Azuba and Nathaniel sent Mr. Walton an invitation to join them at the hotel's *table d'hôte*. They sat in the hotel dining room at their customary table beside the window.

"I came on the *Liverpool*," Simon said.

Nathaniel raised his eyebrows.

"An iron steamship," Simon went on, so nervous, Azuba saw, that he barely knew what he said. "Constructed on the Clyde. It is an extraordinary ship. They took us on a tour of her. Watertight iron sections. Staffed with experienced surgeons. Carries fire annihilators. I had a first-class berth for eighty dollars. I'm glad it was recommended to me to take a thin India rubber coat. It rained a great deal, and I . . . I liked to take my exercise on deck. Twelve days to cross the Atlantic. Quite remarkable."

"Where are you living back home?" Azuba asked, keeping her voice matter-of-fact.

"With my parents and sister. The house is large. I've made a studio in an upstairs room. When I return, I'll seek a place of my own in Saint John. I've been gone for three months."

The dining room windows were open so the diners might enjoy the military band that played in the square every evening. There was a rattle of carriage wheels on cobblestones, the garbled clink and gabble of voices and cutlery. Every table was filled. Waiters swept past, eyes preoccupied, trays held high. Azuba noticed Nathaniel and Simon exchange a glance shaded by doubt, a yielding of previous assumptions. She gazed at the flowers in a window box just beyond the open, paneless window.

"Did you encounter any bad—" Nathaniel began.

"We were starving," she said. It was like the moment when she had spoken the truth to Nathaniel's mother. Long-withheld feelings, like split seeds, began an uncertain life. She leaned forward, her hand gripping a knife set crosswise. Her voice was low, urgent. "Food was stolen from the ship in Callao, and we were trapped in the doldrums. We ran out of food. I thought we'd die before reaching land. I thought our ship would be found adrift, filled with skeletons."

Nathaniel turned to her. He laid his hand on her shoulder. "Azuba. Please."

Her eyes filled with tears. She stared at Simon. "Our water was the colour of tea. Our soup had weevils in it. Carrie became so weak that she could do nothing."

She felt vast grief at the spectre of what might have been. She had kept it at bay, but now it came, a confession: what she had done to her child, to herself, to Nathaniel. And Simon's implicit connection.

Simon sat with his hands in his lap, eyes on the tablecloth.

Nathaniel spoke, after a silence. His voice was stiff. "We were still alive, however, by the time we reached the Isle of Wight." His wrist was brown against the starched cuff of his shirt and lay incongruous amidst the silverware, fingers loose on the facets of his goblet stem.

There was another long silence. Azuba's face burned.

I did not mean you were a bad captain, she thought. *I did not mean to accuse you.*

The waiters—two to a table—deftly slid plates of trussed snipes in front of them. Each tiny bird's head and neck was twisted beneath its body. The legs were fastened together with a wooden skewer. Neither man moved until Azuba reached forward and drew the skewer from her bird.

"You were feared lost," Simon said. His voice was gentle. "I read of it in the paper. It was a great day, I'm sure, when news of your arrival reached Whelan's Cove."

Azuba drank water to calm herself. They occupied themselves with the birds, tearing slivers of meat from frail bones.

"Were there . . ." said Simon. He pushed away the plate of twiggy bones. "How was the . . ."

"It was a hard voyage," said Nathaniel. "But no harder than most. We were not sailing in an iron ship, and we had no surgeon. We suffered a loss, one seaman who fell from the mast. The weather around the Horn was as one expects it to be. All's well as ends well."

Nathaniel looked hard at Simon, and Azuba saw that his curiosity was not for the man but for what his wife might see in him.

"What brings you to Belgium?" He assumed an answer that could have no reference to his own interests, excluding Simon from his fraternity of captains and their talk of weather and cargo.

Simon leaned back as a waiter set down a plate of steaming beef. "I feel that one is born with a predilection. My father does not believe in such an idea, and I let myself be persuaded into the church. I felt, at first, that I could be a minister. I was wrong. After I left Whelan's Cove . . ." He said it with composure. "I went to Fredericton. I made my decision when I realized the commercial potential of photography. I've wasted time. I hope I've not hurt anyone in the process."

He planted the tines of his fork in his beef, glanced at Nathaniel as he drew his knife. "And you, Captain Bradstock?" Simon said. "Did you choose your profession?"

Nathaniel stared across the room, oblivious of crystal and silver, women with ringleted hair, brocade drapery. Azuba saw that he was on the quarterdeck beneath racing cloud shadows, reviewing every line, yard and man, knowing where each was meant to be.

He rotated the goblet's faceted stem. "Everything in our house came from foreign ports. I grew up with two older brothers, both sea captains. Their letters were read aloud. We lived in expectation of their news, and their return. It was a man's life, as far as I was concerned. I don't remember a time when I did not plan to be a ship's captain."

His jaw locked down. In his voice was emotion that he would rather have kept hidden.

The following day, Simon took up what Azuba had thought of as a courtesy invitation to tea. He arrived with the hopeful mien of loneliness. Nathaniel was formal, but could not, Azuba saw, remain hostile. He treated Simon like a man beneath his contempt. Simon was calm. He accepted their invitation to return, and came the next day and walked with the family on the promenoir by the river. On the third day, he arrived when Nathaniel was away.

"I should leave," he said.

"No, Simon. It's perfectly fine. Lisette is here, and Carrie."

"I thought to paint a picture of Carrie," Simon said.

Azuba set the baby's cradle in a patch of sunlight. She sat rocking it with her toe, humming. Simon took out his water-colours and bent over the marble table. Carrie sat upright on a chair with blue velvet upholstery, ankles crossed.

He made Whelan's Cove feel less like a dream or a picture in a book.

"Remember the time we were picking blackberries in Mr. McIntyre's pasture?" Azuba said.

He laughed. "Ah, the bull. My shirt."

They laughed. Carrie laughed. The door opened, and Nathaniel entered.

"We were reminiscing of home," Azuba said. Their laughter died, but their faces remained happy.

When Simon had gone, Azuba apologized. "Do you mind, Nathaniel? He's lonely. And he reminds me of home."

"No," he said. Impatient. "I don't mind."

"Do you still—"

He flicked the back of his hand as if the words were a fly. "Pompous little man," he muttered.

"He is not."

"Suit yourself."

Nathaniel went on a spending spree. He bought Carrie a doll the size of Bennett, with real blond hair, face, arms and legs made of china, a little red mouth and leather black button shoes. She had an entire wardrobe—a blue silk cape with jet beads, kid gloves, satin sashes and a nightdress with seed pearl buttons. He bought Azuba dresses, gloves, dress patterns and silks. He suggested that they buy a Persian carpet for the sail house, and they spent an afternoon finding one, and in the process bought china, linen sheets and pillow slips, and pillows filled with the down of the great white albatross. Nathaniel ordered the shops to pack these things and ship them. By the end of the day, Azuba was exhausted and could barely remember what they had purchased.

Over wine, after supper, Nathaniel bent a speculative look at her, as he did when making his moves at the checkerboard. "That carpet will look well in the parlour," he said.

"Yes, but you must be certain to remove your boots."

She avoided his eyes. They were eating alone on this night in their suite. Since Simon had arrived, Azuba felt livelier. She remembered how she had been accustomed to storing things up to show Simon, or tell him about—things of light and evanescence, like fog drifting over daisies, or the chalice of a poppy seed pod. They were things that he would capture and save for her, in drawings, paintings. There was a part of her that corresponded to these things, a love of beauty that she could not share with Nathaniel. She loved, not Simon, but his appreciation of things frail and fleeting; she loved his acknowledgement of this part of her. And he reminded her of home, that vivid year after the miscarriage when her heart had been breaking, and was then healed by the companionship they had enjoyed.

Yet even as she thought these things, Azuba felt duplicity seeping through the fine cracks of her marriage.

"You must be certain to remove your boots," she had said to Nathaniel. And waited to hear him smile, and agree that, yes, he would. Indicating that he had bought these things—china, linen and pillows—for the life they would have together in the sail house when he and she and the children returned home from Antwerp. He would take over his father's business. He would become an important man of Whelan's Cove, a town councillor, a deacon. They would go together to cotillions; to the launching of new ships; to church. They would walk on the headland with their dog. And watch their children grow.

All this went through her mind in the moment it took to slice a fat chunk of beef and lift it to her mouth.

They were so simple, those unspeakable words.

What are we going to do next?

Most of the other captains' wives had already left with their husbands, or else were packing their trunks to return home.

He was gazing up at the cathedral tower, visible in the topmost panes of the window. "We'll have to take Carrie up there before we leave Antwerp," he said.

Nathaniel had made an arrangement with a flower shop; every fourth morning, a maid arrived with a fresh bouquet. Azuba wondered if he remembered the shrivelled plants she had thrown overboard. Today, there were lilies: ivory and pink.

There was a knock on the door, and she opened it with a lily in her hand.

"Good morning, Simon!"

Under one arm were tucked two books: *Harper's Handbook* and *Baedeker.* There was a worried frown on his forehead. He remained standing in the hall. "I met Captain Bradstock in the street just now. We exchanged greetings. Perhaps I should come back on another day. When he's here."

"No, Simon. He is perfectly happy to have you visit. He doesn't think . . ." She trailed her hand, embarrassed.

Still Simon stood by the door, prepared to retreat. He was not, she saw, challenged by Nathaniel, as were her brothers, but lessened—made to feel effete. *You are not,* she wanted to say. *You're not like any man I've ever known.*

She took him by the hand, pulled him into the room. "Come in, come in!"

And surely Simon feels the same way about me as I do about him, she thought. Although lately she had begun to notice something catlike about him, a wary self-absorption. And it was somehow reflected in herself, a thing that she disliked, and tried to ignore.

Carrie came into the room. "*Bonjour, Monsieur Walton.* Are you going to take us somewhere today?"

"Well," he said. He looked down at the books under his arms. "If you have no other plans?" He glanced at Azuba. It was like being in a sanctuary, going places with Simon. A kind of blessed secrecy.

But wrong, she realized suddenly. It was wrong.

"No, we have no plans," she said. "Other than returning at noon to feed Bennett."

They gathered shawls and bonnets, went down through the lobby and out onto the sunny street.

"The *Palais du Roi,*" Simon pointed with his walking stick. "Built in 1745 for a wealthy citizen, then used as the residence of Belgian kings. And there. The home of Rubens's parents. Newly restored. Corinthian columns, do you see? And the bust of Rubens, there at the top."

"Yes."

Her eyes followed the direction of his stick. She did not mind his instruction. It was like learning the names of crustaceans and wildflowers, an innocent pastime. Nathaniel became impatient when she asked questions, stabbing his finger at the compass, or at sails, or at storm-bearing clouds. His teachings were imbued with the harsh prickle of survival.

Passersby, Azuba thought, *might think that Simon and I were husband and wife, walking with our child.* The thought made her uneasy, and she reached for Carrie and walked one step farther away from Simon.

They turned down a side street, emerged in a small, quiet square, Place Leopold, where they entered the botanical museum. Inside, there was an irregular patter of dripping water, the smell of sunstruck soil. The glass ceiling was tinged green. Stone pathways were cushioned with moss, as soft to the feet as a layer of felt.

They drifted, stopping to inspect the veined petals of orchids, or to point out snails sliding along twigs, or to read Latin names. They tipped their heads to see the uppermost branches of palm trees bent by the ceiling, their trunks strangled by lianas and vines. Azuba let Carrie run ahead.

The air was cloying, reminding Azuba of the doldrums when she and Carrie had sat half-naked in the insufferable humidity. They sat on a stone bench. Simon removed his hat, passed his fingers over his forehead.

"What did you do with all your specimens?" she asked. She spoke as if in a church, hushed.

"They're packed away in crates. Waiting for me to find studio space."

Bird chatter came from the ceiling, and Azuba looked up and saw a flash of scarlet and aquamarine. She turned to share her discovery and saw that he had become preoccupied, sitting with one leg crossed over the other, hands clasping his knee. His foot stirred, and he stared at the mossy stones. His eyes were perturbed, excited. He smiled, and his eyebrows raised, his mouth twitched. She saw that he was conducting an inner dialogue.

He's thinking of someone.

She felt a sear of homesickness for *Traveller,* for the saloon, and a particular night when Nathaniel had sung "Shule Agra," and Gig had laid his head in her lap, and she'd felt the narrowness of the dog's skull, so close beneath the soft fur. She realized, suddenly, that it was necessary for her that Simon be lonely. Otherwise, she could not justify this friendship and should not be here with him—a married woman, alone, without her husband. She had fostered the illusion of herself as being nothing more than attentive, even motherly, to a lonely young man from home.

She sensed that he was not lonely. That perhaps he, too, felt an obligation to be with her. She plucked at the front of her dress. Nathaniel had tightened her stays so tightly that she could not take a full breath.

"Simon," she said. His clothing, as always, smelled of some astringent sweetness. As from sachets. Or a woman's perfume.

He started, raised his eyes to hers.

"Do you remember the gannet?"

It had been a perfect specimen, a northern gannet blown off course by a hurricane. It was dead, and they'd laid it in Azuba's cape and lugged it up the steep path. Carrie had tried to help, but had fallen, scraping her arm. Simon, too, had taken a fall from a rock. The hurricane's remnants had made the September day wild and windy, and the gale had broken every sunflower and rendered the corn patch a mass of dirt-clung roots and tangled stalks.

In the kitchen, Simon had rolled up the leg of his trousers. He had done it discreetly, but Azuba had noticed and swept around to see. His leg was torn and bleeding.

"You mashed your shin?"

"Ah, yes. My shin."

She'd bathed it with a soapy flannel, after she had cleaned Carrie's arm. She remembered herself thinking, as she did so, how a woman loves, occasionally, to mother her husband, and how Nathaniel had never allowed her to do so.

Simon had sat on Grammy's hooked rug before the parlour stove and played with Carrie and her ark while Hannah and Azuba made supper. The gannet remained outside on the porch. Afterwards, Simon had walked away into the wind with the bird wrapped in a cape and slung over his shoulder.

She had thought to remind him of how she had mothered him, and so excuse their intimacy. Yet she saw that he flushed, as if for him the memory held a different meaning.

Pat-a-pat of Carrie's leather shoes. "Mama, come, come! Look!"

Carrie had found a chameleon. It crouched beneath a twig. Its skin faded from emerald green to brown in such a subtle suffusion that even as they watched, the transformation was effected seamlessly, like the moment between dusk and darkness.

16. Flemish Feathers

NATHANIEL AND AZUBA WERE SEATED AT A CAFÉ overlooking the River Scheldt. Wild ducks skimmed low over the water; blackbirds clung to sedges tossed by the wake of passing ships. Azuba wore a cobweb grey dress sprinkled with tiny red, blue and green flowers. She lifted the silver coffee pot. Prisms sparked from her diamond.

"Sometimes," she said, filling Nathaniel's cup, "I can't believe I'm not hungry. I find myself thinking that soon I'll start to be hungry again . . . That's such a dainty cup! It looks like a thimble in your hand." She reached across the table to put a hand to his wrist, felt a sear in her belly as their warm skin touched.

He smiled at her and set down his cup without drinking. He took her hand and looked away. She saw pain in his eyes.

"I have something to tell you," he said. He looked at a barque being towed upriver by a sidewheeler. Captain and mates stood at the starboard rail. She saw a muscle move in his cheek, the narrowing of his squint lines.

"I've booked passage home for you and the children. I'm taking a cargo of coal to Hong Kong. I've engaged a new crew, although I'll keep my officers, my steward and Mr. Lee. You'll leave from here on the London-bound steamer. I've secured rooms in one of the best London hotels. I've booked passage on the *Liverpool,* the same ship that Mr. Walton came on, as you recall. She's bound for New York on September 15. From New York, you'll take the schooner to Saint John. I'll leave for Hong Kong shortly afterwards."

She stared at him. "I can't believe you would do this," she said. "I can't believe you would decide on all of this without one word to me."

A woman at the next table glanced at them.

"How can you," she whispered. She began to mash her blackberry tart with the back of her fork.

He reached over and lifted the fork from her fingers, laid it on his own plate. He took her hand and turned the ring on her finger. "I thought of the children," he said.

"I think of the children, too. We could discuss them together, you and I." She pulled away her hand. She felt a sickening feeling sweep over her, her own diminishment—as if she had lost everything she had gained and were once again the girl she had been when she married him.

"Well. We'll discuss it now, then. I know that parting will be hard. But you *must* understand, now, why I did not want a family on board my ship."

Through her fury, she caught a cast in his eyes, like pleading, begging for her understanding in spite of the harsh tone in his voice.

"I can't be both things—captain and father, captain and husband. I'm divided in my attention, in my responsibilities. Sometimes I have to act in ways I'd rather you didn't see."

"But on the other hand, Nathaniel, you've seen that I have a role to play on your ship. I might not be Mrs. Marshall, but had I not been there, you might—"

"I would not have killed him," he said. Belligerent, a flush of colour burning beneath his eyes. They both glanced at the next table. "And for Carrie to have seen Andrew Moss lying dead on the floor of the cabin, laid out on the same place she played with her doll; for her to have been present when they stormed into our quarters; for my family to go without food—it was intolerable. *Intolerable.* I don't know how other men do it."

She watched the barque, now nearing the stone-walled Grand Basin. Her yards were festooned with men, as *Traveller* had been festooned with birds on the night that they waited for Nathaniel to return from the Isle of Wight.

He took her silence for acquiescence, and his voice lightened. "After a short, comfortable trip, Azuba, you'll see your family. Bennett and Carrie will be with their grandparents and their cousins. You can open up the sail house. You can . . ."

He opened his mouth to continue, but she leaned across the table, her voice so low that it became like a musical phrase, low and dark. "*You* may be accustomed to loneliness. I'm not, nor do I ever wish to be. I don't see it as an honourable attribute. Now I can picture your life, but you still can't picture mine. At first you'll be alive in the children's minds—Carrie's, anyway—oh, yes, and we'll talk of all the wonders we saw, and the things you taught her, and what you did together. Her shining father. Then, after months have passed, I'll show them your picture. *This is your father. Remember him?* But after a while they'll barely remember. Bennett will never truly know you. As years go by, they'll humour me. You'll become nothing but a story. I'll take them down to the cove. They'll stand with me on the shore. I'll gather feathers. I'll point with them. *Your father,* I'll say, *is somewhere out there. Maybe this bird flew over his ship.*" She paused, took a breath. "You know there's a position waiting for you in either of two fine shipyards. You could live in the most beautiful house any couple could wish for. I had hoped that we would go home together and start our life as a family."

His lips twisted downward within his beard. "Azuba, *I am a sea captain.* I know nothing else. I have no other skills. I have worked since I was a boy to become who I am today. Have you no knowledge of what I am capable of?"

"Yes," she said. "I do. I do. But some men change their—"

"Ah," he interrupted. "I see once again you are thinking of your admirable Mr. Walton."

Contempt made his face ugly. She rose to her feet, lifting her skirts with both hands. A sparrow flew up from beneath the table, a crumb in its beak. She walked away, reckless with agitation, knowing that every person at the café watched her.

He did not follow her. She walked the few blocks back to the hotel, holding her parasol tipped to hide her face.

Lisette sat with her embroidery hoop. Bennett lay on a white blanket, pedalling his legs in the air as if seeking escape from his starched gown. Carrie knelt at the window. She rolled a toy horse and carriage along the sill.

Azuba shot her parasol into the elephant leg stand. Her hands were still shaking. "We're going home."

Lisette's hands went to her chest. Carrie left her toy on the windowsill and slid from the window seat. "Are we going home to Whelan's Cove, Mama? To our house?"

Azuba nodded.

"With Papa?"

"Papa is not coming with us. He is taking a load of coal to Hong Kong."

Lisette covered her face with her hands, fanning her fingers so she could see Carrie from between them. Her eyes filled with tears.

"Mama! Why is she crying? She'll meet everyone."

"She won't be coming with us, Carrie."

And this, Azuba saw, was the end of the small, happy world

assembled in the Hotel Antoine—the sunny, flower-filled rooms, the sound of church bells and carillons, the blue monkeys, the toy shops and clean dresses, Lisette's warm voice with its French lilt. Carrie ran to Lisette. Lisette took her hands from her face and reached for Carrie.

"We can't leave her, Mama!"

Azuba picked up the baby and walked to the window, her hand making circles on his back, comforting him although he was the only one not upset. The sunny square below was warped by her tears as she thought how Carrie's sympathy for Lisette, and protest over her loss, was like a sketch whose faint shape would be filled with the full-coloured absence of her father.

Their trunks, hat boxes, carpet bags and sea chests were delivered to the suite.

"There," Azuba told the porters, pointing. She stood in the middle of the room, arms crossed, watching the men as she had been used to observing Slason, or Mr. McVale. "And there, please."

The calf-hide trunks darkened the elegant rooms, as if *Traveller's* stuffy saloon had come into the suite. For days, the trunks remained opened, unfilled.

Azuba sat at her writing table.

"What are you doing, Mama?" Carrie asked, coming to lean against her, watching the pen's nib cutting the paper.

"Just trying to make order of all this," Azuba said. Her voice was tight. "What to take in the cabin, what to take with us but put in the hold . . ." What was to come later, but on another ship. What of Nathaniel's should accompany him to Hong Kong, and what of his could be shipped home. Occasionally she would rise and begin making one pile, and then would change her mind and crumple her list and stand at the window, looking down on women walking in the square, bone-handled parasols held in gloved hands, the nets of their chignons glinting, skirts animate in the dust.

At the end of the day, Nathaniel was weary from the work of provisioning the ship. They avoided one another's eyes, and he occupied himself with the children.

One evening, Carrie and Nathaniel sat at a low table, playing checkers. The air was warm, dense with carriage dust reddened by evening light.

"And then what?" Carrie said.

"Then I'll be homeward bound, with a cargo of silk and rice and tea."

"And tea sets!"

"And tea sets."

"Toy tea sets?"

"Those, too. Coming home, I sail back down the South China Sea, across the Indian Ocean, around the cape of Good Hope and up the coast of Africa."

Lisette came into the room, carrying Bennett. Azuba unbuttoned her dress and Lisette lowered the baby. He began to suckle, tiny hand spidered against the plump flesh, fingers flexing. The young woman paused; there was nothing left for her to do, and yet she lingered. Light from the window lay in the weave of her white cotton cap.

"*Bonsoir,*" she whispered. Her eyes were on the baby, and her lips were parted.

Nathaniel glanced up. His eyes, like Azuba's, followed Lisette as she left the room, soundlessly save for the shiver of her skirt.

"And then I come home in time for Christmas." He hitched himself closer to the table, propped his elbows on his knees as he squinted at the piece Carrie held. "Now if you put down that piece there, missy, your papa will be in terrible trouble."

"Christmas?" She tilted her head and quirked her eyebrows. His pipe bobbed from the corner of his mouth.

"I meant next Christmas. The Christmas after this one."

What was to happen next, Azuba saw, was something that Carrie understood but which had no meaning: as remote, as story-like, as any event in a child's future.

Carrie, Azuba and Simon walked decorously, their feet unimpeded by muddy ruts or grassy hummocks or puddles. Simon's walking stick tapped on the paving stones, and Azuba thought how accustomed she'd become to city life: the rumbling rattle of wagons, carriages and omnibuses; women's skirts so voluminous they could barely pass one another without stepping into the street.

Simon was gazing up at the mullioned buildings, using his stick to mark the place he would next step. "I'm storing up my impressions," he said. "Saint John will seem like a very small city."

Azuba watched the tips of her shoes snouting from beneath her hoop skirt. They were on their way to visit the church of St. Jacques, which had over a hundred different kinds of marble and twenty-three altars.

"I've written to a studio in Saint John, requesting a position as an assistant." He said. His steps quickened as he imagined his future. "I'll be sailing back on the same ship I came over on."

"The *Liverpool?*"

On a balcony, a maid was holding the corners of an eiderdown, shaking it vigorously. A cloud of feathers came pouring from it, and she leaned over the balustrade. There was a tear in the fabric. Another maid appeared. They bundled the eiderdown and dragged it back through the window. Feathers circled on the air.

Simon reached up, made a snatch, but did not succeed in catching the feather. He thrust his walking stick at Azuba and rushed forward, picking feathers from the air, and then went down on one knee to pluck up a few more. People paused to stare. Azuba saw him, for the first time, from Nathaniel's point of view.

"To draw," he said. "Flemish feathers."

And seeing him on his knees, she felt a spear of nostalgia, remembering Mr. Perkins, at Nathaniel's command, gathering the knives that had clattered to the deck, and how she had been standing, panting, at the captain's side.

Simon returned with a handful of feathers. He reached for his walking stick. "Thank you."

"Simon, are you leaving on September fifteenth?"

"Yes, from London."

"Oh, but . . . we'll be on the same ship. Nathaniel won't be with us. He's going to Hong Kong, but we're returning home. Me, Carrie and the baby."

He stared. "Ah," he said. "I don't think . . ."

She saw his doubt. It rushed upon her what Nathaniel would feel, knowing that she and Mr. Walton were together on the *Liverpool,* spending evenings in the reading room, where pools of light fell from lamps with tasselled shades.

Simon looked away, tucked the feathers into his breast pocket, patting them. "I . . . ah . . ." His face was preoccupied, as it had been in the botanical museum when he had conducted an interior conversation. And she felt as distant from him as when she had been alone in her bed on *Traveller* and had summoned his image to assuage loneliness or fear.

He began to walk. "I actually didn't mean . . . I haven't

purchased my ticket. The fifteenth would be a possibility, and it would be nice . . ."

She wanted to stop him, embarrassed for the ineptness of his lie.

"But I also have a plan to return to Paris for a time. I may wait, just a bit."

He will change his life to avoid being alone on that ship with me. Why? Is it because he fears Nathaniel? Or the gossip once we reach home?

"I understand," she said. Her voice was dry, and she could hear the pinched sound of hurt.

She no longer wanted to visit the church. Neither did she want to return to the half-packed trunks. She wanted to be somewhere where she would be whole, happy, her life unfolding—and could not imagine where such a place might be.

She took Carrie's hand. It was warm, smooth as eggshell. Comforting.

Later that day, after they had returned to the hotel, it began to rain.

The windows were open. Rain seethed on the cobblestones, and she could hear horse hooves and the chitter of sparrows. She and Lisette sat over their sewing. The air smelled of wet leaves and roasting coffee. Lisette clucked her tongue, picking at a piece of torn lace.

Azuba made a savage stab with her needle. Nathaniel and now Simon had chosen paths that did not include her. She felt superfluous, humiliated.

She looked out the window at the rain, watching the colourless drops spinning earthward. And remembered the life that did, in fact, await her. Her carriage in the shed, protected by canvas. Linens and quilts packed away in the attic. Her silver coffee set in Mother's dresser drawer.

Return home, she thought, leaning forward to peer up at the rain-darkened cathedral. *Accept my situation, make the best of it.* Even, if she wished, live in luxury, as Nathaniel urged. She could hire another maidservant, another man. She could befriend the other captains' wives.

And who would she become? Cosseted? Obsessed with quilting bees, tea parties, Flower Sunday? Afraid to move for fear of tearing a bit of lace? Sour-voiced and demanding?

She remembered what they had said, those other wives: "Want to sail with your husband? Oh, Mrs. Bradstock! Have you met any of those women? Seen their skin? Observed their manners? And *think* of what we read in the papers . . ."

She slid her needle into the pink-flowered cotton and tugged the thread gently so as not to make a pucker. Now she knew—was forced, in part, to agree with them. It was not her sister sailors she objected to; it was the voyage itself, and its terrors, and what she had subjected Carrie to.

She thought of who she had been before her disgrace, when she had longed to join Nathaniel. She saw herself striding on the headland, the hood of her cape tossed back. Picking berries, planting seeds, driving her horse, visiting Grammy. Kneeling with Carrie, walking the little animals through the dandelions. It had not been so bad.

This is who I am. A married woman who lives without her husband. Loves him, writes letters to him, and enjoys his furloughs.

She stitched steadily, making an effort to visualize herself as this woman. To see how she might be strong, happy.

Then she pictured the sail house on the day of her return. She imagined herself walking up the stairs and going into the bedroom and finding Nathaniel's coat hanging in the closet. And then she saw the world she was homesick for collapse and blow away like a rent spiderweb. Without Nathaniel, it had no heart. It was without reason, or joy. It was as monotonous as small surf—washing forward, drawing back.

In the next stitch, she realized the stark fact. She had no choice. Nathaniel refused to take her and the children on board his ship, and he refused to return home. And she no longer knew what she wanted. She felt a frustration akin to fear, the abject sense that she had gained nothing from her travails.

She summoned the energy of self-respect. There was nothing else to do but raise her chin and do Nathaniel's bidding with wounded pride. *I will go home, yes. And I will make my own good life. Without him.*

"Lisette," she said. She bit her thread. "I've done making lists. Today we'll begin packing."

She tossed down her sewing, turned towards the half-filled trunks. She felt a grim energy, and sensed that she would learn to replenish it at a cost to herself.

The waiter set down tureens: potato soup, sprinkled with parsley; islands of melting butter; a smell of pepper.

"We've grown plump again," she said. "Even you, Nathaniel."

He cast a significant glance. She bit her lips, chased the butter island with her spoon.

Last night, he had slid his hands beneath her gown. They had run up her spine and caressed her shoulder blades, then come over onto her shoulder, pressing until she rolled onto her back, her arms thrown up against the pillow. He had slid his leg over her and kissed her, while his palm circled her belly.

He smiled, putting spoon to lips. "And you," he said. He wiped his moustache with the thick linen serviette, lifted his wineglass. The wine was the colour of sun-bleached straw.

A breath of air came over the table from the open window. It smelled of rain-washed stone and woodsmoke, and a vision rose in Azuba's mind of the city with its walls and towers, and how she would soon be alone, without Nathaniel, in the formless space of the sea.

"Azuba."

Last night's intimacy displaced his captain's sharpness. All day, he had seemed like a man basking in sun—loose, peaceful. They sat in silence as the waiter removed the tureens.

"Perhaps after a few more years, I'll consider hanging up the anchor."

She put a hand against a spear of pain in her throat.

Carrie and Bennett. The baby was oblivious of his fate. Carrie, bravely cheering her father with assurances of how quickly time would pass, could not imagine the days, weeks and years that stretched ahead.

"Having you sail on a ship like the *Liverpool* makes it bearable."

Lamb, flaking crust, a quiver of red jelly. She wondered if food would forever be imbued with wonder and a degree of disbelief.

"I'm glad that Mr. Walton told us of the wonders of steamship life."

"Yes," she said. "I'm glad to know there are surgeons aboard."

"He may well need one, next time he sails."

"Who?"

"Your Mr. Walton."

"What do you mean 'my' Mr.—"

He raised his palm and lowered his voice. "A man may be forgiven a bit of jealousy when his wife has befriended another man. In this case, however, I'm not overly concerned."

"You are so exasperating, Nathaniel. You *know* that my

friendship with Simon Walton stems from the time after my miscarriage. When he was my pastor, and I—"

"Azuba. Azuba, please. I'm sorry. Please hush."

"—and I was alone, and he took the time to have enough concern for my well-being to—"

"—spotted," he interrupted, "is all I meant to say, by Mr. Dennis."

Her heart was pounding so rapidly that she felt stifled, her cheeks flaming. They sat staring at one another. He, too, was agitated. She felt a flash of fear in her belly.

"What did you say?"

"Mr. Dennis, I said, informed me that, for several weeks now, he has spotted Mr. Walton visiting a boarding house notorious for its popularity with sailors. He has been seen with one of its lovely ladies, taking the air of an evening."

He busied himself with his knife and fork. His iceberg eyes darted up.

The red jelly on her plate, heated by the lamb, quivered and slid sideways. Nathaniel speared a forkful of food into his mouth. His moustache rose and fell.

"Mr. Dennis does not know Simon well enough to know that it was him," Azuba said. "There are many men who look the same."

Nathaniel raised both eyebrows and made a stirring motion with his fork as he swallowed. "No, no, it was him. Mr. Dennis was not mistaken. He saw him several times."

"What was 'your' Mr. Dennis doing in the vicinity of such a place? More than once?"

"Perhaps the same thing as Mr. Walton. Lonely men look for comfort wherever they can find it."

"So what you condone in Mr. Dennis you condemn in Mr. Walton?"

"I didn't say I condoned or condemned either man. I

simply observe that they both take a grave risk and may at some point in the future need attention from a medical man."

He chewed. He lifted his wineglass and looked away as he drank.

She set the tines of her fork on the cooling slice of lamb and drew her knife along the grain. She lifted the meat to her mouth.

Nathaniel ordered a third glass of wine. And when the waiter brought the custard, Azuba did not lift her spoon but stared at her dessert. It swept over her that she had wanted Simon to remain single and lonely so that she would be the most important woman in his life—the person he would turn to, confide in. By rekindling this friendship, she had crushed the intimacy that had sprouted between her and Nathaniel in the last days of the voyage. And she saw, clearly, that it was not so much Simon she wanted as the control and stability she could never have in her marriage. For this illusion she had already, once, changed the course of her life. And now, this time, she risked destroying both the respect she had earned from Nathaniel, and the woman she had been on the brink of becoming.

The bells began to chime the hour. Nine o'clock. Dusk spun its forgiving veil, and waiters went from table to table, lighting candles. Nathaniel rose, came to her side, and held out his arm. She did not meet his eyes.

She woke in the night, words clear in her head.
This is my time. My time to sacrifice.
Nathaniel lay with his back to her. During the day, he carried himself straight-backed, his body unyielding. But at night the quilt followed the curves of his body as he slept, his knees pulled in toward his chest.

She slid to a sitting position against the headboard, and reached over quietly to light a candle.

She thought of the words her husband had said, over and over. "Azuba, I am a sea captain. It is what I do. I know no other life."

He had foreseen that it would not be a simple matter for her to come with him, the difficulty of her learning who he must be on board his ship.

She saw, now, that she must understand and embrace the man in his entirety. And match him. She must fight beside Nathaniel in her own way, become the steady, courageous woman she had been when the chicken flew at Carrie. When she had dropped Carrie's animal buttons into the mortar. When she took the gun from Nathaniel's hand.

She listened to Nathaniel's deep sleep-breathing. Simon. She dropped her face in her hands picturing Simon and his lady friend. She had loved the part of him that she could not find in Nathaniel. The part of him that did not object to her tender instincts, and shared her appreciation for the world's beauty: sunsets, shells, feathers, wildflowers. But she was more, far more, than these things. And if she was more, then so was Nathaniel. Ah, that terrible day in the Chinchas when the men had jumped from the cliff—and she thought of how he had sung, and the song he had chosen, "Shule Agra," and how it had brought tears to her eyes.

On the *Liverpool*, with its hot baths, reading room, and men walking the decks in India-rubber coats, heading west while Nathaniel sailed in the opposite direction, she would begin her slow reconciliation to her life alone in Whelan's Cove. And she pictured the house as they would find it upon their return. It would exhale dampness, no matter how long Father had kept on fires. The wallpaper would have loosened from bulging plaster. The roses would be overgrown and hanging from the trellis, and shingles, blown from the roof, would lie like bones in the grass.

Years would pass, and she would become another sort of woman—unsmiling, with the stripped, unvoiced sorrow of a woman who is never caressed.

Her mind raced with the fierce thinking of nighttime.

This is my last chance. Else the marriage will wither. There will be only a storied half-stranger, returning. Gracing us, for a while.

She lit a candle on the bedside table, then gently shook Nathaniel's shoulder. He rolled over violently, forearm raised against a blow.

"Shhh." She reached for his hand, drew down his arm.

He pushed himself up, eyes wide, instantly on guard. He wore a white cotton nightshirt with blousy sleeves.

"What is it?" he said.

"I need to talk to you."

The candle flame guttered, thwarted by an impurity in the wick. He disentangled his legs from the covers, sat on the edge of the bed. The headboard's shadow loomed.

"What?"

"If we don't come with you on this voyage it will be the end of our family."

"What do you think would happen to our family?"

"It will never again be the same as it is now. Tonight we're here, together. And if we rip ourselves apart . . . I can't say . . . I don't know what will happen."

"Are you wanting another husband? Someone more like Mr. Walton?" He spoke in a straight tone, as of something he had pondered.

She was silent. It might become true, should she live alone on the headland.

"I want to try again to come on *Traveller*. I think we paid a price, with the first voyage. Surely, the next will be blessed."

He reached forward and passed his finger through the candle flame.

"I'm going into the tropics, Azuba. I may encounter typhoons. The heat will be unbearable."

"We won't run out of food this time."

"No."

"We will not fall into the doldrums."

"Probably not."

"We'll take Lisette. She can have the storage cabin, she won't mind. She's longing to come with us. Bennett will be in a sailor's cot in our cabin. We'll leave you to your devices, Nathaniel. I understand, now. How it is for you, on the ship. "

He said nothing.

A carriage passed on the square, the horse hooves like a clock, separate and tired.

She touched his shoulder, felt the muscle beneath wash-worn cotton.

"Look at me, Nathaniel," she whispered. "Look at me."

He studied her. Then he cupped her face with his hands. In his eyes, she saw sadness tempered by relief.

"All right, my dear," he said. "All right. Perhaps it is our fate."

A half-smile touched his lips, and he gathered her to his chest.

August 30, 1864

My dearest Mother and Father,
 It is with deepest regret that I take up pen to write you this letter.
 I feel that I have caused you more anguish than I am

worth, but hope that you will think otherwise when I explain my circumstances. I will not be returning on Liverpool. *Nathaniel has had a change of heart, and has decided that it will be best to keep our family united, and I am in agreement with this decision. He and Carrie have forged a bond that is beautiful to behold, and while I know she would accept his absence with the good humour with which she is heartily endowed, her heart would ache, and we fear the damage to her spirit over time. Bennett, also, is at an age where to be in his father's arms has more import than we may think.*

It will not be long, I dearly hope, for Nathaniel has agreed that, after delivering this consignment of coal to China, we shall return via Liverpool, and so be home in another year, all of us, himself included, for he acknowledges that he needs a furlough.

Mother, please be happy for me, for our nursemaid, Lisette, is going to accompany me to help with the children, and will, of course, provide the female companionship that I sorely missed on our last voyage.

I am writing this on the morning after we made our decision so that I can send the letter on today's steamer. I shall soon be in a frenzy, for since our plans have changed so abruptly, there is much last-minute detail to care for. Carrie is sad not to see you, and has told me so, yet time, for her, has as yet little reality, and so she feels it will not be long until she is home again. In the meantime, she is filled with excitement. I am afraid your granddaughter is a real sailor, and she cannot wait to move back into her own little cabin.

In truth, my dearest parents, this decision seems to me to be the right one. I have heard that the trip to Hong Kong is not difficult, and you may be assured that we will not be tempted to continue on and go 'round the Horn again, but shall return to England via the Cape of Good Hope.

She lifted her pen. It nodded, minutely, registering her heartbeat.

One day I hope that all those I love may be together, but as of now, I beg you to forgive me for setting sail, once again, on seas I hope will be calm, and with winds to blow me quickly home to you.

With all my love,
Your daughter,
Azuba

August 30, 1864

Dear Simon,
Nathaniel has changed his mind.
He has decided that we should keep our family united, and so we will set sail with him. I have enjoyed our visits, and I thank you for making the time to accompany me and Carrie. I wonder if you have found what you desired during your time in Europe. I hope that you will be happy and profitably engaged once you have returned to Saint John.
I, too, shall be too busy for any more visits, and so I bid you adieu and bon voyage.
I do not know when I shall return.

With sincere best wishes,
Azuba G. Bradstock

She laid down her pen, tented her hands over nose and mouth. She read over her words and thought that he would never know how, as she wrote, memories burst like sparks in darkness: his hand, helping her climb a seaweed-slippery rock; his socks, steaming over the stove; Carrie, absorbed by the furled, twitching tip of his paintbrush.

They reached the sea by the early afternoon of September 5, 1864. The tug turned back at the mouth of the river. *Traveller* lifted to the swells. Cold, salty wind displaced the earth-scented breeze. Lisette, white-faced, went to her cabin, promising to attend to Bennett if he woke. Carrie and Azuba climbed to the quarterdeck, where they watched the crew scramble up the ratlines, cast off the gaskets and set loose the sails. Every man on board—including Nathaniel, the mates, Mr. McVale and even the cook—tallied on to heave up the main topsail.

Carrie gazed up at the billows of canvas, bent and taut as the necks of horses.

"She's happy, Mama," she said. "*Traveller* is happiest out at sea. She's back home."

Part Five

HONG KONG BOUND

17. Safe Anchorage

IT WAS A HAPPY SHIP.

The saloon became the women's precinct, littered with scraps of fabric, a half-pieced quilt, Carrie's slate, nappies strung to dry, music, French lessons scrawled on tablets, preparations for pudding or ginger beer or doughnuts. Lisette was like a light-hearted sister to both Carrie and Azuba. They made popcorn on the saloon stove. Mr. McVale carried pies and puddings to the galley to be baked, kept them supplied with hot water, irons, flour, lard. Nathaniel poked his head in the door and raised his eyebrows, even smiled at the womanly chaos.

Soon after leaving Antwerp, he transferred all of his navigational equipment to the deck house, and he worked in the saloon only during days of storm, of which there were blessed few. It was a good crew, he told Azuba, and there was no chance of mutiny. Nonetheless, he took his pistols and billy jack up to a strongbox in the deck house. Cigar and pipe smoke drifted down through the saloon windows, coming from the quarterdeck.

In the evenings, after Lisette and the children were in bed, he came to the saloon. He and Azuba sat surrounded by the day's projects. Sometimes Azuba sat cross-legged on the floor, leaning against Nathaniel's chair, bent over her knitting or quilt piecing. She repeated Carrie's whimsical phrases or recounted stories told her by Lisette. Nathaniel told her of miles made, or of the sailor's enterprises—a shark caught, mollyhawks killed and strung from the yards. He read aloud from old newspapers or *David Copperfield*. Or they sat at the round table, observed by the canaries, and played checkers. It was like the evenings after their marriage, the first few months in the sail house when they'd sat by the Franklin stove and Azuba had thought they would always be together.

They spent a week provisioning in Cape Town. Then Nathaniel set his course due south until he encountered the steady, eastward-blowing winds of the high latitudes. The temperature plummeted as *Traveller* leaned to her course. By late October, they had begun their journey around the bottom of the earth. Water froze in buckets. They dug shawls, mittens and cloaks from sea chests.

They encountered no land until, on November 28, midway between Africa and Australia, they passed the island of St. Paul's, an extinct crater whose cliffs rose eight hundred feet from the sea. To the north, they could make out Amsterdam Island. They saw no other ships, save that once they spotted a wrecked vessel, floating bottom-side up, covered with barnacles. Everyone on board stood at the railing, watching in silence. It rose sluggishly with a swashing hiss, then rolled, groaning, into the next wave.

Nathaniel shifted his course northward and entered the West Australian Current. Heat increased as they approached the equator, and they packed away their winter clothing. The sailors went barefoot, wore hats with floppy brims and rolled back their sleeves, revealing the blue tattoos that fascinated Carrie. As they had in the doldrums, the mates erected awnings. Nathaniel made a playpen for Bennett, a shaded wooden crate filled with pillows, fastened to the deck with hooks and eyes. Mr. Perkins made a canvas hammock with a twine fringe. Azuba allowed Carrie to wear nothing but a white cotton shift. Schools of flying fish skimmed the surface of the sea, and the waves were broken by the black tooth-shaped fins of dolphins.

Four days before Christmas, on a hot, cloudy afternoon, they heard the cry—*Land ho!*

Carrie stood beside her father, who held a spyglass to his eye. A lurid light set a sheen to Nathaniel's white shirt and Carrie's red checkered dress. Azuba, Lisette and the baby sat in chairs beneath the awning. Men clambered from the fo'c'sle, stood along the bulwarks.

They had travelled six thousand miles without seeing land, save for the islands of St. Paul's and Amsterdam.

Eastward, the volcanic islands of Java and Sumatra rose from the sea, cone shaped, purple-grey. Nathaniel barked an order, motioned to Mr. Dennis. They went back to the deck house to consult their charts. Men gathered at the bows with the lead line. Nathaniel changed course, headed north by northeast. Just after sunset, *Traveller,* like a white-winged butterfly, sailed beneath the mountainous slopes, entering the broad passage between the Indian Ocean and the China Sea: the Sunda Strait. They dropped anchor off a beach on the coast of Java.

The next morning, there was not a sound on the ship. Every person on board was asleep, save for one lookout in the bows. *Traveller,* too, was at rest, rocking gently. A breeze rippled the green water; light dappled the ship's hull.

Azuba lay curled contentedly beside Nathaniel. Even at

daybreak, sweat glistened between her breasts. She felt the now-familiar relief of arrival, of safe passage. She listened to the birds. Their cries came clearly, and then as if from a distance, and she pictured them, black against the peach-silver sunrise, spearing into the canopy of palm and teak. She could smell smoke, and she imagined the shore as it had been when they dropped anchor yesterday—cooking fires in the warm darkness, an improbable thread of life suspended between sea and mountains.

Nathaniel lay on his side, facing the wall. She listened to his slow, deep breathing. She pressed her forehead against his back, slid her arm over his waist.

"Nathaniel?" Azuba whispered. She raised herself on an arm. "Nathaniel?"

He rolled onto his back, flung an arm over his face. Its hairs were bleached white against skin whose uppermost layer was translucent, dry as parchment. She lifted the sheet, drew it downward in increments, stopping to observe neck and chest, flour-white, with freckles like nutmeg; the button of his navel; shadowed hipbone hollows. He lifted his arm, looked down at himself. He snatched at the sheet, pulled it up, rolled over, pressing Azuba to the pillow.

"Exposing me," he growled.

"The baby's asleep," she whispered.

Sticky skin. Taste of flesh. The bed shifted in its gimbals. The small square porthole was open, and they could hear voices on shore and the soft plashing of paddles.

They stayed in their safe anchorage for three days, to celebrate Christmas.

Parrots and cockatoos flitted from tree to tree with flashes of flame- and lemon-coloured feathers. Mist made a cool, mysterious veil at the tips of the jungle-clad volcanoes. Children stood in the shadows beneath the palm trees.

Traveller was swarmed by bum boats filled with coconuts, sweet potatoes, poultry, Java pumpkins and caged monkeys. They were paddled by bare-chested, long-haired men wearing sarongs. They traded for tobacco. Nathaniel went ashore and made arrangements to purchase enough fish and meat to last them until Hong Kong. He brought back a small evergreen tree, which he nailed on a stand and placed next to the pump organ, and a cage of Java sparrows for Carrie's Christmas present, which he smuggled aboard and hid in the deck house.

On Christmas Eve day, Azuba made doughnuts, rolling the dough into rings and sending them back to the galley for frying. She worked at the saloon table. It was covered with a cloth, and her sleeves were rolled back, her hair tucked beneath a white cotton cap. Flour dusted her sun-browned arms. The fried dough smell rose over the ship, along with the percussive snaps of popcorn, which Lisette lifted from the saloon stove and shook into a bowl. They had opened all the doors and windows and wore thin clothing.

"Perhaps Santa will pay us a visit," Azuba said.

"Will he find us?" Carrie asked. She, too, was twisting dough, rolling it on the floury cloth.

Azuba raised her eyebrows. "Well, Carrie, if he found us in the Chincha Islands, he *may* be able to find us here. You never know."

She wiped sweat from her forehead with the back of her wrist.

Back home. Christmas Eve. Mother, Father and any visiting relatives—Grammy, uncles and aunts from Saint John—sitting up late to label their parcels and decorate the tree and fill the

children's stockings. So cold that branches creak. Mutter of surf.
Stars over the sea, lamplight in a neighbour's window. The thud
of hooves on rolled snow, and the jingle of bells.

For the first time, she saw this as a place that was busy and
self-contained. People were used to her absence, even her own
parents. They had become accustomed to Nathaniel and
Azuba as a seafaring family. "When they return . . ." they'd
say, their voices matter-of-fact.

Lisette probed the warm, white popcorn with the tip of
her needle.

Mr. McVale entered carrying a tray of hot doughnuts. His
eyes went to Lisette, and she looked up, pricking her thumb.
She exclaimed, blushed. She wore white, and her cheeks were
like the feathers of the tropical birds—red-pink. Mr. McVale
stood straight-backed and sweating, correct in his cloth jacket
and black neck ribbon. He stared at Lisette until Azuba
nudged him with a tray of unbaked doughnuts.

He set down the tray he carried and took the new one
from Azuba's hands.

"If Santa *does* come," Azuba said, after the young man had
left, covering her smile with the back of her hand, "he'll be
happy to see our tree."

That evening, Nathaniel came below. "Come and see the
stars." His voice was light, excited. "All of you."

"Are there shooting stars, Papa?"

"You'll see."

As they stepped from the aft cabin door, a flare went off
from the bow and the ship's foghorn boomed. From the darkness came Santa Claus. It was one of the sailors, his shirt and
pants padded. He wore a wig and beard made of manila rope,
separated and combed out to a frizz. They trooped back to
the saloon and gave Santa ginger beer and a doughnut to take
away with him, explaining to Carrie that he was hoarse from

speaking to so many children and could not tarry for more than a minute.

Santa bowed to Carrie, doughnut in one hand, ginger beer in the other. She hesitated and then bowed back. She threw her arms around Nathaniel, who knelt to hold her as Santa turned his back and lumbered away, like an ungainly bear.

On Christmas morning, rain came like a brush sweeping the water, raising its nap, making a hushed rustle. It pattered on the cabin roof and drummed from the waterspouts into tin kettles.

Before Carrie woke, Nathaniel hung the cage of Java sparrows from the saloon ceiling. A shriek came from Carrie's cabin. "Santa came!"

She stood in the doorway, holding a bulging stocking. Then she saw the birds. "Take them down," she said. "Oh, take them down." She knelt on the carpet, put her finger through the bars. "I'll hang them in my bedroom when we get home. I'll take them to meet Grammy Cooper."

Her stocking was filled with toys bought in Antwerp. Jacks, a red and blue rubber ball, a silver bracelet, a thimble, buttons. "Look, buttons! I'll start a new collection."

At the foot of the stove were a few odd packages, wrapped in bits of canvas, tied with twine. "From Santa?" she asked, picking one up and sniffing it. "It smells of tobacco."

"No," Azuba said. "Those are from the sailors."

There was a ball made of twine; pieces of tortoiseshell and mother-of-pearl; a doll, carved of wood; five sperm whale teeth. Carrie laid these things in a row.

"You may thank them after dinner," Nathaniel said. "They'll come visit us."

"Into the dining room?"

"These are good men." He spoke gently. "You needn't be afraid."

Lisette looked back and forth questioningly, but no one spoke. They had not told her of the mutiny or the other hardships. She did not understand why Carrie returned to her buttons, picked them up, one by one, and rubbed them against her cheek.

Bennett sat gnawing a wooden block. He could be sat down like a small toad and would stay where he was put, but if laid on his back, he was able to flip himself onto his belly. The mates had informed Nathaniel that the sailors called the baby "Mr. Bradstock," or "Captain."

Carrie offered him the twine ball. "Here, Captain," she said. "You have this."

They had their Christmas dinner at four in the afternoon.

They drank muscatel wine, with restraint, since the Sunda Strait was renowned for piracy, and two lookouts remained in position at bow and stern. Mr. McVale returned again and again, carrying trays of sugary ham, turkey, boiled vegetable marrow, sweet and Irish potatoes, boiled onions, stewed cranberries, pickles and jelly. They finished with mince pies and Indian pudding.

"Call in the crew, and then come sit with us," Nathaniel instructed Mr. McVale. The young man returned and sat beside Mr. Dennis, who poured him a glass of wine.

"To our families and loved ones at home," said Nathaniel, lifting his glass. He looked around the table. "Halifax," he said to Mr. McVale. He turned to Lisette. "Antwerp. Mr. Perkins, to White Head Island." The big man bent his head, stretched his arm out, glass raised. "Saint John, Mr. Dennis." Mr. Dennis sat on the edge of his chair, elbows on the table. He nodded, curtly, raised his glass once. Nathaniel turned, last, to Azuba. "Whelan's Cove."

Rain drummed the deck. There was a trampling, the creak of hinges. The crew came down and arranged themselves around the little room, pressed against the walls.

"Someone fetch Mr. Lee."

A sailor went back for him. The crew had been fed Christmas dinner; everyone cheered the cook as he entered. Nathaniel offered the men rum or ginger beer, and Azuba handed each man a cigar. The room was humid, hot. It smelled of gravy, sweat-soaked cotton, tar. The floor shifted, and Azuba leaned back in her chair, content, only wishing she could undo her dress and loosen the corset that she had worn for this occasion. The men raised glasses to the captain, and then to his family. Mr. McVale, she saw, took the moment to speak his love for Lisette by gazing into her eyes, and she saw how Lisette took a breath and returned the gaze—timid, thrilled. Carrie looked past her father into the saloon, thinking about her sparrows. The baby was asleep in Lisette's arms.

Traveller, coal-filled, settled deep in the green, rain-stippled water, and the tropical dusk came swiftly.

Nathaniel had screwed a hook into the ceiling of Carrie's cabin for the sparrow cage.

"Look, Mama. They're sleeping," Carrie said. She was tucked up beneath a sheet. The Antwerp doll was on the sea chest, propped against the wall. Carrie clutched Jojo.

"Did you have a nice Christmas, Carrie?"

Traveller rocked, like a kindly being.

"Yes." Her eyes wavered, glazed. "He found us. Santa found us."

"He'll find us wherever we are," Azuba whispered, bending

to kiss Carrie. She felt a prickling rush of tears. It was as she had felt in the cathedral, gazing at the Virgin's bliss.

She closed the door and went into her own cabin. Bennett slept in a sailor's cot, hung from the ceiling with ropes. It, too, rocked, so slightly. The baby slept on his back. She stroked his cheek, pushed back his damp hair.

In the saloon, moths batted against the oil lamp's smudged chimney. The high windows opened onto the dense blackness of the equatorial night. She sought her workbox, curled on the couch. Lisette had gone to bed. Over the water came a tinge of smoke, drumbeats and the faint, metallic din of insects.

She leaned over her knitting, waiting for Nathaniel. The wool was greasy, and the fatter sections of the homespun clung to her fingers, or were snagged by rough spots in her wooden needles.

Hong Kong. Then the return journey.

And then what?

"Azuba."

She started. She had fallen asleep.

He bent, put his arms around her, kissed her. "Happy Christmas," he said. He sat beside her, hands behind his head, legs outstretched. Footsteps passed overhead. They were aware of Lisette, asleep beyond the thin wall.

"I was picturing Christmas at home," she said.

"Do you wish you were there?"

"Maybe. A little. I'm happy now, here. With you."

The oil lamp guttered, but he did not adjust it. She could see the pinched, determined corners of his mouth. His eyes were shadowed. "It's been a good voyage," he mused. He stroked his moustache.

"Having Lisette . . ." she said.

"Yes."

"Imagine," Azuba said, "if she marries Mr. McVale. And we continue on, like this."

Nathaniel reached for a moth. Oily wings, crackle of the dry body. "What do you think about the children?" he said. "No grandparents, no cousins. No school, no friends. Is this a life for them? Would you take them 'round the Horn?"

She was silent, then said, "Would *you?* Would you take them 'round the Horn?"

He stared at the crushed moth. He wiped his fingers on his shirt. "I'd rather not."

She heard regret in his voice. And a hint of indecision. Perhaps he *would* take them around the Horn.

She hesitated, not knowing anymore what she dared desire. She felt that she was braided into Nathaniel's world, almost had become part of him. In the belly of the great ship. Everything in place: sails, men, cargo. Behind them, a good passage marked by Nathaniel's grace. And now, looming over them in the luminous night, the mist-wreathed, teak-sided volcanoes.

She reached for his hands, placed them on either side of her face. She bent her fingers over his thick palms, clutching his indecision close, like a scarf. Embracing his hesitation as her own.

18. Like Dragon's Wings

THEY PASSED THROUGH THE SUNDA STRAIT AND BEAT their way northward, passing the Krakatoa Islands, where an enormous volcano rose from the jungle. They sailed up the Java Sea against the rain and squalls of the northeast monsoon, went through the Gaspar Strait and so, finally, came into the South China Sea.

"Soon," said Nathaniel, in answer to Azuba's question. He motioned to the coast of China. This evening, they were near enough to see the scroll of hills, smoky blue against darkening clouds, and to smell land. "Perhaps tomorrow."

They were eating supper beneath the awning on the quarterdeck. It had rained steadily all day, but by late afternoon had ceased, leaving a soft haze and a heavy bank of clouds in the west. The last red rays speared through, and so the table was set.

It had been Lisette's idea—an interlude for Azuba and Nathaniel, to mark the completion of the voyage, since once they arrived, Nathaniel would have no time. Dinner, Lisette had told them, would be served at sunset. It was Mr. McVale's plan, too, she'd added. Azuba and Nathaniel had been ushered to their seats, and Mr. McVale had poured wine into their glasses.

Azuba pressed her goblet to her chest, as if making a

gesture of obeisance to the god of good fortune. "Letters!" she breathed, staring at the blue shore. "Oh, that all is well."

They had not eaten alone together since the day Nathaniel had invited Azuba to coffee, that morning in Antwerp when they sat by the Scheldt and he had informed her that she would be returning on the *Liverpool*. She felt now the changed atmosphere: Mr. Walton shrunk by distance, his whereabouts unknown, his life nothing to do with either of them; and Nathaniel and she become, it seemed, a captain and his seafaring wife, having dinner—nothing unusual about water droplets misting the bread cloth, or a hand arresting the slide of a fork, or clothing so damp it stuck to skin. Between them now were thick strands of experience—the good, the terrible.

Mr. McVale set down plates of boiled beef and potatoes. Lisette was walking back and forth along the deck on the far side of the ship, carrying Bennett, who was fractious and would not be put down.

"*Alouette, gentille Alouette,*" she sang, softly. "*Alouette, je te plumerai. Shhh, mon petit choux. Shhh.*"

In the rich light, her red shawl glowed like a fanned ember. She pulled it forward, tucked it around the baby.

Nathaniel's eyes flicked between Lisette and Mr. McVale. Then he smiled, reached across the table for Azuba's hand.

And she took it, knowing they shared the same thought: tangled sheets, fallen pillow, the smooth slope of lip and thigh, breath and skin commingled—the groundwork, dark and fertile, that spread beneath their daytime lives.

The lookout sang out. "Vessel to port." Azuba looked towards the land. A ship loomed from the haze. Its shell-shaped sails marked the curve of intention: they were snug, graceful, frail. She gazed, lulled by its beauty. The human presence and her thoughts of Hong Kong connected like a bridge, speeding the transition to cobblestones beneath her feet, carved red-lacquer boxes, breakfast tea and the smell of flowers.

"A Chinese junk," she said. "Isn't it lovely?"

Now she could see the high, carved bow and stern, the broad sails, segmented like a dragon's wings. Long oars rose and dipped. Flags, kites and silk banners—fringed, bright as parrot feathers—hung from mastheads and bows.

Nathaniel was on his feet in an instant, spyglass to his eye. "Mr. Dennis." He pointed. "Vessel to port." He strode to the deck house, returned with his pistol. He and his mate stood side by side, both staring intently through their glasses. The ship was making good headway, coming straight towards them.

The haze thinned, and far off, between the junk and the mainland, red light lay briefly on the sea.

The boat was close enough now that Azuba could make out the faces of a dozen sailors. They lined the railing, grinning, waving.

"Want pilot?" A man held a speaking tube to his mouth and gesticulated in an encouraging, hopeful manner. "Want pilot for make harbour?"

Azuba, relieved, turned to look at Nathaniel. His lips were pushed forward, lines drawn in his cheeks. He took down his spyglass. His eyes were slits. His put his own tube to his mouth. "No." His voice was hollow, magnified. "Not landing here. No." He motioned for them to stand off.

"Pilot? Want pilot?"

The junk came closer. From a distance, it had been swan-shaped, graceful as any ship on a quiet sea. Now, as the junk's bows lifted, Azuba could see barnacles and streaming green seaweed. She saw its two red flags and the plaited bamboo of its deck house, streaked white with bird excrement. She could hear voices, a wind-borne babble that grew loud and then abated, even as the faces grew more distinct, grinning, now, without friendliness.

"All hands on deck," Nathaniel commanded, turning his tube forward towards the fo'c'sle. Azuba turned in the same direction. She saw Lisette standing by the galley, Mr. McVale with bent head close to her.

Azuba rose from her chair. Where was the baby? Yes, yes, still in Lisette's arms. *Carrie.* No sign of Carrie. Below decks, of course; she was below decks, playing with Gig, singing good-night songs to the birds.

Mr. Perkins opened the aft cabin door. He stumbled on the top step of the companionway, blinking his blond-lashed eyes, his fingers slow on jacket buttons. Sailors spilled from the fo'c'sle, treading on each other's heels.

"Quick, hurry, all hands on deck." Mr. Dennis's voice lashed with a raw tone Azuba had never heard.

A cracking of loosened sails. A thud. The junk came up hard against *Traveller.* The deck jolted.

Where? Where should she go? *Bennett. Lisette. Carrie.*

Hands on the gunwales, bodies lifting in easy springs. Pistols. Shots rang out, instantly, unprovoked, and Azuba fell to her knees.

Why? What have we done?

A man, one of their sailors, spun on his heel and fell face first on the deck. Blood came from beneath his arm.

She put her arm over her head, waiting for the blow, but there were more shots.

"Mr. Dennis!" Nathaniel was shouting. "Mr. Dennis! My pistol . . ."

She began to crawl backwards.

Hoarse, wild shouts. More pistol shots. Ring of steel. *Traveller,* untended, broached, her sails cracking. Their table overturned with a crashing of plates.

Her arm was seized. She screamed, pulled away.

"Azuba." It was Nathaniel. She threw herself forward, walking up her dress, tearing it from beneath her feet with one hand, the other wrenched by Nathaniel as he half-carried her down the companionway, hands at her waist, turning to pull her, lift her. The companionway door shut behind them, and they stumbled through the dining room and into the saloon.

"Mama, what is happening? What?" Carrie kneeled with her arms around Gig, who stood stiff-legged, barking.

Nathaniel locked the saloon door. He went to the horse-hair couch. "Sit," he said to Azuba and Carrie, stretching out his arms for them. "Quiet," he said to Gig.

He sat erect, his body quivering. "Mr. Dennis," he said softly, turning to Azuba so Carrie would not hear. "I saw him go down. Shot."

"Nathaniel. The baby. The baby and Lisette."

"Didn't see them. Must be hiding." He breathed the words. "Quiet. They are in control of the ship."

"The baby." She began to rise.

He pulled her down. "We have to put our trust in Mr. McVale," he mouthed into her hair.

Steps on the companionway. Shouts and then silence. Footsteps coming through the dining room. The door was rattled violently. Kicked.

"Your pistol," Azuba whispered.

"Knocked from my hand. Wouldn't fire, anyway."

Carrie shrank against Azuba. The dog flew into a frenzy, broke into a hysteria of high-pitched, begging yelps, flung his body at the door.

Nathaniel rose to his feet, staggering with the ship's broken motion. He pulled the dog from the door, cuffed his face. Azuba slid her hand over Carrie's open mouth. Gig slunk on his belly, white-eyed. Nathaniel opened the door. Three men stood there.

One stepped forward into the saloon. He stood in the place where Carrie sat to cut her paper dolls. The canaries and sparrows were silent.

Do not move, Carrie, do not move. The baby—where is my Bennett? Where is Lisette? The baby, the baby, the baby.

The two other men were peering over the first one's shoulders. Their eyes slid over Azuba and Carrie. A woman, a child, a dog. Searching further, cataloguing.

A parley. The first man, demanding gold and opium. "We get it," he said, "no kill." Pointing upward, making tying motions in the air, indicating that the remaining sailors were unharmed but trussed. "We leave ship."

"We have no gold," said Nathaniel. He held his hands out, palms up. "We have no opium. We have coal. *Coal.* Only coal." Nathaniel swept his arm around, a mockery of welcome. *Please. Look.*

He backed to the couch, sat beside Azuba.

Backs, faces, hands: pulling, bending, tugging. Overturning drawers of Nathaniel's desk. Money, stuffed into sacks. Brass candlesticks. Chests opened. Grunts. Rapid-fire exclamations. Azuba's jewellery box. Into the steward's pantry.

Footsteps as they went above, lugging the sacks.

Carrie slid into a motionless heap, her face buried in Azuba's lap. Nathaniel rose, lifted a fan from the floor, sat back, handing it to Azuba. Azuba waved it over Carrie.

Stir the air. Slow, slow.

"Will they return?" Azuba whispered.

They could hear footsteps, occasional exclamations. No more shots, no sounds of violence. Heavy thuds, as of objects dragged, hatchways dropped.

"I think it likely," he said. His whisper was barely audible, his lips drawn back over his teeth. Fingers on Azuba's shoulder, gripping. Carrie was seized with spasmodic shudders, like the dog.

They will kill us.

Wild surprise in her mind. Wonder. Not like the slow degrees of starvation.

Why? What have we done? The baby, the baby, Bennett, oh Bennett—where is he?

"I think they'll spare you and the children. They'll kill me, if anyone."

"How? How will they . . ."

Swords. Knives. She had heard the ring of steel, seen curved sheaths tucked through belts.

"Let us hope," he breathed. "Let us hope for a merciful death."

He stared at the opposite wall, where the mirror slid and scraped, tipped from its nail. No lamp was lit; darkness had fallen. Azuba could not tell whether Carrie was asleep. Her shuddering had subsided.

Last moments.

"Nathaniel." The word came from her mouth, stark, stripped.

He reached for her hand. They stared at the open door.

Steps trampled in the companionway, came through the dining room. In the doorway stood one of the three men, the one Azuba thought of as the chief. He had drawn his sword. Carrie made a convulsive huddling, pressed into the sofa, hands covering her face.

Nathaniel rose to his feet.

The chief raised the sword, brought its flat side down against Nathaniel's shoulder.

Nathaniel stepped to his desk, eyes on the man. He turned his hands palms up, gestured toward the desk. The man nodded. Nathaniel reached for a small drawer the men had overlooked. He tugged it, and it flew open, spilling pound notes. The chief paused. He motioned Nathaniel to the couch, set his sword back in its scabbard. He made a gripping motion with his hand as if striking a flame, pointing to Azuba. She rose, found a candle, lit it, set it on the table. She backed to the couch. The man carefully picked up the money and examined it. He stuffed it in a deep pocket. He called out sharply, listened for a response. He left the room without looking back.

Silence fell with night. *Traveller* wallowed, every spar jolting in its fittings, blocks swinging, the sails heavy, hampering. They could hear the slap of the junk's sails, the splashing of water passing between the two ships, and the rasping where the junk shouldered *Traveller.*

"They're waiting for daylight," Nathaniel said.

No sounds of a hungry baby. No screaming. No shots. No sound of steel. The smell of woodsmoke from Mr. Lee's stove. Rice. A murmur, a laugh.

"Carrie is asleep," she whispered. She could not speak Bennett's name. Her mouth would not shape the word *baby.* It was the shape of her life as it had been, and was no longer. Nathaniel's shoulder was hard as granite, yielding neither to despair nor sleep nor speculation. Hard as the chief's eyes. She held her own eyes on the candle. Why had the man made her light it? Speculate, yes, she would: surely it was a kindly gesture, something to help them through the night, until daybreak, when they would be released into a new life, gaping into the maw of a murdered, innocent baby.

She slept, woke. Sat. Hand against her cheek, bruised by its loll against Nathaniel's shoulder.

Steps on the companionway. Nathaniel put his hand on her knee. "They are only checking," he breathed. "Playing cat and mouse. They came before, when you were asleep."

It was the chief. His demeanour was changed; he was under the influence of drink or drug, his eyes were wide, the whites exposed, his steps looser, his gestures wide.

Carrie sat bolt upright, jolted from sleep. Hair shining black, mouth open. Azuba glanced down only long enough to see her terror.

Nathaniel made the gesture with his hands, palms up and open. *Welcome. Please. It is yours.*

Sword, flashing from scabbard. Flat side striking Nathaniel's head. Once, twice. Carrie screamed. Azuba caught the child to her. They clung together, faces buried. They heard the shush of sword into leather, a long silence, then footsteps. He was gone.

Carrie began to cry.

"Shh. We will be safe. We will be safe. Papa is here. Papa will take care of us. Shhh." She put her head on Carrie's. Smell of scalp. They had talked of hair ribbons today.

"Are you hurt, Nathaniel?" she whispered.

"No."

They fell asleep, woke to an awareness of pale light touching the room. Beneath the table, Gig lifted his head. Footsteps on the companionway. Footsteps coming through the dining room. They came slowly, much more slowly than they had before. Nathaniel tensed.

A man stood in the door. He was small, furtive. Opportunistic. Pistol in his hand. His eyes swung to Azuba, skipped her face and went to the bodice of her dress, at the point he would grasp. He glanced at Nathaniel, as if taking notice of him for the first time. There were sudden shouts above decks, a trampling of feet, screams. Scream after scream.

Lisette.

Nathaniel jumped to his feet. The man lifted the pistol and fired. Nathaniel's arms flung out, he staggered forward, and his head struck the table with a crack. He twisted, fell sideways onto the floor. His head bounced. The dog leapt at the man, barking. Azuba threw her body over Carrie. They heard the dog's bark bend, choke to silence. A heavy thud. Running feet. Gone, the man was gone. Azuba and Carrie knelt beside Nathaniel.

"Papa, Papa, Papa."

Carrie's whisper, her hands on his cheeks. Azuba's fingers, reaching, probing.

Where is the wound? Feel for a pulse . . .

Blood, the hot, sickening smell. Blood pouring from Nathaniel's head, sticky on their hands, skirts, pooling on the floor.

Steps, once again, in the companionway, coming down.

"Carrie. Lie down. Lie by me. Don't move. Pretend to be dead."

They slumped on the floor beside Nathaniel. Azuba put her head next to his, let blood pour over her face. Carrie curled beside her.

"Sprawl. Lie on your face and put your hand . . ."

There. In the blood.

The steps approached, stopped.

Heart hammering.

Don't move.

Dim, the candle was almost out. Dawn, not yet daybreak.

Someone stood in the door, surveying the scene. There was a rustle of fabric, as in an arm raised to shoot. Click. A quick step to the desk.

No sound from Gig.

Impatient stirring of papers. Sharp shout from above. Pause. Whoever stood by the desk crossed the floor. Quickening steps. Retreating. Running from the saloon.

"No. No. Don't move."

"Papa? Gig?"

Azuba slid her hand to Nathaniel's neck. She felt a pulse, strong and steady.

"Thank God. Thank God. Papa's alive."

They heard Lisette's voice. It was remote, a throb of yearning and decline, like a forest thrush. "*Captain, Madame. Captain, Madame. Cap—*"

Azuba rose on one arm. There were fewer steps on board. Men were running past the cabin. Crash of glass. A block of wood was hurled through the window. It struck Azuba, flew off, knocked Carrie backwards as she began to rise. The child fell onto her back, stunned. Her small hands went to her temples.

Silence.

Shouts, now, on board the junk. Slap of rope, creak of rigging. Rhythmic splash of the junk's long oars. The sounds diminished until all they could hear were their own ship's random protests of abandonment. The slag and flap of loose sails. The long torture of wood—stretched, settling back. The smell of smoke, stronger now.

Carrie rose to her hands and knees. The sun had broken over the sea, and the bamboo bars of the canary cage were golden on one side. Carrie crawled across the floor towards the doorway. She made not a sound.

Azuba worked her fingers through Nathaniel's blood-soaked hair. Her knuckles rose up through the tangled matt, breaking sticky clots.

"Carrie, you must help me."

The child lay with her arms around her dead dog. One hand patted, patted.

"Carrie, quickly, I need your help."

A wail burst from the child. High, unearthly.

"Carrie." Azuba's voice trembled. She kept her back to the

grieving child. "You must help Papa."

Carrie scrambled to her feet. Blood soaked the skirt of her dress. There was a blue-black bruise on her cheek, finger-streaks of blood. Her mouth was slack, weeping.

Nathaniel's eyelids fluttered. He muttered. His fingers flexed.

"Carrie. You must put your hands on his wound," Azuba said. "Just here. Press. Keep pressing. I must go above decks. Be brave. I will be back."

Azuba lifted her bloody skirts to step over the dog. She made her way through the dining room, snatching first at the table, then careening against the wall. Jars and crocks rolled on the floor; she jolted to port, shouldered the wall, was flung back to starboard. She stepped up the companionway stairs. The door flew open. She screamed, shrank back, arm raised. It was Mr. Perkins.

"Captain? The child?" he said.

"Safe," Azuba said. "Injured."

"Mr. Lee. And two sailors." His voice shook. His thick fingers worked at the corners of his mouth, reddened from a gag. "Only ones besides me still alive. Mr. Dennis is dead. They left the dead where they lay. Had no reason to kill us once they had the ship. Got myself untied."

She stared, willing him to state the unspeakable.

"They took the girl. Took her off on the junk." He turned to look in the direction the junk had gone. The stubble of his beard glinted silver in the rising sun. Skin like a rash, his eyelids swollen. The wind was warm, steady from the east. Wavelets flurried westward, pink diamonds enfolding black ones.

Azuba stepped over the sill. Steam rose from the warming deck. The smell of blood. Bodies were sprawled like bundles of clothing.

The fo'c'sle doorway opened, revealing Mr. McVale, holding Bennett.

"Fire!" Mr. Perkins roared, pointing at flames.

Bennett began to scream, held his arms out to Azuba. She ran forward, snatched him up.

"Fire! Fire!"

She scrambled up to the quarterdeck, dropped him into his playpen. His arms, reaching for her.

She ran back down. They had set a fire in the empty stalls next to the deck house. The fire, wind-fanned. Making a dry rustle. Bennett, screaming. Carrie, below, hands pressing Nathaniel's wound. Nathaniel, bleeding.

A wet sack in her hand. Mr. McVale, Mr. Lee, Mr. Perkins. The two sailors. The fire, here, there. Here. Her hands engulfed, searing. The wet sack. She bent at the waist, raised it over her head, a man roaring, or was it her? Beat, beat, beat, beat. Furious. Mr. McVale, scooping water in the slush buckets. Beat, beat, beat. *Over here. Spreading onto the . . . catching my skirts.*

"Mr. McVale, help me!"

Water thrown at her skirts.

A fresh blaze.

Azuba fell to her knees, coughing. Men were ripping boards, throwing them into the sea. Hiss, the feeble smoke.

The fire was contained.

She ran back to Bennett, grasping her collar and tearing open her best dress, worn for their sunset meal. She put the baby to her breast, suckling him as she stepped back down the quarterdeck stairway, heading for the saloon. The baby pulled his mouth from the nipple to take deep, shuddering breaths, his diaphragm, like a pendulum, in the thrall of motion.

Mr. McVale. Panting, hand to his side.

"Where were you, where did you hide?"

" . . . he cried. All night . . . hid in the fo'c'sle." He could not complete a sentence. His teeth chattered. " . . . muffled . . . piece of sacking . . ."

They stepped into the saloon.

Nathaniel was sitting up, leaning against the sofa. Carrie knelt, both hands buried in his hair. The bleeding had stopped.

The ordinary sun. Revealing what had been a parlour. Sheen of black horsehair, hungry canaries making their insistent chorus, and the sweeter, jungly song of the Java sparrows. Sheet music, bloodstained, slippery underfoot. Willowware porcelain, now shards. The oil lamp, its chimney cracked. Silk-covered boxes, lids flung open. A hair comb. A tortoise shell.

Nathaniel's eyes went from the baby to Mr. McVale. The young man put one hand to the table. His body slumped, from no injury. He had gone far away inside himself and could not see, although his eyes were wide open. Carrie opened her mouth but did not speak. She stared at Azuba and the baby, her hands still in Nathaniel's bloody hair.

"Who is left?" Nathaniel said.

Mr. McVale looked to Azuba. He did not know.

"Mr. Perkins." She shifted the baby, slid onto a chair. "Two sailors. And Mr. Lee. The rest are dead."

The silence. Not like silence. Like a silken coil of unbroken water, then the white froth, the spume. The roar of a seething encounter.

"Quickly," Nathaniel said to Mr. McVale. "Get it over. Tell us."

"Standing. By the galley. She had the baby."

All the long wooden poles meant to bend steadily, and in unison—yards, gaffs, masts, booms—resisted one another as the ship tossed, unmanned. Nathaniel put one hand over his eyes.

"A man came. Put his arm. Across her throat. Held a knife to the baby. She. Handed him. To me. Begged. I took him."

"Where."

"Ran. To the locker. In the—"

"Fo'c'sle. Ah."

A deep, narrow locker filled with fence pickets.

Then Mr. McVale's eyes swept the saloon. "Where is Lisette?" he said.

Nathaniel looked at Azuba. The words raked. The wound that would never heal.

"They took her off in the junk," she said. "Alive. You must ask Mr. Perkins."

Mr. McVale turned to leave. He raised a foot to step over Gig, put one hand on the door frame.

Azuba spoke again. "Forever . . ." she began, ". . . grateful . . ."

"Azuba," Nathaniel said, once the young man had left. His voice was drained, stunned. "Azuba, I am . . . please."

"Mama, he's falling."

Azuba plucked Bennett from her breast, laid him in his cot. There was a shocked pause, and then the baby began to scream. Carrie and Azuba put their arms around Nathaniel, tipped his head back against the sofa.

"Fetch me soap and water, Carrie. And clean handkerchiefs from my drawer."

Azuba passed her hands over Nathaniel's face. It was as if she had never seen it before. Like death more than sleep, less peace than absence. The brown skin, the grooves in his cheeks like the boards of a weathered barn. Lips soft as mushrooms.

She mopped the wound, mopped, mopped. It was a long laceration made by a bullet that had grazed his forehead and scalp.

"Carrie, my sewing box."

The wound began to spurt in time with his heartbeat as the water melted the clots.

"Find me my finest needle, please." Her voice was no longer steady. "Thread it for me."

The baby's voice was like a freshet in full spate. Running feet, shouts. Carrie froze, but it was just men taking charge of the fallow ship.

"Only our own sailors," Azuba said. "The needle, hurry."

She pulled the needle through the skin of his forehead. She made six stitches, tied six bloody knots. "Now we have to braid his hair."

Grammy. Did this. The time that man . . .

They made tiny braids on either side of the wound, Carrie's fingers working faster than Azuba's. They tied the braids tight across the gash until the bleeding stopped.

Carrie sat back on her heels. Her dress was covered in her father's blood. She sat with her bloody hands spread in the air. She stared at her dog. He lay sprawled, stabbed in the chest.

Carrie scrambled to her feet, ran to her cabin. She tore the quilt off her bed, had not quite reached the first pool of blood, now spreading, rivulets running beneath the organ, the horsehair couch, the rolltop desk.

"No, Carrie, don't put the quilt in the blood."

Carrie stopped, dropped the quilt over a chair. She fell to the floor next to Gig, one arm around him, her face buried in his fur.

They went to the quarterdeck. On the way, Nathaniel held Azuba's arm, nauseated and dizzy. He sat in her chair, dropped his head in his hands. He spoke through clenched teeth. "Azuba, you will have to steer. Tell them to hoist a distress flag."

"Mr. Perkins," Azuba called out. "Distress flag."

She climbed to the grating, put her hands on the wheel, waited for the ship to take the wind. She called out Nathaniel's muttered instructions to Mr. Perkins, who relayed them to Mr. McVale. Even Mr. Lee climbed the ratlines. Laboriously, sails were clewed up, until only the foretopsail remained.

Azuba stood with arms spread wide to the wheel. Her skirt was stiff with brown blood. Her face was streaked with soot, and the bodice of her dress drooped, revealing the bulge of her milk-taut breast over a stained chemise. She held her eyes on the compass. The burns on her arms and hands began a fierce throb, making her half-crazy with the desire to press them against her cool skirt. She made herself imagine Grammy's soothing burn recipe—olive oil and laudanum. The ship shuddered and came alive, began to rustle forward. Azuba saw how the slightest motion of her hands on the wheel shifted the great sail.

Look at the sail. The compass. The sail.

They could not bury the men at sea. There was no one to sew the canvas.

Mr. Perkins lugged the bodies to the fo'c'sle, laid them side by side in the lee of the raised deck. He covered the dead men with an old sail. He went from corner to corner of the square of bodies, as if the canvas were a blanket. He tucked it beneath torso or limb, squatting to lift an arm, shift a shoulder, poking at the canvas with his thick hands.

The stern waggled; the sail luffed and swelled. Azuba's eyes went from the compass, in its box, to the sail, back to the compass. Behind her, the wake was an uncertain, wandering passage.

Mr. Lee stood on the deck with a mop and a bucket. He swirled the mop in the bloody salt water, lifted it, slapped it onto the deck. No smoke came from the stovepipe.

Bennett slept in his playpen. Carrie sat in her little chair, clutching Jojo, sucking her thumb. Her eyes were either wide open or closed in the sleep of exhaustion.

By late afternoon, Nathaniel and Carrie had not moved from their chairs, nor eaten, nor changed from their bloodstained clothing. Nathaniel sat slumped forward, elbows on knees, bloody-clothed head in hands. He kept his eyes closed, except once, when he sat back, gripped the arms of the chair and cast his eyes over the ship. The charred stalls. The place where the lifeboats had been—stove in and sunk, to prevent their escape. The sail-covered bodies. Mr. Dennis. His flute. His wife in Saint John.

Azuba stood with both hands gripping the wheel until a man was freed up to take it. Then she went below and put salve on her burns and changed her dress. She returned to the quarterdeck and sat cross-legged, feeding Bennett. Her mind made dangerous swoops, like a gull changing course. It flew low and straight towards Lisette.

"Mama," Carrie said. She huddled against Azuba, arms crossed over Jojo, keeping the doll's face pressed hard against her chest. "Where is she?"

Nathaniel had said that likely they would sell Lisette. She would receive a high price. "I'll find her," he had said, when he returned to consciousness. His hand had wandered to his wound and felt the braids. Azuba had been kneeling before him, sitting back on her heels, hands holding a piece of torn sheet. "What have you done?" he'd said, lifting his hand and staring at it. She had not answered. He'd turned his eyes to hers, and they'd looked at one another like people who have been parted for a long time.

"Papa says they won't kill her," Azuba said, now, to Carrie.

"We'll tell the British authorities. They'll find her."

If not, she'll live out her life over there. Brocade and satin, if she's lucky; a garden, and walls to shape the sky.

She reached over Bennett and patted Carrie's knee. "They'll find her."

Carrie did not reply. She stared at the blue coast of China, now only a line in the air, vague as a bank of clouds.

The wind remained steady, and *Traveller* made good speed. Off in the east was a ship, approaching fast.

Nathaniel lifted his head, squinted. "We're too far out," he said. "The junks only attack close to shore. That ship is in the lanes; they'll be friends. We'll take on sailors to help us dock."

Nathaniel did not have the bell struck. Azuba wondered if it was because it would toll like the church rouser, one clang rebounding from the next, one continuous voice, the finished present become the next moment. As if, should time begin, hope would end.

Part Six

HOMEWARD

19. Rabbit Pie

CARRIE WOULD SPEAK ONLY TO AZUBA OR THE BABY.
She would not speak to Nathaniel. Her steady, penetrating
stare absorbed but did not reflect. Black eyes grown darker,
she gazed at waiters, chambermaids, visiting women. She listened to questions but would not answer. Her eyes were clear,
and yet Azuba could not tell what was passing through the
child's mind.

Azuba put down her book, anguished.

My beautiful, sweet, tough child.

The air smelled of rotting vegetables. Carrie knelt at the
open window, looking down at a donkey pulling a wagon
loaded with green turtles. There was a clatter of rickshaws,
the slip-slap of feet. Men passed wearing silk caps and black
linen robes, moustaches hanging to their chests, pigtails to
their heels.

They were at the best hotel in Hong Kong. Once the
news of their story spread, there was an outpouring of sympathy from the English community. The harbourmaster
alerted the authorities, made arrangements with the morgue.
A rescue mission was launched for Lisette, and a hunt for
the pirates.

Nathaniel lay on the bed with his eyes closed, arms at his

sides. His vertigo was so intense he could not walk. His ears rang, and he could barely hear Azuba's voice.

There was a knock at the door.

Azuba admitted a tall, anxious English doctor who had visited several times and had so far been unable to make a prognosis. He wore a vest with a watch chain, and a sack coat whose too-short sleeves exposed delicate hands. She led him to Nathaniel's bed. The doctor sat on a chair. He questioned Nathaniel, examined him, raised his spectacles to peer closely at Azuba's stitches.

"I have determined that he is suffering from apoplectic cerebral congestion," he said, finally. He sat back in the chair. "A result of the smash to the head."

Nathaniel lifted his head from the pillow, straining to hear.

"How long will it last?" Azuba spoke loudly. "The dizziness. The ringing."

The doctor turned away, fussing in his bag. "He will have short-lived episodes," he said. "They will be of differing duration but will be intense. You will not be able to predict them."

The street sounds were like a symphony, the clack of heels and hoofs a percussion beneath atonal birdsong.

"And when they come, how long will they last?"

"One can't say. Perhaps a few minutes. Perhaps days. Sometimes a week or more."

"Will I ever be shed of it?" Nathaniel's voice was harsh.

The doctor raised the fingers of one hand, a hopeful gesture that chilled Azuba's heart. "Perhaps."

She saw sympathy in his eyes before he cast them down.

They went to the living room, where Bennett slept. Carrie sat on a chair and stared at the doctor as he listened to her lungs, shone a light into her eyes.

"How old are you?"

She stared at him.

"What is your name?"

The doctor sighed. He would make an appointment, he murmured, turning from Carrie, with a specialist in matters of the brain. He looked at Azuba's burns and gave her a salve.

She saw him to the door.

Through the open bedroom door, she could see that Nathaniel had lifted an arm and laid it over his face. His body was unmoving, not at rest but submitting. Carrie had returned to the window. The nape of her neck was a white stem beneath the tiny bun.

Bennett came from sleep with a single cry, like the crack of a shell. *Coming from bliss,* Azuba thought, *into this hot, sticky world.*

They needed her, all of them. Who should she go to first?

She plucked up the baby and walked in a circle, rubbing his back, her heart racing.

After three days, Nathaniel made arrangements to hand over *Traveller* to another captain. He wrote to his parents. He put the off-loading of the coal into the new captain's hands, as well as the procuring of new cargo.

They booked passage to London on a steamer. There was nothing to do but wait for its departure. Nathaniel sat on the sofa and read the newspaper. His idleness and Carrie's silence filled the room. Only the baby talked and laughed, delighted with books, food, his twine ball.

One day, authorities came for Nathaniel, asking him to identify some captured pirates. He went, walking unsteadily, one hand running along the wall, the other gripping a cane.

He returned, distraught. He had recognized the man who had visited the saloon and beaten him with the sword. He had recognized the man who had shot him. Lisette had not been with them, and they had denied knowledge of her.

He sat, dropped his cane. He put his head in his hands. "They will be hanged," he said to Azuba beneath his breath.

His forehead was zigzagged with red thread and blood-blackened knots, making him seem to be perpetually frowning.

That night, in the stuffy bedroom, Azuba woke to see a dark shape against the window—Nathaniel, sitting on a chair, staring out towards the harbour. She sat up, put her hands to her face. It was wet with tears. In her dream, she had been embracing Lisette's mother.

"Nathaniel," she whispered. He did not hear her. "Nathaniel," she repeated, clearly.

He rose, tottered. "Damn."

They could see only the shine of each other's eyes. He sat heavily on the bed. His body was without impetus.

"I was dreaming of Lisette's mother," Azuba said.

She kicked away her sweaty sheets, slid next to him, put her arm around his waist, her head on his shoulder. He put his head on hers. After a while, she felt the shudder of his silent weeping.

They visited the specialist in matters of the brain.

He pronounced Carrie to be suffering from mutism and, like Nathaniel's doctor, could offer no cure and no prognosis.

Carrie had still not begun to speak when, after three weeks in China, they embarked for London. Nathaniel's vertigo was, as the doctor had predicted, episodic—gone for one day, then back for three.

Azuba refused to go home via San Francisco. She would not go around the Horn, whether on steamer or sailing ship. So they took the longer route, travelling westward on a Pacific

Mail Steamship Company liner that called at India and the Cape of Good Hope.

On the steamship, they kept to themselves in a spacious stateroom. Their story was widely known, and neither Azuba nor Nathaniel could tolerate fascination-fuelled sympathy. When the baby was asleep, if Nathaniel was dizzy, Azuba read aloud from English novels. They were in the southern latitudes and through their porthole could see a sullen sky.

Carrie sat hunched over Jojo, sucking her thumb.

Nathaniel smiled at her, but Carrie only stared back. Solemn, puzzled.

"Why won't you speak to Papa, Carrie?" Azuba whispered. Nathaniel pretended not to hear, filling his pipe.

Carrie's perfect hands, still brown from the ship's sunshine, pressed against her mouth. Eight fingernails, shells. She stared at Azuba and shook her head.

She doesn't know, herself. She simply . . . can't.

Later, when the children were asleep, Azuba and Nathaniel sat in their self-imposed purdah. Azuba had no energy for imagining, and tried to forget, but could not.

Lisette. Sitting on the saloon floor in her chemise, humming, dreaming of Mr. McVale. Mr. Dennis, lips sweet on his flute. Carrie, standing with legs set wide, hands on her waist, looking up. "Main royal. Mizzen topgallant." Or leaning to the ropes of her swing, fearless over the tipping deck. Or bravely crunching the buttons. "This one, Mama?" Her cheek on Gig's silky head. Smiling, peaceful. Innocent. Borne into each day by expectation. Life—miraculous, blossoming.

Nathaniel slid his fingers into his hair, thumb pressing cheek. Azuba made a cave with her palms and breathed into it.

Someone else was navigating. They felt the thrum of engines, driving the ship forward—wind or no wind.

In London, they stayed again at Thomas's. Their rooms overlooked the willows of St. James's Park. On days when Nathaniel's vertigo had gone, they went on excursions. Azuba took him to the places she and Carrie had visited when he had been too busy to go about with them. They went to Madame Tussauds, and the Thames Tunnel. They stood by the wind-rippled round pond and cast crumbs to avaricious swans.

They were months, now, from the event. Lisette had not been found. Letters had been sent to the wives and families of the murdered sailors. In Hong Kong, Nathaniel had spent an entire afternoon writing to Mr. Dennis's wife. He had sat for a long time with his eyes closed before sealing the envelope. They had found a letter waiting for them in London. Nathaniel had read it and passed it to Azuba without comment.

Thank you for sending me his flute, his diaries and other effects. The funeral service was very beautiful. I wish you and Mrs. Bradstock had been able to attend. I do not know what I shall do without my beloved.

Although they had booked passage on the *Liverpool,* Azuba felt that they were a homeless family, without purpose in the thin sun. She thought how they would appear to strangers. A father, mother, little girl and baby son standing in the greening, wormcast park. The spring wind lifted skirts, exposed wrists and shirtwaists. The mother held the handles of a baby carriage, the father gestured to the child. He carried a cane. The wife watched him, worried.

Azuba tried to see—*How are we? How might we appear?* As if, should she be a bird looking down, she might glimpse some elusive detail that might identify them and reveal their place in the world.

Where they were meant to be. How they were meant to live.

Azuba and Nathaniel took advantage of the hotel's nurse-maids, went out to dinner and to the theatre. Afterwards, they drove through Regent's Park. It was raining, and the carriage wheels shed a necklace of drops. Azuba sat facing Nathaniel. Lamplight glimmered through budded branches.

Nathaniel turned, tapped on the window. "Drive anywhere," he called. "Until I tell you to return to the hotel."

The driver lifted his whip, the brougham turned, and there was a changed energy in the horse, a quickening.

"We'll drive in circles for a while," Nathaniel murmured, as if to himself, looking out the window. His eyes were bitter.

Azuba leaned forward. Her body swayed with the motion of the carriage. She reached for Nathaniel's hands. She had been lying in bed of a morning and picturing her life from the moment of her birth until now. It was like turning the pages of a picture book—one drawing leading to the next. She had begun to see her life's pattern.

"Nathaniel, I'm sorry." Her face was gaunt with effort. "I should have been content to stay at home. If I had, Carrie would still be . . ." Her voice wavered.

Nathaniel's hands lay unresponsive within hers. He frowned at the raindrops that inched sideways across the carriage window, paused and then jagged onward at a new angle. "I could say the same thing," he said.

She felt a shock of surprise. They were speaking, for the first time, to the private person each had discovered in the other.

Traveller and the sail house, on opposite sides of the globe, hung in her mind like miniatures in a locket. Masts, wind-bellied sails, waves, rigging. Gables, daisies, shingles. Each one was fragile, as if sketched by the finest nib. Each one was beautiful.

Nathaniel took a breath that lifted his chest. It cleansed but did not relieve pain. He laid his palm on the seat next to him. "Sit by me, Azuba. There is room."

She stood, took a step in the rocking carriage and thought of the moment she had entered the rowboat leaving Whelan's Cove—the sense she'd had of being in a precarious place, without bounds. Expectant, like a bird with wings half-spread.

She reached for his hands just as they lifted, cupped in the shape of her face.

"Azuba," he said. "It was not your fault."

At this instant, as they kissed, they were as equal as she had ever imagined they might be. They were a family, return-ing home. But now they were bound by what they had lost. What they had broken. What they must fight to restore.

In mid-April, they embarked for Whelan's Cove, travelling first class.

The *S.S. Liverpool* had two black smokestacks, raked, and three fully rigged masts in case of engine failure. There was a figure of Lord Liverpool on her bow, the coat of arms of Liverpool on her stern. There was steam heating, and fresh sea air supplied by ventilator shafts. Generous windows granted long views over the cold, grey Atlantic. Five hundred steerage passengers filled the third deck. On the second deck was a dining saloon with a curved ceiling ten feet tall, walls of Spanish mahogany and chairs upholstered in red velvet. A teak stairway, lit by a stained glass skylight, led from the main saloon to the promenade deck.

Nathaniel had obtained first-class family quarters—an apartment comprised of a large bedroom, a bath and a parlour. In the bedroom were extra berths with leeboards, hooked to the walls during the day; trinket drawers; bookshelves; a Turkish rug. The bath was crowded with a marble tub and salt water shower. The parlour had chairs with blue velvet seats, and leaded paned windows that opened onto the starboard deck.

Every morning, a uniformed boy arrived with a tray of coffee. There was tiffin at one o'clock, and dinner at six. At the evening meal, Azuba paged through a menu offering macaroni soup, boiled mutton with caper sauce, tongue, bacon and cabbage, roast beef, chicken, ham and jelly, baked pork and beans, mutton pot pie, giblet curry and rice, plum pudding, cake and fruit pies.

Nathaniel had hired a girl, Miss King, to help with the children. Miss King stayed in servants' quarters on the third deck. She sat with the children at mealtimes, or took them to a special saloon for children and their servants. She was thin, with prominent, crooked front teeth and large hands that swivelled from bony wrists. She summoned pinched, pained smiles. She would accompany another family on the return trip.

Carrie would not speak to her, nor had she said a single word to anyone else.

Azuba explained it to a few other women, knowing that the story would spread, and then questions would cease. "We were taken by pirates. Her nanny was abducted."

Azuba spent her days walking with the children, or sitting on the shade deck, blanketed from the cold spring air, or visiting with other women, or sewing in her own parlour.

Nathaniel went about with his cane to the smoking room, the library, the barbershop. He made the acquaintance of the ship's captain and the first mate. He walked the decks with Azuba, carrying Bennett, holding Carrie's hand.

Four times around the upper deck constituted one mile. They did one mile, at first, then extended it to two. Eight times around the deck.

"One," Nathaniel said, as they passed the window of their own parlour. Through the leaded panes they could see Miss King, plumping pillows.

He took a deep breath, bent to look at Carrie. "Invigorating. Eh, Carrie? Plenty of food, and plenty of time to walk it off." Azuba and Nathaniel had agreed upon patience. They would not ask her to speak.

The ship ploughed through the waters. They'd been given a map of the Atlantic, and monogrammed pencils, and were told their position every night at dinner so they could chart their progress, for a keepsake. Twelve days to reach New York.

"Two," Azuba said, as they passed their window again.

"Three," said Nathaniel, the next time. He gave Carrie's hand a shake, and she looked up at him. He smiled down at her. "You're a strong girl," Nathaniel said. "Like your mother. Good sea legs. No need to lash anything down on this ship. See how she goes? Like an old horse. Trysails and staysails up today, see, Carrie?"

He jutted his chin at the sails, since his arms were occupied with Bennett. The sails, wind-filled, were oddly diminished, made superfluous by the black, smoke-spewing stacks. Aft, the ship carved a deep, foam-edge wake. It crested and then settled, spreading into a white sheet that grew broad and pale, and whose absorption they could not see.

In the dead-middle of the Atlantic, they were no longer in London, with its marble facades and swans, nor yet in Whelan's Cove, with its spruce trees, pebble beaches and wooden houses. In between, Azuba felt that she belonged to neither. Her own small family—Nathaniel and the children—became, for a time, sharply alone, clearly delineated, like a tree against sunset.

The air carried a new essence: the smell of ice.

After dinner on the seventh night, Azuba sat reading. The children were asleep. Bennett lay in a crib, Carrie curled in her fold-down bed. The door opened and Nathaniel came in. He sat, preoccupied, and worked his cane into a safe resting place.

"What did you see?" she asked.

He began to speak, stopped himself. The first mate had taken him on a tour of the engine room.

"Nathaniel?"

He made a frustrated gesture. She marked her place with a strip of tasselled blue leather. She closed the book, set it on a table. She crossed her arms, watching him closely.

"I can't . . . he showed me something so complicated I don't know how to put it into words. If it had been described to me, I couldn't have imagined it. These are not sailors on this ship. They are marine engineers. Slide valves, steam chests, rods, pistons. Circulating pumps. Steam-jacketed cylinders. This and that, I can't remember it all. The engines are forty-seven feet from base to top. There are two of them. The crank shaft alone weighs . . . I forget. The coal bunker occupies the full width of the ship. They call the men stokers. Or greasers."

He stared at the floor with a bruised, twisted expression.

As when a man returns home, dismissed from his job, she thought.

They could hear the ship's engine, a vast, dispassionate throb. She remembered the discussions on *Traveller,* when Mr. Dennis and Nathaniel had discussed Maury's book on navigation. It would change the seas, they had agreed. It was a kind of taming. Captains would no longer be at the mercy of incalculable forces. They would use their accrued knowledge and become scientists, of a sort. The *Liverpool* seemed the result of such thinking. Her captain did not stand on the deck, hand on supple hemp. Her sailors worked below decks, in heat and roar of sound. The ship did not so much ride the waves as cleave them.

She thought of Nathaniel's pride when he had shown them the frozen barque, and how it had chilled her. She suddenly understood that it had been not so much pride as a kind of joy. A relationship he'd had with the sea.

What will replace it?

That morning, a full-rigged ship had been sighted. A shout had risen. Passengers had hurried to the port rail. They had caught her up and sailed past, near enough to see that she bore patched sails, the soft ones. They piled like pillows, swelling. Her bow bucked and plunged. They could see men in the rigging. Nathaniel had said nothing as they came broadside to the ship, although all around people passed comment. He watched as they left her far behind.

Azuba's bare feet were soundless on the carpet as she rose from her chair. She curled on the floor at Nathaniel's feet. She leaned against his legs. After a minute, she felt his hand resting on her head.

They spent a week in New York. It was late April, and rain pummelled the purple-veined crocuses by the doorway of the Fifth Avenue Hotel. They toured the city in a carriage, driving past private residences on Madison Avenue, entering Central Park and passing by beds of daffodils, blossom-drifted green grass. They went to Trinity Church, and Azuba and Carrie ascended the steeple to see the celebrated view of the city and the bay. Nathaniel, dizzy, sat in the vestibule with his head pressed against the back of a chair, making faces at Bennett. They went by omnibus and ferry to Greenwood Cemetery, advertised as "the most lovely resting place for the dead."

Then they took a coastal schooner to Saint John. On a cool, bright morning in May, they stepped onto the steamer to Whelan's Cove. They stood along the port railing as they came up the Bay of Fundy. The red cliffs were fringed with forests or stamped with sloping pastures. They pointed at farms on the sunstruck headlands, at villages in the shadowed coves. Ayrshire cows browsed behind split-rail fences. Smoke drifted from chimneys. Pink pin cherries fluttered in the hedgerows.

Everyone, Azuba thought, would by now have heard their story, would know that Nathaniel had been injured, that they had left *Traveller* in the command of a new captain. As they rounded the headland and headed into Whelan's Cove, she could see that the dock was packed with more people than was usual for the steamer. Sun brightened the waters at the harbour entrance but had not yet reached the church steeples, nor dried the wet timbers of the dock, nor stroked the shipyard roofs. White flakes came into view, fluttering over the people.

"Handkerchiefs, Carrie," said Azuba. She reached for the child's hand. "They've seen us."

At her side, Nathaniel held Bennett. Carrie pressed close to Azuba. They were borne towards the waiting people, and even as she leaned over the railing, waving, Azuba felt the pluck of ending: the press of Nathaniel's arm, Carrie's gloved hand in hers, the baby between them—a time of self-absorption in its final moments. At their feet were hatboxes and leather cases. Azuba wore a new silk dress, blue-green, with detachable sleeves. It had been made for her in Hong Kong, since her only other good dress had been ruined by bloodstains. Both she and Carrie wore hats whose wicker bands pulled forward to shield their faces. Hers was trimmed with braiding and jet beads. She wore gloves with mother-of-pearl buttons and carried an ivory purse with pink silk dividers. She remembered their appearance when they had sailed up the Scheldt into Antwerp. Carrie, then, had been waving—eager, excited, unaware of her stick-thin arms or her stitched-together dress.

Now the child stood straight, blue skirts fluttering above her oiled leather boots, a plaid cape clasped at her throat, staring fiercely with knit brows.

The steamer came 'round, bumped up against the barnacle-encrusted piers. Azuba saw her parents, familiar as worn furniture. They had aged, and yet seemed innocent— like ancient children. She felt like a stranger who would never be able to explain her past.

On the wharf, there was a surge towards them. Parents, brothers, sisters-in-law, cousins, neighbours, aunts and uncles. A clamour and babble. Carrie ran straight to Grace. Azuba saw her mother kneel, throw her arms around Carrie, saw her father go down on one knee, patting Carrie's back. Azuba had warned them, but they had not believed, she saw, that Carrie would not answer their pleading, loving questions.

Grace stood, turned from Carrie, dazed. Azuba held Bennett. He wore a wide-skirted wool dress, thick blue stockings and a knitted cap. His eyes were as round as Carrie's, as wide—only his were innocent.

They went to Grace and Joseph's house for dinner. Grace had made up beds for them, but Azuba and Nathaniel wanted to go home. After eating, Grace took Bennett on her hip. She carried him up the stairs, took him into every bedroom. She showed him the views out the windows. Azuba, in the downstairs hall, heard her say, ". . . then the sails *flew* away . . ." She talked in a calm, singsong voice, as much to the baby as to the silent little girl who followed.

They arrived at the sail house at four o'clock. The buggy wheels crunched to a stop. The mare tossed her head, and the bit jangled. The sun had not yet dropped behind the headland. It warmed their faces, glazed the shingles of the roof.

All the stories, Azuba thought. *All the times I recalled this house to keep us from fear.*

"Carrie," she said. "This is it. This is our house."

The house hunched beneath the sky, its shingles rain-rutted, sleet-scoured.

Waiting, as if the house were animate. A stalwart, welcoming presence, even weathered, empty, silent.

Waiting.

Nathaniel made fires in all the stoves. For supper, they ate a rabbit pie made by Grace, with boiled potatoes and fresh rhubarb chutney. Azuba made the beds. She smoothed the coverlets, and sensed a change in the way she moved, here in the same rooms. Her hand moved more slowly over the cold quilts—competent, heavier, burdened with regret. Passing through the parlour, she paused by Nathaniel's photograph. She picked it up, traced it with her finger. She put it back, ran her fingers over feathers in a jar. They were dusty, decaying. She plucked one. Its shaft had been inhabited and partially destroyed by some insect.

Everything was the same but worn and oddly angled, not quite as she had remembered it, yet as familiar as her own body. She was inside the house now, looking out. Its wood, its curtains, the way it shaped the view brought her up against how she had longed for it, when trapped on *Traveller.* And yet how she had longed for a life aboard *Traveller,* when she'd felt trapped within the house.

It was late, and they all went to bed at the same time. As she tucked Carrie into bed, she heard Nathaniel coming up the stairs. His cane tapped the treads. His dizziness had intensified over the day.

Carrie curled on her side gazing at the candle flame. She clutched Jojo.

"Your own room, my love," Azuba said, leaning to kiss her.

"Goodnight, Mama," Carrie breathed. Her eyes drifted shut—a glitter before they closed. Her hand loosened on the doll.

Azuba stood listening to the ticks and creaks of darkness. She took the candle, went down the hall and into her own bedroom, where Bennett lay sleeping in a crib and Nathaniel sat on the side of the bed. He wore his long underwear. He had opened the window, and the smell of spring wavered through the room. Wet soil, buds. Faint chime of peepers. A thread of air made the lamp flame quail.

"I wrote to my father from London," Nathaniel said. "I told him that I would begin work at the shipyard as soon as I returned."

They had not discussed any particulars of their future. They had only agreed that they were returning to the sail house.

She sat beside him on the bed. They listened to the waves breaking on the rocks at the foot of the cliff.

It was what she had always wanted him to do. Yet this moment was like when he had told her she would go to sea. What she desired, when it finally arrived, offered only confusion, without a sense of pleasure or fulfillment. She could not be joyful for herself when now her mind unfurled, for him, the dusty offices, the ledger books, the sawmills, the mould loft. And then she imagined him at his desk on *Traveller*—

grim, focused, a controlled desperation, his hard hands on protractor and compass, his pencil scrawling bird-track marks across the charts. Tossing down the pencil. *I'll get us around.*

"How long do you think you'll work at the shipyard? When you're well again, I thought perhaps you . . . we . . ."

"I won't be well again."

He stood. He staggered slightly, and put a hand to the footboard.

He walked to the window. She did not follow him. A wave broke—a complicated undoing. They heard the pebbly wash as it expired up over the sand, and then the rushing sigh of its retreat.

"I'm done," he said. "I'm done with the sea."

Azuba knew Nathaniel's condition as soon as they wakened. He raised his head from the pillow experimentally. He sat slowly and if dizzy made his way to the dresser with a hand held out before him. His mood was dark, quelled. He watched Carrie with despair. He sat on the parlour floor and introduced Bennett to the animals of the ark. He did not go to the shipyard until the vertigo was gone.

Azuba lay awake nights and wondered how long this epoch of their lives would last. The moon slid across the sky, one day passed to the next, and they lived like people in a lifeboat who hold on—enduring. Waiting. For any destination, any landing place.

She did not attend bees or teas. The women would pity her, or, worse, she would feel their hidden vindication. "Didn't I say; didn't we tell you." She refused to speak of Carrie's mutism or Nathaniel's apoplectic cerebral congestion. She wanted only to make an attachment to place, like the plants growing in her garden.

The house was in need of airing and scrubbing. Bedding and linens were damp. Mice had invaded drawers and closets. Even though Azuba had stored the Star of Bethlehem quilt wrapped in paper, sprinkled with pepper, a mouse had nibbled one corner. Feathers drifted from pillows. The garden had gone to lambs' quarters and mustard.

Hannah and Slason returned. Slason hitched his white horse to the plough and turned under the weeds. He brought a wagon of rotten manure and harrowed it under until the garden was a bed of black loam. Then Azuba knelt in the windy warmth, set wrinkle-skinned potatoes in trenches, sprinkled carrot seeds. Bennett crawled on the grass, or slept in a cloth-shaded basket. Carrie worked beside Azuba, handing her seed potatoes, or wandered in the field, strewing dandelion clocks. By suppertime, Azuba's back ached and her hands were sunburned. Lisette hung like a pendant from her neck, bumping up against her.

Two weeks passed, and then a third. Seeds sprouted, swallows made nests beneath the overhang of the barn roof. Joseph gave Carrie a puppy. She whispered to Azuba that she had named him Andrew Moss. Azuba knelt in her flower garden, planting sweet william, honesty, herbs, hollyhocks. One day, Slason brought pullets in cotton bags, tipped them out into the chicken yard. Hannah made pies with the first wild strawberries.

Azuba and Carrie walked down the road to visit Grace. Andrew Moss, the puppy, frolicked at their side as they walked up the driveway, speckled by the sparse shade of young elms.

"Well, then," Grace said, touching a finger to Carrie's cheek. She put a bowl of water on the porch for the puppy. She sat Carrie at the kitchen table and gave her gingerbread and tea sweetened with maple syrup. There was a fire in the cast-iron wood stove. From her place at the table, Azuba could see the silver shine of the sea. Grace resumed her calm busyness: scooping flour from a crock, offering it to the table like casting seeds to chickens, caressing the pile to spread it. Her hands lifted dough from a bowl, set it on the floury table.

Wind rustled the lilacs. Leaves swept the air, beginning their day's work.

Azuba sipped her tea, watching Carrie, who watched her grandmother's hands. Dough like a fat belly. Folding it forward. Then the heels of her hands—pressing away.

Azuba saw the dark thoughts in Carrie's face.

Mr. Dennis, turned into a sausage roll of canvas. Gig, Andrew—eyes fixed in a sightless stare. *Captain! Madame! Captain! Madame! Lie in your father's blood.*

Granny kneaded the dough. Over and down, press, press.

Knead the pictures away, Carrie, Azuba thought, watching the little girl with anguish, longing to return her to who she had been—her brave, eager child. Freed of Andrew, Lisette, Gig, Mr. Dennis. *Softly, softly,* she pleaded in her mind, and she reached out to touch Carrie's shoulder.

Almost every day, Azuba sent Carrie to visit her grandmother. Carrie and Grace spent most of their days outside. They carried woven baskets made by the Indians. Carrie's was round, made from cedar bark. Grace's was black ash, with a handle of carved spruce.

They picked fiddleheads and strawberries. They gathered bark, roots and flowers for making dyes: hollyhocks, gold-enrod, rhubarb root. They picked dandelions and blue-berries. They went to the hedgerow beside the marsh, where men were scything hay. Thorny vines drooped, top-heavy with blackberries. They made jam—black, seedy, spread on hot white bread.

The night they made jam, Carrie sat bolt upright in her bed and cried out, "Mama!"

Azuba came to her.

"The jam. Papa's head."

Azuba sat on the bed and rocked Carrie. "Think of Granny's clock," she whispered, rocking Carrie. "Tick-tock, tick-tock."

Azuba thought, but did not say, how it was a sound that erased the moment that came before, and made a new one.

"Shh," she whispered. "Tick-tock. Only jam. Blackberry jam."

"Any minute now your grandfather will be home for supper," Grace said to Carrie, ignoring the child's silence. Grace was lean and strong—like a wooden rocking chair, spare lines built for comfort. "He's happy his grandchildren are living here. He had you in mind when he built that house." She glanced at Azuba. "He had that little bed of yours special-made."

They were sitting on Grace's porch, stripping summer savoury leaves from woody stems. The plants were limp and warm, and an oily, herb-bitter smell rose from them.

"They call it the sail house, Granny, but they don't know," said Carrie.

Grace and Azuba looked up sharply; their hands faltered on the aromatic stems.

"Don't know what, Carrie?" Grace said.

"What a real ship is like."

"No, I don't suppose they do. Doesn't matter, though."

"Why not, Granny?"

"They call it that for the way it was wrapped up. Hopes and dreams hidden behind sails. It was a beautiful sight, up there against the sky. Those patched old sails, fluttering like moths. Wasn't it, Azuba?"

Azuba could not answer. She bundled her summer savoury in her apron, slipped from her chair and went to the porch railing. She could see the shining white square of their house.

"Could you see the sails from here?" Carrie said.

Granny set her work aside and pulled Carrie close. "Yes," she said. "Your mother and I watched them snapping in the wind."

The air smelled of autumn—bright, clean—and carried the wild, uncaring tang of the sea. From the chimney came woodsmoke, and out through the doorway, the smell of roasting chicken and potatoes.

She is talking. Oh, Carrie is talking. I can't wait to tell Nathaniel.

Gazing at the sail house, Azuba remembered the winter when her father had begun building it. She had watched the oxen labouring up over the headland, and had not known how her life would unfold. She had been filled with love for Nathaniel, and the freedom implicit in her imagined future. The two feelings were spliced together into hope. Now, listening to Carrie speaking to someone other than herself, she felt her heart lighten. Hope was a familiar feeling, yet was changed by having been lost. Now, hope contained less yearning, less dream; it had itself become precious, equivalent to life in whatever guise.

20. The Orchard

A SHIP'S HULL TOWERED OVER THE BUILDINGS OF THE shipyard. It was black, with gold trim; in the summer evening, it exuded the smell of paint and tar. It had no masts yet, and without them the ship was squat, blunt, reminding Azuba of wrecks she had seen, lacking the fragile shudder, the light-catching ephemera of sails.

Bennett was now two years old. He wore trousers with a gusset in the back, and suspenders, and a cloth cap. Beneath blond hair, his eyes were blue, like Nathaniel's, only darker.

"Do you like her?" Nathaniel said, squatting to put his arm around the little boy. "Next time you come, we'll go on board."

Azuba stood with Carrie at the window of the company store. They could see bags of Java coffee, and lead-lined tea chests, and pyramids of yellow sugar cones.

"There are my boots, Mama," Carrie said. She made blinders around her face, stood on tiptoe and pressed against the glass. There was a pair of leather boots that she longed to have. Their buttons were as black as snake eyes.

She is getting so tall, Azuba thought. *No longer a little girl.* She was helpful, handy with Bennett, quick with her needle. She and Azuba were piecing together a new dress for school. They were using bits of an old one of Azuba's and an old one of Carrie's. Together they pored through *Godey's Lady's Book,* exclaiming over lavish dresses with hoop skirts and crinolines. She was eager to start school and had met her teacher, a lovely nineteen-year-old woman from Montreal.

She never spoke of the voyage, or of her memories. *Life stretches ahead for her,* Azuba thought, peering through the glass, *exciting as those boots.*

The door of the mould loft opened, and Mr. McVale stepped out. Nathaniel had made him the yard foreman. He went with them down to the carriage shed. Even after a year, Nathaniel was awkward with horse and harness, glancing at the horse's head as he tugged at buckles and straps. Mr. McVale helped him, and then handed up the family. Azuba and Nathaniel sat in the front, the children in the back. Mr. McVale gave Bennett an extra swing through the air before landing him on the seat. Azuba and Nathaniel leaned forward at the same time, waving to him, urging him to come visit. He was Bennett's godfather, and came to their house on every occasion—Christmas, Easter, Thanksgiving, birthdays.

Nathaniel settled his hat, pulling with both hands. He lifted the whip, flicked it, clicked with his tongue. They turned up between the buildings. They were going to visit Grammy Cooper, who had taken to her bed.

"Taken to her bed," Grace had said, and Azuba had felt foreboding. In her lap was a loaf of fresh-baked bread, steam moistening its cloth, and held between her feet was an iron kettle, filled with soup, its lid secured with a piece of rope.

They turned off the main street onto the hill road. Bits of gravel and dirt spat from the wagon wheels. They passed a blacksmith's shop with its smoking chimney. Houses fell away until there were only close-cropped rocky pastures with cedar trees and bony cows. The maples were frost-reddened.

Along snake fences grew rambling, thorny branches of black-berries, red and black, the black ones dulled by dust.

Carrie held a jar of crabapple pickle in her lap. Bennett's solid little body leaned against her. She fished in her pocket. "Here," she said. "Granny said you could have this." She handed him a button. He held it in his palm, entranced. It was shiny brass, with a pattern of a square-rigged ship, all sails spread. He closed his fingers over it, pressed his fist against his chest. "Don't put it in your mouth," Carrie said.

The sun hung in the sky as they went up the hill, although by now those in the town below saw only fiery clouds burning in the silver-blue west.

The people caring for Grammy Cooper were loading their wagon. The horse was already hitched. The woman came forward. Her head was wrapped in a shawl. Cold came down out of the trees.

The woman spoke to Azuba in a low voice. "Took the chamber pot to her. Spoon-fed her, but she don't care to eat. We've a good fire on. I heard tell you were bringing food. She's had nothing but water." She glanced at the children. "The rugs, she . . ."

"Yes," Azuba said. "Thank you."

Azuba went ahead. She pushed open the door. It yielded against an unaccustomed resistance, and Azuba stood on the threshold, looking down. Half-lit by the lamp and the dusky light, the room was cave-like, darkened by rugs. Every inch of the floor was covered with Grammy's hooked rugs, the best ones usually laid away in chests or kept on the floors of upstairs bedrooms or hung on walls.

Grammy was in a bed by the south window, propped against pillows. She raised one arm, made a clutching motion with her fingers. Azuba stopped to remove her shoes. She lifted her skirt, looking down as her sock feet crossed the nubby knots. Trees, apples, mermaids, pansies, shells, whales, churches, clouds. She crossed them and knelt by the bed. "We brought soup, Grammy," she said. "And oatmeal bread." She put her hand to her grandmother's temple, stroked back the white hair.

The children came to the door. They, too, stopped, surprised, and Nathaniel came up behind them. Grammy Cooper repeated the clutching motion with her fingers. Nathaniel and the children removed their boots. Nathaniel carried the pot of soup to the stove. He pushed back a rug, stippled by sparks that had fallen from the grate.

"Don't matter about the sparks," Grammy said.

The fire hissed, a quiet sigh of steam, like breathing, and the room filled with the soup's herby scent.

They sat around Grammy's bed and watched the sun slip behind the hill. A ship was coming up the bay, its sails still holding the light. It was the size of the ship on Bennett's button.

Grammy sighed, turned her eyes to the ceiling. "Tired . . ." she murmured. One arm hung loose over the side of the bed, the fingers relaxed as if they had gathered up all the images from the carpets and then let them spill back.

Azuba gazed at the beloved face, its flesh loose on the frame of bone, and behind the eyes a lifetime of desire and hope, courage and fear, despair and acceptance. She looked at the carpets, their images fading in the dusk. Pieces of a life, laid into a kind of pattern, that Grammy had wanted them to walk across.

She took her grandmother's hand, feeling its improbable strength, like the wing of a moth.

∽

They sat up with Grammy's body for two days. The house was filled with autumn flowers, brought by the village women. Pot marigolds, black-eyed Susans, phlox. Azuba took up the rugs, since it rained the next day, and the next, and the yard was chopped by the wagon wheels into a muddy soup. They covered the mirrors, stopped the clocks.

On the day of the funeral, they carried her out feet first. The church bell tolled eighty-five times. The men wore black silk hatbands, and the women wore black crape shawls, with hoods of white silk. They buried her in the hillside cemetery. Wagons, buggies, victorias and landaus wound up along the coast road. Horses paced with bent necks, faces turned leeward. Women snatched at hats and the fringes of shawls. *Home,* women breathed, as the wooden casket went into the soil. They folded their gloved hands. *She's going home.*

After the funeral, the family gathered for supper at the sail house. No one could speak of sorrow so deep, memories so private. Instead, they spoke of the season just past—of the new ships, of the summer's gardens, of hay and wild berries. Later, they carried sleeping children into the cool air. Nathaniel and Azuba stood with their own children, watching as the carriages went away down the road. Light lingered. It was early September, and a chill was in the evening. The sun had travelled northward, and light slanted from behind the hills, as if emanating from Grammy's house.

After she had put the children to bed, Azuba stood in the door of the dining room, contemplating the remains of the meal. She saw the shapes of plates and serving dishes, the glint of silverware. Smell of cold, greasy meat. Of syrup-soaked pie crusts. Of tea.

"No, no." She had waved the women away. "Hannah and I will do it."

Nathaniel came to the doorway, put a strong arm around her, pulled her so her back was pressed against his chest. She had let her hair grow. There was no longer any reason to keep it short: no lack of fresh water, as on *Traveller;* no lack of privacy. Some summer mornings, she held her face into the wind and let her hair blow like a petticoat on the clothesline. She wore it, now, in a chignon, netted at her neck.

His hand slid to her belly, where a new child slept. She was four months pregnant. He pressed a kiss to her temple. She turned and put her arms around his waist and laid her cheek on his chest.

"I'm sorry," Nathaniel said. "You loved her."

"Yes."

She stood with her ear pressed to his chest, listening to his heart. It was as comforting as a clock, only less monotonous. Subject to pauses. Irregularities within its rhythm.

The children were asleep in their spool beds. Beneath the floor was the foundation of fieldstones and the cool cellar. She realized that as long as Nathaniel was her companion, and they felt compassion for one another, it would not matter where they lived. She would never be homesick. She felt the pulse of life, like his heart—an animating presence, dispelling the dreary, dead longing that had once torn her mind.

"I can hear you thinking," she whispered. "Your heart betrays you."

Every morning, white fog shrouded the nearby fields and hid the bay. By noon, the fog thinned, and streamed across the spruce trees. The trees loomed, vanished and then reappeared, each time more fully, until the fog was only a cool, salty breath hanging in shadows.

Nathaniel had woken dizzy, with ringing ears. He did not

go to the shipyard but sat on the porch, holding the arms of his chair, his eyes closed. Azuba sat beside him, sewing. They listened to a wagon passing within the fog. The sound of hooves was soon swallowed—a gravelly crunch, one step following the next, dwindling.

Carrie had returned from school the previous day talking about a man who had come to take photographs. She told them, at the supper table, that it had been Mr. Walton, and that he had spoken to her. He had asked after her parents. He had made the children gather around their teacher on the school steps.

"I've heard that Mr. Walton is becoming successful," Nathaniel remarked suddenly, opening his eyes and looking down the mist-shrouded bay. "People are talking of his studio on Prince William Street."

It was the first time, since Antwerp, that either of them had spoken his name.

Below, the church steeple emerged from the fog. Then, gradually, the masts in the harbour and the shipyard roofs. Azuba touched Nathaniel's arm. "Look, how beautiful."

They watched the emerging village. Gulls wheeled. They could hear the sounds of the shipyard, less frantic now, since the ships were complete, waiting to be towed to Saint John for finishing.

"I wonder," Nathaniel said, "if he isn't . . . if he and his ilk—" He broke off, and his chest lifted as he took an exasperated breath. He motioned towards the village, the harbour with its forest of masts, the red-cliffed bluffs. "I wonder what will become of this place. It will not survive."

"Don't be ridiculous, Nathaniel."

"Think of the *Liverpool.*"

He leaned back and closed his eyes. In the village, he was called Captain. The people of the cove were delighted to claim him as one who had seen the world and had returned to them, no matter what the circumstances. Yet he would not speak about his life as a captain, would not be drawn into discussions of ships or sailing, only smiled beneath watchful, ironic eyes. He carried a silver-tipped cane, wore a hat like a businessman. Throughout the first year that he was home, as if with painful effort, he had restrained himself from reading the sky, from studying the wind-sheared bay or drawing out his spyglass to watch passing ships. Lately, he had begun to relax back into these habits. He always knew the whereabouts and status of *Traveller.*

He spent evenings at his desk, while Azuba sat in her chair, tired from her day of supervising Hannah and Slason, or running after Bennett, or hoeing weeds in the wind. Occasionally he picked up his personal ship's log, which he had taken from *Traveller.* He read it, sipping his pipe, smoke drifting from his lips. Then he set the log back on its shelf and stared at the wall. Azuba glanced at him and then looked down, not wanting to intrude upon his thoughts. She watched her fingers looping grey homespun.

True, it was, and barely believable. What she had witnessed. Her husband. On the quarterdeck. Legs braced. Hard blue eyes, ice-riddled beard. Roaring: *All hands on deck!* Men spilling from the fo'c'sle. *Carrie.* Finger pointed inside a soaked mitten. *I am your captain, and* Traveller *is your ship . . .* The following waves, the terrifying greybeards. The ship, lying on her beam ends. Nathaniel, compelling men to swarm ice-coated ropes and cling like rag dolls a hundred feet in the air.

"What could become of it?" Azuba asked now, motioning towards Whelan's Cove. She could not imagine it deserted—its slips rotting, no sawmills spewing yellow clouds skyward—nor the forests empty of labourers.

He patted his breast pocket for his pipe, bent forward to

shield his match. Smoke trailed from his lips. He narrowed his eyes at the town, assessing facts and probabilities. Then he motioned with the stem of the pipe at the shipyards, fully staffed, dominating the village. At the wooden ships, so numerous as to be like the flocks of birds blackening the skies in their annual migration. "The day of the wooden ship is over," he said. "In twenty or thirty years, I imagine this place will be a ghost town."

She shook her head. "No, Nathaniel. I can't believe it." She picked up her sewing and felt his reflective stillness beside her on the porch, and she was reminded of the moment, on the deck of the *Liverpool,* when they had passed the full-rigged ship and he had stood on the deck, watching as they left her far behind.

Nathaniel decided to become an orchardist. He bought a large parcel of land behind the house, with a declivity where trees would be sheltered. He sent away for a book on horticulture, *The American Fruit Book: Containing Directions for Raising, Propagating, and Managing Fruit Trees, Shrubs, and Plants.* He studied chapters on grafting, budding, pruning, soil management, pests, irrigation, marketing.

In the evenings, now, he did not read his log but sat at his desk with ruler and pencil, designing his orchard. Cox's Orange Pippin. Snow Fameuse. Golden Russet. Ashmead's Kernel. He designed storage barns, made lists of what he would need: wagons, ladders, barrels. He would make a greenhouse for starting seedlings. He had begun to attend horticultural lectures. He brooded over his calculations, erasing and redrawing.

"I will ship apples to England," he said. "Boston. And New York."

Here on land, and in his own way, he was still a captain, although he muted his air of command. Lately, he attended political meetings and came home smelling of tobacco, grave with decision-making, flush with the excitement of Fenian raids and the birth of the Dominion of Canada.

Azuba resumed the things she had done when Nathaniel was away: tending to the kitchen and pantry, housekeeping, assigning Hannah's tasks, caring for the children. Her hands were skilled, strong. She worked, walked and talked with quick-minded decisiveness. Her eyes had less liveliness, less curiosity. They were wide and direct, steady. Her mouth was drawn at the corners and had lost its humorous cast. There were new lines in her cheeks and beside her eyes. She wore a cloth belt on which were suspended three chains—one for keys, one for scissors and one for a tiny book with ivory pages and a pencil. They purchased a second horse so that Azuba could drive herself to the village. They did not always discuss, of an evening, what each had done during the day. Respect was like a space between them that made them think before they spoke and clarified each to the other, like a lens.

She hired a dressmaker to come to the house and help her and Hannah make silk dresses. After their initial seclusion, she and Nathaniel had been gradually drawn into the community. First they had attended a church event, and then a cotillion. Soon they were going to teas and dances at Nathaniel's parents' house, were absorbed into boisterous family dinners at Azuba's family home. Uncles, aunts, cousins. Sledding parties in December, and then the New Year's Eve dance.

And they settled into the sail house, shaped by its gracious beauty. Azuba stretched to place sun-warmed sheets on shelves. Nathaniel slung his coat on a hook, sat smoke-wreathed at his desk. The smell of molasses and ginger per-meated curtains and quilts. The dog curled on the hearthrug,

Carrie read in a cane-seated chair, Bennett rummaged in his toy chest. Tall windows framed storm clouds, apple blossoms, sunsets. Wind sighed over sills, and the roar of surf was only a distant thunder, less present to their minds than their own happy voices, or the crunch of horsehooves coming up the lane.

Love, like hope, changed. It was buried in small moments and came most strongly when least expected. Freedom, Azuba saw, came at the same time, and so was not a matter of choice, but of grace. One could not find it, but rather was swept by it, as when she stepped from her corset and sighed, soothing with her fingers the welts on her skin. It was a kind of relief, a brief tumble into unbounded clarity.

Some nights, dizziness overcame Nathaniel as he bent over his desk. He reached for his cane, but she stood and put out her arms.

"Hold me, Nathaniel," she said, as if she had not noticed.

They went together up the stairs. She kept her right arm looped around his waist, carried a brass candleholder in her left hand. He took the banister.

Companions, going up towards the glimmer of light in the hallway.

Stand by for stays! she heard him roar, in her mind. *All hands on deck! Hold, hold.* Waist-deep green water, the fury of wind in the rigging, and *Traveller* on her beam ends.

"Nathaniel," she said.

He looked down at her. He was weather-beaten, strong, with his white squint lines. The left eye, narrowed by the thickened lid, was still compassionate; the other, unhooded, was still bold.

Yet in his stern face, as they stood facing one another on the stairs, was no shred of anger, or command, or coldness.

Only love, like a reflection.

Epilogue

THE COOL AIR CARRIED THE THROB OF CRICKETS AND the smell of goldenrod. Fog shrouded all but nearby things. It was a golden fog, spun with the hidden sun. It made Azuba think of Rubens's paintings in Notre Dame.

She was cleaning lamps. The table was covered with smoke-smeared chimneys and brass fittings, a bowl of water, baking soda, twists of rags. She felt a flush of nausea, faintness. Cornbread baked in the oven; green beans and potatoes simmered on the stove. Hannah's forehead held beads of sweat, and her freckled hands worked competently among the pots and kettles.

"I need to lie down, Hannah," Azuba said. "I'll just go upstairs until this passes."

Bennett sat on the kitchen floor playing with the ark. He had set the animals in a long, curving row, two by two, and had set the ark beneath the table. One of the elephant's trunks had broken off, and a horse was missing. On every piece, the paint had faded or been chipped or worn. The windows were open, and white curtains blew out into the light-filled room, stroking the invisible current.

Bennett made crooning admonitions or stern commands. He grasped the animals with his fat, sturdy hands and made them walk. *Captain,* the sailors had called him. Those same sailors had been killed, and so Azuba and Nathaniel would never tell Bennett this detail of his own story. The child did have an air of command, Azuba thought. This morning he had helped catch some stray hens—running through the lifting mists, his arms spread, he had headed off their frantic, galloping spurts.

"I'm going upstairs, Bennett," she said. "Be good for Hannah."

He did not look up, as Carrie would have. His absorbed busyness brooked no interruption.

She went into the front hall and up the stairs, her hand on the banister. Even after four months, she was still queasy when she woke. She had not yet felt the baby's first kick, but her belly was swelling. She glimpsed herself in the mirror. Brown flowered dress, white apron, a hand to her cheek.

She thought of the young woman she had been, and of how only in retrospect could she see herself wrought by events, each one like a hammer stroke. She saw herself wearing white, the night she had met Nathaniel. She remembered the moment she had realized that she and Simon were trapped by the tide. Or when she had stepped aboard *Traveller* for the first time. She saw herself staring at the Horn, with its silver-winged birds, and then the storm. Nathaniel's cold voice, announcing that food had been stolen. Carrie's whisper, "Is he dead, Mama?" and Mr. Perkins lifting Andrew's parcelled body. The doldrums. The brown hen, swallowed by the sea. The pirates. Mr. Dennis. Lisette.

Azuba stopped in the door of her bedroom. Even now, a year later, the feeling swept over her. *What if I had not gone?*

She lay on the bed, watching the wind-stirred curtains.

Carrie now spoke to everyone and had become to all appearances as she had once been—bright, capable, serious.

But she looked at her mother steadily, as she looked at pictures in books or food on her plate or a fly on her finger—always on guard, it seemed, against danger or betrayal. And Azuba saw sadness in Carrie's eyes when she curled close to Nathaniel and he cupped her head with his hand or stroked her shoulder.

Lisette. Nathaniel had done everything within his purview to find her, writing to agents of the British colonial government in Hong Kong, hoping for new intelligence. Nothing came of his inquiries. Hope, like memory, dimmed. He wrote to Lisette's family. He sent them money, and informed them that he had not given up trying to find her. In the last few months, two separate rumours had reached their ears of a European woman living in China. Nathaniel had written both to Lisette's parents and to the British authorities, but had not yet had a reply from either.

A cow shambled into view, moving across the close-cropped pasture towards the clifftop. *In any case,* Azuba thought, watching the cow, *Lisette is no longer the person she was. If she has made a life for herself, it is in spite of her circumstances.*

She sat up against her pillow.

As Nathaniel and I must do. Carrie's sadness enveloped them in equal portion, as did the loss of Lisette.

The nausea faded and was gone. She remembered how, when seasickness passed, she had lain in the rocking, gimballed cabin bed, watched the wave-tossed light on the white walls, and felt the simple peace of health spread from head to toe.

The smell of cornbread filled the house. She heard Bennett's footsteps running, and Hannah's exclamation, and the clatter of stove lids. Carrie was at school. Azuba pictured her little girl, once her best and only companion. At ten years old, she wore her hair parted in the middle, clasped in the back and falling loose.

Woodsmoke spiced the cool, salty air coming over the windowsill. Azuba's eyes cleared of the grief that had darkened them at the thoughts of Lisette and Carrie. She gazed around the room. She saw the bow windows framing the bay. She studied her china wash set on its stand: blue and white bowl, pitcher, covered soap dish; the stand itself—yellow, with painted black and red flowers, a linen cloth tucked over its railing. The room was comfortable and spare, as she loved things to be. It was pieced with beauty: white quilt with red and blue stars; white wallpaper with silver stripes; noon sunshine warming the spruce floorboards, lighting Grammy Cooper's hooked rug. It was the rug they had taken on the voyage, so familiar as to be part of her, with its white-sailed ships, and village, red, purple and yellow houses, the colours of a late summer garden, hanging on the hillside—half-tipped and without proportion, like a dream.

She sat up, swung her legs over the side of the bed. Nathaniel's presence, rather than his impending absence, filled the house, and she felt it in the rustle of the wind, in the narrow, deep quiet.

She went to the window.

Nathaniel stood in the field behind the house. As if he were on deck, his legs were set wide, his hands folded behind his back. He was gazing out over the wind-rippled grass at all the empty places where he would plant his little trees.

Glossary

aft: at or towards the stern (rear) of a ship.

austral: southern.

baize: a coarse, usually green woolen material resembling felt.

beam ends: when *Traveller* was lying on her side, her masts parallel to the surface of the sea, she was lying on her beam ends.

belay: to stop and secure a running line around a cleat or belaying pin.

belaying pin: a metal bar fitting in a rail that serves as a cleat.

bend a sail: to join a sail to the yard.

binnacle: a built-in housing for a ship's compass.

blackbird: a kidnapped black or Polynesian slave.

blackbirder: the captains who abduct black or Polynesian slaves.

blocks: wooden pulleys.

box the compass: recite the points of the compass in the right order.

brace the yards: trim the sails by tightening the braces.

braces: lines (ropes) used to pivot the yardarms.

broach: to come broadside, or sideways, to the wind and seas.

brougham: a four-wheeled carriage.

bulkhead: an upright partition.

bulwarks: the part of the sides of the ship that rises above the deck to create a wall-like structure.

bum boat: a small boat carrying or selling provisions to a ship.

bunt: the middle part of a sail.

buntlines: lines used to haul the foot (bottom) of a sail up to the yard for furling.

butts: large casks (e.g., "water butts").

Cape of Good Hope: a mountainous promontory south of Cape Town, South Africa.

capstan: a revolving cylinder with a vertical axis, used to wind an anchor cable.

chafing gear: any of various mop- or brush-like appurtenances used to keep the lines from wearing. The material to make this gear was made on board the ship from "junk" (old fabric), which the sailors separated into strands, knotted together and spun into yarn.

clew: the lower corner of a sail.

clew lines: ropes used to haul the corners of the sail up to the yard for furling.

clew up: to haul the corners of the sail up to the yard for furling.

corozo: any of various tropical palm trees yielding palm oil.

corozo nut: a seed of one species of palm; when hardened, the seed forms vegetable ivory, used to make, for example, Carrie's buttons.

crazy quilt: a patchwork quilt whose patches are made of various materials, shapes, sizes and colours, often with a random pattern.

crinoline: a generic term for stiff, full petticoats, taken from early 1850s petticoats stiffened with horsehair. By the time of Azuba's voyage, the term was applied to all hoop-shaped skirt supports (whalebone, cane or steel).

deadeye: a round hardwood block, attached both to a ship's railing and spliced into shrouds and backstays. Used to exert tension.

deadlights: heavy shutters that could be closed during storms.

deal lumber: fir or pine timber, especially when sawn into boards of a standard size.

dogwatch: two short watches, 4–6 p.m. and 6–8 p.m., used to shift the watch hours so that each group of sailors took the night watch on every other day.

Fenians: a militant nineteenth-century organization founded among the Irish in the United States, dedicated to the overthrow of the British government in Ireland. Raids were made from the U.S. into Canada.

fiddles: a wooden barrier around the edge of tables and counters to help prevent objects from sliding off in heavy weather.

fo'c'sle: forecastle. The crew's quarters in the bow of the ship. Also a short raised deck at the bow.

gaff: a spar to which the head of a fore-and-aft sail is bent.

galiot: a light, single-masted, flatbottom Dutch merchant vessel of shallow draft.

gam: to meet socially, exchange gossip, chat (a whaling term).

gamming chair: a chair for conveying women from a dory onto a ship.

gaskets: bundles of small rope to wrap around sail and yard after sail is furled.

gig: a light ship's boat.

greybeards: enormous waves.

guano: the excrement of seabirds, used as fertilizer.

halyard: a permanent line used to hoist or lower a sail or a yard.

hardtack: a ship's biscuit.

hawser: a thick rope or cable for mooring or towing a ship.

heave to (hove to): to adjust a ship's sails so as to greatly reduce forward motion. A ship's captain might order this done in rough weather, or to speak another ship.

holystone: large squares of soft sandstone used to scour the deck. This whitened and softened the wood. The stones were also called "prayer books" or "bibles."

The Horn (Cape Horn): the southernmost point of South America, on a Chilean island south of Tierra del Fuego. Notorious for its storms.

japanned: furniture finished with a hard, usually black varnish, called *japan*, and brought from Japan.

jib: a triangular staysail from the outer end of the jibboom to the top of the foremast, or from the bowsprit to the masthead.

jibboom: a spar fixed to the bowsprit to extend its length.

junk: old cables or rope cut up to make chafing gear; also, a sailing vessel used in the China Seas.

lazarette: a space between decks used for storage.

lee: the side away from which the wind blows.

lee shore: a shore to leeward. Very dangerous for a sailing vessel, as the ship will be blown towards, or onto, a lee shore.

leghorn: fine braided straw; a hat of this.

lines: ropes.

lobscouse: "biscuit pounded fine, salt beef cut into small pieces, and a few potatoes, boiled up together" (from *Two Years Before the Mast*, Richard Henry Dana).

marlinspike: a sharp, pointed iron tool.

mizzen mast: the mast closest to the stern.

mollyhawk: a sailor's term derived from the Dutch *molle muck*, meaning "foolish gull." Applied to a smaller species of albatross, or sometimes to jaegers or immature gulls. (from the endnotes to *Quite a Curiosity: The Sea Letters of Grace F. Ladd*, ed. Louise Nichols, Nimbus Publishing).

mould loft: a large floor for making half-models of the hull of a vessel. The models were carved from blocks of laminated wood. Full-scale sections were laid on the loft floor, and full-sized moulds of the sections were put together here.

nainsook: a fine, soft cotton fabric, used especially for baby clothes (from the Hindi *nainsukh*).

oakum: a loose fibre obtained by picking old rope to pieces, used especially in caulking.

paling: a fence made with pointed pieces of wood.

patten: a shoe or clog with a raised sole set on an iron ring, for walking in mud, etc.

phrenology: the study of the shape and size of the cranium as an indication of character and mental faculties.

pilaster: a rectangular column, especially one projecting from a wall.

promenoir: a paved public walk.

quarterdeck: part of a ship's upper deck nearest to the stern, reserved for officers of the ship and their families.

ratline: a rope tied between shrouds. Ratlines form a ladder that sailors climb to get up to the yards.

reef: to roll up a sail to reduce its surface area in a high wind.

reticule: a small handbag, usually with a drawstring closure.

running rigging: lines used to work the sails (halyards, braces and sheets).

sack coat: a loose, unlined, semi-fitted jacket with long sleeves.

sailor's valentine: intricate designs made with shells, usually framed.

scuppers: holes in bulwarks through which water drains overboard.

sextant: an optical device used to measure a celestial body's angle of elevation above the horizon. Used together with a chronometer to find a ship's latitude and longitude.

shroud: a rope run from the mast down to the side of a ship to help support the mast.

sidewheeler: a steamboat with large paddlewheels mounted on its sides.

slatting: shaking of the sails by the wind if the sails are not properly set.

snake fence: a fence of roughly-split logs stacked in a zigzag pattern. Also called a "snake-rail fence."

spanker sail: the fore-and-aft sail set on the mizzen mast. A spanker is gaff-rigged and looks like the sails on a schooner.

spars: a catch-all term used to describe masts, booms, gaffs and the like.

speak a vessel: to communicate with another vessel at sea.

spun-yarn winch: a simple wheel and spindle used to make chafing gear.

standing rigging: ropes or wires used to support the masts.

stay: a part of the standing rigging, which supports the mast. A rope run from the masthead behind or in front of the mast.

staysail: a triangular fore-and-aft sail set between the masts.

taffrail: the rail at the stern of a vessel.

tiffin: a midday snack or light meal.

trade winds: winds blowing continuously towards the equator and deflected westward.

treenails: long wooden pins used to fasten planks to structural members. Pronounced "trunnels."

variables: an area of light, unsteady winds north and south of the trade winds, and between the trades and the westerlies; also known as "horse latitudes," because if water ran out, horses were thrown overboard.

wear ship: to turn a sailing vessel's stern, rather than bow, into the wind, in order to change tack.

weather: the side of the wind (as opposed to "lee").

weevils: any insect that spoils stored grain.

westerlies: broad westerly wind belts in both the northern and southern hemispheres.

wind cake: a cake in which egg yolks are beaten in water until foamy, then egg whites are beaten until stiff and folded into the batter.

Yahgans: aboriginal inhabitants of Tierra del Fuego; as described by Charles Darwin: ". . . at night, five or six human beings, naked . . . sleep on the wet ground . . ."

yard: the spar perpendicular to a mast upon which a square sail is set.

Acknowledgments

My gratitude to the brave and little-known women who sailed with their captain husbands on merchant and whaling vessels in the nineteenth century. Details of their lives, and some of their adventures, are woven into this novel.

Thanks to the authors and researchers whose books illuminated time, place, and technicalities. Some of them are: *Women at Sea in the Age of Sail,* by Donal Baird; *Hen Frigates: Passion and Peril, Nineteenth-Century Women at Sea,* by Joan Druett; *The Sea Letters of Grace F. Ladd,* by Louise Nicols; *Flying Cloud: The True Story of America's Most Famous Clipper Ship and the Woman Who Guided Her,* by David W. Shaw; *Around Cape Horn,* by Charles G. Davis; *The Way of a Ship,* by Derek Lundy; *Life and Times: Recollections of Eliza Cox Carter,* edited by Judith Baxter and Beth Quigley; *The Great Guano Rush,* by Jimmy M. Skaggs; *Two Years Before the Mast,* by Richard Henry Dana; and *Cochin-China and My Experience of It,* by Edward Brown. For a complete bibliography, please visit my website: www.powning.com/beth.

I used a great deal of original material: women's diaries, captains' logs, a master's thesis, photographs and letters. For these, I am indebted to the New Brunswick Museum

Archives, particularly the assistance of Janet Bishop. For questions answered, books supplied, and an invaluable day spent viewing wedding dresses, underclothing, workboxes and the like, thanks to New Brunswick Museum curator Peter J. Larocque.

For microfilm of the *Weekly Telegraph* (1862–64), thanks to the staff at the Saint John Regional Library Reference Room.

For allowing me to experience life in the nineteenth century, and for letting me explore their costume department, thanks to the staff of Kings Landing Historical Settlement, Kings Landing, New Brunswick.

Special thanks to Lucy Loomis at the Sturgis Library, Barnstable, Massachusetts; and to Glenn Gordiniere, ship's historian at Mystic Seaport, Mystic, Connecticut. For medical details, thanks to Edith Konesni, PA-C; Dr. Suleiman Khedheri; and Dr. David MacMillan. For help with creating characters for the novel's earliest draft, thanks to illustrator Twila Robar deCoste, biologist Inka Milewski and chef Russell Dobbelstyne. My grateful thanks to Ann Patty and Sue Sumeraj. Thanks to Barbara McIntyre at the Quaco Museum; and to Patricia McCaig, Catherine Thompson, Jesse Williams, and Emily Upham.

For meals, peace, birds and kindness, thanks to Sister Kate and the retreat house of the Cistercian-Trappistine nuns of the Notre-Dame de l'Assomption Abbey in Rogersville, New Brunswick.

For the place where the book was born, I am grateful for those who facilitate the Leighton Artist's Colony at the Banff Centre for the Arts, Banff, Alberta.

For reading and fact-checking an early draft, thanks to sailor/luthier Karl Dennis. For advice in the beginning, and for fact-checking in the end, much gratitude to sailor/author Derek Lundy. Any errors are mine.

Acknowledgments

Deepest thanks to the terrific team at Knopf Canada: Diane Martin, Marion Garner, Deirdre Molina, Amanda Lewis, and Nicola Makoway.

Thanks to Terri Nimmo for the gorgeous jacket and Jake Powning for the novel's website design.

Heartfelt thanks to my editor, Angelika Glover, for asking the right questions, for making me dig deep, for patience on the long journey and for shepherding the book from start to finish.

And to my dear friend and most amazing agent, Jackie Kaiser—I am profoundly and endlessly grateful.

For help with research, and for her inspiring passion for New Brunswick history, thanks to my daughter-in-law, Sara Powning. To my mother, Alison Davis, for her careful reading and commentary on several drafts. To my father, Wendell Davis, for enthusiastic support. To my son, Jake— for love. To my granddaughters, Maeve, Bridget—for joy.

To Peter, husband of forty years, thanks for always lightening the darkness with your belief in me, and for your love.